A chance meeting beneath the mistletoe, a stolen glance across the dance floor—amid the sumptuous delicacies, glittering decorations, the orchestra swells and every duchess and debutante, lord and lackey has a hopeful heart. There's the head-strong heiress who must win back her beloved by midnight—or be wed to another . . . the spinster whose fateful choice to relinquish love may hold one more surprise for her . . . a widow yearning to glimpse her long-lost love for even one sweet, fleeting interlude . . . a charming rake who finds far more than he bargained for. And many other dazzling, romantic tales in this star-studded collection from the Word Wenches . . .

Praise for the Word Wenches and *Mischief and Mistletoe*

"A coterie of multitalented historical romance authors, who blog together as the Word Wenches, provide short stories that truly showcase the styles they are noted for. These romantic, passionate, humorous, exciting quick reads are delectable tidbits, confections that charm and delight, like the holidays themselves."—*RT Book Reviews,* 4 stars

"In this stellar anthology, eight authors present a holiday-inspired, Regency-set novella . . . there isn't a single literary lump of coal here."—*The Chicago Tribune*

"Touching, gently funny, satisfying, and short enough to be read in one sitting, each story in this delectable anthology is a holiday treat."—*Library Journal*

"Heartwarming anthology . . . a sweet gift for the reader."
—*Publishers Weekly*

"Whether you like a Victorian England romance or a more modern one, there's a holiday story for you in these two anthologies."—*Parkersburg News and Sentinel*

"These cheeky stories were fun to read."—*First: for women*

"You'll find stories to enjoy!"—**Heroes and Heartbreakers**

"Each romance is light-hearted fun, starring likable protagonists who bring alive the holiday season in the Regency British Isles."—*Midwest Book Review*

The Last Chance Christmas Ball

MARY JO PUTNEY
JO BEVERLEY

Joanna Bourne 〜 Patricia Rice
Nicola Cornick 〜 Cara Elliott
Anne Gracie 〜 Susan King

ZEBRA BOOKS
KENSINGTON PUBLISHING CORP.
http://www.kensingtonbooks.com

ZEBRA BOOKS are published by

Kensington Publishing Corp.
119 West 40th Street
New York, NY 10018

All Kensington titles, imprints, and distributed lines are available at special quantity discounts for bulk purchases for sales promotion, premiums, fund-raising, educational, or institutional use.

Special book excerpts or customized printings can also be created to fit specific needs. For details, write or phone the office of the Kensington Sales Manager: Attn.: Sales Department. Kensington Publishing Corp., 119 West 40th Street, New York, NY 10018. Phone: 1-800-221-2647.

Zebra and the Z logo Reg. U.S. Pat. & TM Off.

First Kensington Books Trade Paperback Printing: October 2015
First Zebra Books Mass-Market Paperback Printing: October 2016
ISBN-13: 978-1-4201-3859-7
ISBN-10: 1-4201-3859-6

eISBN-13: 978-1-4201-3860-3
eISBN-10: 1-4201-3860-X

10 9 8 7 6 5 4 3 2

Printed in the United States of America

*To our intrepid editor, Alicia Condon, who gave us
the lovely idea of a Christmas ball and then had
to do the intricate editing to fit all the pieces together!*

*And to the readers of the Word Wenches blog,
who make our online community such a pleasure
to create and share.*

CONTENTS

PROLOGUE

Jo Beverley

"*Y*ou write a neat hand, dear."

Clio Finch looked up at the elderly lady and smiled. "Thank you, Lady Holly."

The Dowager Countess of Holbourne preferred to be called that and Clio was happy to comply. She'd do almost anything for her generous benefactress, but she knew she was lacking in one respect. She couldn't match the lady's bright jollity.

Lady Holly looked her seventy-odd years, but in the best possible way. Her hair was silver rather than gray and bubbled out from under pretty caps. Plumpness softened her wrinkles and her eyes were the brightest blue.

She always dressed in the latest fashions. No eternal black for this widow. Today she was in a high-waisted gown made of a vibrant flowered print. During the three months Clio had been here as her companion, Lady Holly had gently pressed her to wear brighter clothes herself, even offering to buy them for her. Clio hated to disoblige the kind lady, but she couldn't, she simply couldn't, so she used her own mourning as excuse, even though her traditional mourning period was over.

Writing out the invitations to the Christmas ball was a rather tedious task, but Clio welcomed it. At last she was truly being useful. She'd make quicker work of it without Lady Holly's interference, but the lady had taken a seat beside her at the table in the light of the window and as usual, was chattering.

Lady Holly picked up the list she herself had written out, so Clio felt free to dip her pen and continue the set phrases.

. . . at Holbourne Abbey on Thursday, the twenty-eighth of December . . .

"It's my fiftieth, you know."

Clio looked up again. "Fiftieth?"

"Ball, dear! Fifty years."

"My goodness, that's extraordinary."

"It is, isn't it? I never imagined that when we held the first. I'd always adored Christmas, but my husband's mother was the sort not to encourage 'dissipation in a holy season' as she put it. Once George was earl, however, and his mother removed to the dower house . . . So lovely, don't you think, that neither John nor Elizabeth has ever suggested that I move there. Once we were free to do as we pleased, what could be more splendid than a glittering event in the dead of winter? Everyone attends, and it has quite a reputation by now. So many matches have begun or been accelerated by my Christmas ball."

Clio smiled again, but her logical mind said that an annual event was likely to intersect with many a courtship at some point, rather than the event itself having any power.

"That's why I'm inviting Miss Langsdale and Miss Fenton this year. I will be writing those, dear, so you can note that on the list." She passed it over and Clio made the mark. "I hope some of the magic will rub off on them," Lady Holly said, "for I fear this might be their last chance. Allie Fenton means to take employment, can you believe, and Sarah Jane Langsdale speaks of opening an orphanage!"

"They don't usually attend, ma'am?" Clio asked.

"I have always invited them, of course. They're goddaughters of mine. But Allie has had to take care of her mother, and then her father, and Sarah Jane ceased attending some years ago. I fear she feels she's past frivolity. So foolish."

Clio could sympathize with that. She couldn't imagine ever indulging in frivolity again. Perhaps the young women also felt a little out of place. They weren't truly in the Holbourne Abbey circle any more than Clio was, which was why she was a companion rather than a guest. She had no faith in the ball magically making such ladies desirable brides.

"And Clary Douglas is to come this year from Scotland, along with several others," Lady Holly said. "She's not on the list because I invited her in a letter some weeks ago, pointing out the significant anniversary. It's so long since we saw her and our Scottish friends. Perhaps they'll show us how to celebrate Hogmanay."

"That will be interesting, ma'am. I understand the Scots have their own special traditions and don't celebrate Christmas much at all."

"Except in the religious sense. Christmas has become so dull in England these days. I've heard people say that holly and mistletoe, and especially the Yule log, are pagan. Such nonsense! The German members of the royal family bring whole trees into their houses at Christmas and light them with candles. I have thought of doing the same, but even after all these years, the Germans aren't very popular, are they?"

Clio ignored that tricky question and began a new invitation.

Dear Lord Claymott, Lady Holly requests the pleasure of . . .

"The first ball was in 1765," the old lady said. "The king was young and the regent a mere lad. Everything seemed set to be splendid. We had no notion of the Americans turning away from us, the revolution in France, and that dreadful Napoleon Bonaparte. But the ball has been held every year since then, come what may. Even weather has never interfered. That must mean it's blessed, mustn't it?" She added the last sentence rather anxiously.

"It must." Clio put as much conviction into it as she could, for she could see where Lady Holly's mind had turned.

Kim Stretton, the younger son of the house, had chosen a career in the army and fought at Waterloo. By God's grace he'd survived, but he'd been badly wounded. He'd returned home to heal, but had set up camp in the old tower that was attached to the modern house. His servant came and went, but even his family was excluded. Clio had never seen him.

She wished she could. It wouldn't matter how hideously he was disfigured, she'd treat him warmly. As she would have treated Will if he'd returned to her, no matter how crippled or scarred. She fought tears. It would never do to blot her work with teardrops, and her sorrows were her own.

"And then there's Caro," Lady Holly said, moving on as if they'd completed a silent conversation. "I do hope my granddaughter will attend, with Camden, of course."

"I'm sure they will."

"I'm not." Lady Holly could be trenchant when she pleased. "Everyone tries to keep unpleasantness from me, but I know the gel's dancing with scandal in Town, and as good as living apart from her husband. Too young to wed. Perhaps I should have said something, but they seemed to be in love."

"Best not to interfere, ma'am. Lovers never listen."

"It is a madness, isn't it?"

Clio agreed, but Lady Holly's tone seemed nostalgic rather than disapproving.

"I do hope the insanity strikes Edward soon," Lady Holly said. "It's time he wed, and we must have an heir."

Edward was Viscount Brentford, the elder son of the house and an admirably steady man. The Strettons were a solid, pleasant family and Clio felt blessed to have been given refuge here. She prayed events would work out splendidly for all of them.

Lady Holly considered the sheet of names again. "I'm not sure there's a lady here to suit him and I can't think of anyone to add. He's known everyone hereabouts all his life. There is Roxie, of course. . . ."

Roxanne Hayward had inherited an adjoining estate and ran it herself. She'd grown up as part of the Stretton family and was in and out all the time, red hair wild and clothing more practical than fashionable. Would she actually dress up in finery and attend a ball?

"I'm just about to write that invitation," Clio said.

"Oh, no, leave that to me as well. She's as good as family. It would be an excellent alliance—two estates running together—but I did think at one time she and Kim had a *tendre*."

"Time changes people," Clio said, then realized it was an unfortunate comment and looked for something else to say. "The next name is Gower. Are they family connections?"

Lady Holly wrinkled her nose. "John Gower's wife was a distant cousin. I had her daughter Mary here a few times when she was a child. Gower hinted so broadly for an invitation that I felt I must give in. I suppose he wants to dangle that poor girl before eligible men. I hope he doesn't have his eye on Edward."

Clio's eye had moved on. "Who's Lord Gabriel Quinfroy?"

Lady Holly's face lit. "A charming scamp and an addition to any social occasion. Son of the Duke of Straith and wealthy in his own right. Of course, it's spoiled him and women tumble at his feet, but he's too delicious for anyone to mind."

I mind, Clio thought, tempted to strike the vile seducer from the list. It wouldn't do, but when she wrote out his invitation she tried to imbue the ink with a powerful repellant force.

My True Love
Hath My Heart

Joanna Bourne

CHAPTER ONE

December 24, Christmas Eve

*H*e watched her emerge from the servants' stairs into the hall, a neat, straight, slender figure in a dark dress and white apron. He'd known she would come. He'd been waiting for her—not patiently, but with his blood pumping in anticipation.

Nick Lafford stood at the window at the end of the corridor, backed by the light. A good place to observe and remain unobserved. When he saw the door open, before Claire—his Claire—stepped into the hall, he turned toward the window as if he were interested in the scene outside. He hid his face.

It was midmorning with a gray sky and heavy snow falling. A carriage, emptied of its visitors, was being driven around to the stables. Nothing else moved in the landscape of outbuildings.

She'd notice him as she headed down the hall—the outline of a man looking out at the weather—but she wouldn't recognize him. She didn't know he was at Holbourne Abbey. She'd dismiss him as another well-tailored guest here at Holbourne Abbey for the house party. A friend of Edward's maybe, the right age to be a soldier, newly discharged.

She was dressed as an upstairs maid, neat and proper and trying to be prim. If he wanted to be picky about it, her clothing was a little too fine, the fabric too expensive for a servant to wear at work. Her mobcap trailed a pair of long flirty ribbons at the back. That was vanity on her part and he loved her for it.

A plump older maid, a brown hen of a woman, bustled along the hall ahead of her, all good humor, chattering. Claire followed with the air of a sleek cat that had somehow been adopted into a family of chickens. She carried clean towels and a jug of water. She'd stuck a white dusting cloth into the waistband of her apron. That would be an indictable offense among housemaids, he imagined. The housekeeper would scold her if she got caught.

She was jaunty and intent, thoroughly herself in her borrowed persona. Even the mobcap perched on her head in an impudent, Claire way. If she'd been walking down Bond Street dressed as she should be in one of her flowing, jewel-colored frocks, heads would turn when she passed. Female heads, envious and a little disapproving. Male heads, in admiration.

When she and the other maid had gone inside Gower's room, Nick stayed where he was, watching the door, being ordinary. Just another guest here to enjoy the festivities of Christmas Eve.

But he and Claire weren't ordinary. They were both outsiders. A little dangerous sometimes. Disingenuous at best, downright liars at worst. They were made for each other.

Claire followed Anna down the hall. The housekeeper sent the maids out two by two when they went to set the rooms in order. She'd paired the newly hired London maid with plump, good-natured Anna, who knew the foibles and secrets of all the guests and didn't mind sharing them.

Anna turned the knob and pushed the door open with

her hip. They were in Gower's bedroom at last. This was the Red Room, with walls the color of aged burgundy wine and fierce, masculine hunting scenes in the pictures. The bronze figures on the mantelpiece were, on the left, Mercury in a hurry and, on the right, some unhappy Celt with an arrow in his thigh. Maybe Gower was given this room in the hope it would shorten his stay.

"A fine-looking gentleman." Anna was looking back at the door. "Interested in ye, I think."

"Who?" Her mind wasn't on the burning question of fine-looking gentlemen. She was planning how to rifle the room.

"The gentleman in the hall. He was sneaking a peek, I think. Ye have an admirer. More what ye be used to dealing with, I imagine."

There it was again. Everyone from the butler to the scullery maid knew she wasn't what she pretended to be. She might fool the guests, but the servants had figured it out before she'd been in the house an hour. They played along, but she hadn't fooled them one jot.

She could hardly ask what mistakes she made.

Feeling baffled, she tossed pillows off the bed and stripped down the sheets, airing them out for a minute before they remade the bed. She said, "I've given up men altogether," which was true enough.

"Ye'll be one of the few. We'll have some fine old giggling and bussing tonight, now they've hung the kissing bough in the kitchen door. Them valets up from the south are a cheeky lot."

Gower had tumbled his bedclothes off the bed on both sides. Be nice to think that was a night tussling with a guilty conscience. Probably a restless night after gorging himself at the table.

Gower's daughter, who had the Rose Room down the hall, left barely a dent on her pillow. She must lie still as a doll all night long. The daughter had brought dozens of expensive dresses, but not one single jewel. Only two empty jewel cases.

So many secrets a maidservant discovered. She'd had no idea.

Anna continued talking, ending up with, "He'd warm a bed on a cold night, that one. Fine figure of a man, don't ye think?"

It was a measure of how little she'd been paying attention that she had to say, "Who?"

"Bless ye, child, no. The man watching you in the hall. Something familiar about him I canna put my finger on, but he looked a proper gentleman."

"I didn't notice." There was only one man she was remotely interested in and he was in Paris. Or Lyon or St. Petersburg. Wherever the Foreign Office needed someone to pull chestnuts out of a fire. He was far away, in any case, and she didn't care in the least.

Redoing the bed came next, before she dusted. There were orders of precedence in the cleaning of a room, as strictly kept as any royal processional.

"Hold a twitch while I scrub. I'm that mucky from tending fires." Anna plunged her hands in the water bucket up to the elbow. "There was a time I would 'uv spared a glance for a man like that. A glance and mayhap a smile."

"I will bob a curtsey at him if the chance presents itself." She'd practiced her curtseys. She was proud of them.

They pulled the sheets and blankets back up the length of the bed. Smoothed and retucked everything, layer by layer. The coverlet came last. "Grab the corner, dearie," Anna said, "and up we go. What was I talking about?"

"Kissing, I think. You were in favor of it."

"Aye. I wouldna have *done* anything, mind you," Anna said. "I was more than happy with my John William all those years. But a girl should look. The good Lord made men to be appreciated."

"I'll make a point of looking him over if he's still in the hall when I leave." But she wouldn't. She'd only just shaken herself free of one wellborn, arrogant, son-of-a-bitch aristocrat. She had no intention of acquiring another.

"Ye do that, love." Anna went back to mending the fire.

As duties were divided, the other maid's part—her part—was to chase dust. So she ran a damp cloth over every surface, looking into all the corners as she went. She didn't expect any useful revelations. Gower wouldn't hide the *Coeur de Flamme* anywhere a maid dusted. He wouldn't hide it among his clothing in the tallboy. His valet would sort through that and Gower wasn't the man to trust his valet.

Nick would have searched this room foot by foot, painstakingly, meticulously. He'd have gone flat on his belly, peering and prying underneath that tallboy and that dresser and the desk. Nick would—

She had no intention of thinking about what Nick would do.

She opened the window and shook her cloth out in the falling snow. It would be hard to get out of this window using a rope ladder. Someone skilled or desperate might try it.

Anna leaned back on her heels to admire her work with the fire. She gave the tiles of the surround one last loving swipe. "Neat as ninepence."

Close the window. Set the latch. "Why ninepence, I wonder? Is a sixpence less tidy? Are shillings sluttish?"

"Wouldn't surprise me." Anna shot her one of those sidewise looks that meant, "You are odd as a three-legged cow," and stood, one hand pressed to her back, huffing out a little sigh of relief. "I'll leave ye to the dusting, then, and be off to see if Miss Effington has pried herself upright this fine morning." She collected her brushes and scooped dirty towels from the floor. "It's a wonder rich folk don't get bored, lying abed till the day's half done. And on Christmas Eve, too. If you ask me, the gentry don't have half the fun we do downstairs."

"Shouldn't wonder."

She was one of the rich folk, she supposed. Her shops brought in more income than most estates. Trading jewels in Antwerp was even more profitable. But every day of her life she'd been up with the sun. When she was young, it had been to grind coffee, keep order among the apprentices, prepare the shop for opening. Her grandmother kept old-fashioned ways. Nowadays waking early let her catch the sunlight for her work. She matched jewels by natural light, always.

"No accounting for gentlefolk. Kittle cattle." Anna wended her way with a click and clink of her pail. She left behind the privacy nefarious deeds require.

"All mine," Claire whispered, turning in a circle. Was there anything more satisfying than being solitary in a room you planned to poke about in?

She pulled out drawers and opened glove boxes to her heart's content. Studied Gower's collection of poorly cut rings and shirt buttons in the flat box in the top drawer. On top of the oak wardrobe, a hatbox with a hat in it. Opening the doors, she found boots standing in a row along the front. Behind that, a stack of hand luggage and boxes.

Promising. Promising. A riding crop on top. Under that, a gentleman's traveling kit with recesses for comb, brush, scissors, soap, razor. Most of that was laid out on the washstand. Next down. A portable writing desk. Ink, quills, sealing wax, and blank paper. A ledger that was coy about the accounts. She'd cut her teeth on account books and recognized shady dealing when she saw it. A hidden drawer—all of these writing desks had a hidden drawer—full of banknotes.

Fascinating though this glimpse into Mr. Gower's mind might be, it wasn't what she wanted.

The next box down was ... the kindest word was "unlovely." The workmanship was poor and the proportions ill-chosen. But the contents rattled and shifted when she picked it up.

And finally she'd come to something that was locked. Oh good.

She set it on a shelf at eye level and went to work with her bent probes. Even an amateur—she was happy to consider herself an amateur in the craft of lock picking— needed only a handful of minutes to get it open. In more exigent circumstances she could have broken the box apart with a rock. Or pried the lid up with a kitchen knife. Or tucked the whole thing under her arm and walked away with it. Obviously, in the life of a housemaid the opportunities for theft were endless.

The lock turned.

Behold jewelry. Here was a tray holding a dozen jewel cases, each about the size of her palm. Florentine leather, blue and green. She lifted out the tray and found a melee of gold and bright jewels tossed together haphazardly.

Gower kept his daughter's baubles locked away in his room, hidden in the bottom of the wardrobe. Why? It looked as if he'd emptied the contents of two or three jewelry boxes in here and carted it off. A monkey trove of treasure, with a monkey's feckless disregard for scratched pearls or dented gold.

There'd be a mean-spirited story behind this. A fight between father and daughter. Punishment? She could almost feel sorry for the woman.

She ran her fingers through bracelets and tangled necklaces and felt the shapes in the small velvet bags. She couldn't help thinking the stones were ill-suited to the daughter's pretty fairness. She priced as she fingered through—this was her business, after all. Thirty guineas for that sapphire bracelet. A fussy design and the stones were poorly matched. Forty for the topaz pendant. This huge brooch should be broken down for the stones because it was hideous.

The *Coeur* wasn't in this angry jumble. Gower, who tossed fragile pearls and brittle jade into that clinking chaos, probably kept his diamond cushioned safe in one of these pretty leather cases. A diamond that was almost impossible to damage.

The upper tray, then. The first leather case held a ruby necklace. Very nice. The second case was lighter. She—

"I always wondered what housemaids did in their leisure time." The voice came from the door. "Theft, apparently."

CHAPTER TWO

$\mathcal{T}$here was an instant like lightning—filled with a flash of recognition in the midst of blank surprise. She recognized him at once. How could she not? Nobody else spoke like silk over steel. Like honey and granite rock. Rough with laughter, sarcastic over the card table, whispered across a pillow—that was not a voice one forgot. She turned slowly to face him.

Nick Lafford stood in the doorway, a man not taking his dismissal seriously. She was furious with him. She was impatient and unforgiving. And everything inside her, heart, mind, and spirit was glad to see him.

He closed the door behind him and strolled into the room. Time flowed sluggishly around him, giving her a long opportunity to feel five or six emotions in a row, all of them complicated and contradictory.

"Picture of a maid dusting the jewelry," he said. "How thorough of you."

"Searching it, actually."

"We rise above the banal, then. I always enjoy rising above the banal with you." He came to look past her into the box on the wardrobe shelf. "We have the very likeness of plunder. I feel quite piratical. Is it immensely valuable?"

"Not so far." She closed the leather case with the rubies and put it firmly back in the tray. "If they were vegetables, this would largely be a pile of potatoes."

"Not counting the *Coeur de Flamme*." Nick wore one of his deceptively open expressions.

"Not counting the *Coeur*, which I haven't found yet. What in the name of sanity are you doing here?"

"I appear to have joined you in ransacking with intent. Embarrassing if I'm caught at it." He leaned to look into the jewel box and they touched, just a little. A brush of his jacket on her shoulder. A feeling of warmth at her side. Nothing really.

He said, "I'll bet these dainty little boxes contain the good stuff."

"Almost certainly. Go away, Nick."

"I don't think so. You may, eventually, be glad I'm here." He stirred a finger into the jewels, inquisitive. "Or, of course, you may not. But I'm here anyway."

This was so typical of him. Ready to filch jewels at her side or lead her onto the dance floor in Vienna in front of the assembled nobility of Europe. Once, he'd helped her relocate an inconvenient body. Once—

Blast him for being Nicholas. For being sneaky and single-minded and never giving up. For being clever enough to move her like a chess piece to this time and this place. For saying he loved her.

Blast her for being happy to see him again, even for a minute.

She squashed down the anticipation and gladness that was springing up inside her like so many bubbles rising to the top of beer. She concentrated on being stern. He'd taken her by surprise. That was all. Nothing had changed.

He hooked up entangled necklaces and bracelets and let them dangle. "What a hoard for a man to lug about the north country. They almost beg to be stolen, don't they?"

"No."

"I hear their siren call. 'Pick me up and carry me away,' they say. Surely he won't miss a few."

"I'm busy, Nick. I don't have time for this."

"And we're not thieves, like the regrettable Mr. Gower." When she didn't comment he said, "The money doesn't matter, does it? He didn't just cheat you out of money. He stole your work. He tried to steal your good name."

Nick understood. That was what made him so insidious. He'd always understood her.

She batted his hand out of the way and picked up the next leather case. "You contrived this. It's not some cosmic mischance."

"Humbly, I admit it. I arranged for a guest list to the house party to land in the papers. You saw it. You're here."

"I should have been suspicious."

"I'm delighted you weren't. It means you're here." He gestured a circle, taking in the jewels, the rest of the room, Holbourne Abbey, and Northumberland. "Instead of breaking into Gower's town house. He keeps guards. With guns."

"Guns in his garden and the unbreakable safe he brags about. I hope someone robs it one fine evening, but it won't be me. Damn you for interfering."

"I can't help myself, you know. Indulged from childhood. No self-discipline."

He hadn't changed a whit in the months since she'd sent him away. Still the perfect English aristocrat, casually confident, wrapped in the armor of first-class tailoring. Still the long, intelligent, handsome face that didn't show a tenth of what he was thinking. Brown hair in fashionable disorder. Brown eyes carefully controlled in what they revealed.

She said, "I don't have time to chatter with you. Anybody could walk in."

"The door's locked. You don't think I neglected to steal a key." He reached past her and selected a leather jewel case, flicked it open, and found emeralds. "This is nice."

Very nice. Trust Nick to see that. "It's famous—both the bracelet and the central stone. Spanish work, from stones plundered out of the New World. Owned by a noble French family for the past few centuries. Stolen a decade ago."

"It must cringe at the company it keeps. May I confiscate it for you in my capacity as representative of the British government?"

"You may put it away."

"Do you know, you're almost impossible to give jewelry to, my sweet."

"Well, you can't steal it for me."

"I can't buy it for you either, alas. I've tried." He set the emeralds aside. His next leather case held a necklace of citrine and gold.

Her choice held a diamond brooch, the stones cut at least a generation ago. "This must belong to the daughter. Her name escapes me—"

"Mary."

"That's right. I expected to find this yesterday when I searched her room. He must hand her trinkets out to her, one by one, and take them back at night."

"One of several petty punishments. They disagree over her choice of marriage partner."

The English nobility were particular about who they let marry into the family. Wasn't that the root of her own unhappy problem? "Who would be the daughter of a Gower? I'd rather scrub and dust for a living."

She opened the next case. Opals. Then the next . . . and held her breath.

Nick whispered, "Well, well, well."

Here was the *Coeur de Flamme,* the Heart of Fire. She spilled it into her palm, the gold chain, the delicate setting of red gold and rubies, the heart-shaped diamond. It fit, gentle and familiar, in her hand after the hours she'd spent with it.

Nick said, "That is fairly magnificent."

"It's an old stone. Legendary. I think Gower acquired it with his wife's dowry."

"The stories don't do it justice." Nick's breath was warm on her face. In her hair.

The *Coeur* trembled with the movement of her breathing. Red fire danced along the great flaw at the center that made the stone unique.

For one instant she felt the lust to possess. She was brushed by the greed men feel for the great jewels of the world.

Then it was gone. She was a jeweler, daughter of a long line of jewelers. She traded gems. As a craftsman, she served them. She was a moment of their long history. They passed through her hands and she opened her fingers and let them go.

"Good, then. You have it. I don't want to hurry you, Claire," Nick said, "but I suggest you stuff that in a pocket and we run. This seems a moment for all deliberate haste."

"I'm not here to steal."

"You've just dropped by to say hello." From the corner of her eye she saw Nick's familiar lopsided smile.

"Something like that."

"Let us say, '*Bonjour, Monsieur Coeur de Flamme.* Sorry we're in such a hurry. We'll chat another time,' and shuffle along." He reached out to touch the diamond, once, lightly, stroking it.

Involuntarily, she shivered. He didn't notice. She thought he didn't notice. He didn't look at her anyway, only at the stone. He said, "That setting is yours. Even if I didn't already know, I'd recognize your work anywhere."

"Mine. My work." She'd set the *Coeur* in red gold that twisted like tongues of flame. Dozens of tiny, table-cut rubies rippled up those curves, feeding color into the diamond. "That's why I went to Paris last summer. To make this."

"And be cheated."

"He said I'd chipped the stone. He didn't pay me for my work or materials and I lost the bond I'd posted. The magistrate sided with him."

Nick said, "Paris is occupied by an English army. Gower's an Englishman."

"And I am a woman and a merchant and not English. Not even French."

"So, of course, you lose a case at law."

"I do not chip stones entrusted to my care. Nobody chips a diamond. It's ridiculous."

"He attacked your reputation with that lie. I've been waiting for something bad to happen to him. Something fiendishly subtle."

"That is my intent." She put the *Coeur* away in its leather case. She lowered the lid of the wooden box, relocked it, and restacked it with the others in the back of the wardrobe. She closed the wardrobe doors.

Done. The stage was set. The *Coeur* was ready. A lesser woman would have grinned.

"I had pictured the two of us in wild flight to the nearest port." Nick sounded regretful. "Wild flight usually comes into play at some point when I'm embroiled in one of your convoluted schemes. I even brought riding horses."

She said, "You are not embroiled and I do not scheme."

"You scheme, plot, connive, and machinate. You are a credit to gentle womanhood." He strolled over to the line of glassware on the dresser at the window. "Brandy?" He held up a decanter.

It was a challenge. He dared her to stay here with him, to take the chance Gower might come back.

Tremors of excitement fluttered in odd corners of her body, the old anticipation of a plan ready to unroll. Nick was beside her and that was five or six twisting, shivering feelings all by itself. She felt alive in every corner of her being. She didn't try to disentangle why.

She should leave. She should get out of here. Get away from Nick. For his good. For hers. Hadn't she decided that was the only way?

She said, "Thank you."

He poured into two glasses. "We will drink to our not-so-much chance meeting."

He was shameless. Had always been. She said, "I'm furious at you."

But she wasn't. She couldn't make herself be angry.

"You have every right to be. May I say in my own defense . . ." He tasted the brandy. "This is rather good."

She took a quick swallow. "Very nice."

"A well-chosen and expensive tipple. Let us take a moment to appreciate it. Do housemaids generally help themselves to the good brandy?"

"More often than you'd think. We add water to the decanter so nobody notices the level falling. I'm surprised there's a glass of drinkable brandy in England." She clicked her glass against his. *"Proscht."*

She chose a Swiss toast to remind him—to remind herself—she was a foreigner in his world. Not English. Not upper crust. Not wife material. Not suitable in a hundred ways.

He replied, "Cheers."

Nothing had changed between the two of them, had it?

He sauntered across the room and deployed himself into the chintz armchair by the fire, his legs stretched out long. He'd stopped being a housebreaker and become a dandy of the *ton,* at ease, all loose limbs and carelessness. Her dangerous, deceptive Nick Lafford in his natural disguise. Her Mad Nick, who went his own way and did whatever he damn well pleased, impervious to reason. The man she'd sent away for his own good. And for hers.

She came to him, close, warming herself with the impudence and laughter inside him. Appreciating the well-polished suavity. He was as much a work of art as anything she designed. He was one of those jewels she might hold for a while, but could never possess. It was just as well she understood this.

Pity she couldn't work up a proper spout of anger. That was why she hadn't trusted herself to talk to him for three months.

When she went searching inside herself for fury and outrage, all she found was exasperation. Nicholas could exasperate paint on a wall. Probably, she sighed. "You were about to offer some weak excuse for maneuvering me into the frozen wastelands of Northumberland and interfering in my dealings with Mr. Gower."

"I was. I am. Just give me a minute to marshal excuses." Meek words. He was a man of many cordial, placating, mild words. His true intentions would always be considerably harder—flint dipped in honey. "I'm madly curious about your intentions here, by the way. Silly of me to think you'd be straightforward. You're not going to steal the *Coeur,* are you?"

"Not exactly. Or anyway, not now. You're changing the subject."

"How you do see through me."

Nick didn't drink his brandy, just held the glass in negligent fingers, resting it on the arm of the chair. A year ago they would have been talking her plan over, refining the weak points, considering alternatives and possibilities. They would have been partners.

Now, they weren't.

He might have read her mind. He murmured, "It's been a while."

"Three months." Three months since she'd put an end to whatever it was they had between them.

"Four days short of three months, if we were counting. You never told me why."

"I told you." But he hadn't understood. Strange that he couldn't see how impossible it was. He was the god of shrewd judgment when it came to everybody else. He had none for himself.

"Tell me again," he said.

"We've become a scandal."

A dismissive gesture. "We kill scandal by getting married."

"You know that's not possible."

"Why not? Remind me." Nick's gaze didn't leave her.

That determined attention caught at her like a strong wind. Pulled at her. It was hard to remember common sense and harsh realities when Nick was being persuasive.

She said, "Your family—"

"The ones I like are wildly in favor. The ones I don't like will—" He sat up abruptly. "A complication is about to arrive."

She'd heard maids going about their business in the hall outside. This was different. A man's boots came this way, heavy and impatient.

"Gower," she said.

"Most likely."

"He doesn't know me. Never met me."

"Good."

Nick grabbed her wrist and pulled her onto his lap. The glass of brandy disappeared from her hand and found its way to the table. He covered her mouth with his own and kissed her.

He tasted of soap and brandy and insistence. Of memory. Of indulgence and sweet, sweet nights together with no thought of the future. She was immersed in him as if she'd been plunged into an ocean of Nicholas. *I don't want to fight him.* Mindlessly, she let go and fell.

The footsteps slowed and stopped. The handle of the door turned. Rattled. A key scraped angrily in the lock. Nick pulled up her dress to show leg and stocking as far as the garter, creating a vulgar scene. A housemaid and her lover.

Nick whispered into her ear, "We have ten seconds. Let me kiss the hell out of you for that long."

She cut off his last words, grabbed into his hair and pulled him to her mouth. Kissed him deeply. It seemed longer than ten seconds, but it wasn't long enough.

Under half-closed lids she saw the flicker of light and

dark as the door opened. Caught the impression of dark clothing and the outraged flapping of a bat sweeping in. Gower.

Even at that last minute and past it, she didn't let go of Nick. She held on to the kiss. She was a child unwilling to take her hand out of the candy dish.

Gower yelled, "What the hell is going on here?"

Time to play her role.

She squealed and hid against Nick's shoulder. Gower didn't know her face and she wanted to keep it that way. "Oh, lawks. Oh, my dear lord. Oh, no."

"How dare you! In my own room! Get out. Get out now," Gower snarled.

She pushed Nick's hand off her thigh and pulled her skirts down. Held her apron over her face and ran for the door.

Behind her Nick murmured, "You are so very much *de trop*, Gower."

The kitchen was the warmest room in the Abbey and full of people, not one of them silent. It was haven, sanctuary, and retreat at the moment. Exactly the sort of place she could hide from members of the aristocracy.

Claire slid onto the bench at the big table, feeling she'd had a narrow escape.

Grace, who carried coal and water up and down stairs and had complicated teeth, was drinking tea. She made space, whispering, "Ye are in so much trouble."

Betsy, kitchenmaid, on the other side of the table with the other cup of tea, murmured, "Worth it though, I bet."

"Hah!" Margaret, undercook, thumped a crockery bowl full of raisins in front of them. "Here. Make yeselves useful. And ye, Mistress Claire, ye can keep out of mischief for a while. Such goings on."

Of course Gower's bellows had been heard. The who and

where and why had raced ahead of her. One of the footmen looked smug. There were no secrets in this house.

She scooped a handful of raisins out onto the table, took one of the sharp, battered little knives from the side of the bowl, and began the sticky job of taking out the seeds. When she was a child she'd seeded raisins in just this way in the blue-and-white tiled kitchen of her grandmother's house in Geneva. The oak of the table there could have been sliced from the same tree as this table under her elbows.

Tabby, also kitchenmaid, stopped lifting lids and stirring stock at the big closed stove and pushed in companionably to share the work, damp-haired and cheerful.

"They do say it be Master Nicholas they caught you with," Betsy said.

"Kissing him. In the Red Bedroom." Tabby ducked her head and lowered her voice, a careful eye on the cook at the head of the kitchen. "And mebbe up to other things. I dinna believe that, though."

Claire deseeded another raisin and slid it to the pile that was growing between the three of them. The kitchen smelled of cinnamon and something else. "I didn't kiss him," she lied. "We just talked."

"Oh, right. Right." Betsy was quick to reassure. Obviously she didn't believe a word of it.

"He's not one for troubling the maids, our Nicholas," Tabby said.

"If he did trouble 'em"—Betsy dealt with a raisin—"he'd do it in his own bedroom. Plenty of space and privacy there."

"He has the most beautiful manners," Grace said.

Tabby nodded. "Been coming here since he were a boy and never a bit of trouble out of him."

The cook scraped nutmeg into a bowl, using a little grater. He was old, white haired, stick thin, and French. In spite of his great dignity, he was listening.

Nutmeg. That was the other smell in the air.

Grace spoke up. "When I bring Mister Nicholas's shaving water mornings, he looks right at me and smiles. Thanks me. Not like that Gower. Bug under his boot is what Gower thinks I am."

"Cursing and swearing like this was Donnybrook Fair." Betsy shook her head. "Brattle and brabblement ye could hear all the way down in the parlor."

"Not a gentleman, Gower," Tabby said. "Only invited because that sweet daughter of his is a relative of milady on her mother's side."

"A distant relative," Betsy sniffed.

Tabby shrugged. "Blood's blood. Mister Nicholas ain't nowt closer related, not really."

"Difference is," Betsy said, tapping her knife on the table for emphasis, "he's a Lafford. Different stable he come out of. Different altogether."

"Even if he's picked up careless ways from all that gadding about in foreign parts, he won't bring 'em here, to milady's house. But we wondered . . ."

Silence, while they concentrated on raisins and the cook visibly leaned in the direction of the conversation. The pots on the stove lifted their lids, attentive. Even the Christmas puddings—two of them, one for the family and guests, one for the staff, brought out from the pantry and resting on the sideboard for tomorrow—were listening.

"We wondered . . ."—Betsy looked at her sidewise—"if mebbe ye knew him, you both being from London and all."

More silence, filled with avid curiosity.

People spoke of a pride of lions and a murder of crows. They should add an inquisitiveness of maids. "London's a big city," she temporized.

Tabby murmured, "Oh, a great huge place, to be sure."

"They do say there's houses as far as the eye can see," Betsy agreed.

Grace said, "Ever so large."

She hadn't convinced them. She knew that because they immediately started talking about Miss Effington's maid, who insisted on drinking cocoa in the morning as if she were a lady herself. The lack of further question and comment about Nick meant they'd made up their minds.

They'd decided she was having a mad affair with Nick. Apparently, they approved.

She seeded raisins and ate a few and watched the weather being changeable at the window. Right now, it was a haze of thin blowing white that sparked and dazzled in the light. But there was a clear patch coming. If her plans went well tomorrow, Christmas Day, she'd have to race about outdoors for a while. She'd have to hope the snow lifted for an hour or two.

She took the next fifty raisins in hand and dealt with them briskly, listened to some interesting gossip about Gower's treatment of his horses, and mentally reviewed her plans for vengeance. Then the housekeeper bustled in and sent her upstairs with a basket of seasonal greenery.

CHAPTER THREE

$\mathcal{N}$ick didn't hurry leaving Gower's room. He ignored the comments that followed him down the hall and the slam of a heavy door. A fashionable of the *ton* doesn't hurry and, besides, he had thinking to do.

Claire's plans for revenge were his second worry. Claire herself, as always, was the first. Claire was the reason he'd come here. The reason for many of the choices he'd made these last years.

They were under the same roof. A big roof, admittedly, but it was better than knocking on her door on Bedford Street and being told blandly that *mademoiselle* was in her workshop and could not be disturbed. That *mademoiselle* was not at home. That she was not receiving visitors today.

"Nickie." That came from his left, from one of the doors he'd already passed in the corridor. Maybe he should have been walking faster.

"Nickie! Over here!"

With some reluctance he turned. The door was cracked the merest inch. An eye peered from the opening. When he stopped, a pretty blond head poked out and looked both ways along the empty hall.

"Is Papa angry at you?"

"Yes." Because he was famed for his superhuman self-control, he didn't tell her to use her ears. This was Cousin Mary, after all.

"Why?"

"Nothing to do with you, fortunately." But Gower was a bastard so he added, "Stay out of his way for a while."

"I have to *talk* to you," she whispered.

"Downstairs. Pick a parlor, I'll meet you there."

She darted out into the hall and grabbed his arm. "In here. In private."

Claire, the woman he wanted beyond all others, fled like a roe deer before the hounds. Cousin Mary tried to drag him into her bedchamber.

He stood his ground. "I never enter a woman's bedroom without immoral intent. I'm fond of you, but not that fond."

"We can't talk in the hall."

"We are talking in the hall." He leaned past her and pulled the door to her room firmly closed behind her. "Come downstairs, sweet, and regale me with your problems as we go. By the way, why are your pretty jewels tossed together in a box in your father's wardrobe?"

"He's a swine."

"Well, of course he is. How is he being swinish at the moment?"

"He stomped in and took everything out of my jewelry box and carried it off."

To lure Claire back, he'd involved himself with the Gowers. Not the most favorite of his distant cousins. Somehow this meant playing knight errant to Cousin Mary. God knew she needed one. "How odd of him. Why?"

"So I can't take my jewels and run away." She pressed her lips together, looking like a desperate and harassed white rabbit. "What am I going to do?"

"I'd discuss that with Charlie if I were you. Let us seek him out and you two can consult."

"Papa watches me. His valet spies on me. The lady's maid he hired for me—"

"Spies on you. I'm sorry about that. There are crowned heads of state who gad about with more freedom."

"He's probably bribed the housemaids here to watch me."

"Very possibly. I have a secret emissary among the maids. I can ask her if she's been bribed."

Mary wrinkled her forehead and became a worried rabbit. "I could escape if you'd get engaged to me. He'd stop watching if I agreed to marry someone he approves of."

"I doubt he approves of me at the moment."

"But he does. He really does. You're rich and you're related to everyone important. You could be duke someday."

"Not unless I arrange the death of seven male heirs, three of them children. Not in the best of taste, slaughtering one's relatives. Though, on a selective basis, I've been tempted."

Mary paid no attention. She was, he thought, a good bit smarter than she let on. She fell into step beside him, which was to say he walked slowly and she hopped at his side, looking at him instead of where she was going. He hoped Charlie had more patience with this sort of thing than he did.

She returned to her argument. "We don't have to be engaged long."

"The prospect is naturally enticing. But no."

"Charlie and I could elope. You could lock Papa in a dungeon to give us time. They probably have dungeons here."

"Not a one. When I was a boy, we looked. I'm also not going to knock your father over the head or drug his brandy or set highway men on him. I am not a gothic novel."

She looked blank. More than usually blank. "Will you sneak into Papa's room and steal my jewels for me?"

"I was hoping to get through the holidays without stealing those jewels. We shall see."

His family. His interwoven and nearly limitless family with branches and twigs of it sprouting off in every direction and every one of them madder than the next. Why did he let himself get drawn into these things? Claire was enough complication to last a man for his lifetime.

He said, "Charlie doesn't need your trinkets. He's not poor."

"They belong to me and I want them." Now she looked like a sly and devious rabbit.

They'd come to the top of the stair that led downward. Clatter and roistering surged through the front hall. A dozen of the younger guests, skates in hand, were headed for the ornamental pond at the end of the garden and ice-skating. Mary took his arm and leaned on him all the way down the stair.

At the bottom he detached her. "Find Charlie," he said. "Go ice-skating. Your father's not going to be watching you out there."

She frowned again. She had a pretty frown, like a kitten or some baby animal. That was something else he hoped Charlie appreciated. She said, "We don't have much time. Papa wants to find me in a compromising position with one of the men he's picked out. I don't know how he's going to do it, but that's what he's planning. It could be you, Nickie. You have to help me."

Because he'd known her since she was a wobbly three-year-old, he said, "I'll do my best."

If anyone wondered why he spent his life flitting between the major cities of Europe, it was to escape his family.

Around them in the entrance hall the pack paired off for skating, laughing, acutely aware of each other, collecting coats and scarves from the footmen. Through the door of the Tapestry Drawing Room he could see a dozen older guests ranged comfortably by the fire.

Charlie wandered out from behind a pillar and saw Mary. His head snapped up like some questing hound. There was an almost audible click in the air and he started toward her.

"I'm going to marry Charlie. I don't care what Papa says." The white rabbit had become a determined white rabbit. Love did that to you.

"I'll see if I can get him for you." That might even be a good use for the pair of reliable riding horses he'd brought. The border with Scotland was spitting distance away. How hard could it be to travel ten or fifteen miles in this weather? His coachman would know. Or he'd ask Claire's advice. She was always sending messengers across Europe with a fortune in jewels stuffed in their smallclothes.

He left Mary in Charlie Pearson's capable hands and went to track down the woman who was in no shadow of any possibility a fool.

CHAPTER FOUR

It was surprisingly difficult to pluck one maidservant from the flock at Holbourne Abbey. Nick finally found her in the maze of service halls on the lower floor. When she left the house, she carried what appeared to be a basket of festive plant materials—holly, bay, pine, fir branches possibly.

They pushed through the wind and snow, her leading, him following, around the house. Then they stood awhile, each in their separate bit of landscape. He was getting cold, even if she wasn't.

He'd admit he didn't know the minutia of a housemaid's work at Holbourne Abbey, but he'd wager it didn't include long, chill intervals inspecting the bushes outside the house. The bushes directly under . . . He leaned against a brick wall that separated one anonymous garden from another and counted windows, matching them to his mental floor plan of the house. She was exactly under the Red Bedroom. Gower's room.

That was interesting. He would have gone to help if she'd been doing something industrious, but she just stood and considered the shrubbery. Probably she was thinking. She could do that as well without him as with him.

He was utterly charmed by the intensity with which she ignored him. It seemed impolite to break through that. She knew he was here. He hadn't been secretive following her out the back door and around the house. So now they both stood about getting snowed on and he kept watch in case she needed help. He passed the time guessing what that ingenious woman might be up to.

It took five or six minutes for Claire to discover all she needed to know about that patch of icy ground and snow-covered bushes. All was satisfactory, it seemed. She set her basket neatly on the ground, removed a top layer of prickly green, and took out what was underneath. That turned out to be a rope ladder with iron hooks on top. It was very much like one they'd used in Vienna. He could even make a good guess as to which shop she'd bought it in near the docks in London.

She pushed in among the bushes, scattering snow, and everything shook for a while. He didn't have to see to know she was unrolling those ropes over branches and along the ground, making it look as if it had fallen from the window above. When she came out, dislodging more snow, she left no obvious sign of what she'd done. The ladder wouldn't be seen unless you happened to be walking by and looked closely. Another hour of snow and even that would be hidden.

So now he knew what she was up to. Not the final cunning details, of course, but the overall plan.

He clapped slowly, not making noise, using broad gestures. She turned in his direction, radiating displeasure, but didn't come over and say anything. She'd evidently decided to reserve comment for another time and place. A warmer one, he hoped.

She picked up her holly and pine, replaced it in the basket, and headed off. He followed twenty paces behind on the cold stomp back to the house, playing the lovelorn swain, which he was. Whatever she was up to, from here he could keep an eye on her.

CHAPTER FIVE

Once inside, Claire didn't dawdle getting to the Tapestry Drawing Room. Mrs. Taft wanted the holly and green boughs put out, the good luck distributed to the household, and everybody in the kitchen on hand to help with the dinner.

Nick strolled along behind her with his signature insouciance, keeping up. He must be freezing to death. She'd wrapped up in her cloak when she went out, the warm, red wool that was a practical countrywoman's wear. He'd followed her without getting his own coat. He'd stood in the wind wearing nothing but his jacket. Idiot.

Down the long hall past the kitchen. Up the stairs. She was full of images that had nothing to do with here and now. She remembered Nick skimming down the rope ladder in Vienna, holding it taut and steady for her as she came after him, awkward in skirts. Nick absolutely silent while he loaded a gun for her and went out to meet a pack of mountain bandits, unarmed. Nick taking the cold spot in the bed.

She'd made the right decision when she cut the ties between them. She'd known it was going to hurt. It did.

She stopped at the door of the Tapestry Room and let him catch her up. She said, "We have the room to ourselves. If you have something to say, this is the moment."

The Foreign Office dispatched Mr. Nicholas Lafford to

the far corners of Europe to lie for his country. In Prague or Paris he sliced Gordian knots and disentangled complications for king and country. Cunning as a fox, knowing as one of the more successful Medicis, accepted everywhere. He raised aristocratic blandness to high art. It was a pleasure to watch him work, except when his particular skills were directed at her.

"Ah. Good. Do you know where we are?" he asked.

The answer to that was not the "Tapestry Drawing Room off the main Hall," obviously. "Guessing games?"

"Of a sort." Nick took the basket from her and held it in one hand. He used the other to tilt her head up. "Look."

For an instant she didn't see what he meant.

He said, "The kissing bough's hung. Those clever footmen." Gently, one hand along her cheek, he brought her to face him. He laid his lips over hers.

They'd shared a thousand kisses. This was different.

Nick had brought the cold in with him on his clothes and his skin. Cold filled the air around him. Rose from his damp jacket. When she took his face between her hands, she felt the chill scoured into him by the wind. His hair between her fingers still held snowflakes.

He didn't offer an amiable kiss, a friendly kiss, a comfortable kiss. This wasn't even the passion he took and gave so fiercely. This was Nick stripped to stark demand, the pretenses gone.

It was unsettling to think of what Nick might be, stripped of pretenses.

He ended it before she did. He took the hand she'd laid on his cheek and kissed it, as formal as if he'd been taking liberties with a duchess. "I wish kisses could convince you," he said. "But they won't."

"No."

She felt him shrug. "Let's exchange some of those words you've been running away from for the last three months."

The face of Nicholas Lafford changed when he wasn't

telling lies. He looked both older and younger when his defenses were down. Younger face. Older eyes. He was still beautiful as the dawn. Maybe that came from being an aristocrat and bred to it.

She felt her heart twist in her chest. Felt her lungs clench as if a giant fist squeezed around them.

"I'd rather not have this conversation."

He nodded. "Not so easy to say it to my face, is it?"

"Painful," she said. "For both of us. You'll probably wish you'd just walked away. I know I do." She pulled her shawl around her and crossed to the great mantelpiece over the fireplace. He was right. It was time to say these words. No more avoiding it. No more hoping she could tear apart the ties between them without this final confrontation.

When she looked back, he was plucking one single white berry from the mistletoe of the kissing bough. He tucked it in the pocket in his vest before he picked up the basket and joined her.

She must say good-bye to Nicholas with complete finality. She must marshal the facts that would convince him. But she was in no hurry to come to that inevitability. She could wait five minutes. Or ten.

"I have my own mantelpieces here," she told him. "My own assigned picture frames and mirrors, plinths and odd corners. Mrs. Taft—she's the housekeeper—makes use of me extensively in the matter of mantelpiece decoration. She thinks I'm filled with artistic talent. It's because I come from London."

"A woman of perspicacity." Nick helped himself to one of the parlor chairs. "Where do you want this?"

"I'll get one of the ladders from—"

But he'd already pulled his jacket off and draped it across the seat so she could stand on it. "Where?"

Gallantry. It came from his excellent good manners and from that great generosity he mostly kept hidden. She was about to hurt him in several significant ways so she accepted this gesture. She said, "Let us go left to right as if we were reading. Put it here, on the left side."

The footmen had brought up baskets of useful green bits and pieces. She knelt and went through her inventory.

Nick stood beside her, arms folded, looking down. "The holly and the ivy. A basketful of tradition. We did this together last year," he said. "Remember?"

Last year they'd crossed the Channel in cold weather and ridden up from Dover to arrive at her house in London the day before Christmas. Outside was rain that froze as it hit the cobbles and a stiff wind coming up the Thames. An unlovely day. But they'd been warm and cozy in her parlor. They'd walked to her parish church at midday and Nick had stuffed the poor box with banknotes on his way out.

Yes. She remembered.

"This isn't so different. Just grander." She lifted red ribbons tied into bows and sewed tight. Took wide white ribbon still on the spool from the top of the basket. "We have hectares of holly and miles of ribbon. Enough to decorate East Anglia."

"A county badly in need of embellishment."

"I've always thought so."

Last year on the way home from church they'd bought Christmas wreaths and pine branches from a cart in Russell Square and carried armfuls home in the rain, prickly and awkward and dripping. They'd stood laughing on her doorstep to shake the water off before they went inside. She said, "My grandmother used to take me to the Winter Market to buy gingerbread. It doesn't taste the same when I buy it in London."

"I envy you that gingerbread." He sounded perfectly serious. She looked up sharply. There was nothing in his face but a kind of serious intensity. "I envy you a childhood in the house on Verdaine Street in Geneva with the mountains all around. Learning a trade at your grandfather's knee. Sorting citrines and topaz by the window. Rolling your hoop across the Place de la Madeleine down to the docks on the lake. I envy you sitting on a stool in the kitchen, eating gingerbread."

"I know how lucky I am."

The smells and sounds and sights crowded around her. She was overdue for a visit home. She'd go there when she was finished striking back at Gower. Grandpapa spent most of his time drowsing before the fire these days, but he'd laugh when she told him about it.

Nick put a touch on her shoulder. Three fingers, just holding her attention. "Claire, let me tell you about growing up a Lafford."

"You don't have to—"

"I'm making a rather lengthy point. Bear with me." He went down on his haunches suddenly, beside her. They were face to face. "Show me what you're doing with this greenery. Twining it together?"

"Holly twisted with the ivy and tied. With this." She picked thick black string from the selection of threads and strings. "We can talk about something else. I don't need to know your secrets."

"Yes, you do." He was competent with the holly. Mostly, though, he looked at her. "I want you to imagine a great mansion. A house grander than Holbourne Abbey, but silent and formal. A cold perfection from the topiary in the garden to the paintings on the ceiling. That's where I grew up, spare son of a spare son. I doubt my parents could have picked me out of a crowd. I don't know how old I was when I realized I was an annoyance who must be provided for. I was quite indecently glad to go away to Eton."

Nick—so totally self-possessed, such entertaining company. Men do not build a shield of caustic wit unless they need shields. Unshakable self-sufficiency comes from having no one to depend on.

She said, "I thought it would be something like that."

"I stand before you, transparent as well-blown glass."

Nick took the scissors from her and snipped off a length of black string. Twenty inches or so. "I'll need yards of this, so keep it handy. Claire, why did you kick me out of your life?"

"You asked me to marry you."

"I did, didn't I? Not usually the signal for panicked flight."

Could she tell him he offered everything she wanted? That she'd sent him away before she weakened and said yes.

He'd opened a little muslin bag. "Do you want tiny gilded pinecones or gilded walnuts? I have both. In some ancient time an aged aunt of the Stretton household painted these. They use them every year."

She accepted them from his hand. "You used to spend Christmas here?"

"They took in a distant cousin. I didn't willingly return to that mausoleum my family lives in. More string, please." He held out his left hand, palm up.

She obliged with the string. "City Christmases for me. The manager of my London shop—the shop in Bond Street, not the exchange in the City—invites me to his house on every holiday." She had to smile. "He has a fat wife, a yappy white dog, and an abundance of children. We speak German." She added, "You can't put gilded pinecones, even small ones, on ivy. Ivy doesn't have pinecones."

"My ivy does."

"Then use the thread. There are needles here some-where. Do it right, if you must do it."

" 'There's a divinity that shapes our ivy, rough hew it how we will.' If you marry me we'll put pinecones on apple trees in every city in Europe. I'll catch blackmailers and petty thieves. You'll buy the discarded gems of princes." He ges-tured, asking for a threaded needle. Black thread. They were complex gestures. "It'll never be dull with me, Claire."

She complied. She gave him fine black silk thread to anchor his inappropriate pinecones. "It can't work."

"I'm not conceited enough to think sharing a bed with me is going to change your mind. I don't expect to overwhelm you with kisses, though it'd be fun to try. But we've been friends. We've been accomplices, partners, lovers. Tell me why we can't take the next step. I deserve to know why you've sent me away. Tell me."

There was a universe of patience inside him, all of it waiting for her to answer.

Then a woman stood in the doorway. One of the guests. She choked out, "Oh, Nickie," and stumbled toward them, crying.

CHAPTER SIX

*T*he girl in the doorway was pretty. Lovely even. Slender and graceful, with the gold and rose English coloring. And oh, so young.

Claire thought, *This is the sort of woman Nick should marry*, and was sad and angry knowing that.

The girl launched herself at Nick and began sobbing into his cravat. Nick was precisely the sort of man one would want to sob upon, having mountains of sangfroid at his disposal and the likelihood of handkerchiefs. He was performing the necessary soothing and patting and looked gratifyingly annoyed with the whole business.

"Papa found us in the library together," the girl choked out. "He ordered Charlie to go away and never see me again."

"You can ignore that," Nick said. "It's not possible to snub somebody at a house party. You're going to find yourself sitting next to Charlie at every meal. I'll arrange it."

"Charlie left and Papa hit me and called me a stupid little slut. He hit me, Nickie. He said I'd been—"

"Hush. It's over. He won't hit you again." Nick folded the girl in against his chest. "I won't let it happen."

Quiet words, firmly spoken. The reassurance you'd give a child. But this was Nick making the promise.

Nick met her eyes over the girl's head. Sometimes his mask slipped and the ruthlessness that made him so useful to the diplomatic corps showed through. His features held nothing but a certain immobility. It was his eyes that gave him away. They had become entirely cold.

It was unwise to hurt someone Nick was fond of, as he was fond of this girl. . . .

Who needed help. Claire pushed branches and leaves and bows of red ribbon out of her lap and crossed the room to her.

Gower's daughter. Heiress of some reasonable amount of money, owner of that box of gaudy jewels, darling of the *ton,* cousin to the sort of people who lived in country mansions, but still not someone to envy. All kinds of lessons to be learned from that.

"He's looking for her right now." Nick interpreted the mumbles coming from the region of his chest. "He went to her room and didn't find her." More mumbles. "Fortunately, by that time she'd gone to hide in my bedroom."

"Where you were not."

"Where I was not because I was following you hither and yon about the property."

"You lead a charmed life, Nick."

"And because I was harmlessly engaged in following you, Gower didn't find me with Mary, doing this"—he lifted his hands an inch, indicating what he held —"in my bedroom."

"That would have been a merry meeting. The daughter, your bedroom, and an already-enraged father." Gently she disengaged Mary from Nick's shirtfront and turned her. "Let me see, pet." She coaxed blond hair back from a pale, blotched face. "Where did he . . . ?"

She saw—Nick saw—a reddened cheek that resolved into the print of a spatulate hand.

Shock filled her, and then anger. No woman who worked for her in her house, or served in the shops, or repaired jewelry at the benches in the studio would face this. Every woman of them knew there was a place to go for help and someone to protect her. Mary Gower needed that protection.

"I made him angry," Mary said in a little voice. "I should have—"

"A pox on that. You didn't make him angry. He made himself angry." Her own vengeance against Gower was feeling more and more trivial. She touched Mary's cheek. "We'll get some ice to put on it. There's certainly enough around the place."

Nick said, "He's looking for her right now."

"Then he won't find her. We won't let him."

Nick was already calculating, going over the same possibilities she was. "Where is she safe?"

She could answer that. The simple answer. "With Lady Holly. Absolute protection."

"Until Gower takes Mary back to London."

Mary started crying again, not making any noise, just standing there between them, trembling, with tears running down her face. Nick put his arm around her shoulders, muttering, "Damn it. Where is Charlie when I need him? I suppose he has to run off with her. Gower's never going to let them marry."

He must have felt the question. He met her eyes. "Charlie is the best of good fellows. He has an income and a small property somewhere."

"In Kent," Mary said in a wavering voice.

"But he doesn't move in the highest circles. He's Edgerton's bastard. Gower has higher ambitions."

"Like you," Mary said.

"That's all very well." It wasn't, but if Nick could deal with Turkish bandits, which he could, he could depress the ambitions of a Gower. More important—she peered into Mary's face and asked, "Do you want to run off with Charlie? Elope? Is that what you want?"

"Yes," Mary said simply and stopped crying.

"Then you shall, Mary mine. I will arrange it." Nick

grinned his insidious, wholly unrepentant grin. They'd done some of their best work when he was grinning like that. "Which means we can't give you over to Lady Holly because it's not polite to involve one's hostess in an elopement."

Nick with the bit between his teeth. Sometimes the man needed the voice of reason. "It's not that easy."

"Your definition of easy has always eluded me, sweetheart. She wants to run off with Charlie. Charlie, for reasons of his own, doubtless good ones, wants to run off with her. Simple."

"So you say. In any case, they can't go today." She gestured toward the window. White flakes in various stages of torment writhed outside. "You couldn't elope to the garden wall in this weather, let alone Scotland."

"Tomorrow. We'll send them off tomorrow."

"If the weather clears." She lined up problems in her mind, one by one. "If we can distract Gower long enough. If they want to go."

Mary—she'd almost forgotten Mary—piped up, "We do."

"We keep Gower away from her," Nick said, his voice hard. "He doesn't come near her. Pity she can't just lock herself in her room for a day or two."

"She can." It was possible. More than possible. This would work. "Mary has a headache. Mary has a fever and—I don't know—chilblains and the migraine and fits. She needs nursing. She needs that scary old bat who haunts the attic. The old nanny."

"Mrs. Locksley. I used to be terrified of her when I was a boy."

"You still are, if you have any sense. We will bring the old lady down and put her on a trundle bed in Mary's room. Even Gower won't get past Mrs. Locksley."

"There are Prussian regiments who would retreat in disarray before Mrs. Locksley."

"You talk to Lady Holly. I'll . . ." She could feel the seconds ticking by. Gower would be going room to room, looking for his errant daughter. Only a matter of time before he showed up at the Tapestry Room. "I'll get her out of sight."

"Where?"

"As well here as anywhere else."

There were no places to hide in the Tapestry Room. Nick didn't look for one. He knew she'd have a plan. "What do you need?"

"I'll use that chair. That one. Bring it over "—she picked a spot—"here. And take your jacket with you. You'll want it if you're visiting distant attics to fetch down crones."

He'd already lifted one of the baskets to the chair, and moved the other closer. "She can't really hide behind this," he said.

"She'll do well enough. I need your handkerchief."

He was carrying a nice large one. Perfectly clean. She folded herself down to the ground, muttering, "Ribbon, thread, and needle. And a handkerchief. Thank God some men can be relied on."

Now she needed Mary. She looked up. "Come here." She pointed. "Sit. No. Closer to me. Facing away from the door."

Mary was all bewilderment, but willing. She set herself down rather gingerly on the hearthrug.

"White ribbon." That was for Nick. "Around her waist. Tie it in back as if she's wearing an apron." More words than she needed, really, with Nick.

"Right. Where are the scissors—Good." Nick pulled out two arm's lengths of wide ribbon. Snipped it off. Circled it around Mary's waist and into a neat bow. "But will he recognize the dress?"

"I don't understand." Mary did not seem to be one of the world's speedy thinkers.

"You're going to pretend to be a maid." She said that to

Mary. To Nick, she said, "Dark blue velvet. We're lucky. Half the maids are wearing dark blue wool." She had the needle threaded. "A dozen feet away he won't be able to tell the difference." She began the huge, hurried stitches that would shape the handkerchief into a rough cap. Fast and clumsy. It would do for a single glance from the doorway.

"Maybe. Maybe." Nick danced backwards six steps. Ten steps. All the way to the parlor door. Fast and facile. Sword-fighting moves, so graceful it hurt to look at him. Hurt her, anyway. He said, "It's good. The basket hides you, mostly."

He came back to make minute adjustments to the placement of baskets.

"We are maids putting out decorations. Nobody looks at us. And we will be even less conspicuous when you are gone, Mr. Lafford."

"Then you need this." He dropped to one knee, reached among the ivy and pine, and spilled a huge inventory into Mary Gower's lap to hide the lack of an apron.

He said, "Claire."

"Yes." Stitching, she didn't bother to look up.

"Love . . ."

That got her attention. Not in the best way, perhaps, since he was saying it in front of his cousin. She said, "You should—"

He leaned across the Christmas trimmings and the disorder of greenery and kissed her quickly, but firmly and thoroughly. At her ear he whispered, "Take care of yourself, as well as that fool Mary. I need you."

She didn't think of a reply before he was out the door and gone. Then she thought of five or six.

CHAPTER SEVEN

Claire said, "Almost done." The mobcap turned in her hands, receiving the final stitches that attached the ribbon trimming. It was large and floppy and would cover most of Mary Gower's hair. "It's not authentic close up. But then, if anyone comes that close, the game is up."

"Am I supposed to wear that?" Mary's face screwed up into mild distaste. "It's very ugly."

"Isn't it? You're not nearly as stupid as you act—nobody could be that stupid—so you're used to wearing a disguise. Lean over and let me put this on you."

A quick, shaky laugh. Mary took the crude cap from her, pulled it on, and began a competent job of hiding her distinctive blond hair. "If I'm a fool, nobody pays attention to me. If Papa thinks I'm stupid, he doesn't watch me carefully. Sometimes I get away with doing exactly what I want." She tilted her head, fingering the edge of the cap. "Will I pass as a maid? I'll keep my head down and be very occupied with this." She picked up some of the sprawling decoration in her lap.

"We both will. I want your father to walk past this room with a single glance and see two maids putting up the Christmas decoration. Nothing else."

"When Papa's angry, he doesn't give up. He rolls over everything and everybody. He'll—"

A clatter from above. Someone was coming down the

great staircase. But the noise quickly became four or five on the stair, their voices lighthearted together, tossing laughter back and forth. That wasn't Gower. Not yet.

Mary had frozen in place. "He'll be so angry when he finds me." She squeezed her hands together and pressed them against her belly. "He'll come here."

"But he'll go through the obvious places first." Claire kept her voice entirely calm. "The attics and storerooms. He'll go pounding on the doors of locked bedrooms and stomping through the kitchen, making himself a nuisance. He'll be tired and impatient and humiliated and he'll never imagine you'd be here, in plain sight, on the main floor."

"I wouldn't imagine it either," Mary said.

"Then let us play the role fate has assigned. We'll keep our hands busy making perfectly splendid festoons. Black thread." She held up a spool. "I'll show you what I want done with the holly."

They worked, making the garlands as she wanted, turning them in a curl that would surround the Christmas candle set in the middle of the mantel. Holbourne Abbey would get exactly the sort of decoration she put in her own parlor, except twice as long. She murmured, "Use more string," and "Turn it so the leaves face in the same direction. Like this," and "We're putting tiny gold pinecones on the ivy," and "Don't ask me why."

Mary's hands stopped shaking when they had something to do.

After a while, Mary whispered, "You're not a servant, are you? You're the shop girl. Nickie's shop girl."

"I own shops." This was what it meant to be scandalous. In her own world she was respected and deferred to. In Nick's, she was an object of mockery.

"Cousin Lavinia—Nickie's sister, you know—calls you 'That Shop Girl.' She makes up a lot of vicious nicknames."

"I'm not entirely surprised."

"She calls me the Idiot Mouse and smiles when she does it. But she doesn't smile when she talks about you."

"I've met her."

"Then you know what she is," Mary said. "I'm not sure Nick does. You can't tell what he's thinking."

Nick was the shrewdest of men, but even shrewd men could be blind when it came to a sister. He didn't listen to her today, but years from now, when it was too late, he might.

Nick's sister had come to the house in Bedford Street months ago, mincing into the parlor, pricing the furnishings in a fretful, dissatisfied way, looking for vulgarity and not finding it. She'd perched on the edge of a chair and explained crisply that the affair between a shopkeeper and a Lafford must end. That it was ruinous for him. That the Foreign Office would ask for his resignation. That his family was disgusted with him.

Mary would appreciate this—"She said she'd make sure no one came to my shops if I didn't give her brother up."

That got a genuine smile. "Oh, but she'd like to have a tenth that much power. She's nobody in the *ton*. She doesn't realize they're sneering at her most of the time. They tolerate her because of Nick. What did you say?"

"What any little upstart foreign shopkeeper would say. I told her she should have asked for Austrian crystal when she replaced the jewels in her bracelet. Birmingham glass is sadly obvious."

Mary choked on laughter and pressed her fist to her mouth to keep it inside.

That was what Gower saw when he passed in the hall and poked his head into the Tapestry Drawing Room—two housemaids sitting tailor-fashion on the hearthrug, half-hidden by baskets and chair and long garlands of shiny green leaves, whispering together, doubled over laughing.

Gower snarled, "Damned lazy sluts."

Peering sideways, Claire saw high boots, a gold-and-green waistcoat, and the florid, self-indulgent, pug-nosed fury of a bully.

An inch away from her, Mary's face drained of all color. Claire took her forearm and squeezed hard, telling her to stay quiet. Do nothing. There was no way to call back their laughter, but it was natural enough for a pair of giggling housemaids to be startled and dismayed and fall silent.

She said, "Sorry, sir," in a muffled voice, not moving, trying for a bit of Northumberland accent.

"I'm looking for Miss Gower. Where is she? Have you seen her?"

"No, sir." Mary, beside her, was shaking. She wanted to say, "Stay still. Still as a rabbit that sees the fox. Still as ice in a frozen stream."

She had to get him out of here before Mary fainted. Claire stood up slowly. It would be unnatural to do otherwise. A good housemaid is polite to the guests.

She spread her skirt in a half curtsey. It hid Mary behind her. "Is owt wrong, sir? Should I fetch up Mrs. Taft to ye? The housekeeper, sir?"

She watched his face. Gower had already discussed matters with the housekeeper.

"We'll go look fer yer Miss Gower. I'll just run get Mrs. Taft."

It routed him. He snarled, "No, God damn it," and slammed the door back against the wall as he left.

And they were safe.

CHAPTER EIGHT

Just before midnight Claire wrapped herself in her wool dressing gown and crept from her bed among the sleeping maids. She felt her way down the dark attic hall, one hand running along the wall. The window over the stairs was full of darkness and rattling windowpanes. Christmas was riding in at the back of the North Wind, but it was coming.

Maybe the weather would clear tomorrow. Maybe it would be a day of elopement, the rescue of fair maidens, and clever vengeance. She indulged in some mindless optimism since that was suited to the season.

The servants' stair was cold as the attics and as dark. But she knew these stairs by heart, having been up and down them a good many times. The upper floors were all silence. A knot of men stayed up, drinking and playing billiards in privacy at the back of the house, but most of the guests had gone to bed early. Some of them would go to the village tomorrow for Christmas service in the little church there, even in the face of the storm. It was a tradition for the Strettons. For the guests . . . it made an excuse to be vigorous in the open air. Some of these former soldiers found civilian life dawdling.

The grand rooms of the ground floor were drafty caverns, lit here and there by candles set inside glass chimneys. The double doors to the Tapestry Drawing Room were closed. In this well-maintained household they made not a single squeak when she opened them and slipped through.

A fire burned low in the hearth, giving plenty of light to guide her through the room. The hunting scenes hung on the wall were muted into contours of black and gray. She couldn't see the horses rearing and dogs leaping, huntsmen bounding into the fray, maidens cheering them on from the side of the wood. But she knew they were there.

At the center of everything the Christmas candle stood on the mantelpiece surrounded by the swirls and twists of the Christmas garlands she'd made.

Lady Holly had lit it before sunset. Family, guests, and everyone from downstairs crowded into the room to watch. It would burn all night, on this night, at the heart of the house.

She came close to the fire, getting warm on one side, still cold on the other, and looked up at the candle flame. She'd fallen into an odd mood, no longer gnawing away at plans for tomorrow. She had an inexplicable certainty that everything would work out.

"Mary's safely settled," Nick said, behind her. "I checked after supper. Nobody's getting past the Demon Nanny. She'll meet us in the library tomorrow morning."

I knew he'd come. "You have allies among the servants. Somehow, they all know Gower hit her."

"The servants always know. It's part of their charm." Nick came closer. "It means every eye will be turned elsewhere tomorrow, glued to a roast on the spit or the Christmas pudding aboil—"

"Letting Mary elope."

"If we have good weather." After a minute he said, "You're cold."

"December in Northumberland."

"Of course. The very rocks in the ground are shivering."

There was no distance between them now. She felt the warmth radiating from his body, then a brush of his clothing as he opened his coat and took her in his arms and wrapped the coat around both of them. He held her. They stood like the old friends and lovers they were, sharing their bodies' heat.

She snuggled her back against him and wrapped his coat tight. She encountered his hands, doing the same. A coat for two. She put her hands over his and said, "You remembered I like to watch Christmas come."

"I like it myself. I like it better when I'm with you," he said.

Chill wisps of wind whispered past them, gathered together, and blew up the chimney in a long, low, deep column of sound. She said, "When I was a child, in Geneva, we used to dress up warm and walk to the Cathedral of Saint Pierre. We'd stand outside and listen to the bells at midnight. The most beautiful bells in the world, they say."

"They say that in Geneva."

"We are nearly always right."

It was an entirely perfect moment. They were together, keeping each other company. Holding human warmth between them. The air around them was empty and waiting. The huge stone house around them, perfectly silent.

She said, "I've made decisions—"

"Not tonight," he whispered. "Nothing here tonight but you and me and Christmas."

Christmas came then, striking the first three deep notes at the great case clock in the marble entry hall, spilling from parlor to parlor to breakfast room to conservatory to ballroom, chiming and tinkling, filling the house. Voices, just at the edge of hearing, ceased. She and Nick weren't the only ones listening for Christmas.

The last notes, small and sweet, sounded here in the Tapestry Room from the French ebony-and-gilt clock on the table under the window.

She stayed where she was for a long time, leaning into Nick's arms. They said very little. At last, reluctantly, they moved apart. Nick walked her upstairs to her room in the attic and waited till she went inside.

CHAPTER NINE

She was going to be clever and vengeful today, Claire decided, and possibly criminal. Since it was Mary's jewelry she'd be tossing into the snow with Mary's tacit permission, this wasn't technically illegal. Gower cheating her in Paris had not been technically illegal. It would be especially satisfying to deliver a backhanded blow to Gower and stay carefully within the law.

She'd awakened at dawn in the long attic room with the comfortable sound of three other maids snoring gently. Christmas Day splatted snow against the window. Not promising weather.

But a few hours later Holbourne Abbey could have been inhabiting a different country or a different month. The sky was a clear and transparent blue, the air, dry and crisp. Guests, family, and every servant who wasn't absolutely needed in the kitchen would go to church in the village.

A perfect day for going to church or for an elopement or to enact a long-awaited revenge.

She went to the library to await events. Nick brought a roll up from breakfast and offered it to her. When she shook her head, he ate the roll slowly, tearing it apart and consuming it bite by bite as he strolled about, looking at the titles of books. He had the air of a man prepared to be entertained by a difficult day, rather like a lion tamer at the Roman coliseum getting ready for the fights.

Eventually Mary arrived, leading a sturdy, brown-haired young man—Charlie—by the hand, being surreptitious. They darted into the library, closed the door behind them, established themselves in a sheltered nook, and started kissing.

Not yet. Not yet. Nothing could be done till the house emptied. Claire stayed at the library window. It was cold enough and the wind was strong enough that heat was sucked out the windowpanes and all the spaces of the frame leaked cold. From time to time Nick came over to appreciate the view and went away without comment.

From here she could see the stables and the path to the village. Grooms had been out early, leading carriage horses back and forth to pack down the snow. Hearty souls began the tromp to the village, strong young men and women arm in arm with the older ones. Three sleighs, piled with furs and blankets, came last, carrying the ladies of the family and the guests. Gower rode in the third sleigh.

Nick rubbed the fog of their breath off the windowpane. "It's time."

"We have a lot to do before Gower gets back," she said. "Keep an eye on those two."

She hiked up her skirts and took the main staircase two steps at a time. Nobody to complain about it. For all practical purposes she had the house to herself.

The jewelry box was where she'd left it in the wardrobe, still sliding and clattering when she picked it up. She lifted the lid, found everything in place. The leather case that held the *Coeur de Flamme*—yes. All present and accounted for.

She opened the casement window before she left. Wooden box hugged to her chest, rattling slightly, she ran through the empty house, down the stairs, into the library.

She detached Mary from her frantic hold on Charlie and showed her the box.

"These are mine. They were my mother's." Mary pressed fingertips to one leather case and then another. "Papa sold most of her jewels. These are the only ones left. I won't let Papa have them."

"We won't." They packed the cases, one by one, into the top of Mary's satchel. Claire took out the Heart of Fire. This was the last time she'd touch it, probably. The currents of fate were unlikely to bring it back in her direction. She laid it across Mary's palm.

"I was going to wear it at the ball," Mary said. "I had a dress made to match it. Pink."

"Pink?"

"Pink silk with little embroidered flowers. And a double flounce at the hem." Mary pressed her lips together. "I like the new setting. I didn't at first, but it's kind of pretty."

Kind of pretty. "Thank you. The *Coeur* is very old. Nine hundred years old. From India. Stories say it gives courage to anyone who wears it."

Mary closed her fingers around it and she gave a shaky laugh. "I could use some courage."

"Put it on, then. Under your clothes." Quickly, she fastened it around Mary's neck. "Wear the Heart of Fire on your way north. Wear it at your wedding. For luck. For courage." It occurred to her that Mary had lived with Gower her whole life and not been cowed. The fragile-looking blond girl had her own kind of courage.

They'd come to the tangled magpie nest of jewelry in the bottom of the box. "What about these?"

Mary had already turned away. "Papa bought those. He can keep them."

Claire trudged up the little hill at the far reaches of the garden, clutching Gower's ugly jewelry box to her chest. Down there was the ornamental pond where the guests had skated yesterday. Behind her were clumps of rhododendron and holly. Nick waited beside her with his usual catlike patience.

"It's not that far to Scotland," she said. "There're carts

and carriages on the road. Lots of help if they get into trouble."

"They'll be fine. They aren't wandering in some howling wilderness."

Mary Gower and her Charlie, riding Nick's borrowed horses, would be through the village by now and out on the main road north. "There are farms and houses. It's not deserted," she said.

"Charlie Pearson was in the retreat from Corunna. A little run up to Scotland is a stroll in the park for him. And you'll give them a good head start. That"—he gestured to the box she held—"should distract Gower."

"Such is mine intention."

"You'll doubtless explain what we're doing here. In your own good time." Nick was warmly dressed, but he hadn't stopped to fetch a hat. When the wind blew, snow sifted down from tree branches and fell into his hair, sparkling against the black. "I think I know, but tell me. I like to see how your mind works."

Of course he knew. "This is where the thieves stopped to divide their loot. Right here."

"That would be the thieves who went out the window in Gower's room. Their ladder broke and they fell into the shrubbery. That's why there's rope among the bushes."

"Those thieves," she agreed.

"After they fell, they limped all the way through the snow to where they'd tied their horses."

"They are hearty and determined thieves."

"Oh, naturally. The horses were tied . . . here." Nick knocked snow off a couple of the lower boughs. "Oh look. Somebody's been by with horses. How convenient."

"There's a pair of hardy souls that gets up early to ride. A man and a woman. I see them out of the window on the top floor. They generally stop here for a while."

"Verisimilitude scattered all over the ground." Nick kicked at it.

"Thank you. One uses the materials at hand. So . . . my thieves quarreled in this picturesque spot. A fistfight at the least. Maybe knives."

"They're desperate men," Nick agreed, "as well as robust and determined." He was always ready to get into the spirit of these imaginings. They'd laid many plots and contrivances together in the last years. For some reason the memory of that didn't hurt anymore. She didn't stop to explore why this should be so.

She opened the wooden box. "I was going to take my revenge today. I'd waited a long time. But this is for Mary Gower." The gold was cold between her fingers when she scooped out a fistful of necklaces, bracelets, rings, and threw them in a wide arc across the snow.

Nick cocked his head. "Are you being a bit too enthusiastic?"

"I'm making Gower grub about in the snow. He'll keep looking and looking for the valuable pieces—the ones Mary has. He'll only find this trash." She upended the box. Brilliant red, green, purple, and gold fell into the snow at her feet.

It went against the grain to misuse even these badly cut, badly set gems. She was a dealer in gems, accustomed to trading pieces of great value, but she was also an artist and craftsman in love with their beauty.

Last of all, sudden and hard and brutal, she threw down the box. It broke facedown, wood shattering, hinges sprawling.

She stood for a while, looking down. Nick came crunching across the last two feet that separated them. Maybe he'd seen that last instant of regret. He always knew what she was feeling.

He started unbuttoning his overcoat.

She said, "If you even think of taking that off and wrapping it around me, I will strip you naked and leave you to die in a snowdrift."

"Is that a promise?" He used his warm, sensual voice, teasing her with it.

"I hate it when you're gallant."

"That's what makes it so much fun. You put me in my place. Everyone else takes me seriously." He looked around the countryside and back toward the house. "We're standing here in the open. Is there something unpleasant that needs doing? You can hand it over to me."

"You're being gallant again." She shook herself. The sun dazzling on this vast expanse of snow made her eyes water. "Nick, have you ever been a coward?"

"Frequently."

"Now you're lying."

"It's the simple and sad truth. I am not cast in the heroic mold. I've walked away from more battles than you can imagine."

As you walked away from Mary Gower. And the miserable old woman in Leipzig. The shopkeeper in Prague. That fool of a second secretary in Vienna. She shrugged. "Maybe."

He said, "I do not spend my life wandering the far corners of Europe because I'm fond of bratwurst and borsch. Are you taking your clothes off? I'm delighted, but this seems a chilly spot."

She ignored that.

The whole time she'd been at Holbourne Abbey she'd carried the copy under her dress, above her own heart. There was no need for modesty in front of Nick. She wriggled her hand under her cloak in back and loosened the tie at the nape of her neck, lowered the bodice of her dress, and unpinned her counterfeit jewel.

He looked at what she held in her hand. "And yet another of them. If that's a copy, it's a very good one. So good it's making me nervous."

"It's glass, but the color match is almost perfect. I did it from memory."

"Another skill I did not know you possessed. Useful in your work, I should think."

"It's one of the great, unteachable arts, seeing color. If I hadn't possessed it, my grandfather would have patted me on the head and sent me off to make tarts instead of taking me into the workshop."

She did up her back. It was an excuse for not looking at him. "When I sent you away, it was because I was afraid."

"Of what? Me?"

She shook her heard fiercely. "Not you."

"How gratifying. You're afraid of what, exactly?" And he waited.

She'd avoiding talking to him for two months, three weeks, and—what was it?—four days. She could put off the discussion for a few more minutes.

She pulled her cloak around her and knelt down in the snow beside the welter of jewels. She knew this spot. She'd walked this little hill a dozen times, picking the exact place to drop the jewels. The rocks she wanted . . .

Snow had fallen since she'd last been here, but she found the rocks she was looking for.

Nick went down on his haunches beside her, warming her face with his breath, shielding her a little from the wind, watching what she was doing. "Cowardly and afraid of what?" he asked softly.

She brushed snow away lightly. She said, "Your family. My family. The rest of the world."

One rock was flat granite, part of the ground, an ordinary inhabitant of this soil, here since the beginning of time. The other, next to it, was a heavy, smooth, oval-shaped lump the size of two fists. She'd found it in the garden and brought it here.

"That's inclusive. Where shall we start?"

"I'm afraid you want to marry me to spite your family." She set her copy of the *Coeur de Flamme* on the flat stone.

An almost imperceptible pause. "It's the sort of thing I

might do," he conceded amiably. "But it happens I want to marry you because I love you."

"Oh." Her hand was clumsy, holding her pretty copy. Glass clicked on granite.

Nick said, "I don't lie to you, Claire. To other people, maybe. Never to you."

She picked up the carefully chosen hammer stone in her right hand. "When I was only your friend and lover, your family could ignore me. Marriage makes it a scandal and an outrage."

"You've been talking to my sister, haven't you? You really shouldn't. I have a wide choice of family, all of them better company than Lavinia. They'd be delighted to see me marry a fortune. It's what the younger sons of younger sons do."

"You have a tidy pile of money." She shifted the rock in her right hand. She'd made this copy with some care. It was a pity. . . .

"You have more. My great-aunt Edwina—you will have the terror and privilege of meeting her in London—says you are a provident and farsighted choice. She approves. And your grandfather approves."

She'd lifted the hammer stone. She set it down again carefully.

"Grandpapa? You went to see Grandpapa?" There was nothing Nicholas Lafford wouldn't do. Nothing.

"It's customary and I have excellent manners. He said he'd been expecting me."

"You went to Geneva?" She could not visualize a meeting between Nicholas and Grandpapa. What would they *say* to each other?

"On my way back from Florence a month ago. I spent a week with him in your family home. A revelatory week. What that old man doesn't know about the skeletons in the closets of the great families of Europe is not worth knowing."

Secrets. She'd never before noticed how much her grandfather had in common with Nick. "We buy and sell jewels. We know secrets."

"He said you'd hold your own among any grand aristocrats. He's right. In the salons, in the ballrooms, you shine like a star."

"You stalk like a prowling wolf. They just don't see it."

"I am discreet and invisible and benign. Your grandfather approves of me."

Grandpapa and Nick. They were both canny and cynical and a little ruthless. Of course Grandpapa liked him.

She took up her hammer stone and rapped it down sharply on this fake of hers. This false claimant. This imposter.

One tap. The heart shape cracked neatly and fell into a dozen pieces.

"That's . . . thorough," Nick said.

"I'm used to working with glass. It does what I tell it to."

"Let me guess. This is where the thieves dropped a diamond and it unluckily hit a rock and broke."

"Or a horse stepped on it."

"Or lightning struck." Nick's mobile lips tucked in at one corner. Bright, appreciative eyes laughed at her. "A diamond is the hardest substance in the world, Claire-my-jeweler. You don't crack it open on a rock."

"Gower says a jeweler can chip a diamond just laying it in a setting of soft gold." She smiled. "He'll come. He'll find his hoard scattered and the valuable pieces missing. His diamond, destroyed." She stood and stretched and threw the hammer stone deep into the wood. "Or stolen and out of his reach forever. Come, Mr. Gower. Come and admire the 'chipped diamond' I've left for you."

"A proper revenge." Nick was enjoying this. She'd known he would. "Who were you going to give the *Coeur* to originally? Before you met Mary?"

"Talleyrand. Minister of France. Grand intriguer of Europe."

"Good God, why?"

"Because a hundred years ago the *Coeur* was stolen from Louis XIV. It's gone through a score of owners since, but one could argue it's still property of the French throne. If Talleyrand got his hands on the *Coeur,* Gower could hold all the legal tantrums he liked. He'd never touch it again."

"Remind me never to make you angry," Nick said.

CHAPTER TEN

She would have gone back to the house, but Nick reached his hand out. He said, "Let me show you something."

They followed footprints that led toward other footprints and then to the edge of the ornamental lake. It was empty of skaters now, a clouded, windswept mirror gray under the bright sky. Glittering white shaped the banks broken by the stark black of the thickets and branches.

"The bridge," Nick said. "In all your time being useful in the house, you probably haven't seen this." And so she let him lead her to the stone bridge that arched over the frozen river that fed the lake. "Look," he said simply.

She didn't see at first. Then suddenly she did.

At the far end of the lake a walkway led into the gardens. Some whim of a long-ago gardener had shaped the trees into a row of arching branches. The drifts against the enclosing walls and arcs of snow held by the branches made the walkway into the shape of a perfect heart.

"Only from this spot," Nick said. "Only in the winter snow, only sometimes, you can see that. I hoped today might be one of those days."

"It's beautiful."

"Nice in summer, too. Will you marry me? Will you

come back here with me someday and walk through the gardens in June or July?"

One last time. One last time she'd try to make him see reason. "We don't match. Merchant and aristocrat."

"No woman in the world is a better match." He took up her left hand and held it to his right, palm to palm. "Perfect. All we have to do is hold on to each other."

"Don't say that." Because it was what she felt.

"If you love me, we'll launch ourselves into this great hazard." He took her shoulders, drew her close to him. "We'll grab the world by the scruff of the neck and make them accept us."

She couldn't look away. She couldn't make her face show anything but the truth. She whispered, "I want you."

"Will you take the risk? Make a life we can share?" He smiled one of his long, slow smiles. "A bed we can share?"

"I'd like that," she said.

His careful, knowledgeable fingers twined into her hair. His thumbs caressed the planes of her cheeks, memorizing skin and bone, speaking to her with persuasion and demand. He kissed her forehead. These were the first notes of the prelude to something he did very well indeed.

"We won't have an ordinary life," he said. "Not a quiet one. We'll solve these little problems England gets herself into, and you will buy and sell and make art of the great jewels of the world. We'll see ballrooms and the courts of kings, bazaars, the shops of your merchant friends. Maybe even visit a seedy back alley or two."

"I would consider it a very dull life without the occasional back alley." She had so much to look forward to, not least the strong, sleek body she pressed against.

He'd sneaked his overcoat around her while they were talking. She was warm inside it, with him. So she snuggled close.

He said, "I can't give you that heart-shaped diamond filled with fire, alas."

"I have the only heart I need right here." She put her hand flat on his chest. "This heart. This fire."

My true love hath my heart and I have his,
By just exchange one for the other given.

A SCOTTISH CAROL

❧

Susan King

CHAPTER ONE

Edinburgh, Scotland, December 1815

"Sir," a young man called. "Lord Cranshaw—Dr. Seton, if you please!"

At the steps of the Advocates Library, Henry Seton, Viscount Cranshaw—he preferred Dr. Seton, come to that—paused as one of his students approached. A wintry wind riffled the capes of his greatcoat as Henry grasped his hat brim. He waited as Charles Hay, youngest and brightest of his students, walked, aided by a cane and hampered by a coat far too large for him.

"What is it?" Henry asked. The lad likely had a question about the arduous task assigned in anatomy class, he thought. Less capable students had already complained, although this young fellow would no doubt complete the task easily.

He glanced down the street looking for his coachman, arriving soon with the carriage to head south to Cranshaw Castle, Henry's country estate. In a few days, his sister would meet him to travel down into England to attend a Christmas ball—one Fiona wished to attend, but Henry did not, particularly. Before leaving Edinburgh for Cranshaw, though, he intended to browse the library's medical collection for texts written by his now-deceased colleague Dr.

John Douglas, whose brilliant work would aid a piece Henry was writing.

"Dr. Seton," Charles Hay said. "A question about the assignment, sir."

"Did you not listen, did you not take notes?" Henry asked brusquely. In the few months since he had replaced Dr. Douglas as medical lecturer, he had needed to establish authority quickly. Just thirty, with a lamentably public reputation as a courageous surgeon who had saved lives at Waterloo while wounded himself, he did not feel like a hero, yet was regarded as one. To distance himself from that while teaching, he relied on his tall, imposing physique, with an added touch of gruffness and a glare that could cow the boldest student.

"I know the assignment, sir, to read and review some texts."

"Yes. Read Bartholin's *Institutiones Anatomicae* in French if you have no Latin."

"I have read Bartholin in the original, sir." The boy seemed nervous. "And I am researching *Philosophical Transactions of the Royal Society* to find every piece written on diseases and conditions of the heart, as assigned."

"Good." Something quivered within Henry's own breast. It felt suspiciously like sympathy. Sometimes young Hay looked bewilderingly familiar, yet Henry could not place him.

A university student, Hay looked an adolescent—slight, beardless, and blond, his voice faintly husky. He depended on a cane, but despite all challenges topped the class. Anyone would feel compassion and respect for the lad, Henry thought.

But Dr. Henry Seton, Lord Cranshaw—physician, war survivor, and lecturer in medical sciences—did not succumb easily to sympathy these days. The change suited him. He had been too trusting once, too willing to follow his heart.

"Sir, our papers are due on Christmas Day," Hay said.

"A week is time enough. I will not be in my Edinburgh rooms then, so the papers must be delivered to Cranshaw Castle by twilight on December twenty-fifth. My estate is two hours south of here. You and your fellows can hire a courier to bring the whole lot at once, if you wish."

"But it is the Yule. People should be with their families that day."

Henry hesitated. Had he grown so cold? "Doctors, even in training, must forego holiday privilege. And you know we do not widely celebrate Christmas in Scotland—shops are open, merchants and laborers go about their work. Doctors attend, and students study."

"Will you not accept papers after the Yuletide?"

"I will be traveling then." On the insistence of his sister, whose husband was unable to attend the ball, Henry would be off to Northumberland. "I intend to read the papers before the New Year. Since Scots celebrate Hogmanay robustly, you will have your holiday, sir."

"I plan to be traveling on Christmas Eve," Hay persisted.

"Then finish your task early. Good day. I am off to find Dr. Douglas's treatises on the heart, and I suggest you do the same." He turned on the steps, ducking into the wind.

"Dr. Seton!" Henry turned as Hay mounted another step. A burst of wind tilted the slight lad, who stumbled. Henry caught his narrow elbow.

"All in good order?"

"Aye." Hay pulled free. "I am familiar with Dr. Douglas's work. See." From a pocket, he extracted a volume to show its title: *A New Treatise on Diseases and Conditions of the Heart.*

"His last book! How did you get this? The library does not loan its volumes."

"His writings are all—in my father's collection. I am reading this one again."

"Impressive. It is not for the novice. This is one of his

later works, after Douglas became convinced that heart disease is as dependent on sentiment as on physical causes. Many thought it rather a medieval theory."

"Are goodness and happiness not healing in their own way?" Hay smiled.

"Somewhat." The boy's smile was damned familiar, but how?

"Sir, please keep this copy. My father's library is mine now. I want you to have this."

"Thank you." Surprised, touched, Henry accepted the book.

Hay nodded, but Henry frowned. Somehow the boy affected him, weakened his deliberate gruffness. That mysterious resemblance was like the past tapping him on the shoulder.

"Blithe Yule to you, sir." Hay touched his hat brim. The wind tore at the overlarge hat, unfurling long, curling tendrils of golden hair, feminine as a girl's.

Girl. *Dear God.* Henry frankly stared. He glanced down, up—down again, noticing curves beneath baggy clothing, long hair tucked under a collar. How had he not seen this before?

Recognition burst like sunlight. "Clarinda Douglas? How—what—"

She crammed her hat down and stepped back, lurching with the cane. "My carriage—there—good day!" She hurried toward a waiting chaise.

Henry stared. Clary! John Douglas's only daughter had been nineteen last Henry had seen her, seven years ago. And here she was, posing as—Hay?

Years ago, Henry had been welcomed in the Douglas home as he collaborated with his mentor, sharing family meals—later, sharing a good deal more with Clary, until that came to a sudden end. She was beautiful and shy, with a weak leg from a paralytic fever in childhood. She had intelligence, courage, a soft smile, and he had loved her. But her father had discouraged Henry's suit—surprisingly, it seemed at the time—and Clary had soon married another.

Henry had joined a regiment, determined to let the past go. But he had not been able to forget Clary.

Yet she had been under his nose these months and he had not noticed. What the devil was she doing in boy's kit, attending anatomy lectures? She knew more about academic medicine, having edited her father's writings, than most of his students. Women, even professor's daughters, were forbidden to enroll in the university—but Henry would have let her slip into his lecture hall had she just asked.

Stepping into her carriage, Clarinda Douglas paused. Her wide gray eyes met Henry's intent gaze. Then she all but tumbled into the vehicle, and the coachman slapped the reins.

What a fool he had been, Henry thought, so preoccupied of late, set on ignoring the world. He had not even seen Clary in front of him. The war, the brutal memories of a battlefield where he had fought to save each life under his care, still shredded his sleep and his concentration and had worn icy ruts in his heart.

But even before the war, he and Clarinda Douglas had moved on. Henry had never married, did not know if he would. Clary had married a cousin, a Perthshire landowner who had died within the first year. Hay—that was the fellow's name. Sir William Hay.

Ten times the fool. He swore under his breath. She was a widow—she was Clary—yet he had not recognized her, had spoken curtly. Loneliness stabbed him. He still missed her.

Now Clarinda Douglas would never return to his lecture hall for the blazing awkwardness of it, if nothing else. She had pride. Well, he did, too.

Henry turned to head into the library, shoving open the wide door.

CHAPTER TWO

Snow whirled from gray skies as the carriage wheels and horses' hooves shushed along the road. Clary leaned her head against the window, watching the icy trees stream past. Over two hours ago, sky overcast but still clear, she and her coachman had departed Edinburgh for Cranshaw Castle. Her stomach knotted and she fiddled nervously with the packages beside her.

She would rather walk back to Edinburgh through snow, with her foot-dragging gait, than see Dr. Henry Seton, Lord Cranshaw—especially now. How foolish she had been to attend his lectures, even disguised. Feeling so lonely, she had sought out his lecture hall, watching him, soothed by his voice. She had finally found the courage to approach him, but she should have left well enough alone.

Today was Christmas Eve and she was bound for a ball, she reminded herself, and the lacy snowfall was beautiful. She would appreciate her luck and make the best of it. As a child she had loved Yuletide—her Highland grandmother had celebrated Yule with songs and special treats, and Clary's mother had kept those traditions. But her family was gone now, Papa most recently. With no one close to celebrate with this year, Clary had found some happiness in surprising her servants with small gifts that morning.

But the little maidservant who was to travel with her had contracted a bad head cold, so Clary had decided to make the journey alone—just a trip to Cranshaw Castle to meet her friend, Mrs. Fiona Seton-Graham. What needed real courage, she knew, was the risk of seeing Fiona's brother, Dr. Henry Seton, Lord Cranshaw, who was also attending the ball.

A new qualm rippled through her. She was mad to do this, especially after he had recognized her last week. An hour past when the snow began, she had begged her coachman to turn back.

"Naught to fret over, Lady Hay!" Mr. Kendrick had replied jovially. "I will see ye safe to Cranshaw. My mother lives nearby, so I will be there for supper and the night—won't she be surprised! I'll fetch ye back a week from today, as we've arranged. Giddyap now!" He urged the horses onward.

Her rendezvous this afternoon was only with Mrs. Seton-Graham, she reassured herself. With luck, Clary could avoid Lord Cranshaw, even at the ball. They were all invited to a grand Christmas affair hosted by Lady Holbourne, a friend of her father and her cousins, at Holbourne Abbey in Northumberland, to take place in four days. Fiona had kindly offered to include Clary in her traveling party, assuring her—knowing Clary's misgivings—that Cranshaw would travel separately while lending his larger coach to comfortably accommodate the ladies, their maids, and luggage.

Nervous about the ball but dreading a lonely Yuletide even more, Clary had accepted Fiona's suggestion. Her cousins, who lived in Bellsburn near Holbourne Abbey, were also invited to the ball, and Clary would stay with them. Their welcoming reply was tucked in her reticule.

Surely Lady Holly's annual Christmas ball would be so grand, so thrilling and crowded that Clary would hardly see Henry—and with luck, he would not see her.

She patted the packages beside her, small gifts for Mrs. Seton-Graham and her English cousins, and a large packet for Cranshaw containing the papers completed by his students. As Charles Hay, she had offered to send them to Cranshaw via a "cousin," Lady Hay, visiting there.

What a kerfuffle this was! Now Cranshaw knew she was Charles Hay. She winced, thinking of the moment the wind had loosened her hair, while he stood glowering.

But she could not risk his discovering how madly, stupidly, cow-eyed in love she had been with Henry Seton, her father's handsome, brilliant protégé. Her heart had been sore broken, but that was in the past. She lifted her chin.

Through a snowy haze, she saw Cranshaw Castle in the distance, a picturesque structure merging a windowed façade and ruined tower. As the coach rolled along, Clary drew a steadying breath. Fiona would be there and they would soon head south. All was well.

Smile, she reminded herself. As a child, she had learned to hide fears and frailty behind a cheerful, plucky nature. It kept well-meaning sympathizers at bay. *Poor little Clarinda.*

Squaring her shoulders, smoothing her gray woolen skirt and pelisse, straightening her bonnet, she rested her gloved hand on the heavy packet meant for Lord Cranshaw.

May his great burden of reading, she thought, give him no time for anything else.

Snow fell steadily now, Henry saw, glancing through the tall windows of his study and library, where he sat in an old wing chair. He felt contented in this cozy room filled with high bookshelves and illuminated by hearth flames, content in this old, blessedly silent house, while his deerhound napped at his feet and snow fell peacefully outside.

No matter that it was the eve of Yule and he was alone; he had never celebrated the holiday much. Besides, he had work to do and now the time to do it, with his sister no longer coming to the house, and his servants gone for a few days as well.

Butler to housekeeper, cook to coachman, the servants had left that morning, since Henry had planned to be gone for a week. They lived locally, with Cranshaw Castle shut part of the year. But shortly after their departure, a courier had brought a note from Fiona. She wrote that she could not attend the Holbourne ball after all, as her three small daughters had chickenpox and she would not leave them; she hoped Henry would attend and was not too disappointed. She assured him that she had also sent apologies to Lady Holly and the Edinburgh lady who had planned to accompany her.

Henry had written back with recommendations for the children: baths with finely ground oatmeal to soothe rash and willow bark for fever, a tincture of which he included in a packet. Suspecting heavy snow was on its way—he sensed it in the air—he had paid the same courier to dispatch his messages quickly, sending his own regrets to the Dowager Countess of Holbourne as well: *My apologies, dear Lady Holbourne, but a family matter and winter weather prevent my sister and me from attending the ball. . . .*

He was not disappointed at all, and intended to savor this time to himself.

Sipping the whisky brose that Mrs. Johnstone, his housekeeper, had prepared before she left, he felt the comforting warmth of the concoction—whisky, cream, oats, and honey—spread through his chest. Settling back, he turned a page in the volume that Clarinda Douglas, as Charles Hay, had given him from her father's collection. He was determined not to think about the giver, only the thoughtful gift and its important contents.

Reading Dr. Douglas's description of angina pectoris, he turned pages, stopping when a folded paper slipped free. Creased and yellowed, it fell open and he saw John Douglas's handwriting. Curious, Henry peered at the note, perhaps a diary page or part of a letter. The note read:

*Physicians must distance ourselves and yet keep
compassionate hearts in our breasts. We know how
important the heart is to the body—now, late in my life,
I understand how essential it is to life. The workings of
the heart and the blood are science, but doctors must
remember that the heart and the emotions can create
poison or cure.*

More of John Douglas's conviction about feelings and
the heart, as if the two were one. Henry frowned, skeptical.

*Keep the heart in good physical health through
sensible means. Nurture its full health through love
and compassion. You have known love. Claim it again.*

Henry frowned, feeling as if Douglas whispered like a
ghost in his ear. He looked at his glass—Mrs. Johnstone's
brose was strong stuff. Love and compassion! Science sat
better with him than sentiment. Douglas's note was directed to someone personally. That was all.

Yawning, he leaned back, soothed by the hot crackle of
the hearth fire. His deerhound yawned, too, stretched out
near the hearthstone. The vast old house creaked, filled
with memories and ghosts and silence. His housekeeper
had prepared a few meals for him, and the forester and his
wife would look in on the house later. No matter the snow
or the holiday—all was well.

Times past, his family would sometimes open the great
house for the Yuletide season, candles blazing in the windows and chaises coming up the drive bringing guests for
soirees and teas and luncheons. His mother in particular
had enjoyed Yule. But now his parents were gone; there was
only Henry and Fiona, who had a family and homes in Edinburgh and Mid-Lothian.

Cranshaw Castle was his property in its entirety, and he
loved the vast estate with its farms and possibilities. He

was not ready to fill the house with his own family yet. Someday.

For now, he had lectures to prepare and articles to write for an Edinburgh journal. His only concern was receiving his students' assignments. The snow could delay a courier, but as long as the papers arrived, Henry would not quibble over timing. Just let them think he would.

He would not see Hay's paper, though. He sighed.

Raising a mock toast to the snoring dog, he sipped the brose. "Good Yule, my friend," he murmured, then took up the book, yawned, and settled back.

"Lady Hay," Kendrick said, handing her down, "There's no one about here."

"Mrs. Seton-Graham will have arrived by now," Clary replied as she stepped down to the snowy gravel. "I must not delay you further, Kendrick. You are anxious to see your mother."

"I am," he said, unstrapping Clary's small clothing trunk to set it on the ground. "My lady, I'm a bit concerned about the snow. If this gets worse, will ye be welcome to stay here?"

"It is only flurries. But yes, I suppose I could stay if need be. Leave the trunk there with the packages. One of Cranshaw's servants will move them for me. Do go see your family," she urged. "Blithe Yule to you!"

Lifting the hem of her pale gray woolen gown, using her cane in her left hand, she climbed the entrance steps, turning under the portico roof to wave as Kendrick drove away.

She rapped smartly on the door. Silence. She waited, knocked again. The large double door, not quite latched, opened slightly. Hearing quick footsteps, she was startled when a large dog poked its great head and shoulders through the doorway. The deerhound, its thick gray coat catching snow, gazed at her with dark, gentle eyes.

"Good day!" She patted its head. Fiona had said to expect few servants at the house, Clary remembered. She glanced back as the carriage rolled down the snowy approach, and then pushed the door open, stepping into the foyer with the dog. "Pardon me! Is someone here?"

The vast interior was dim and quiet. Had she arrived first? She glanced around the spacious foyer with its painted floor and soaring walls. A curving staircase swept into darkness.

Clary smiled at the deerhound. "Are you the butler? Please tell Mrs. Seton-Graham that Lady Hay has arrived."

The dog walked down the main hallway, turning back expectantly. Light emanated through a doorway there. Clary followed.

Seeing the man seated, asleep, there—hair black as his coat, shoulders broad, crossed long legs in black boots—she gasped and wanted desperately to flee.

Instead, she mustered courage and stepped forward.

CHAPTER THREE

"**S**ir."

Firelight glowed and snow fell, and Henry dozed in the chair. The remnant of a dream stirred yearning, loneliness. He frowned.

"Sir." A whisper.

Henry opened his eyes. A vision stood in the dim light of the doorway, an angel or a ghost clothed in mist and frost. A tall guardian hound stood by her side. The exquisite spirit watched him gently. Henry went still, wrapped in her spell.

"Lord Cranshaw. Pardon me. It is Yule Eve, and I am expected." Slowly the figure came toward him. She limped, the dog buttressing her carefully.

His dog. And—*Clary?* Henry sat up, cleared his throat. "Pardon me," he said gruffly.

"My fault," Clarinda Douglas protested. "I did not mean to startle you."

He got hastily to his feet. "I was just . . . reading."

"I do apologize. You looked quite as if you saw a ghost."

He tipped his head. "In a way I have," he murmured. "Miss Douglas. Greetings. I believe it is Lady Hay now?"

"Yes. Though I am widowed." She moved, a tap of the cane, a slow step.

"I had heard. My condolences." He took her hand, cool and slim in its soft little glove.

"Thank you." She watched him. With those gray-blue eyes and flaxen hair, that pale coat and bonnet, she looked a fragile ice princess. No wonder he had thought her a ghost.

How strange to stand so close to her in the intimate warmth of his study, with neither of them knowing what to say. He released her hand. "To what do I owe the pleasure?"

"I expected to meet your sister here." She smiled— tremulously, he saw. He knew the spectrum of her smiles, anxious, sweet, mischievous . . . seductive. "Mrs. Seton-Graham and I are going to Lady Holbourne's ball down in England."

"You are my sister's traveling companion?" He blinked, surprised. "She never said."

"We are good friends," she explained. Henry nodded, aware, although Fiona rarely mentioned Clary. "I was also invited to the Christmas ball at Holbourne Abbey, and Mrs. Seton-Graham kindly offered to share her coach. She said you . . ."

"Would not be here?" he supplied.

Her fingers flexed on the cane's ivory handle. A gift from her father on her sixteenth birthday, he remembered. "When your sister arrives we will leave, and be no bother to you."

"You have not heard? Have a seat, Lady Hay. Here, Maximilian, out of there." He moved the dog away from a low, scroll-end settee beside the fire.

She sat tentatively, primly, gloved hands clasped. "Heard what, Lord Cranshaw?"

So formal, despite all. He scowled slightly. "Fiona is unable to attend the ball, as it happens. She sent a note today by messenger, and sent word to Holbourne Abbey and to you as well. Her children are ill."

She gasped. "The little girls, are they very ill?"

"Only chickenpox. They will soon be hale again. I take it you did not receive word?"

"No." She pulled at her gloved fingers. "I must have left

home before it arrived. Oh, dear," she added, glancing at him.

"Indeed," he murmured.

"But my coachman just left," she said faintly. She straightened her shoulders. "Perhaps your coachman could bring me to him? Kendrick has gone to see family who live nearby. And Fiona lives west of here, I think. I could go there, perhaps. I would not trouble you, but . . . I have no other transportation." She looked distressed.

"My own coachman has left for the holiday, but I can take you to meet your man," Henry offered. Hastening Clary away seemed a very good idea. Memories were crowding him already. "Fiona's home is fourteen miles west, quite far in bad conditions. And if you have not had the chickenpox, I would not advise visiting. I can easily run you to meet your coachman."

"I could not impose."

"You must, if you wish to leave here," he said, "and go to your ball."

"Since your sister said you were attending, too, I thought you might be gone already."

"I agreed to escort Fiona, but with her message and the worsening weather, I sent my own regrets by courier this morning." He stopped. "Do you—require an escort to the ball?" He craved his solitude, but time was he would have done anything for Clary Douglas. That was still true, he realized in dismay.

"My driver can take me to my cousins' home near Holbourne." She bit at her lower lip. "I am not sure what to do. The weather is turning rather poorly." She glanced at the windows.

"All is well. I will drive you to meet your coachman." What the devil was in that brose to make him so biddable? But it was Clary, he knew. She'd always had a damnable effect on him. He felt so willing around her. The feeling came rushing back now, here, with her.

"Thank you, Lord Cranshaw."

"Where is your coachman's family home?"

"I do not know. The name is Kendrick."

"Tenants of mine. They live a few miles from here. I can easily run you there. First, take some refreshment. You must be cold and weary after your journey."

"Should we not go now, before the roads are slick?"

Henry glanced out to see trees already whitening. He frowned. "Perhaps your driver should return you to Edinburgh instead, Lady Hay."

"He is a sensible driver, and we are expected in England." Clary shivered. "Oh. A hot drink first would be nice, though, if the cook or the housekeeper has something ready." She glanced toward the door. Max now lay flopped over the threshold, a guardian decidedly off duty.

"My servants," Henry said, "are gone."

She blinked. "All of them?" She sat ramrod straight on the settee.

"Most. The forester—my groundskeeper—and his wife have a house on the property. He is also the parish minister, but the living is small enough that he keeps the Cranshaw grounds, too. Their son is one of the grooms. I'll have him harness the chaise. With luck, he is in the stables looking after the horses. The other servants have left for the holiday. I expected to be away the week, until plans changed. We are alone here," he finished, "but for Max."

"Then we must leave soon. It is so—improper."

"A bit awkward," he agreed. "But we will keep it our secret, and be off soon enough. As to refreshment, my housekeeper left a good brose, and there is claret. We could manage tea."

"I do not want to be any trouble." She did not look at him.

Trouble? She had always been the sweetest form of trouble. But those days and those feelings were gone, he told himself.

"Tea, then," he said, sensing she needed it. "I'll go down to the kitchen."

"Let me prepare it," she offered, standing.

"I am quite self-sufficient. It comes of having been in a regiment."

"Yes—I heard that you had gone to Ireland, then Belgium, and made a good showing."

"Quite," he said curtly. He stepped over Max, who leaped up to pace between his master and his new friend. Then the deerhound trotted over to sit beside Clary.

Henry paused. She was having the same damnable effect on the dog.

Remembering the packages left outside in the elements, Clary hurried through the foyer, cane in her left hand assisting her weak right foot, and opened the front door. The dog followed and stepped out with her. Breathing in sharp, cold air, Clary watched snowflakes spiraling downward, covering the ground. The storm had not lessened. She descended the steps carefully, her narrow leather boots and gown hem powdering with snow.

Alone with Henry was what she dreaded most. Meeting him at his home without the anonymity of the lecture hall felt intimate. Dangerous. Seeing him moments ago, so tall and broad-shouldered, curly hair black as his jacket, jaw firm against the creamy tucked cravat, buckskin trousers snug in high black boots—and seeing his summer-blue eyes—had made her breath quicken raggedly. But for the new scar jagged over his temple and a deeper seriousness, he was the Henry she knew, and had tried to forget.

The young Henry Seton had brought her joy and then heartbreak, leaving her life so suddenly. Now he still drew her like a lodestone, more compelling, intense, so handsome. Yet he seemed bitter, taut—was it the war? The thought broke her heart all over again.

She inhaled cold, exhaled mist. The atmosphere in the house was heavy with unspoken past and present. Soon she would ride with him to the Kendricks' home, just a half hour in a chaise. Yet she felt sad to leave him rather than relieved.

Dusting the snow off the packages, she gathered them in one arm and headed back to the door, while Max, in tailwagging eagerness, stayed close by her side. Already the world seemed blanketed in white—ground covered, trees like bridal lace, snow dancing in airy veils.

Beautiful indeed, but driving would be risky now, though she trusted Cranshaw's judgment. Otherwise, she could be stranded here alone with him. She gasped at the thought.

In the distance, a wide path led to the stables. There she saw a tall figure in greatcoat and hat going into the building: Cranshaw looking for the groom.

Distracted, Clary took a step, and her boot heel found slick ice. Her weak foot slid out from under her—the dog broke her fall, but her shoulder, then her head, hit the ground.

Stunned, she lay still while snow flurried on her cheeks and the dog nudged at her.

Henry set down a silver tray loaded with china and tea things—steaming teapot, milk and sugar, cups, a small plate of cakes. He had found a kettle of water simmering in the hearth and rummaged about setting tea to steep. Then he had grabbed coat and hat from the hallway to head out to the stables, finding the groomsman gone and the horses bedded with oats and water nearby. He could harness the chaise himself or go to the groundskeeper's house, over a mile down the road. But the tea would be ready, so he had hurried to the kitchen.

Finding Clary gone, he peered into the corridor. Hearing

the dog bark, he realized the girl must have gone outside. He opened the door to see Max testing the steps anxiously—and then noticed Clary sprawled in the snow. He rushed down the steps to kneel beside her.

Blood trickled over her brow and her eyes were closed. Henry touched her arm, heart slamming. "Clary!"

Her eyes fluttered open. "I'm fine," she said, trying to sit.

He pressed her down. "Not yet. Be still." He slipped his hand under her head, relieved to find no blood there. "Try to sit now. Slowly." He braced her.

Touching her head, she winced. "I fell. My cane—my packages, where are they?"

"Over there. Let's get you inside." He stood, assisting her to stand, and swept her into his arms. Though she protested, he carried her up the steps into the warmth of the house and then to his study's firelit coziness. The dog followed.

He put her on the settee. "Take off your bonnet, please. I am all thumbs with frippery."

"You never were," she said, voice muffled as she freed the ribbons to remove her hat.

Henry almost smiled at her candid remark. So her memory was intact despite the blow. Good. He waited while she removed hat and gloves. "Now the coat," he said, helping her ease out of it. "We will have your shoes and stockings, too, if they are wet. This weather is better suited to pattens than thin little shoes. Why ladies refuse to wear sturdy boots—"

"These are very good boots. I did not expect to be walking through snow, and I cannot manage in pattens. Perhaps you've forgotten."

"I remember," he murmured.

"Truly, I'm not hurt." She smoothed her skirts, and Henry saw her hands trembling.

"You're chilled through. There's hot tea, but first let me

look at your head." He perched at the edge of the settee, his hip pushing against her skirts and thigh beneath. Warmth stirred there. He touched her head, her hair curling fine and fair about his fingers. Silent, he felt for the wound. The dog snuffled at them and settled by the fireside to watch.

"Ah," Henry said when Clary gasped in pain. "A considerable bump, and a cut." He took a handkerchief from his pocket to dab and clean the wound, then plucked a clump of snow from her pelisse to hold its cold to her forehead. "Snow is just the thing."

"How fortunate that we have an abundance of it." She smiled ruefully.

"I'll fetch more, but I want to know you're not hurt. I need to test your limbs, if I may."

She nodded, pressing the handkerchief to her head. Henry ran his hands down her skirt, over knees, ankles, waggling her left foot in its slender laced black boot. Heat plunged through his body—he ignored its allure. He'd thought he might never touch Clary again, and here she was, but in his doctoring hands. He frowned, concentrating. "Pain here? Or here?"

"Just stiffness after a foolish fall. Not the right foot, please," she added.

Henry did not touch the smaller foot he knew was twisted inward. "No injury there? Good." Next he touched her shoulder, and she sucked in a breath. "That hurts?"

"A bit. It's nothing."

He eased his hands along her arms, rotated her wrists, and moved her hands. She felt like heaven—warm, soft, supple, wondrous. Something within him felt dangerously close to melting. Focus, he told himself. Calmly, he took her face between his hands, resisting a sudden memory of kissing her, and tilted her head this way and that. "Pain?"

"Truly, it's nothing, Lord Cranshaw. I do hope we will be leaving soon."

"Look at me, please." He lifted her chin with a finger.

Her eyes were clear, their misty gray depths, dark-lashed, simply beautiful. He eased his fingers back to her curls, his touch lingering. He sat back. "With such a knock to the head, you should rest."

"My cousins expect me tonight, and we still must find my driver."

"Rest first," he said firmly. "Have tea, and I will fetch snow to ease the bruise. Then we can discuss traveling."

"I cannot stay here," she insisted.

"Better to wait a bit than to swoon publicly at the Holbourne ball."

She grimaced. "That would be dreadful."

"Quite." Henry picked up the teapot.

"Do let me pour," she said, beginning to rise.

"No matter, we often did things for ourselves in the regiment." He poured the tea, steam rising, and Clary sank back. "Milk? Though a lady fainting away might be the talk of the ball. Sugar?" He lifted the little tongs.

"A dash of milk. But the ball is not for days. I will be quite well," Clary said. "Besides, they will have much to talk about at this ball. My cousin wrote that some are calling it the 'last chance ball.'" She accepted the cup he handed her along with a small seed cake. Henry poured himself a cup, stirred milk and sugar, sipped it while standing. He frowned, perplexed.

"Last chance?" he asked. "Why so?"

"Some may hope to find a match there, or see an old . . . love." Quickly, she crumbled a bit of cake and nibbled it, her cheeks blushing rosily.

"There's a bit of matchmaking at any ball."

"True. Though I wonder—" She glanced at him, and then away.

"Fiona bringing us together there—or here?" Realizing it was possible, he frowned. "My sister ought to know better."

The flames in the grate snapped and a log broke, sending sparks. Clary jumped, nearly spilling her tea. "It will be a lovely Christmas ball, and I was so looking forward to it. *Am* looking forward to it," she added, and sent him a quick smile.

He had missed that smile. So genuine, fairylike, the bow curve of her lips held brightness, sensuousness, and was utterly Clary, all he knew of her and loved in her, or had once. She beamed hope, forgiveness. Uncertainty, too.

He turned toward the window. Sleet tapped the panes and daylight was rapidly fading. The weather was increasingly poor, and Clary was hurt, though she might deny it, and should not travel, regardless of weather. She would have to stay here, alone with him. A hot surge of need sank through him, deeper than physical, ardent and disquieting all at once.

"I'll fetch that snow," he said abruptly, taking his empty teacup as he left the room with Max at his heels. Outside, he scooped snow into the cup and found Clary's cane. While the dog nosed through snow, he looked about.

The snow was no longer airy, pretty stuff. Now it slanted wild and sleety, shawling the trees, burying the ground, obscuring the distance. His boots were inches into the stuff, and ice pelleted his hair, his coat. No wonder Clary had fallen. Certainly they would not travel tonight.

Noticing her trunk and packages, he stuck the dish of snow in his pocket, grabbed the smaller things under his arm, and carried them, trunk and all, inside. Whistling for Max, he kicked the door shut behind him.

Clary sat up slowly, head spinning, shoulder aching, and stood, unwilling to submit to weakness. She bounced on one foot, hoping Henry remembered her cane. She would show him that she was ready to travel. Staying here was madness.

"Not yet, please." Henry entered the room and set the

packages and cane aside. He took her arm, his hands so warm and strong, sure and wonderful, that Clary sat without protest. Then he dumped snow from the teacup into his handkerchief to make an icy compress. As she pressed it to her head, he lifted a shawl from a chair. "Fiona keeps this here. Says the place is drafty."

She touched the fringed paisley wrap patterned in red and gold. "It's beautiful. But I would spoil it—my skirt is damp."

He spread the shawl over her. "Wet, more like. You may have to change."

"My trunk is outside. Truly, I cannot inconvenience you further."

"I brought your things inside." He stood regarding her, all easy elegance and contained power, the firelight pouring golden over his long, fit form, over dark curls and blue eyes. Then he pointed toward the window. "The storm is building—soon it will be unsafe to travel."

"Oh!" She glanced there, surprised. "It's snowing quite heavily now."

"It is, and the roads may become impassable. We are at the head of a glen here, and the drifts can pile quite high. A local trip might still be possible, but your driver will not want to risk a long journey. And I do not think you should leave yet, with that injury."

She raised her chin, head aching, and managed a smile. "I've had far worse."

"Stubborn girl," he said quietly, so naturally that her breath caught. "You let nothing hold you back, God knows. But this is no simple snowstorm, and a cranial injury can be serious. Nor will a charming smile seduce me into saying otherwise," he added with a tilt of his head.

His gentle intonation, that hint of affection was so like the old Henry she remembered that Clary felt a swirl within of unexpected hope. "But we cannot stay here."

"There are rooms aplenty, as far apart as you like,

though your safety is assured. And my housekeeper left food enough for a medieval siege."

"I meant that we are alone. It is not proper."

"We are hardly strangers." He gazed at her evenly. "I am acting as your physician, which provides a certain exemption. Compress to head, please, madam."

She obliged. "Intractable man."

"Exactly." He pressed his lips together as if to suppress a smile.

"Tomorrow, first thing, we must go to the Kendricks'," she said. "I believe my driver was planning to stay the night, so he will be there with my vehicle to take me into England."

"Perhaps. This sort of weather can prevail for a day or more. But I could fetch the forester's wife up to the house if she will come. Her joints ache miserably in the cold."

Outside, Clary could hear sleet and wind thrashing against the windows. "My Northumbrian cousins expect me for Christmas. What of the holiday?"

"They may have bad weather, too, or will hear of the storms in Scotland, and in either case understand your delay. The holiday means little to me, my dear," he finished.

Was that casual endearment politeness or habit—or intentional? "I must send word to my cousins soon," she said quickly.

"You may arrive on their doorstep sooner. This is Sunday. The ball is Thursday. If the weather improves and workers can clear the roads to the south, carriages should be traveling in a day or two. If our sled was in good repair," he added, "I would consider it, since you seem quite eager to be gone despite the conditions. Please understand, Lady Hay, that I am more concerned about your wee cranium than your timely transportation."

"I know." She appreciated his calm wisdom in what seemed an untenable situation. "When the roads are clear, will you attend the ball?"

"I have already sent my regrets. It would be rude to appear when a dinner plate is not counted for me. I sent a token of my remorse—a couple of bottles of an excellent Highland whisky that some cousins of mine make in their, er, distillery. I never ask whence it comes. But," he went on, "if you require an escort to the ball, I could risk discourtesy."

"Lady Holly and her son and his countess would no doubt be happy to see you, and you could easily explain, if you wanted to go. You have friends there, your sister said. A Lord Harris, I believe? And one of Lady Holly's sons?"

"Her grandson, actually. Captain Stretton's father is the current earl. Lady Holbourne kindly invited me with a note of thanks for her grandson's survival, but sheer luck saved Kim and Ivo, not me. There was an explosion—their actions were brave, but their wounds were grievous. One sustained a terrific blow to the head, the other—well, several injuries." He frowned.

"Angels watched over them," Clary supplied softly. "A doctor appearing at the right time can be a miracle in itself. How fortunate you were there."

"I was a member of the Scots Greys," he said, staring out the window. "Hardly an angel—did little enough for a couple of years, acting as a regiment physician in Ireland until we were sent over to the Low Countries. We narrowly missed Quatre Bras—perhaps you've heard of it—but we were at Waterloo. I needed more than my physician's skills that day. Thank God, my father had been a surgeon and made sure I knew his craft as well as my own. He was tougher than any officer, I vow." He glanced at a portrait hanging over a mahogany writing desk. "I was able to step in when one of the surgeons was killed."

"I am sorry that you had to be there, at Waterloo."

"Don't be," he said brusquely. "I was glad to be of some use."

He glanced away, hands in pockets, and Clary sensed

that those battlefield patients, and the experiences there, meant far more to him than he would reveal. She had heard that Henry had saved lives there while injured himself. That long scar on his forehead had not been there last she had seen him, before the war. He must have taken a bad blow to the head, she thought, frowning.

"At any rate, I had planned to stay here at Cranshaw and attend to my work. You are welcome to share my solitude."

She smiled. "Any port in a storm?"

He waved a hand. "Such as it is."

Clary settled back with the cold cloth against her brow. "This is a lovely house. I vow it has seen many wonderful Yuletide seasons."

"It has," he agreed, sitting in a wing chair, crossing one booted leg over the opposite knee. "My mother was English and loved Christmas. She kept it here when my sister and I were young. But I am a Scotsman and keep a scant Yule. Besides, the past is done."

Setting aside the cloth, she smoothed the patterned shawl. "When I was a girl," she said, "we sometimes visited my grandmother in the Highlands in December. She would sing beautiful songs and we would make cakes and bring in pine boughs and string dried rowanberries. We were not dour at Yuletide, even though we were Scots."

"Catholics," he said, his lips twitching. "That accounts for it."

"Dreadful Papists," she admitted, laughing. "And my father a Protestant."

"If you want to attend church tomorrow, we may not manage it in this weather."

"We kept a Scottish Yule at home in Edinburgh, so I am not accustomed to attend. You might remember," she added. "Papa would see patients or lecture that day, though my mother would sing the old songs and bake cakes and have the cook make a fine feast. Sometimes she would take us to church. Papa tolerated it all rather amiably." She smiled, remembering. "It is interesting that both our mothers celebrated Christmas, though Scots often do not think it an important day."

"Would you truly want to go out in this blizzard to drag in pine boughs, and then light candles and sing until midnight? I warn you, I have not the heart for it."

Clary felt her throat tighten. "Some Yuletide celebration, even a small token, is a lovely tradition to have." She did not want to add how much she would miss it this year in particular.

"I do not find it necessary," he said.

She tilted her head, studying him. "You have changed."

"I needed to," he said. "So I did."

"The war?" she asked cautiously. "How awful it must be to endure such frightening, distressing things. I would flee. I could not face it."

"You?" he said. "You would easily summon the courage. I did what I could there," he went on. "It was chaos—the cannon fire, the screams, the charges, and stray shots. We worked fast, tending men with terrible injuries, broken bones, wounds that needed surgery. Some were gravely injured. For others, infection set in fast." He shook his head. "One detaches for sanity's sake. That, along with other matters . . . made me realize the benefit of relying on the mind over sensibilities. Just let the heart pump, as it were." He gazed at her.

Clary tipped her head, listening. Did he truly mean that? As for other matters, she hoped she'd had no role in hurting him, but someone or something had. She felt a surge of empathy, of anger, and protectiveness sensing what he had endured and knowing she had not been there for him, even as a friend.

"I am sorry," she said. He shrugged. "Did you read my father's book?" she asked then. "His treatise on the heart?"

He tapped the cover of the book beside his chair. "Here. Medieval ideas, much as I respected your father. The heart is a strong and critical muscle. Emotions—are another matter entirely, and not to be confused with science. Feelings can be contained, controlled."

"Some can do that. I am not adept at it."

"Well." He shifted, seeming keen to change the topic. "So we will have a workaday Scots Christmas, you and I, while it continues to snow. We can both attend to studies. Have you finished your assignment? Oh, and I believe you have something to tell me . . . Mr. Hay?"

She nodded, gulped, knowing she must explain. "That large packet is for you. Open it."

"This?" He reached for the package, pulling away string and brown paper to reveal several slim manuscripts. "Ah. Not a Yule gift." His gaze was piercing blue. "Thank you."

"Yes," she managed.

"Now," he murmured, setting the papers down. "About Charles Hay."

CHAPTER FOUR

Clary exhaled. Her head ached dully. "After my father died last spring, I missed him dreadfully. My family was gone. My husband as well."

"Sir William Hay. Was it sudden? Forgive me for asking."

"Yes. You were in Ireland then, I think. He was a Perthshire laird. A baronet."

"I know. A cousin of yours. A match arranged when you were a child. Go on."

She wanted to explain—the longstanding debts eased by the match, by promises made by others that wrenched her life in an unwanted direction. But it would not matter to him now. "William had a bad fall while riding," she said. "He was reckless, hotheaded, had to prove that day that he was a better rider than his friends. He died instantly. We were married six months."

He murmured a wordless sympathy. Clary could not seem to look at him.

"I went back to live with Papa," she said. "But since his death, it has been very hard. I've been lonely despite good friends, but what has been most hard was having so little to do."

"You often helped your father with his medical writing."

"And nothing else interested me quite so much. I'm not very good at needlework." She tried to smile. "Friends tried. Your sister insisted on taking me to concerts and soirees and such. I never saw you," she added quickly.

"I stayed at Cranshaw after my return, until I accepted the lecture post. So you decided to try a university education? I wish you had come to me." His words were clipped, low. If he was displeased, she could not blame him—but she sensed a frisson of hurt. "There might have been a way—an exception, based on your need to finish your father's writing, or some such."

"I wanted to tell you—but I could not bring myself to try." She paused. "But when I heard that you would lecture in the same hall Papa had used, I needed to be there." She was uncertain how to say it. "I wanted to hear you."

"Me." The inflection revealed caution, not pride.

She closed her eyes, remembering how she had longed to see him, hear his calm voice, even run to him and be welcomed in his arms again. But that was the yearning of her starved heart.

"I wanted to hear about medicine, science, things Papa and I discussed."

"How on earth did you manage to act as Mr. Hay without discovery?"

"I knew the university well from Papa's days there. So I put on my husband's old clothing, went to your lecture hall at the proper time, took a seat and always left just before the end of the hour. I gave my name to you that first day, do you recall? I dared not use Douglas, so I took Hay. You never noticed. It was a risk, I know."

"I noticed you," he said gruffly. "As the best student in the class. I did not recognize you, I admit. Should have." He shook his head. "But I understand."

She blinked. "You do?"

"You felt closer to your father there, took comfort from familiar surroundings. But you could have come to me," he added.

Relief washed through her—he did not condemn her.

"Women are not permitted in lectures." Not the whole reason, but it would do. "We are frail, weak, might faint away if exposed to topics unsuitable for young ladies."

"Not you."

"Or Charles Hay," she added brightly.

He smiled a little. "Very well. I'll speak to the provost to arrange for you to attend my lectures."

"Do you think it is possible? I would like that so much."

He nodded. "You must have missed your father very much to do what you did."

"Still do, especially at this time of year. Thank you. It is kind of you to help."

He frowned then, reaching for the stack of papers. "Thank you for bringing these. I should get started. There's quite a bit of reading here."

A dismissal? But she wanted to talk more about Yule with him, share good memories. She wanted to know what the holidays had been like at Cranshaw, and tell him what her family did in that season. She wanted to sit close beside him in warmth and peace and safety, with the fire crackling in the grate, the dog asleep by the hearth, the wind and snow fierce against the windows while all was golden and secure within. Yet he did not look at her, turning pages.

Tears stung her eyes. Something in him was lost, and she did not know how to reach it. She had to know why he had changed so. Was it to do with her? She hoped not, but—

"Henry," she said impulsively, desperate to ask.

His hands stopped, but he did not look up. He waited.

She opened her mouth, but a yawn took her over so suddenly, so loudly, that the dog awoke.

"You should rest, Lady Hay," Henry drawled.

She sat up, head suddenly woozy. "Oh!" She touched her bruised head. "Wait, I must ask." A fog of pain and fatigue swamped her. "Why did you—leave so abruptly that day, years ago? I never—oh!" She put a hand to her head.

"Come upstairs." Henry moved toward her. "I'll take you up to bed."

"To bed?" She stood, dizzy, setting her hand on his chest, all sturdy wool, soft linen, solid warmth beneath. She rested her brow on the pouf of his cravat. "You'll take me with you?"

"What? Good Lord." He took her arm, draped the shawl over her shoulders. "Are you feeling unsteady? Confused? It sometimes happens with head injury, and quite suddenly. Can you manage the stairs?"

That did it. All the remorse, the hurt, the dismay, the embarrassment over what she had just inadvertently said—all the unfulfilled wishes, too—tumbled through her. Clary pushed away and snatched her cane. "Dr. Seton," she emphasized, "you know I never complain, not about stairs or wet clothes or snow or—" *Or loneliness. Or missing you.*

"I know," he said softly. Kindly.

She walked away, head spinning and shoulder stiff as she used the cane, too aware that she likely looked an old woman, shawled and bent, and she felt a spark of anger. Lifting her chin indignantly, she hurried toward the stairs. The dog followed, paws tapping along the floor.

"Wait." Henry strode past her and lifted her trunk. He took it upstairs, disappeared for a few moments, and descended the stairs again with the easy athletic grace that she had loved about him once, and discovered that she still loved now.

She took the stairs in her usual manner, leaning on cane and bannister. But the height made her dizzy. She stopped.

"Slowly, my girl." Henry was there, just there, his arm bracing her. She let him help her to the top step while the dog scampered up with them.

Reluctantly, she stepped away from him. "Thank you. Which room?"

"I set your trunk in there." He indicated the closest doorway. "Mrs. Johnstone readied the room for Fiona today, hearth and all."

"Thank you," she murmured, hand on the door. "Please pardon what I said earlier. I sometimes speak before I think."

"I always rather liked that about you," he said. "Rest for now. Meet me downstairs for supper later. Mrs. Johnstone left soup, bread, and cheese in the kitchen."

"That would be excellent." She shut the door.

"Clary." His voice through the door was close. "Call if you need me."

Silent, she pressed her brow to the door. *I always needed you.*

Turning, she was pleased to discover a small water closet built into a corner, and a basin of water with fragrant soap. Refreshed, she removed her gown—glad she had worn garments she could manage without her maid—and knelt in shift and petticoat beside her trunk to sift through her folded things to change.

She touched her ball gown wistfully, lavender silk and flounced hem, and wondered when she might wear it. Given the weather, she might not attend the Holbourne Christmas ball. She sighed, and chose a prim slate-gray gown, long-sleeved with rows of black ribbon marching along front and hem. She had fulfilled two years of widow's weeds, but was in half-mourning for Papa now. Besides, the somber gray reminded her that she was but a shadow in Henry's past.

The hearth fire warmed the chill from the room, and fatigue overtook her. She lay on the bed's blue coverlet and drew the paisley shawl over her. Just for a few moments, she told herself, and slid into sleep.

CHAPTER FIVE

When words and ink swam under his gaze, Henry set aside the student manuscripts. Unsurprisingly, Charles Hay's paper was the best of the lot. He shook his head, bemused.

Curious about the storm and needing vigorous activity after a long bout of reading, he shrugged into greatcoat, top hat, and gloves, found a shovel by the kitchen door, and went back to the entrance to clear the snow from the portico steps. No servants were about to do it, nor did he mind physical work. Years as a doctor, rolling up his sleeves to deal with many unpleasant matters, and tending to chores in his regiment days left him no undue pride about what was proper to do or not do. And in a snow-stranding, needs must, he thought.

The steps were covered again nearly as fast as he cleared them. In gathering darkness and tearing winds, he trudged toward the stables, grateful for sturdy high boots. The horses were content, happier when he petted and spoke to them, found more blankets, poured water and oats for them. Then he headed for the house, whistling Max back more than once.

Pausing on the top step, he recognized a near blizzard: strong winds, bitter cold, steady snowfall. Travel would be impossible tomorrow and perhaps for days.

The Christmas holiday that Clary so loved would be

spent in isolation with him. Her anticipation, her hopes, and happiness, her disappointment, too, all depended on him. And he was loath to admit that he cared for Yule—or for Clary.

Her question earlier echoed again. *Why did you . . . ?* But what haunted him even more were her father's words seven years ago, on the day Henry had asked permission to court Clary. *Ridiculous, Seton. She's set to marry her cousin Hay. If she's led you to believe otherwise, well, you're a fool, sir.*

Scowling, remembering, Henry went inside, stomping and shaking off the snow.

Hours later, Clary still had not come down for supper. At first, Henry was glad the stubborn girl had taken his advice to rest. The cook's hearty soup still simmered, a crusty loaf was warming, and the larder supplied cold meat, cheese, apples, butter, and chilled cider. Henry waited his own meal, feeding the dog and returning to his study to listen for a light, uneven step on the stairs. He looked forward to that sound.

Gloom gathered, so he lit a few beeswax candles and stoked the fire. Hearing a noise at the doorway, he glanced up, seeing only Max. The longcase clock in the hallway ticked steadily, and Henry stood at the window, watching snow plummet.

Finally, he pivoted and strode toward the stairs, increasingly concerned.

Knocking at the bedroom door, hearing no answer, Henry eased it open. The room was dark but for the hot glow of the hearth. She was asleep, he saw, cozied with the shawl. He moved forward. "Clary?" he whispered.

Bending, he listened to her breathing, watched her for signs of distress, and saw none. In the firelight, she was lovely, pure, her hair curled and mussed over the sweet curve of her cheek, one bare arm resting on the patterned shawl.

She slept peacefully. He did not need to stay. But he lingered, brushing her hair back, touching her brow; he felt no fever, and noted the wound was improving. Rest would help her head. But first he had to know that she could wake easily.

He touched her shoulder. "Clary."

She shifted a little, mewled softly as a kitten, and the sound plunged hard through his body, surprising him. She wrinkled her nose, shifted to her back, the shawl sliding down, revealing the creamy tops of her breasts, full and luscious. He took in a quick breath.

"Clary." He knelt, nudging her shoulder. "Wake up. Show me you can."

Her eyes opened. In firelight, her irises were gray, lovely. Clear and healthy. She sighed. "Henry," she whispered. She touched his forearm. "I am so glad you're here."

"Always here, love," he said before he could stop the words. "How do you feel?"

"Oh." Those marvelous eyes, smoke and ice, drifted shut. "Tired."

"Sleep. We can wait supper." He brushed the back of his hand along her cheek.

She nodded, her fingers curled over his sleeve. Henry waited to be sure her breaths were even. He brushed her cheek again, following the curve of her jaw. She smiled with such quick, elfin beauty that he smiled, too, in the dark, truly, for the first time in a long while.

He leaned close. Knew he should leave, but instead inclined toward her, his breath sifting her golden curls. She moved her head, and before he could hold back, he set his lips to hers, kissed the soft curve of her smile. She breathed a little moan and her hand slipped to his face as she leaned into the kiss.

Then he was kissing her again, a deep, lush caress and a sigh shared between them. Her mouth opened sweetly beneath his and her arm encircled his neck, drawing him toward her. He touched her then, caging her torso with his hands, sliding his fingers upward, exploring, caressing her cheek and throat with lips and breath, cherishing the exquisite warmth of her mouth against his as he pressed her into a fuller embrace—

He drew back. *Good God.* What was he thinking, to ravish her even for a moment? And how could he relinquish the control he honed and valued, the taut will that kept him apart from everyone, from emotion—from hurt as well as love. He angled away, and rose to his feet.

Her hand stayed his arm, and he caught her fingers in his. He kissed them, then let go.

"Sleep," he said, and left.

Clary woke blinking in the darkness. Had she dreamed that Henry had come to her like a prince, kissing her to life again? She sat up, slid a hand over her face, easing sleep away. As she stood, splashed her face, dressed in the dark gray wool and laced her half-boots, she wondered. But he had been there. The kiss had been magical, but real and sincere. He cared—his heart was not closed off. Hope lifted her own heart like a kite and she smiled, smoothing her hair, pinching her cheeks, fetching her cane as she opened the door.

Down in the foyer, she greeted Max when he padded forward. Resting her hand on his rough, warm coat, she walked beside him toward the library with its cozy light.

Henry sat at a writing desk under the light of a single candle, making notes on some papers, so focused that he did not see her. Not wanting to disturb him, she entered quietly, heart thumping as she remembered the touch of his hands, his lips.

Her attention was caught by the portrait over the desk. Earlier, she had seen it and other paintings hung about the room but had not studied them. She recognized Henry's father, the previous Lord Cranshaw, standing beside the same writing desk, his hand on books stacked beside a row of surgical instruments. He looked remarkably like his son; tall, thinner, equally handsome, he glowered intensely.

An older painting over the fireplace portrayed a robust man unlike the stern, uncompromising surgeon. In a mulberry dressing gown over tartan vest and breeches, he sat at a table littered with an assortment of books, papers, bottles, coins, cups, candles, a dagger, a pistol. Leaning in his chair, he looked out at the viewer amiably. His powerful presence filled the frame.

Clary crossed the room, drawn by the larger portrait.

"My great-great-grandfather." Henry came toward her. "Archibald Scott, a Border laird. He was an apothecary, but was better known as a reiver." He looked up at the painting. "As a boy, I often wished I had known him."

"He looks a spirited rascal," she said. Henry laughed.

"Aye. He kept the Yule well—kept it like a house afire, so they say. Roaring, magnificent Christmases that went on until Hogmanay, and days after."

"Goodness!"

"He's a local legend. He'd invite everyone, friend and foe, for great feasts and bonfires, songs, and whisky flowing. More than one feud was mended and begun during his Christmas celebrations, so it is said. The original Cranshaw tower burned to a ruin during one of his fests. I suspect," he added wryly, "that Roaring Archie, as they called him, celebrated every chance he got with feast, song, fires, and plenty of whisky. He did not particularly agree with the Protestants diminishing Christmas, so he continued to keep it. You would have liked him." For an instant she saw the same mischief in his eyes as in Roaring Archie's.

"He would have gone searching for pine boughs in a blizzard," she said wryly.

"Indeed. Alas, the current laird of Cranshaw is not wont

to do that. How do you feel now? I could fetch you a hatchet so you could get some greenery for the décor, if you are ready to explore the vast frozen arctic."

She lifted her brows. "So bad as that?" Henry nodded. Earlier, she had heard winds howling, had seen the windowsills draped in snow. She went into the foyer, crossing to the door. Henry walked behind her, Max with him.

When Henry reached past her to open the door, Clary gasped to see the vastness he had described—a blurred and pale expanse of mounds in place of steps, drive, hedges, and gardens, even the path to the stables. Winds blew cold and snow fell glistening against a dark sky.

"We are well and truly stranded," Henry murmured, echoing her thoughts. "It could snow for a day or two. Who knows when the roads will be clear enough even for larger coaches."

She shivered in the chill, awed by the grandeur. "It's beautiful."

"And treacherous."

"What of the horses?"

"I saw to them a little while ago. They should be fine tonight, and I'll go in the morning. The groom lives over a mile away and may not get to them soon." He shut the door, closing off the snow light. In the dark foyer, with candle-light far off in another room, Clary looked up at Henry. For a moment, though they did not touch or speak, she felt wrapped in warmth, safety, affection, and more. All that she had wanted and missed for so long was there. Had she imagined that moment, upstairs? She hoped not.

"Lady Hay," he said, voice gruff in the shadows, "shall we go to dinner?"

"You need not call me so formally," she said.

"I must." He offered his elbow. "For propriety's sake. And your honor."

"I am a widow. You are a doctor and exempt, and my

widowhood gives me some exemption, too." She took his arm and he led her to a dining room papered in blue Chinese wallpaper. Candles blazed on the table and the sideboard, where dishes were laid out.

"I brought up what I could find in the kitchen. The soup is a bit thick, having simmered for so long. The rest is good, if simple."

"It's lovely," she breathed.

"I did not want you to eat in the cold scullery, though I would have done were I alone," he said. "Since you are missing a chance to be with your cousins on Christmas Eve, perhaps this will do instead." He drew out a chair for her near the end of the table, and then took a chair at the head, just beside her.

"Thank you, sir." She smiled. "But who will serve us?"

"Max!" Henry whistled. Clary laughed, and he grinned fleetingly. "We will call it a country supper so we can serve ourselves."

"There is no one about to declare otherwise," she agreed.

"Quite." His eyes met hers, and she felt a shared awareness that made her blush.

As she rose from the table, he immediately stood, and as she served herself from the dishes on the sideboard, he came behind her to carry her dish as she limped along to ladle soup and choose cheese, meat, bread. When both sat to eat, Clary sensed a curious tension in the silence—and felt a warm, lush tautness in her body. She was keenly aware of his nearness.

The soup was thick but savory, and she was surprisingly hungry. As they ate, the conversation was quiet, punctuated by Max's soulful gazes. Finally, Clary laughed and relented, slipping crumbles of cheese to the dog.

"He adores you," Henry said. "If you stay, that dog will lose what few manners he has. Down, Max, leave her be."

"I do not mind," she said. "It's Christmas Eve, and dogs

can be spoiled as well as—" She looked away. "I nearly forgot. You do not much care for Christmas."

"It has yet to prove its usefulness," he said. "But you and Max enjoy it, so indulge. I warn you he will be unhappy tomorrow, having had far too much cheese."

Clary lifted her bowl of soup. "This?"

"As you will, Lady Hay."

She set the bowl on the floor and the dog happily slurped. "I do wish you would stop calling me Lady Hay. It is so stuffy, and reminds me of my husband's deceased mother. Lord Cranshaw reminds me of your father. We used to be just Henry and Clary."

"We did," he said, sitting back. "As Lady Hay, do you have lands and such to watch over? What of your husband's family?"

"It was fully five years ago, and they have never objected to my part of the inheritance. He left me a house and a little land in Perthshire. The rest went to his brother and nephew. The house is old, not large, but lovely. And after Papa died—well, I am modestly comfortable now. No one need ever worry about me." She shifted her cane, and tapped it on the floor. "I am a childless widow and a cripple as well, but I am dependent on no one."

"Well done, Clarinda Douglas," he said, elbows propped as he watched her. "If you were home now—if all was perfect in your world—what would you be doing on this Yule Eve?"

His question surprised her. All perfect? She pondered. "Singing," she said.

"Not dragging in green fripperies and berries better left to the birds, and opening your home for wild pagan festivities?"

"Singing," she affirmed, "and having a quiet celebration with people I love and enjoy. And baking—I would make the oatcakes my grandmother made, and seed cakes, scones with raisins, gingerbread and apple tarts like my mother made. The house would be filled with laughter and song and sweet, buttery baking smells. If this was a perfect Christmas Eve."

"Which most assuredly it is not," he said. "I may have to reconsider Christmas. I am partial to apple tarts and gingerbread."

"Ah." Clary wanted to smile, but echoed his mock serious mood instead. Something was happening, and she did not want to interrupt its course. Henry stood and went to the sideboard, taking out two glasses.

"I shall play butler again, if I may," he said. "Fresh cider? Mrs. Johnstone made a new batch. No spirits for you, my girl, until your head is fit for it."

"I have no headache at all, after a little sleep. But cider would be lovely."

He poured, and brought the glasses to the table. She tilted her head, regarding him. He was changed somehow, more open, more the true Henry Seton in the last hour than in all the months since she had first walked into his lecture hall. That day she had found a hard, reserved man with a closed heart—and today she was learning of the grief he had seen and hurt he had endured. She realized that he was simply protecting himself until he could heal and feel whole again.

She had done something similar all her life, building a wall made of smiles and false cheerfulness to ensure her independence. He had drawn inward quickly, efficiently, to give his wounds and feelings time to sort out.

But here at Cranshaw, with its snowy seclusion and candlelight and conversation, with stolen kisses and a simple shared supper, moment by moment she loved what seemed to be emerging between them, some magic she thought destroyed years back. Not for all the world would she tip this fragile balance and have him remember he did not trust her.

That was it, she realized—somehow he had lost trust in her, and then everyone. The effect of war, perhaps, compiled on a heart as broken as hers had been by their separation. Yet now, tonight, he was easing back into himself.

She sipped the cider, and Henry did the same, raising his glass in a toast. "To snowstorms and strandings—and to a good Yule."

"To snow," she toasted. "And a blithe Yule to you, too. What would your sister be doing tonight? Though her children do have chickenpox," she added. "Does she celebrate as your mother did in your childhood? Does she invite you to her home?"

"They invite me, though it is a simple family dinner. She and her husband keep a little Yule for the children. Alan Graham is a tea merchant and does exceptionally well, but his offices in Edinburgh are open on the Christmas holiday. Fiona does some baking with the girls and they perform wee songs, and then there is dinner. Usually, I do not attend." He glanced at her. "So her girls call me Uncle Grumphy. They have not had a Yule gift of me, and believe I should produce them dutifully and often."

Clary laughed. "Uncle Grumphy! And well you've earned it, giving no Yule to wee lassies."

"I do not know what wee lassies want."

"Ribbons," she suggested. "Dolls. Hoops and balls. A small gift and they would no longer call you Uncle Grumphy."

"I am loath to give the title up, for its advantages. And just this morning I sent tinctures for their fevers, so I am not miserly, am I?"

"And you are generous with your snow treatments as well."

"Tonight at my sister's house," he said thoughtfully, "there is also the ceremonial dragging about of the greenery."

"But not the raucous Yuletide of Roaring Archie Scott."

"We no longer burn houses down around our ears at

Christmas." He raised his glass again. "Cheers to quiet holidays, Clarinda."

"At least you are toasting the holidays now, sir," she
replied.

"There is that," he murmured.

Henry carried the dishes down to the kitchen and Clary
followed, insisting on cleaning them in a basin, though he
had not wanted her to risk the rough stone steps to the base-
ment level, or spend too much time on her feet. The chores
were quickly done between them, and enjoyably so, and
again he did not mind the work.

"I have cleaned many a dish and basin myself," he told
her. "Besides, who is there to clean dishes but poor Max,
who only uses his tongue for it? We cannot leave things
about to wait for Mrs. Johnstone's return, nor can we
chance that Mrs. Hall, the forester-minister's wife, will
make her way here soon."

"We?" she had only said, tilting her head in that fairylike
way she had, all gray eyes and gorgeous lips, so that he had
to look away or pull her into his arms.

Later, he sat in the study going over the student papers
while Clary grazed along his bookshelves, pulling volumes
here and there to read, sitting and rising and putting one
book back for another, her cane tapping softly on carpet
and floor.

"Sit, if you will," he finally said. "So much activity de-
tracts from my idea of a quiet, snowy fortress where I ac-
complish all my work before the melting begins."

"Oh," she replied, looking so hurt that he regretted
speaking, "I am sorry. I cannot find a book to my liking at
the moment."

"I thought you enjoyed medical treatises, the more pon-
derous the better."

"I regularly saved my father from writing such, so I

would only want to make corrections on the pages of the books in your library."

"Here, then," he said, and stood to lift down a packet of pages from a shelf. "Try your hand at these." He carried it to her, and Clary sat in a wing chair that matched his own, a chair rarely used. He rather liked seeing her in it.

She sifted through the pages. " 'Treatment of Cranial Injury'—you wrote this?"

"When I returned to Edinburgh after Belgium, I was asked by the publishers of an Edinburgh journal to write about my medical experiences there."

"You've seen a great many head injuries?"

"Far too many. Including yours. So I never take them lightly, having seen the consequences. If you want to make corrections to that manuscript, please do."

"Thank you," she said. "I would be honored."

"Honored! You are my best student," he murmured. "I value your thoughts."

"It is an honor because you are well known for your brave actions in the war."

"Anyone could have done it, had they the training and been there as I was."

"Let people praise you. We need to appreciate heroes," she said. "Acts of courage and humanity in a hellish place like a battlefield inspire other people, restore pride in humankind. What you did there, even if you do not know it, helps strengthen our spirits, our hearts."

Henry watched her, and felt his throat tighten. "It did not feel inspiring at the time," he said simply. "Hellish, yes. But the memories—the thoughts of men I treated and could not save. I have brooded over that these six months, wondering what I could have done differently, how I might have saved this man or that one, what I could have tried. I wrote scores of reports for the regiment, and copied each one so I could study the cases again. Some I know I could save now, if I had another chance. But—" He gestured futilely.

"You have a chance," she said. "Write about all those cases, about field medicine, and let others learn from your experience. You could not save those men, but you could save others through the good work of other doctors."

Henry frowned thoughtfully. "Possibly. But with so many different types of injuries, treatments, surgeries, infections to write about, it's quite a task."

"I can help you," she said. "If you like."

He inhaled, sitting back. "Yes," he said then. "We could work together. Yes." He saw her delight—the elfin, luscious smile that sweetened her face and glowed in her eyes. He smiled, too, and turned back to his work.

The clock ticked in the hallway, and all Clary wanted to do was throw herself into Henry's arms. But propriety ruled, and he always had such reserve about him, though she sensed it beginning to melt. Suddenly, she wished the snow could continue for days, weeks, cocooning them while they learned each other's ways and hearts once again. That would take time; she was impulsive, but he was wisely not. She smiled to herself, anticipating what could come of their renewed connection—and excited, too, to work with him on his treatise about field injuries.

Henry capped the ink bottle, set down his quill, and stood. "I'll look around outside," he said. "Clear some snow, make sure all is well—trees and roofs and so on. Come, Max." The dog only opened an eye and huffed back into sleep. "You rascal, stay there then and guard the lady. I will be back soon," he told Clary, and smiled at her gently before going into the foyer to grab coat, hat, and a lantern. Moments later, she heard the door open.

Clary left the chair to sink to her knees, curling seated beside the dog. She rubbed his thick, warm coat and watched the hot flickering flames, feeling peaceful, happy.

She began to hum, smoothing the dog's fur, lost in thought. The hallway clock rang midnight.

Christmas Day had come. "Blithe Yule to thee, my friend," she whispered to Max. A favorite Christmas song her grandmother always sang in Gaelic came to her, and she lifted her voice, first in the Gaelic, going on to the refrain. *Alleluia, alleluia . . .*

Max huffed in contentment, moving his ears. Clary sang on, now in English, as the poignant, lovely melody nuanced each note to sweeten the air.

> *My love, my treasured one I know*
> *My sweet and lovely one are you*
> *Alleluia, alleluia . . .*

She paused, leaning toward the dog. "I want to stay, Max," she whispered. "Oh, how I want to be here with you and your master, always."

A pure and lovely sound caught his attention. Singing? Henry paused on the step, shovel in hand, and looked around. In the darkness, with lantern light pouring gold down the steps, the snow was a deep cloak, shadowy and pale, mounded over the world. It was beautiful and peaceful—dangerous, too, for its cold and ice and silent seclusion.

He cocked his head, and opened the door. Clary was singing. Stepping inside quietly, knocking snow from his boots, he walked along the hall and stood at the study's threshold.

Her clear, beautiful voice had a pure tone as she sang in Gaelic, then English. Seated on the floor, she rubbed the dog's ears. Max, the scamp, loved every moment of it, watching her with dark, worshipful eyes.

> *My love, my treasured one I know . . .*

Henry leaned against the doorway, watching. Her voice, rich as whisky and honey, filled the room, the house. His heart.

She bent then, whispering to the dog, and Henry would have given all to know what secret she shared. She wiped a tear from her cheek, and leaned her head against Max's.

She did have a damnable way about her, and it was doing its work.

You have known love, Dr. Douglas had written. *Claim it again.*

Suddenly, Henry wondered if John Douglas had written those words for his daughter or for his student, who might read them one day. Perhaps the good doctor wrote to himself—a reminder to never forget the essential importance of love. Of the heart.

Claim it again. Henry stepped back, deeply wanting—but not yet ready.

Hearing the shovel scraping on the steps, Clary got up from the floor, determined to go outside to see what the storm had wrought. She dressed in her warm frogged pelisse, her bonnet, and gloves, and with cane in hand went to the door, Max at her side.

Henry had cleared the steps and was now shoveling snow away from the base of the portico entrance, a valiant if futile effort against the huge expanse of snow that had collected in the several hours since her arrival at Cranshaw.

Max ran ahead of her and she made her way down the steps cautiously. Henry greeted the dog, and turned to see her coming toward him.

"Careful!" Carrying the shovel, he came toward her. "You don't want to fall."

"I do not and I will not," she said, smiling, lifting her chin. "What's this?" Glancing down, she saw a knee-high stack of pine boughs.

"I cut some greenery," he said, and shrugged.

She smiled. "Thank you." He smiled, too, quick and warm. Clary caught her breath, thrilled—then looked around and spread her arms wide. "Henry, it's so beautiful!"

"And the very devil to clear."

"Then leave it. Let the snow fall as it will, let the sun clear it when it will."

"You are in a hurry to leave," he reminded her. "Though I cannot safely take the horses and carriage out yet. Two days, perhaps more. Do you mind?"

She laughed. Henry looked at her quizzically. Clary walked deeper into the snow, supported by the cane, the snow thick enough to both impede and steady her, though her gown dragged and snow slipped icily into her boots. She turned, her skirt and coattails making swirls over the soft snowy surface, and saw Henry standing there, watching her, head tilted.

"I do not mind at all, Lord Cranshaw," she said. "I will stay as long as it takes to clear."

"You may not make it to Lady Holly's ball," he said. "I cannot promise it."

"I do not mind staying." She spun again, arms out. Something filled her, bubbled joyfully within her, the beauty, the peace, the wonder of the snowfall and this haven with the man she loved. The only man she had ever loved. The thought made her stop in her turning. She faced him.

"I have a question," she said.

"Yes." He seemed to expect it.

"Why did you leave—then?"

"I asked your father's permission to marry you. He refused."

"Refused?" She put a hand to her chest. "I never knew."

"He said you had already agreed to marry your cousin. Said I was a fool."

"And I was told I must marry Sir William, and that you had no interest in me at all—that I was the fool. A girl with a lame foot. A cripple." She looked away, in the light-dark vastness of the transformed world. "You are no fool, Dr. Seton."

"And you are no cripple, Clarinda. I have never seen that in you. How long will you stay?" He propped a hand on the upright shovel.

She blinked away grateful tears, and tipped her head. "Well, it is Yuletide, and you do prefer to be alone at this time of year."

"Do I?" He looked around, surveying the place, the mounds of powdery snow glinting in snow light and lantern light. "It is a good place to be alone, but a better place to share."

She pointed to the house, and the lantern light caught the long shadow of her arm. She deepened her voice. "We have no Yule here, just work and solitude for Lord Cranshaw."

He laughed softly. "Is that how you see me?"

She lowered her arm. "Not quite so grim as that." She stood, smiling.

"You know you're like a fairy when you smile. Like an elf. And I wonder what mischief you've got in mind."

Seeing his grin, she laughed in delight. She stepped toward him, but the deep snow trapped her boot and her weak ankle. She tumbled down with a woof of breath.

"Clary!" Henry was kneeling beside her in an instant.

"I'm fine." She looked up at him, grabbed his coat, and tugged down. He braced over her, gloved hands in the snow to either side. "I always loved you, Henry," she said. "Did you know?"

He stared down at her. "I did not. Your marriage, and so on."

"The marriage was my father's idea. Well, my mother's. There was a family debt owed. An agreement—I knew nothing of it until too late."

"Your father mentioned it once, a rather weak apology after the fact. Too late."

"You purchased colors and left. I thought you did not care. You did not argue for me."

"That was my mistake," he said, leaning over her. "I have learned from it."

She looked up at him, holding his lapels. The snow was cold. She did not care. He was a shield over her, his breath warm as he leaned closer.

"I have always loved you, Clary Douglas," he said. "I always will." He lowered to kiss her, his lips a warm blessing in the chill. He kissed her mouth, the snow from her cheeks, then pulled back. "Though I fear I may ravish you right here, in the snow, since we are being improper."

"Whatever will we do?" she asked, half laughing.

"I think I will marry you," he murmured, nuzzling her cheek, the heat and thrill of his breath and his lips melting her inside, no matter the cold. "What say you?"

"Yes, let's do." She tilted her face toward his, took his cheeks in her snow-dusted gloves. "I wish we could marry soon."

"Did I tell you my forester is a parson?" he asked, kissing her again. "And do you happen to have a beautiful gown that you planned to wear at some ball . . . what ball was that . . . ?"

She kissed him deeply, then drew back. "I do have a gown, and I did hear about the parson."

"We could fetch him and his wife and son for witnesses, and have our wedding in the morning. On Christmas Day."

"With greenery for the wedding décor," she added.

"Just so." He stood and helped her up, grabbed her cane, and lifted her into his arms. While the dog romped at his heels, he carried her up the cleared steps. "But there is something we should do first."

Clary rested her head on his shoulder. "And what is that?"

"Make this a scandalous Christmas indeed, so there is nothing for it but to marry, and quickly," he said. "Hey, Max—out of the way!"

CHRISTMAS LARKS

❧

Patricia Rice

CHAPTER ONE

Thursday, December 22, a week before the ball . . .

"*C*areful-like, don't spill it!" a mouse squeaked from behind the fading damask-papered wall.

"It's bloomin' hot, innit?" another mouse retorted.

Mice spoke?

Pinching his nose to wake himself up, Ivo Whitney-Harris emerged from the black depths of his chronic nightmares to examine this curious phenomenon. He couldn't think past the raging pain in his head.

"Leave it here, then scamper quick-like," the first mouse whispered.

Mouse feet scampered. Ivo considered all the vermin he and his men had routinely annihilated in camps over the last long years. He didn't think the mice had raised a vocal protest. Images of mice carrying swords and wearing plumed French caps emerged in his murky mind.

But he was back in England now, driven by necessity and succumbing to homesickness. He now hid behind his own secure walls in Bellsburn—he thought.

Had English mice learned to speak while he was away?

He shivered. He knew this wasn't sunny Italy, but the room was bloody freezing. He'd hoped to be greeted joyfully by the old family retainers who were all the family he had now. Where the devil were the Merriweathers? Although, given his dilatoriness, he probably didn't deserve a prodigal son's welcome.

He rubbed his bandaged temple trying to clear his thoughts.

Bandaged? Hadn't the bandages been removed?

He suffered a momentary terror that he was back in battle after all. He struggled to drag his aching bones to a sitting position, looked for his weapon, and strained to remember his last hours.

Everything in his braincase lurched, and he almost passed out. He had to cling to the bed's—sofa's?—edge to remain upright. He couldn't remember drinking himself under the table since his Oxford days. His mouth didn't taste of week-old vomit as it had then.

He pushed past the pain to remember a frantic rush to board a ship across the Channel—and the letters, the damned letters that had followed him over half of Europe, catching up with him in France. A post chaise might have been involved after the ship. He rubbed his aching head again and fought back the weakness of tears.

His father was dead. That fierce old man wasn't supposed to die before Ivo could talk to him. What a wretched way to die—surrounded only by sheep and servants.

Blessedly, Ivo's nose detected the scent of fragrant, steaming tea. Forcing both eyes open, he noted a faint thin light penetrating the darkness. Holding his bandaged head so it didn't fall off, he turned to trace the source. Deciding there was a window behind him, he groped on the far side of the bed, grasped a handful of fabric, and yanked it aside.

Gray light entered, illuminating his rumpled greatcoat covering an old sofa, and a china tea set on the side table. Steam wafted from the spout—hot tea, thank heavens.

That blue-painted china meant he really was home. Still steadying himself with one hand on the cushion, he reached for the pot and shakily poured tea into the cup, admiring the way the gray light played across old ivory porcelain and faded paint. The image needed a rose on the tea tray—a rose in winter.

A still life formed in his head as the tea warmed his stomach, and he rummaged around until he found his valise.

Head still pounding with all the hammers of hell, he located his sketchpad and charcoal. Sipping the tea, he began to draw. Sanity was in his fingers, not his head, these days.

Returning home from the market, Sarah Jane Langsdale strode briskly through the wintry December streets. In her basket, tucked between root vegetables, was a package that had cost her more than money.

The lace had come at the expense of her pride.

This past year, independence had emerged from the devastating loss of both parents. She'd learned that she was strong and could take care of herself.

Attending the Holbourne Abbey Christmas ball was as good as admitting to her godmother that Sarah still hoped to find a husband, which she most decidedly did not.

"The lace is a foolish waste," she told Mary, already regretting the expensive purchase. "I shall return it tomorrow."

Stout, her dark hair displaying threads of silver, Mary was more mother than maid to Sarah these days. "You cannot ignore Lady Holly's invitation," Mary remonstrated, as she had ever since the invitation had arrived. She adjusted her hold on the heavy basket of apples designated for pies for the church bake sale. "It's Christmas, and our good lads are home safe and sound this year. You must join the celebration."

Not all Bellsburn's boys had returned this past year since Waterloo. Many had been left on the battlefields. And some . . .

Sarah had reason to agonize over the new baron's absence. Abruptly, she turned the corner so they might pass the old Whitney house—the one where she and Ivo had spent half their childhood being tutored by her father, and taught music and dancing by his mother. Those days were long gone, but the memories . . . Should be shoved in a dustbin.

"The orphanage will be a fine thing for the village," Mary said, understanding their change in direction. "Perhaps you can persuade Lady Holly to donate toward the renovations."

"I can't think attending her ball will impress her more than my simply making a call and explaining what we need," Sarah argued.

"Your mourning is over," Mary countered. "It won't hurt to have a bit of a lark before you take yourself off the market. I hear the entire Abbey will be lit with candles."

Mary would enjoy the jewels and gowns and decorations and a visit with her old friends. Sarah's loyal companion deserved that bit of holiday fun.

Sarah supposed she could use her godmother's dreadful matchmaking ball to raise interest in the orphanage. That still didn't justify the lace expense.

"You know the lace is to catch a man's eye, and I have donned my cap," Sarah argued. "I don't wish to smile and gossip and pretend I'm interested."

A flash of blue darting down the kitchen steps of the empty Whitney house caught her eye. "Did you see that?" Sarah increased her pace. "I hope no one has broken in. I told the vicar someone should live on the premises."

"The late baron only left the house to the church, not the funds to keep it up," Mary reminded her.

"Hoping his *son* would fund the maintenance." Sarah tried to keep the bitterness from her voice. She had no right to judge another, even if Ivo Whitney-Harris had turned out to be such a disappointment.

"You can't go in there, it's dangerous!" Mary cried, horrified, when Sarah stopped on the stairs to dig into her reticule for the keys. "We'll ask the vicar to take a look."

"It is Friday. He will be making his rounds. What if it's someone who heard about the orphanage and needs our help?"

"Then they should have gone to the vicarage and not broken into a vacant house," Mary said dryly, but she followed Sarah up the front stairs.

"Perhaps if they're thieves, they will run away and not come back if they know someone is looking after the place." Sarah opened the weathered door.

The lovely papered foyer struck her once more with nostalgia for a more innocent time. She'd always loved the elegance of the blue and gold stripes on the walls. Old Mr. Merriweather would have greeted her and her father with a stiff nod as if they were as important as Lady Holly. His wife, Bess, would have hurried upstairs with a plate of fresh-baked ginger cookies. The house would have smelled of beeswax, and at this time of year—greenery. Lady Harris had loved to fill her house with the outdoors.

But the lovely baroness had died long, long ago. Afterward, her husband had preferred his country estate. He'd closed up the village house after his son Ivo rode off to war. He'd left a skeleton staff these last years, in case Ivo returned, but the scapegrace never had. In the months since the baron's death, the neglect had left the house smelling badly of must and mice.

"The church never should have let the Merriweathers go," Mary muttered.

"I agree. At least as long as they were here, the house was maintained. But the baron couldn't know he would die before his son returned." Although Ivo could have returned any time these last months since the war ended, if Sarah understood rightly. He just hadn't.

"I'll check the kitchen. You look through the public

rooms," Sarah suggested, studying the dim interior. "See if anything has been disturbed."

"Don't be foolish. You stay right here, and I'll go down and see if the door is properly barred. These are dangerous times." Mary set down her apple basket and lifted a brass candlestick as a weapon.

"The baron's executor has already removed all the valuables," Sarah protested, but Mary didn't heed her. Sturdy Mary would make so much noise clumping down the stairs that any thief would have time to flee, so Sarah didn't fret.

Once they had the funding, she would move in here as part of her wages for teaching the orphans. That was a far nobler ambition than marriage.

Boldly, she walked through what would soon be her new home, mentally creating offices and schoolrooms of parlors, study, and library.

CHAPTER TWO

$\mathcal{L}$ost in the crash of cannon fire in his head and slash of brush across canvas, Ivo ignored the creaks of the house. Black smoke curled across his skies. He darkened the oil on his palette, and nightmare horses reared, breathing fire.

And then the mice returned.

"We gots to hide in the attic," the bossier one squeaked.

"They got bread," the naysayer protested stubbornly.

Ivo realized he was starving. Toast and tea would hit the spot.

Reluctantly setting his brush in the turpentine he'd found in the storage cabinet, he abandoned the canvas and limped for the upstairs corridor.

He didn't understand why his beloved home echoed like one of Europe's abandoned churches. He'd always preferred this snug house in town belonging to his mother's family over his father's enormous, isolated country seat. He needed people around him, not sheep.

He clung to the bannister, intent on finding the kitchen, but his aching head and gimpy leg both gave out at the landing. Dizzy, he sat down abruptly and peered into the twilight gloom of the foyer below, hoping for some sign of the missing domestics.

An angel materialized in a spectral light from the foyer windows.

Ivo rubbed his eyes. Angels wore white and had wings. They didn't wear practical gray pelisses and shabby bonnets. But the morning light illuminated porcelain features bearing the perfect demeanor of a heavenly visitor. Huge blue, dark-lashed eyes and rich rose lips turned upward in a smile of pure bliss as she spun about on the black-and-white tiles, then caressed the frame of one of his old paintings.

He couldn't help a chortle of delight at this welcoming vision. "Sarah Jane," he cried. "You make a perfectly dreadful angel."

The blissful smile shattered, replaced by shock as she swiveled from the painting to the stairs. "I—" she started to say, then stiff disapproval froze her expression. "Lord Harris," she said formally.

The never-used title jolted unpleasant reminders that made Ivo's head ache more. He preferred nostalgic recollections of the vicar's daughter—his childhood nemesis. "With your expressive eyes, you should have been an actress," he told her, his addled brain not processing his thoughts before they reached his tongue. "It's been how long? Five years? You're all grown up."

"I was seventeen when you left—hardly a babe," she said in those acerbic tones he remembered with less delight. "What are you doing here? I thought you were a burglar."

The question baffled him. She was the intruder here. Barging into his home was nosy, even for Sarah. This house had always been his haven from his father's chronic complaints about his only son's wasteful pursuits.

Rather than return her question, Ivo remembered his manners and attempted to stand. He saw two of everything, staggered, missed the bannister, and sat down again with an embarrassingly abrupt thud.

She uttered a cry of alarm and flew up the stairs. "You're injured! How did you . . . ?" Apparently thinking better of the question, she called, "Mary, come quickly!"

"Don't shout so loud," he grumbled, pride badly mauled. "I got myself here just fine. Nothing a bit of toast and tea won't cure. Where are Mr. and Mrs. Merry?" He used their childhood name for the servants.

She hesitated, and then sat down beside him to examine his bandage. She smelled of apple blossoms, and he wanted to lean over and bury his nose in her hair.

"That's a dreadful black eye and your nose may be broken." She touched his aching beak. "We should have a physician look at you."

He shrugged. "I've been worse. The mice said you brought bread. I don't suppose you could toast some."

"The mice?" Her brow creased in a frown before she replied in the soothing tones he recalled from long ago, when he'd been abed with some childhood illness. "We can do tea and toast and a bit of Mrs. White's apple jelly. Let's get you back upstairs first."

A sturdy woman in black hurried into the foyer. Not grandmotherly Mrs. Merry, Ivo thought in disappointment.

"Lord Harris has been injured," his angel told the crow. "We need to return him to bed and call a physician."

"Toast," he politely reminded her.

"Tea and toast once you're settled in," she agreed.

Why wasn't she home with her husband? Having Sarah Jane flutter around him as she had done in their youth disturbed him on a painfully personal level.

Ivo steadied himself as he stumbled back up the stairs. His gammy knee still gave out at the most inopportune times, but he could walk.

Apparently, these days Sarah smelled of apples and fresh bread and . . . a delicate fragrance all her own that stirred base desires. Good to know he wasn't dead, he decided, reeling toward the safety of his sofa as soon as they reached the next floor.

"You ought to be in bed. . . ." She bit off whatever else she intended to say. She was doing that a lot.

"No blasted linens," Ivo finished for her. "House all closed up. Should have written, sorry." He leaned against the sofa back and closed his eyes to stop the spinning.

"There's still a few bits in the larder," the crow murmured. "I'll see what I can find, then fetch Dr. Jones. You should come away now."

"Don't be foolish, Mary. I can't leave him like this. There's a teapot up here already. We just need to heat some water and find a bit of tea."

Ivo heard her checking his mysterious china tea set. He'd not packed china in his valise. He might have packed tea. It was the best medicine for homesickness.

"Tea, valise," he managed, dragging pillows behind his back so he could sit upright. "No water though."

"There are a few coals for a fire," his angel said, exploring the room. "Surely there's still water in the cistern. This is a fresh pot of tea."

"Mice made it," Ivo said in satisfaction. "Not me."

That produced a quiet round of whispering. He was enjoying the unfamiliarity of feminine company. Although Sarah was gratifyingly familiar—in an unaccustomed way. Gads, his brain was muddled.

He must have dozed off for a while. He woke to warm soapy water cleansing his grizzled jaw. The scent of apple blossoms and tea forced his eyes open.

His angel's worried frown wasn't blissful, but the sight of a tray laden with tea and toast was the next best thing to Sarah's angelic presence.

"I think I love you," he sighed in gratitude.

Sarah bit her lip at Ivo's inane comment and concentrated on removing the bandage wrapped around his shaggy dark hair. If he had truly addled his wits, she must not allow him to addle hers.

"Whatever have you been doing to yourself?" she asked,

nervously distracting his attention, which seemed focused on her bosom. Ivo was the only man of her acquaintance who loomed over her sufficiently to look down her dress.

He winced and reached for the toast. "Don't exactly remember, but I made it home. That's a good thing, ain't it?"

That was a matter of opinion, if he thought this was still his home. But Ivo had always been a charmer, and she wasn't immune to his grin.

"The war was over last June," she said. "A Dr. Seton wrote that you were injured, but you'd be well enough to travel in a few months."

"Doc Seton! He saved Kim, y'know."

She pressed her lips closed. From all she'd heard, the Countess's son didn't appreciate being saved, but now wasn't the time to tell Ivo about his friend.

"This cannot be a war wound." She examined the swollen gash that the bandage had hidden.

"Likely not," he agreed through a mouthful of toast. "Recollect a bit of a dispute with ruffians. Traveled all Europe without mishap. Forgot good old-fashioned English highwaymen."

That explained a bit. "You were on your way home when you were attacked by ruffians? Then you *did* receive the letters from your father's solicitor?" She held her breath, hoping he understood the situation and was just ignoring it in his own inimitable way.

Ivo wrinkled up his aristocratically straight—but broken—nose, and winced again. "Letters, yes," he said without conviction. "They all caught up with me in Paris. Read the one about my father's death and thought I'd best come home. Haven't made it through the others."

He rubbed at his temple and looked bereft. "He was a surly old goat but too young to die. What happened?"

Oh, dear. Sarah kept her sigh to herself. He didn't know about the house. "It was very sudden. A heart spasm or some such. You couldn't have saved him. You were exploring the Continent and that's why it took so long for the letters to find you?" she asked neutrally.

He brightened. "Museums. The artwork—just incredible. Makes my own efforts seem feeble in comparison. You'd like Italy," he said. "Palaces! They lived in palaces filled with sun and air!"

"You never liked England's winters," she recalled.

"Killed my mother," he agreed through more toast.

His father's death had been a few months after Waterloo, while Ivo had still been convalescing. She could see how mail might have wandered.

She didn't want to be the one who told him about his father's will.

"What about you?" he asked abruptly. "Didn't you marry that Brown boy Lady Holly introduced you to?"

"That was five years ago and all in my godmother's stubborn head," she exclaimed. "He married Agatha Wilson and has two little boys. Their farms marched together, so it was a good match."

Bob Brown hadn't been the one to break her heart.

"Good," Ivo said fervently, before frowning. "Then Lawrence came to his senses and captured your interest?"

"Lawrence?" she asked with incredulity, wondering at the odd path of his thoughts. "He's heir to a viscount and needs an heiress to keep him in horses. I don't wish to marry anybody."

"Ha, the dowager countess is wrong again." He settled back and closed his eyes with what looked oddly like peace.

Worried about his befuddled mind, Sarah finished cleaning around the scab.

"She should give him apples," a tiny voice whispered from the walls.

Startled, Sarah froze. Had she heard an apple crunch?

"Ma said they's good for what ails you," another small voice agreed.

Before she could investigate, she heard Mary returning with Dr. Jones. Sarah breathed a sigh of relief. Now things would be set straight, and Ivo could be removed to his home in the country, where servants anxiously awaited his return. Then she could look for voices in the walls.

Mary ushered Sarah out of the salon so the physician could examine the new Lord Harris. The maid frowned as they waited downstairs in the foyer for instructions.

"Dr. Jones said head wounds are very dangerous," Mary whispered. "The baron could have scrambled his wits, and we must wait to see if he recovers them."

Sarah barely held her gasp. "Not Ivo, surely! He was always so bright and . . ." And there she went again. She returned to pragmatism. "The baron has no heir. For the sake of the people on his estate, we'll hope Dr. Jones is wrong, and he won't be incapacitated."

"You could marry him," Mary said pragmatically. "Then you wouldn't have to worry about funding the orphanage."

"Most certainly not," Sarah said, horrified. She had made peace with her lot in life. She did not need her adolescent hero disordering her hard-won serenity. Ivo had no interest in orphans—or her, as he had so eminently made clear.

"I don't think he's eaten." Sarah returned the conversation to more immediate matters. "If I dash back to the market, I could return the lace and buy meat pies."

"Stop that," Mary admonished. "If he wants pies, he can buy them. He's not one of your charity cases."

But despite her cross words, Mary rummaged in her apple basket. She frowned and tilted the contents toward the light. "I know we bought a dozen," she muttered.

Uneasily recalling a whispered conversation she'd hoped she'd imagined, Sarah checked the basket, too. "The three freshest apples are gone. I specifically remember you saying they would be good for eating if the pie didn't need them."

Sarah glanced back up the stairs. "Perhaps we should search the house now."

"Wait until Dr. Jones comes down." Mary resisted the suggestion. "We can ask him to send one of the butcher's boys to look."

Restlessly, Sarah paced into the parlor to draw back the draperies. The winter light revealed a coating of dust and cobwebs on a pair of old horsehair chairs.

"The paper is too pretty for children. Will you leave this a sitting room?" Mary asked.

"I don't know." Sarah gazed up at another of Ivo's oil paintings. This one was a domestic scene of his mother and an elderly spaniel. They'd both been dead at the time he'd undertaken it, but he'd painted them out of vivid memory and love.

The executor hadn't thought this painting or the one in the foyer worth storing. Ivo would be horribly insulted. She hoped he would allow them to stay.

"I'll have to ask him which things he'd like to take away," she admitted. "For all I know, he might want these old chairs. His father's will left the house, but made no mention of the furnishings. I can't deny him his mother's possessions."

"You'll need beds and desks and such anyway," the maid agreed with fatalism.

So many orphans, so little money, Sarah reflected. "Perhaps I shouldn't have bitten off so much, but after seeing the overcrowded state of the orphanage in Newcastle . . . What else could I do?"

"Too many soldiers dying," Mary agreed. "Poor tots hardly knew their dads, and to lose their mamas, too . . . It's a hard life, that it is."

They heard the physician on the stairs and hurried back to the foyer. Dr. Jones shoved his spectacles up his nose and regarded them gravely.

"The baron has suffered a severe blow to the skull in an area that was not properly healed from an earlier injury. He's in so much pain, I fear internal swelling. He could recover in a day or two, or he could lose his eyesight, or die."

Sarah cried out her despair, then bit back further reaction. Her heart ached for the reckless, talented boy she'd loved, but she didn't know this man who could ignore his home and family for years.

"These types of injuries are exceedingly dangerous," the doctor continued. "He said Henry Seton, the physician who treated his earlier head wound, is lecturing at Edinburgh University these days. The baron claims Seton will be attending the countess's ball, so perhaps he can have a look at him when he arrives."

The ball was a week away!

"Should we arrange transport to his lordship's estate?" she asked, trying to sort out this disaster. "It's nearly ten miles, but he will have the comforts of home and people to care for him. I could ask Lady Holly for her carriage."

The doctor shook his head. "He shouldn't be moved. I don't know how he arrived here, but the damage is already done. He must keep his head elevated to reduce the swelling. He needs to be kept warm, and knowing the lad, he needs to be kept occupied. I fear he is dwelling on the past and is more agitated than he reveals. I would recommend laudanum, but then we'd have no idea if the internal injuries are repairing. He must be undisturbed until we see evidence that the swelling is reduced."

Sarah swallowed and let her pulse steady before asking, "Could we at least move him to warmer accommodations? There's the Abbey. Lady Holly always liked him. . . ."

The physician shook his head. "Have her send servants and coal, but do not move the boy one foot more." He took her hand and patted it. "I'll tell the vicar. Perhaps he knows someone who will help. It's a shame this new vicar has no wife." He shook his head in disapproval at the lack. "The baron certainly can't expect an unmarried lady to wait on him. We'll find someone."

"Bess and James Merriweather," Mary said decisively. "The baron can pay them to return."

The doctor nodded agreement. "Excellent thought."

Sarah couldn't quibble, even if the church was turning the house over to orphans in a few short weeks. Perhaps Ivo would have recovered by then, and he could take the Merriweathers with him to his estate. That would be perfect for all.

"Can you manage until they arrive?" Dr. Jones asked with concern. "I know it's not proper, but Holbourne Abbey is filling with visitors. I don't know if they can spare anyone."

"We'll be fine," Sarah said with more confidence than she felt. "Mary is here for propriety. The Merriweathers aren't far out of town. I'm sure they will be here before dark. If you would send word to the baron's estate, they might arrange for someone to arrive in a day or two, providing the weather holds."

In truth, she'd seldom been to the baron's country seat and had no idea if the servants had stayed on after Ivo's father died. The late baron's solicitor, Mr. Armstrong, had handled Ivo's affairs in recent months. Which reminded her . . .

"Mr. Armstrong has gone to Bath until after the New Year. Do we need to let him know that the baron has returned?"

"The vicar and I will see to that. I'll send a cart for the Merriweathers. If you'll just engage the ladies of the parish to help out, the lad will be well tended. We can hope to see you at the ball," the physician said cheerfully, tipping his hat, before letting himself out.

"Well, and if this isn't a fine kettle of fish," Mary muttered. "I'll set the kitchen to rights and start the soup. You'd best round up a few ladies to sit with him until the Merri-weathers arrive."

It didn't take a second's thought for Sarah to reject that notion. "You saw him. He's not in any state to be seen by gossips. He's used to me nursing him when he's ill. I'll stay until Mrs. Merriweather arrives."

Ignoring Mary's unhappiness with this decision, Sarah chose an apple from the basket and carried it up to the sickroom. She found Ivo slashing red paint across canvas—a sight so familiar from her childhood that she smiled.

Until she saw the nightmare he was painting—and a half-eaten apple on the tea tray. The charming, easygoing Ivo she knew didn't paint nightmares—and apples did not transport themselves upstairs.

CHAPTER THREE

Ivo became aware that his angel hovered in the corner of the room. He'd lived with the ghosts of his lost comrades for so long that an angel or two didn't disturb him. He hoped it didn't mean that Sarah was actually dead, and her ghost peered over his shoulder. That really would be too much for his shattered soul to bear. So he continued pouring gore onto his canvas in silence.

"The doctor says you must rest," she said.

Ah, that was his Sarah. He perked up, despite the pounding headache. She'd start nagging soon enough, but he knew how to get around her. He grabbed a smaller brush, dabbing a new element in a corner of the canvas. His head hurt less when his hand moved.

When he did not reply, she eased closer. He'd always let her see his work. She never offered criticism, only excitement when she recognized his subject.

She wouldn't recognize his nightmare. Ivo winced and finished up the quick sketch in the corner—giving her something fun to see.

"The four horses of the Apocalypse?" she guessed. "I never liked Revelations."

Well, of course, she'd see the main theme first. Stupid of him to think his nightmare was invisible. "Neither do I," he surprised himself by saying. He narrowed his eyes and examined the half-painted canvas critically. She was right.

Fire-breathing horses belonged in Revelations, not in his damned head. "I'll have to read it again, but I rather think this is a more contemporary representation."

"Oh."

He heard her understanding in that single syllable. Guilt for tainting her with the horror of war plunged like a dagger to his gut. Dropping his brushes into the turpentine, he fell back against his pillows, exhausted.

"War haunts you, as it should," she interpreted. She poured tea from the cooling pot and handed it to him. "Close your eyes and rest them for a while. Your paintings are too marvelous to be lost for all time if you blind yourself."

He sipped the tepid tea. "When I was twelve and had the measles, you said much the same thing, although I believe the tirade at the time included phrases like 'you horrid boy,' and 'it's all your fault there will be no picnic.'"

To his ear, her soft laughter was sweeter than the symphonies he'd heard during the Congress of Vienna. Ivo relaxed and finished his tea.

"I apologize," she said, unapologetically. "It was probably not *entirely* your fault that half the village took measles after you came home from school that year."

"Thank you." He opened his eyes again to catch her bending over the canvas. An apple rested in the hand behind her back. "Does the larder contain only apples?"

She jerked upright guiltily and offered the fruit to him, like Eve handing over temptation. "There has been no one to cook for. Mary is starting some soup. Did she bring you the other apple?" She indicated the half-eaten one on his tray.

He frowned. "It arrived while I was dozing, I believe. No idea how it came to be there, but I was hungry enough to eat until the physician arrived."

A small crease crossed the bridge above her nose, but she spoke politely, as if they must be formal. "I can send for meat pies at the market if you're hungry, but Mary reminds me that it is nearly the end of the month, and I have spent the last of my coins. How good is your credit?"

He rubbed his newly bandaged nose in thought. "If I still have my valise, I should have coins. Does old Mr. Blenheim not sell pies anymore? He knows I'm good for them."

"The influenza was very bad last winter. The town lost many of our older citizens, including Mr. Blenheim. There have been quite a few changes since you left," she added sadly.

In less than a minute, she had gone from laughter to mourning. What an amazement she was! After years of listening to men gripe and grunt, get drunk and kill, Ivo noticed that her softer emotions pacified rather than rousing his sleeping tiger.

If only she could lessen the shrieks in his dreams . . .

He rummaged in his valise and produced the shabby vest where he'd hidden his loose cash. "I still don't understand where all the servants have gone. The house used to have a raft of them." He looked up in alarm. "Surely, they did not all die?"

Her fleeting smile of approval at his hiding place disappeared behind a wary expression. "No, of course not. We've sent for the Merriweathers. How did you save your valise from marauding highwaymen?"

Easily distracted, he tried to remember the details. "I vaguely recall playing gladiator, ordering the post-chaise driver to race at a ruffian holding an ancient blunderbuss so I could disarm him with my sword." He snorted at another memory. "I'm fairly certain I fought two-handed, using the valise as a bludgeon to catch the second rogue coming up on our other side. I suspect the horse bolted and my bad knee gave out. That's probably how I cracked my head. It would have been simpler to give them the coins."

"You are accustomed to fighting," she said. "I cannot begin to imagine what you've seen and done these last years."

"Nothing to write home about," he grumbled in discomfort.

"So you didn't," she retorted, then softened her sharpness to add, "Rest your head. I'll run down and see what we can do about meat pies."

After she departed, Ivo glared at his apocalyptic horse. She hadn't even noticed the French mouse he'd added to the corner. Maybe he should add a few more.

He rubbed his jaw and realized he hadn't shaved in days. Perhaps he ought to at least *pretend* he was human—for Sarah's sake—before he figured out what the devil was happening under his own roof.

Carrying a basket of meat pies, Sarah stopped in the foyer to remove her pelisse and bonnet. She halted when she realized she was being watched. Glancing up the stairs, she saw Ivo wrapped in his greatcoat and muffler sitting on the landing. His clean bandage was stark white against his bronzed face and dark curls, and he'd shaved.

She remembered a day when she'd seen him standing on that same landing wearing an elegant navy frock coat, starched white linen, and knit pantaloons, his curls tumbling over his forehead, looking for all the world like a sophisticated London gentleman and not the dirty urchin of her childhood.

She'd lost her heart that day, but he'd not noticed.

She was no longer so naïve as to fall for a pretty gentleman.

"You are supposed to be in bed!" she protested. "What are you doing in a coat?"

"Freezing," he said. "Waiting for meat pies. I'm starved. You have yet to tell me where the Merriweathers are. And the maids. I need more coal for the fire."

The doctor had said he was not to be upset. How could she tell him that his father had given away the only home

Ivo loved, and that the servants who were like family to him were all gone? She couldn't hurt him that way, but lying was so awkward. . . .

"Everyone's on holiday." She removed a pie from the basket. "Now go back to bed or I'll eat this myself."

"You should have bought one for yourself! Find plates and I'll share." Ivo stood and started down the stairs, but grabbed the bannister as if still dizzy.

Worried that he'd kill himself, she hurried up with the still steaming pie. "I've eaten. You haven't. Back to bed, right now. I'll have Mary bring up some coal. We've called for the Merriweathers, but the weather is worsening. I can't promise they'll be here soon."

She couldn't promise they'd be back at all. She only knew that they'd retired to live with one of their daughters in the country.

"I'd not thought about taking them from their family on a holiday," he said in regret, heading back up the stairs. "I've upset everyone by coming home."

Oh, Lord in Heaven, help her. She hated letting him think he was *unwanted*. What a horrible way to spend his first holiday back from war—injured and alone!

"You are the best Christmas gift we could all hope for," she assured him, almost truthfully. "It's just everyone is at sixes and sevens with the Holbourne Abbey ball next week. If your head is better, you could attend, and we'll all have reason to celebrate."

He slumped onto the sofa bed and frowned. "Lady Holly is not still trying to match make, is she? She's incredibly bad at it."

"She matched you with Lily Comfrey, did she not? You didn't seem to object when you announced your betrothal." Sarah remembered in considerable detail her own shock and pain at the news.

"Her father had a prime art collection," he said through a bite of pie. "We got on famously. But Lily wasn't much on waiting. I heard she married Geoffrey Thomas several years back."

He didn't seem heartbroken.

"You got betrothed because you liked her father's art collection?" she asked, not bothering to hide her exasperation. "Then it's a good thing she ran off with Mr. Thomas. You deserved that."

He laughed at her through wicked whisky-brown eyes. Even the bruises and bandaged nose didn't detract from his charm. "You expected me to fall cap-over-heels for a pretty face just as in your silly novels? I didn't think practical Sarah so romantic. No wonder the countess failed to match you up."

"I don't need a man to complete my life. I'll have Mary bring up some coal." She flounced out to the sound of his laughter.

She supposed it was better that he was laughing and not painting fire-breathing horses. The nightmare painting worried her more than she cared to admit.

CHAPTER FOUR

Friday, December 23

𝒰nhorsed by cannon fire, Ivo loaded powder into his musket as the French cavalry galloped toward Kim and his men. He aimed at the nearest soldier, but the overheated weapon jammed. Neither bayonet nor sword could halt the approach of the black fire-breathing monster emerging from the smoke. . . .

He screamed a warning as the horse flew over him.

"It's all right, you're home now," a soft voice whispered over the screams of the dying. "It's just a dream. Sleep, it will be all right."

The shock of soothing murmurs in his ear instead of curses yanked Ivo awake. Still tense, groping for his weapons, he hesitated long enough to smell apples. No smoke suffocated him. No horse crushed him into the blood and mud.

Gentle hands stroked his hair.

He rested against ripe curves wearing little more than thin linen.

Clinging to this lifeline of tranquility, he pulled her into his arms so he might feel a lighter weight than a horse against him. She resisted, but he murmured what he hoped were reassurances.

With human warmth snuggled against his side, he slept more soundly than he had in months, maybe years.

She was gone when he woke.

Ivo lay still, wondering if his nightmare had taken an odd turn or if his dream angel had been real. He could still smell apple blossoms on his pillow. A soft blanket and crisp sheet covered him. He recalled Sarah bringing them the night before, when he'd refused to leave the salon and his easel.

Had she come to him in his dreams?

At least he wore trousers and shirt for decency. He disliked the vulnerability of nakedness when he didn't know if he'd be routed from his bed. He hadn't allowed an unguarded moment in years. His nightmares had awakened entire hostelries.

But no one had ever caressed him back to sleep—not since childhood.

Sarah Jane had soothed him even then—during that bout with the measles. She'd been the only who'd had measles before, and she'd insisted on being his nurse. She'd only been what, six or seven?

An odd warmth spread through his chest at that memory, as if he'd opened a window and sunshine poured in. Feeling better, he sat up.

Remembering the cold, unwelcoming country seat awaiting his return, he almost lay back down again. He needed to find his solicitor and tell him what he'd failed to tell his father—he didn't want to be a farmer. In fact, he *hated* the isolated farm. He needed this house with its warm memories of his mother and friends.

Embers of coal still burned in the grate. He managed to rise without staggering, throw on more fuel, and stir the flames. He found his water pitcher full and swung the hot water kettle to heat.

"We gots to tell 'im," the mouse insisted.

"But then he'll leave," the bossy one argued. "And the lady will leave, too, and there'll be no more pies."

"But I 'eard the lady talk! This is s'posed to be *our* house, just like ma'am said. He don' belong here!"

Ouch. Even the mice didn't want him?

Mice didn't talk. His head was less foggy this morning. He was quite certain that when he'd left England, mice didn't talk.

He was also fairly certain he didn't want to know what they were talking about. So he made his tea and examined the nightmarish canvas. Ridiculous symbolism, he concluded. It needed contrast. Adding French mice was absurd, but he didn't feel inclined to paint this one out. Perhaps he'd use it as his signature.

He waited for some sound that the household was stirring. Had Sarah actually spent the night here? Surely her parents . . . ah, he remembered now. She'd lost her parents over a year ago, to that influenza epidemic. He should have been here to comfort her then, instead of waltzing in Vienna, but he'd thought she had a husband to help her. The damned dowager had told him Sarah was betrothed—and had conveniently forgotten to tell him she'd failed at another match.

The scent of bacon wafted up, and the light patter of feminine feet on the stairs distracted him.

He knew it was Sarah even before she opened the door, and his spirits lifted. His head was ready for verbal jousting this morning, and his childhood companion could be counted on to give as good as she got.

There had been a time in his youth when she'd punctured his pretensions all too frequently, and in his adolescent arrogance, he'd been irritated. Experience had taught him how rare it was to find a woman who knew his mind as well as she did.

Her smile was tentative. "How is your head this morning?"

"I no longer feel as if I need to remove it to air it out," he said carelessly, although the pain still lurked.

He studied her, noticing that her cheeks were extra rosy this morning, less like a porcelain angel and more like an enticing woman.

"I doubt that's a condition of the injury," she taunted, turning her face away from his scrutiny to set a tray on the table. "I recommend regular church attendance to air out dirty minds."

Ivo chortled. "Surely it's not Sunday? I didn't hear church bells."

"This is Friday, and Sunday is Christmas, but you are in no state to attend. I'm waiting for Dr. Jones to stop by to tell us if he's reached the Merriweathers. He seems to think you're not to be trusted alone."

That wiped the grin from his face. Ivo tried to approach her, but she hurried to stir the coals. He had a craving to hold her again . . . as he had last night? Was that why she was avoiding his gaze?

"Did you really come to me last night?" he inquired. "I remember waking . . . and then sleeping more soundly than I have in years."

"You used to have bad dreams when you were little, I recall. Your mother said yours was a sensitive nature." Avoiding the subject, she smiled and flitted around him, toward the door.

"Sensitive, by Jove! I have the hide of a rhino. Sit down and talk with me, Sarah. What is it you aren't telling me?" He blocked the door with his greater size, proving how insensitive he could be.

She met his glare with defiance. "Would you care to tell me everything you've learned these past five years since I saw you last?" At his silence, she nodded knowingly. "Of course not. And neither do I."

"You're not meant to be a termagant," Ivo countered, stepping aside. "And I do not mean to torment you. Please, when you can, come talk with me. It is lonely up here listening to the mice."

She looked startled and cast a glance at the wall. "As soon as we have a little more help, I mean to investigate those mice."

So, she'd heard them, too. "I'll feed them toast and bacon until then," he said more cheerfully as she swept past him and out the door.

The mice were right. His Sarah Jane was keeping something from him.

"He seems a bit better, doesn't he, Dr. Jones?" Sarah asked as the physician descended the stairs later that day.

She was trying very hard not to remember how she'd let Ivo hold her in his arms last night. That had been embarrassingly improper—but it had seemed so *necessary* at the time. He'd relaxed—and smelled and felt so good. . . . She rubbed her cold hand over her hot cheek.

He'd slept. That was what was important.

"Yes, our patient's pupils have returned to normal, and he claims to feel less pain, although the lad has been known to be less than truthful," the doctor said with a chuckle. "But he's anxious to be out and about, so that's a good sign. I've changed the bandage, and the swelling is down. Let's give him another day or two of rest, though."

Sarah tried not to show her relief too obviously. "And have you heard from the Merriweathers?"

He frowned. "They are eager to see Ivo . . . Lord Harris, but apparently a couple of children from their parish have disappeared, and they're aiding in the search. The mist is turning to sleet. It's not a good time for them or children to be out and about."

"Oh, dear." Sarah glanced out on the wintry gray day. "I feared the weather was turning. Perhaps the Merriweathers should come here, and I could aid the search in their place."

"The Merriweathers will know where to look and you

won't," the physician assured her as he buttoned up his coat. "I'll be glad to see this house opened up for orphans. It's difficult these days for the parishes to know what to do with the homeless."

"I hope they remember that when I request more money," Sarah said tartly. "We've not raised enough funds for more than a few beds."

He nodded. "I'll speak with those I know. And surely Lord Harris will contribute once he's on his feet again."

Not once Ivo realized this was no longer his home. It had been cruel of his father to deprive his son of the home he loved.

It had been cruel of the son to deprive his father of his presence. She guessed that made them even but not any happier.

"And I heard the story of how he came by that blow to his head," the doctor said with a chuckle. "His driver claims the baron is a hero, fighting off bandits with valise and sword. The fellow recounts a terrifying experience, but he kept the horse moving when Ivo ordered it. Although it sounds as if the bandits were a trifle green if they couldn't shoot a moving target."

Sarah shuddered at the image. "That sounds more fool-ish than brave."

"Indeed, standing in a post chaise when it's racing down a rutted road probably wasn't the brightest reaction," the doctor agreed, still smiling. "But the baron is a soldier ac-customed to fighting. What he isn't accustomed to is stop-ping. Ivo tumbled head over heels over the side. Terrified the boy even more."

"And so the driver delivered him to his destination and left him injured on his doorstep?" Sarah asked doubtfully.

"He stopped at an inn. Wasn't much anyone could do ex-cept bandage his head, and the baron insisted on travel-ing on."

Which he would have, Sarah acknowledged. Ivo had always considered himself invincible—an exceedingly annoying trait in civilization but probably useful in warfare.

Mary hurried in from the cold shortly after Dr. Jones departed. She carried a basket and a triumphant smile. "I've brought your gown! There is still time to sew on the lace."

Sarah sighed at sight of the old gown that had been a hand-me-down from Ivo's mother when she'd first worn it five years ago. Back then, it had been the most elegant extravagance she'd ever owned. She'd spent hours adapting the seams to the current fashion. Ivo hadn't even noticed it—or her. That had been the ball where he'd announced his betrothal.

"A few more lace ruffles won't transform it into fashion," Sarah said, taking the basket. "But I suppose I could hope that most people won't remember it."

Mary pursed her lips. The baroness's taste had been that of a married woman in extravagant London. Mary had never approved of the lavishly embellished sleeves or the daring garnet bodice, but Sarah loved the tawny-gold velvet skirt. She could wish the bodice were a more appropriate color, but in her heart of hearts, she adored the holiday hues.

She had only agreed to attend the ball if she didn't have to purchase a new gown, so Mary did not dare comment on the impropriety. And Sarah rather thought her advanced age and new independence deserved a bit of boldness.

"The salon has the best light for fine work," Sarah said. "I'll take the sewing up there and keep his lordship company for a little while. Did you also bring over more supplies from our kitchen? I'm uncertain how much longer we must keep up our pretense of this being a proper home."

"I've brought over more potatoes and can cook up some mutton, but we cannot fool him much longer. A man like that expects rich sauces and a selection of meats and fish."

"He's been at war. He should know how to live simply.

And he understands that there is no one to cook for him. It's the *why* that is difficult to work around. I was hoping the doctor would say he was better."

"If you stay much longer, your reputation will be compromised, and he will have to marry you," Mary insisted. "You'd better think about that. He doesn't need a nurse."

"I rather fear he does," Sarah said with a frown, remembering the prior night when his shouts had awakened her. "But it will be good when Mrs. Merriweather takes over."

She couldn't admit—even to herself—that her heart raced with anticipation as she hurried up the stairs. She knew she must refrain from hope, just as she knew she shouldn't attend the ball. But she had not yet learned to entirely stop dreaming.

After all, the orphanage was a dream come true. Almost.

CHAPTER FIVE

Cleaning the black paint from his brush, planning the day he'd like to share with Sarah, Ivo realized with a jolt that he'd not planned anything other than war in years. Even traipsing across Europe after he'd recuperated, he'd more or less gone where events carried him, with no thought beyond the next meal or museum.

He'd been surviving, day by day. After last night, he realized that survival was no longer enough. He missed the camaraderie of friends and family and the larks they used to share. He was even looking forward to Lady Holly's ball, if his trunks arrived in time. Living inside his head was a lonely—and probably unhealthy—business.

His years as a soldier should have proved that his artistic leanings didn't make him less than a man—even if his father was no longer here to express approval. He was his own man now, and it was time to plan the future *he* wanted. He could fill his mother's house with laughter again and think about hiring a steward to run the bleak estate. His head hurt less at that decision.

Sarah arrived with a sewing basket and a tea tray, and Ivo's mood rose another notch. He'd not expected to feel hope again. One of the many reasons he'd postponed his return had been his desperation to remember what optimism felt like.

"I'm happy to see that the physician does not require me

to live on broth and gruel," he said, helping himself to bread and cheese. "Have you heard from the Merriweathers? No matter how much I'm enjoying your company, I cannot think it's proper for you to be here."

Cuddling Sarah to cure his nightmares had most certainly not been proper, but it had been the best night of his life. Admiring her flushed cheeks, Ivo finally admitted to himself that believing his childhood friend had married had been the partial reason for his despair and long absence. He'd thought he had no reason to return. He'd been wrong—in so very many ways.

He would try to make that up to her.

"I don't mind the company while I sew this gown. The Merriweathers are busy, but hope to arrive shortly." She frowned as she spoke and glanced at the walls.

"The mice have been quiet," he said, entranced by her fleeting expressions. "Perhaps they are napping."

"This is a rather large house for mouse hunting," she agreed obliquely. "There is a servants' staircase back there, is there not?"

"An all-purpose staircase," Ivo corrected. "My mother used it often when she wished to complain of the noise I made in the schoolroom."

"You have a habit of running people ragged," she said, settling down with her sewing. "Try staying in one place for a change."

He might at that, now that there was some reason for doing so.

Spreading the velvet evening gown over her lap, Sarah checked the hem for fraying stitches.

"I remember that gown," Ivo exclaimed, glancing up from his painting.

His familiar masculine presence was reassuring, but his looks heated her more thoroughly than the coal fire. She smoothed the fabric, admiring the sheen and avoiding his eyes. "Of course. It was one of your mother's. We were much of a height, and she was always generous with her wardrobe."

"No, no, that's not what I mean. I remember the ball—and *you,* when you wore it," he said. "That was my last Christmas here. I had never seen you so grown-up, and I was thunderstruck. Had I not already agreed to my betrothal, I would have been at your feet that night. You were stunning. I was a bit of a shallow bastard, was I not?"

Sarah didn't know to which of these amazing comments she should respond. He'd thought her *stunning*? *Her*? And he had not said a word? Of course not, he'd been betrothed. She thought *her* head might start aching. "It must have been difficult thinking of home while you were away," she said, avoiding the more personal comments that had her battered, wary heart racing.

"When war is all there is, it's very comfortable not thinking." He didn't look ashamed as he picked up another oil.

She supposed he'd suffered losses as great as the village's. Sarah refrained from flinging her scissors at him, but she couldn't resist a taunt. "Much easier to let others do your thinking for you."

"Possibly." He frowned, glancing in her direction again, and then stroking paint across the canvas. "But in the long run, not very practical. I should like to know what it is that has you glaring at me when you think I don't notice, but it's obviously something you think will disturb my muddled mind. Is that the gown you're wearing to the Last Chance ball?"

"Last Chance ball?" She chuckled at the sobriquet. "That's a shocking name for a lovely holiday lark. The countess enjoys the company."

"That's what the bachelors call it—Lady Holly's ball to give spinsters a last chance to nab them. I thought I'd outwitted her by betrothing myself *before* that last ball." He spread a broad stroke of red across the canvas.

Sarah shuddered to think what the red represented in his nightmare vision.

"You betrothed yourself to the woman she'd picked out for you the *prior* year," Sarah countered. "You always were an idiot, Ivo."

He grinned unrepentantly. "I was all of twenty and still wet behind the ears. If my trunks arrive in time, would you let me escort you this year?"

Stunned, afraid she'd stammer if she spoke, Sarah tried to swat down all her whirling hopes with pragmatism.

He'd hear about the orphanage if they went to the ball. He would never speak to her again. She had to tell him.

A noise from behind the wall distracted them. A whispered exclamation and a not-quiet admonishment followed.

Ivo set down his brush, held his finger to his lips, and gestured Sarah toward the door.

"Is Mary in the kitchen?" he whispered.

She nodded, understanding his intentions. There were four exits in the passage behind the salon: one led to the attic floor, one opened on the corridor outside the salon, another led down to the kitchen. The fourth was a disguised door to the salon so the servants might slip in and out with trays and coals. Ivo meant to block the "mice" from fleeing upstairs by stepping through the disguised door.

She would catch them if they fled through the corridor exit, and Mary would catch them if they ran down to the kitchen.

Standing guard over the corridor exit, Sarah heard squeals as Ivo entered the passage through the disguised door. She waited in anticipation, but no one emerged on this floor except Ivo.

"I'm chasing them down to the kitchen," he asserted, before disappearing into the closed stairwell again.

The dratted man was supposed to be resting!

Lifting her skirt, she took to the main staircase and raced through the house and down the backstairs.

The culprits had already emerged into Mary's startled presence and were heading straight for Sarah when she arrived. Ivo's large form blocked the hidden staircase. Mary stationed herself with a broom at the outside exit. With Sarah blocking their last escape, the two dirty and bedraggled children ducked beneath the long wooden block of a table.

"Your mice, my lady," Ivo said formally, with a bow, as if he'd conquered an army.

She flashed him a grin in memory of their childhood war games when he'd played knight to her rescued princess. Then she turned to the frightened children.

"We won't hurt you, we promise." She sat on the bottom step so as not to scare them. "Although, we might give you a bath before we feed you. I daresay your mother would be horrified to see you in such a state. Do you have names?"

"Evangeline, miss," the older of the two whispered, pushing her grubby blond hair out of her eyes. "And this is Caleb. He's only five and doesn't know much."

Ivo snorted, leaned against the door, and crossed his arms. "Boys just play at being dumb so others will do their work for them."

Caleb beamed. "I'se very good at finding apples."

Sarah felt tears well. She feared that the two lost, brave children who were taking care of each other might rip her soft heart in two. "Well, then, come out from under there and let us see about finding more apples. Although, I think they're in a pie now, aren't they, Mary?"

The maid didn't leave her position against the back door. "Aye, that they are, fresh baked."

"We're orphans," Evangeline said tentatively. "Ma'am said we could live here. But there weren't no one in the place when we came."

"Until *he* came," Caleb said, crawling out from under the

table and nodding at Ivo. "And he didn't eat nuffing. We was hungry."

Ivo looked puzzled. Before he could start questioning again why the house had been left empty, Sarah turned to the pantry, hoping to distract him. "The baroness always loved feeding orphaned larks at Christmas!"

CHAPTER SIX

rowning, Ivo settled on the kitchen bench and watched Sarah and Mary prepare a proper luncheon for two grubby urchins. He remembered his mother giddily helping with pies to take to the church poor. He didn't remember actual orphans in the house.

He still didn't understand why the house had no servants. His father's executor should have been handling estate affairs until he returned. Ivo had left the satchel of official correspondence in his trunk, thinking he'd be home before he had time to read it—

—Or avoiding any more bad news after realizing that it was too late to earn his father's approval. His heart hurt as much as his head, knowing he'd left his father to die alone.

"Where's your mother now?" he asked the children, helping himself to a large bite of the pie Sarah set in front of him.

"She's sick," Caleb said. "She said we's be orphans soon, and she wants us to have a new mommy." He puckered up a little, but the little girl squeezed his hand.

"Just for a little while," the girl explained. Ivo didn't think she could be more than a few years older than the boy, but she had the practical approach of someone who has been looking after herself for a while. "Just until our real mama gets better," she said reassuringly.

She was lying. Ivo recognized the way she shifted her

eyes from him to the boy and back again, as if ordering him to shut up. Damn, but she was a heartbreaker with those big brown eyes and that tiny, trembling chin.

Sarah looked as if she might weep. Ivo didn't want Sarah to weep. He should have been here to give Sarah a shoulder to cry on when her parents died, to tell her she wasn't to worry, just as this tiny little girl was telling her brother.

Only—he hadn't thought of Sarah as a sister since that last ball, and especially not after last night. Damn his ignoble self.

"Can you give us your mommy's name so we can see how she's doing?" Ivo asked when it became obvious the women were too tongue-tied to do so—or hiding too many secrets. Such as, why had the orphans thought they could come to *his* house? That hadn't seemed to surprise Sarah at all.

"Betty," the little girl piped up. "Our daddy was Silas Greene, but he went to war and didn't come home." This time, her lip trembled, and she hastily drank the milk that Mary set in front of her.

"Betty Greene," Mary murmured. "She used to work here in the kitchen."

"The Merriweathers were looking for two children," Sarah whispered back, although if Ivo could hear her, the children could, too. "Go tell Dr. Jones. I'll be fine here."

Mary glared at Ivo. He tried to look innocent, as if he hadn't slept in Sarah's arms last night—and wanted to again, preferably without orphans lurking.

While Mary ran off to find Dr. Jones, and Sarah heated water for the children's baths, Ivo limped upstairs, thinking he would start asking questions as soon as Sarah had a free minute. He arrived in the foyer in time to answer a knock at the door.

He fumbled in his coat for a coin to reward the fellow unloading his trunk, and then stood over his luggage in trepidation. He still didn't want to read his correspondence.

* * *

By the time Sarah returned upstairs, Ivo was shaking with rage and despair. He crumpled a letter and flung the paper at the door. "Why?" he cried. "Why? He *knew* I loved this place. There's nothing of my mother in that ugly stone hovel of his!"

Sarah's heart plummeted to her feet. Here it was, the moment she had dreaded, when all her stupid silly hopes were smashed again. "I think he simply wanted you to take up the reins of the estate that meant so much to him," she said quietly.

"You could have *told* me!" he shouted. He swung around to indicate the foyer she loved so much. "I remember my mother dancing in joy when the new French wallpaper was hung." He gestured at the front parlor. "She used to play the pianoforte and sing in there. And what will it be now? A schoolroom for grubby urchins? Is that what you've planned—stealing my home from me?"

Even hearing his hurt, *knowing* his pain, she was hit broadside by his accusations. Refusing to pander to this man who had so much to offer and who offered so little, she shut herself off as she had learned to do these last painful years.

"It was either an orphanage or let the house fall to rack and ruin while you gallivanted about Europe," she said icily. "We had no one to tell us how you would like your father's will carried out. Don't blame me for your own neglect! Just give me a moment to collect my things, and I will be gone. The Merriweathers should be here shortly. Explain to *them* that you don't want an orphanage here. And Merry Christmas to you, too."

She didn't even shed a tear as she gathered up her beautiful gown and ugly cloak and walked away from the only man she'd ever loved. She would fight for the children's home in the coming days, but not . . . *now,* while her heart was splintering.

Shattered, Ivo roamed from room to empty room, remembering the year his mother had thrown a holiday party, and he and Sarah had sampled the punch, not knowing it had been laced with rum. They'd literally giggled themselves sick.

And the schoolroom! Her father used to grind Ivo's brain with Latin declensions that had no relevance to his need to paint Sarah as she bent over her grammar. He was supposed to give up the *schoolroom*? And his sunny salon . . . the only place in all Bellsburn with sufficient light for him to paint in winter without freezing.

He stopped at the forlorn bedchamber that had once been his. All the personal belongings had been stripped. He supposed Armstrong had shipped them out to the manor. There had once been a braided rug on the floor that Sarah had kneeled on when he'd been an invalid, and she'd soaked cold compresses for his fever.

Sarah! He'd only just rediscovered what she meant to him and now . . .

He faced a bleak and lonely future in a grandiose house he despised, running an estate he had no interest in, looking for old friends who'd married and moved on—as he hadn't.

He should never have come back. Like a wounded dog, he should have kept running.

He returned to the salon and the nightmare painting he'd been working on. The image he'd started of Sarah in her red gown, staving off the wrath of war. . . .

He picked up his bloody red brush again. When the Merriweathers came to find him, he didn't even look up.

Saturday, December 24, Christmas Eve

Sarah slipped down the kitchen stairs of Whitney House carrying packages. Inside with the merrily flickering fire, she hugged Bess and James Merriweather and exclaimed happily over the children slurping porridge at the table. They eyed her packages with interest.

Out for a lark, they were," Bess said. "Their ma is still that ill, but these two aren't orphans yet. Betty must have sent them here when she was fevered."

The Merriweathers had already set to work making lists, heating rooms, and seeing to the "master's" chambers, even though they knew Lord Harris's stay would be temporary. No one should be thrown from their home at Christmas, they'd all agreed.

"I wish I had more to offer," Sarah said, handing over her basket of packages containing warm stockings and caps for the children, who tore into them with delight. They popped the gifts on their heads and hands and held them up for admiration.

She kissed their cheeks, and then glanced upstairs as if Ivo would magically appear. "He's all right?" she asked anxiously.

"He won't come out of the salon," Bess said, shaking her head. "He paints all night and day. It ain't healthy."

She would not care. She *would* not. She would simply wait for Mr. Armstrong to return and settle matters. "There are other orphans who need a home," Sarah warned the Merriweathers. "We can't abandon them."

They nodded in understanding. "It takes the boy time to think things out," Mr. Merry reminded her. "He'll come around."

But Ivo would hate her forever, Sarah knew, just as he hated his father's house.

Sunday, December 25, Christmas Day

Listening to the church bells ringing, Ivo packaged up the dry canvas—and all his hopes and fears—in brown paper. He shrugged on his greatcoat, found his hat under the desk, and with more fortitude than he'd marched off to war with, he set out in the wintry air.

His head no longer hurt, but the rest of him felt as if he'd tumbled off the Cliffs of Dover. He thought he was thinking clearly again, but he wouldn't know for certain until he challenged his demons. He had spent years of war not speaking his feelings. Somehow, that had to change.

He pounded on the door of Sarah's cottage. She'd had to move from the cozy vicarage after her father's death, he'd been told, and was staying in the church guesthouse until she could find better accommodations. He wanted to be bitter that she would be moving to *his* house, but that was part of his head clearing. If anyone should have his house, it should be Sarah.

When she answered the door wearing her ball gown, Ivo's jaw dropped to his chest. Unfinished lace trailed off a bodice that revealed far more bosom than he'd ever seen her expose. He almost swallowed his tongue—as he had the last time he'd seen her in that gown, looking like sin and heaven in the same magnificent package.

"My gift fades in the shade of your beauty," he said in awe. "I couldn't wish for a better Christmas gift than to see you wrapped in glory. Merry Christmas, my Sarah."

She looked shocked. Perhaps he'd been a trifle bold, but he'd never minced words with Sarah. Ivo didn't give her time to slam the door in his face. He shouldered his way in, found the sunniest window, set down his present, and ripped at the paper. "This is for you. I'm rotten at saying what I think or feel, so I'm hoping you'll help me." As she often had, he'd realized these past days. Sarah had been his spokesman to the world, interpreting his emotions when he couldn't find the words.

The room smelled of greenery and bayberry candles, just as his mother's home once had. Ivo politely admired the mantel decorations as Sarah tucked lace into her bodice. She grabbed a shawl to cover herself, but she still said nothing.

When he sensed she was ready, he finished ripping off the paper. Behind him, she gasped at the canvas he uncovered.

Ivo stood diffidently, holding his latest work for her approval. The completed painting revealed a confident goddess in scarlet and gold, holding her hand up as if to halt his prancing, fire-breathing nightmare stallions. Ivo gritted his molars and waited as she studied it. Her eyes widened as she held up her lacy sleeve to compare it to the one on the canvas. He'd done a pretty damned good job of remembering every elegant curve of that gown on her form.

"You think I can stop nightmares? That's a pretty conceit," she finally said.

He'd hoped for more than her usual pragmatism, but she was repaying him for leaving her dangling too long. He deserved her coldness.

"Not a conceit," he assured her. "It's how any right-thinking man would see you."

He waited as she crouched down to examine his signature. In the dark corner beneath a horse's rear hoof was a single mouse wearing a French uniform and a silly grin. She traced this symbol with a finger, and Ivo held his breath as her lips finally tilted upward.

But when she stood, she was rubbing tears from her eyes with the back of her hand. "I like the red," she said, giving him no other hint of her feelings.

She was killing him as surely as his nightmares. But he had not come this far only to give up because of his damnable inability to express himself.

"I love the red. It looks splendid on you." He swallowed, lifted his gaze from the red fabric barely covering her bosom, and tried to say what the painting apparently hadn't. "I have raged and cursed the fates and my father, but I cannot curse you, my Sarah. Even I must admit that it is not the house that I will miss, but the memory of *you* in it."

He'd had his head stove in several times over the past year. Maybe his brains had been scrambled. Or his priorities rearranged, but Ivo couldn't think of Sarah as a sister anymore. She was no longer a child. And he was a man with needs that included the need to be loved as he was—not as a soldier or a baron or even a farmer. He was none of those things. Sarah knew that. But could she accept it? This was the demon he feared. Sarah belonged here in town, nurturing orphans, not sheep. He only knew war . . . and art. Could she accept him as the worthless creature that he was?

Tears coursed down her cheeks, and he longed to swipe them away, but didn't dare touch her without her permission.

"I would give the house back to you if I could," she whispered.

"No, you wouldn't," he said with some return of his notorious humor. "You would tell me I have a perfectly good house in the country and can buy or build another in town should I feel so inclined. Your larks need you and a roof over their heads more than I do. I can hear your sermon without your needing to say a word."

She glanced up with such hope in her eyes that his head disconnected from his heart, and he floundered.

"You hate your country seat," she murmured. "If there were any way to trade, I would."

With just that simple statement, she carved to the heart of the matter. And finally—finally—Ivo understood it didn't matter where he lived. It was who he lived *with* that counted most.

He gathered her in his arms, kissing her as he should have done the moment he'd crossed her portal. "I love you, dear heart," he murmured when he came up for breath. "I will live in your orphanage with you, if you'd let me. Or build you a palace." Refusing to let her reply, he kissed her again, because he knew her heart, had always known her kind, giving, loving heart—and that it had always included him.

Lost in the wonder of Ivo's kisses, Sarah clung to his strong shoulders, letting him feed every dream she'd ever had—because Ivo wouldn't lie to her. She might lie to herself, but Ivo wouldn't lie to her, and she could not hide what had been in her heart for so long.

"Marry me, Sarah Jane. If you do not say yes before the ball, I will tell Lady Holly on you. I shall be ruthless in my pursuit. I will scare away all your other suitors and paint your beauty on every wall in Bellsburn."

She laughed and leaned against his solid chest. "It is too much, too fast," she insisted. "I have just spent these last days trying to eradicate you from my thoughts. You cannot mean what you say."

"Have I ever said what I didn't mean? I take that back," he said quickly. "I lie about little things, I confess. So if you insist, I'll let you wait to answer until the ball. But I am not lying about how I feel about you. That's why you're on that canvas. You're my hero."

She laughed at the thought of being anyone's hero and tried to push away, but she had dreamed of this for so long. . . . "I know you lie about little things. And you wouldn't lie now. But you need to be certain. I've been certain for many years, but for you . . . it's new."

She cast away all her pride to admit that. She'd loved him as a boy. She loved the maddening, charming, conscientious man even more—the kind of man who made the sun rise on a dreary day and made the larks sing at midnight. Ivo brought that kind of light to the world.

"No, my love isn't new," he argued. "It just took a blow to the head to wake me up to what love is. And a blow to my pride, I suppose. I wanted to tempt you with a beautiful house, to offer you something you couldn't have otherwise. Now, you already have what I thought you might want, and I only have a cold and drafty farmhouse to offer."

She sank into his arms again. "Houses don't matter. It's *us*—we belong together. I've always felt that way. We can live in your mother's home where I can teach the orphans their letters, and you can teach them to paint. We can take them to the farm and teach them to love sheep. You can hire the world's best steward and spend all your time painting. Anything is possible—as long as we have each other."

"How did you become so very wise, Miss Langsdale?" he whispered into her hair, tightening his embrace. "I'll fund your orphans with all the money the world's best steward earns for me, and then I shall buy you a scarlet cloak to wear always, so everyone will see my pride in you."

She lifted her head to see the love burning in Ivo's understanding eyes, and she let him ease the heavy burden she'd been carrying. "A cloak to match my gown for the ball," she murmured. "Let them realize that if as unlikely a pair as a nesting dove and a soaring falcon can be happy, there is hope for all."

In the Bleak Midwinter

❧

Mary Jo Putney

CHAPTER ONE

December 26, two days before the ball

$\mathcal{C}$aptain the Honorable Kimball Stretton gazed out the window of the stone tower, his heart as gray and cold as the Northumberland hills. He'd grown up here at Holbourne Abbey, and once he'd loved the drama of the changing seasons, from vibrant spring through lush summer, dazzling autumn, to the subtle shades and warm fires of winter.

The locals called this remnant of an ancient Norman castle the Lucky Tower, and their vehement protests had prevented one of his ancestors from tearing the structure down when the new house was built. The tower had been repaired so it wasn't a public menace, and now a drafty passage connected it to the back of the new house.

As children, Kim and his brother had loved playing up here. Usually Edward was King Arthur while Kim took the part of Lancelot. After Roxie arrived, they'd tried to persuade her to be their Guinevere, but she'd scornfully refused. She preferred playing Morgan le Fay, who had beauty, power, and danger.

Kim's lips curved involuntarily as he remembered the first time he'd met Roxie. The April day had been clear and sunny, with the cool blue sky of the north country. Kim and

Edward had been preparing to ride out into the hills when a small female figure with blazing red hair had appeared.

Their mother had told them of the poor little Hayward girl who had lost her parents in a carriage accident and had come to live with her grandparents on the neighboring estate. Her grandmother was going to bring the girl to Holbourne to visit Caro in the nursery. The new little orphan had nothing to do with the sons of the house.

Then a redheaded sprite with a pale face and dark circles under her eyes had marched into the stable yard. Looking from one boy to the other, she asked, "Can I go riding with you?"

Edward said gravely, "You must be our new neighbor. I'm Edward, Lord Brentford. I'm pleased to meet you."

She bobbed a curtsey. "The pleasure is mutual. I am Miss Roxanne Hayward."

Wanting that intense little-girl gaze on him, Kim said, "I'm Kimball Stretton, but everyone calls me Kim. I'm very sorry about the loss of your parents."

Her lips quivered before she gave a short little nod of acknowledgment, then asked again, "Can I ride with you, *please?*"

Edward was not immune to the appeal in those great gray eyes, but he shook his head regretfully. "Not without your grandmother's permission. Besides, we don't have a pony your size. You might get hurt. You can play with our sister, Caroline."

"She's just a *baby.*" Roxie tilted her chin up, miserable but refusing to ask again. She was so small, so gallant. Unable to resist her any more than he could resist a forlorn puppy or a kitten, Kim said, "You can ride with me."

Edward frowned. "You really shouldn't."

"I'll keep her safe." Kim leaned over and extended his hand. "Come on, Red, I'll show you the hills of your new home."

Her small face blazing with delight, Roxie caught his

hand and he lifted her up and settled her astride in front of him. Kim suspected that his mother and Roxie's grandmother would not approve, but he was used to disapproval. If he got a scolding, it would still be worth it to see Miss Roxanne Hayward's radiant smile.

He'd been a slave to her smile ever since. But he no longer belonged at Holbourne Abbey.

He was about to turn away from the window when a rider cantered over a hill on the path from Haywick Grange, the horse's hooves kicking up dry particles of snow. Pale winter sunshine touched the rider's hair to dark fire, but her grace and superb riding would have identified her even if Roxie had been wearing a hat as a proper lady should.

Though he knew he should turn away, he couldn't make himself do it. Roxie slowed her mount to a walk as she approached the Holbourne stables, and for long moments she lifted her gaze to the tower, her expression sad. She wouldn't be able to see him in the deeply shadowed window, but she knew he was up here in his lair, like a wounded beast who'd gone to ground.

She'd tried repeatedly to visit him when his batman Welles had first brought Kim's battered and broken body back to Holbourne, but Kim had refused to see her or anyone else. He might not be good for much of anything, but at least he could spare his family and Roxie from further grief.

For all their sakes, it was time for him to get out of the way.

Miss Roxanne Hayward, tomboy heiress, glanced up at the old tower as she slowed her mount to a walk before entering the Holbourne stable yard. The gray stones and dark windows of the tower were as bleak as ever. Did Kim ever look out at the wide Northumberland hills with pleasure?

What did he do during the cold days and endless northern nights?

Suffer, she supposed. He'd refused to see her, or even speak through the peephole in the massive medieval door. His only communication had been a note scrawled in an awkward script that was nothing like the smooth, impatient hand he'd used in the dozens of letters he'd written from Portugal and Spain and Belgium. The note told her to forget him. Think of him as dead. She must find a new life with a better man.

Unconsciously, she touched her breast, where the small folded note was tucked between her stays and her shift. The paper was limp after months of acting as a talisman.

Kim had sent no other notes, no word of any kind, since then. Her laughing, beloved companion had promised that he'd come back after Bonaparte was defeated for good and all. Then, finally, they'd marry.

He *had* come back, but with injuries so devastating that he couldn't bear to let even his family near. His servant and protector, Welles, was the only person Kim would see face to face. The batman's occasional reports implied that Kim was gradually improving, but he would never be the man he had been. The Strettons had decided to allow Kim as much time as he needed rather than force themselves in, but Roxie knew his withdrawal was as hard on them as it was on her.

Did Kim think she would stop loving him because he wasn't the same young man she'd fallen in love with? He'd changed, but so had she. She'd believed that their love was true enough and strong enough to endure anything, but he wasn't willing to give that love a chance, the damnable stupid man!

Her lips tightened. Months had passed, and perhaps it was time she took him at his word. By now, her refusing to accept his dismissal was one more burden on a man who had too many other burdens.

Feeling bleak, she rode into the stable yard. Her mood lightened when she saw Edward approaching from the direction of the house. He smiled and stepped up to help her dismount. "You're up early, Roxie."

"The dowager summoned me to servitude since the house is in chaos with preparations for the ball." She slid from her saddle into Edward's firm grip. "I don't suppose your idiot brother has seen fit to emerge from his lair?"

"He hasn't." Edward hesitated. "But last night I did talk with him through the door. I was so exasperated that I told him if he wouldn't marry you, I would."

"Surely he didn't believe you'd make such a dire sacrifice!"

"I wanted to prod him out of his cave. Instead, Kim said that was an excellent idea." Edward closed his eyes for a moment, his expression strained. "He plans to leave Holbourne Abbey after Twelfth Night."

Roxie gasped. "Surely he wasn't serious!"

"Deadly serious."

The last bit of hope drained out of her. As long as Kim was at Holbourne, there was a chance he'd recover and return to the normal world. But if he left . . .

Seeing her expression, Edward wrapped a comforting arm around her shoulders. "It may be the best thing for him, Roxie," he said quietly. "Here everyone knows Kim as he was, and I don't think he can bear that. A new home where he's a stranger will be a fresh start. He said perhaps he'll get a cottage on the south coast, which will be warmer."

"How could he believe that you'd actually want to marry me? The idea is preposterous!" Roxie began moving numbly toward the house, grateful for the support of Edward's arm.

"Is it, Roxie?" Edward said, choosing his words carefully. "During the years when Kim was dodging bullets and fevers on the Peninsula, it occurred to me that if he got himself killed, I should ask if you'd be willing to accept second best. You belong here at Holbourne as much as I do."

"You're not second best!" she exclaimed in surprise. "No need to settle for me just because we've known each other forever and our estates march together. Find a young woman you can fall in love with! There is no shortage of candidates, and not just because you're heir to an earldom. You're quite presentable, you know."

He smiled a little, but shook his head. "Alas, apart from a mad bout of calf love when I first went up to London, no woman has made the least dent in my heart. I suspect it's not in my nature to fall madly in love."

"Nonsense," she scoffed. "You just haven't met the right woman."

He shrugged dismissively. "I always assumed I could rely on you and Kim to produce an heir for Holbourne if I chose not to marry, but he's not cooperating. So what do you think about my suggestion? I've found no one I like as well as you. We've been the best of friends for twenty years. That's a decent foundation for marriage, I think."

Roxie glanced at him as they continued along the path to the main house. Edward and Kim shared a strong family resemblance with their height and dark hair, but Kim's eyes were blue and laughing while Edward's were a warm, serious brown.

She'd loved them both since she was a child, but in different ways. Edward was the brother she'd never had, while Kim—owned her heart. They'd been privately pledged to each other for years.

Now Kim had broken that pledge. She wanted a husband and children. If Kim didn't want her, who better to marry than Edward, her dear friend and one of the best men she'd ever known?

For the first time, she seriously considered him as a husband—and found that it wasn't difficult. She could see them as friends and lovers, husband and wife, sharing a family and a future. The prospect was far more appealing than sliding into a lonely spinsterhood. As an heiress, she wouldn't have much trouble finding a husband, but she had no interest in fortune hunters. She wanted a man she should trust. "I think we'd suit very well," she said slowly. "Are you sure, though?"

"I've been thinking about this longer than you," Edward replied. "And the more I think about it, the better I like the idea. If you accept me, we can announce our betrothal at midnight of the Christmas ball. Lady Holly and my parents would adore that."

"Especially Lady Holly." Roxie drew a deep breath, fighting the wave of pain that swept through her as she thought of giving up on Kim for once and all. "That might be too soon. I need time to think."

"Of course, my dear girl. Take as long as you need." He bent his head to give her a light kiss.

Edward's mouth was warm. Firm. Masculine.

Not brotherly.

He stepped back, and she touched uncertain fingers to her lips. "I will make one last attempt to see Kim," she said, her voice uneven. "I doubt he'll be willing to change his mind, but I must try. If he still wants nothing to do with me . . ." She exhaled roughly. "You and I will announce our plans and move forward to a happier future."

Edward's rare smile lit up his face. "Fair enough. Take the time to be sure. I can't lose either way because I'll rejoice whether you marry me, or whether you manage to lure Kim back to life."

"I can't lose either, if it means that I marry one of the handsome Stretton brothers," she said wryly. "For now, though, we are only considering a betrothal. Either of us can step away if we decide we won't suit, or if we choose someone else."

"You're giving me the chance to fall in love with one of

Lady Holly's wistful young ladies?" he said with amusement. "Very generous of you!"

"One never knows," she said seriously. "Sometime in the next few days, you may look across a crowded room and realize you've found the love of your life."

He swung open the side door into the house. "You, Roxanne, are a hopeless romantic. It's one of the things I've always liked about you."

As Roxie stepped forward, she saw movement in one of the windows on the floor above. The pale oval of a face and a flutter of closing draperies. She gestured upward. "Someone saw us. If they witnessed that kiss, rumors will be flying through the household that an Interesting Announcement is imminent."

"Every house party needs a good subject of gossip," Edward observed. "If anyone asks me about it, I shall raise my brows in my best 'I beg your pardon?' look."

"That will silence the curious," Roxie agreed. "If I'm asked, I'll smile with an air of sphinxlike mystery. That will convince everyone that something is afoot."

"Perhaps something is," Edward said as he set a light hand on her lower back. "We shall see."

He ushered her inside. This short side passage led to the vast, lovely atrium that was the main entry to the house. The chamber rose two tall, columned stories into the air, with vast skylights bringing sunshine into the heart of the house.

Roxie loved Holbourne Abbey. She'd been in and out of the house since moving to Northumberland. She knew every nook and cranny that a child could hide in.

The Strettons had been her surrogate family, particularly in the years after her grandparents had died. The earl and countess had swiftly become Uncle John and Aunt Elizabeth, and she'd been presented in London by the reserved, elegant countess and the much more flamboyant dowager.

Today she looked at the house in a new way. If she married Edward, someday she'd be mistress of all this splendor. And yet, she'd always preferred the rambling warmth and coziness of Haywick Grange, which had begun as a farmhouse and been added to over several centuries.

Kim also loved her house and wanted to live there. They'd be close to his family but with privacy.

Because they were both horse mad, they'd planned to breed horses. Kim had received a good inheritance from his great-uncle Kimball, and they would use that to expand the stables and acquire first-rate breeding stock. It had all seemed so perfect. . . .

She bit back her grief over lost dreams. She was incredibly lucky, the possessor of a fine estate and fortune, rich in friends and neighbors, and now a proposal of marriage from a man she'd loved for years. It was a different kind of love from the intoxicating passion she'd felt for Kim, but equally real.

She and Edward would be happy together. She knew it.

But he wasn't Kim.

CHAPTER TWO

$\mathfrak{M}$outh set in a grim line, Kim turned away from the sight of Roxie going off with Edward's arm around her shoulders. They looked so right, so at ease. He was happy for them, and he couldn't bear to watch.

He leaned back against the cold stone wall, his left hand white-knuckled on his cane as a torrent of memories rushed through him. Roxie had been his constant companion when Kim and Edward returned from Eton for the holidays. She'd been his best friend, as close to him as Edward—until the day he returned home and realized that Roxie was no longer a child, but a young woman.

Their gazes met and a lightning bolt of awareness had blazed through him. Roxie was not just his friend, but infinitely more. Her wide, startled gaze had revealed that the lightning was mutual. From that day on, they were a couple.

They'd been discreet, and no matter how powerfully youthful desire raged, they'd never crossed the line to full intimacy. Only Edward had known how intense their relationship was. He approved and thought it would be a most suitable match when they were both older.

Edward had also threatened to skin Kim alive with a dull knife if he harmed Roxie. The warning hadn't been needed. As much as Kim desired Roxie, he would have skinned *himself* alive rather than hurt her. She was so full of life and intelligence and beauty that no other woman could match her. Though he enjoyed his years at Oxford, he was always mad to return to Holbourne and Roxie.

There had never been any question but that they'd marry. Roxie was as essential to him as his beating heart. Yet during his last year at university, he'd gradually and uncomfortably recognized that he needed something more than Roxie and an easy gentleman's life.

The day he returned home after completing his education, he and Roxie had gone for a ride and ended up on a blanket in their private, willow shaded refuge by the river. They'd barely managed to keep their hands off each other before then.

Though they stopped short of the final joining, they'd learn to please each other with long, intense kisses and intimate touching. Satisfaction came swift and hot. Afterward, they lay panting together, Roxie half naked in his arms. Their families would have been horrified, yet it felt so utterly right.

Roxie murmured, "Now that you're through with university, we can get married. Shall we have Mr. Langsdale start to call the banns this Sunday? I can't think of any good reason to wait." She tilted her head back and smiled lazily up at him, her gray eyes soft with contentment. "I think we've waited quite long enough."

He opened his mouth to reply, then halted, unable to speak. The idea that he'd been pondering on and off for years surged to the center of his mind, too powerful to be denied. He swallowed hard and tried again. "Roxie, my love. You're not going to like this, but . . . I'm going to buy an army commission."

Roxie froze and stopped breathing. Then, very carefully, she pushed herself up to a sitting position and stared at him. Her face was so white that a faint haze of golden freckles was visible across her cheekbones. "Why?"

"The army is a traditional choice for a younger son." Striving for levity, he added, "Surely you can't imagine me entering the church!"

"You don't have to do either!" she retorted. "Haywick Grange is almost as large as Holbourne Abbey. There is quite enough work for both of us."

"I could keep busy," he agreed. "But you run Haywick Grange as well as your grandfather did. You don't need me for that." With a pang, he had a new realization. "You don't need me at all."

"How can you say that?" she whispered. "I love you. I need you every day, every hour. Your absences tear me apart. Again I ask, *why*?"

He hesitated as he sought for words to explain what he hadn't clearly articulated even to himself. "I've had a charmed life, Red. Being raised at Holbourne Abbey, a wonderful family with health and wealth. Most of all, you. I know I've been blessed." He hesitated again. "I feel that I must do something challenging and difficult and selfless to be worthy of all that I have. I need to prove myself."

"You don't need to prove yourself to me!" Great tears were forming in her eyes. "I've always loved you exactly as you are."

"It isn't you I must prove myself to," he said gently. "It's me. And this isn't just about me. Napoleon must be defeated. He's conquered most of Europe, and he wants nothing more than to add Britain to his empire."

He braced to withstand her pleas that he change his mind, fearing that she might be able to break his will. Instead, she sat up fully, her face like carved alabaster as she began refastening her bodice. "Then we'd better not become officially betrothed."

Her pain echoed in him. "I was hoping we could marry before I leave. Then you'll be an official member of the Stretton family."

Her eyes narrowed. "How lovely. You're giving me the

opportunity to become a widow when I've scarcely become a wife. No, thank you."

"Then follow the drum with me. You love discovering new things. Wouldn't you like to come with me to Spain?"

"The idea is not without some appeal," she said reluctantly. "But Haywick Grange needs me. I have a responsibility to the servants and tenants as well as the estate. I can't just go away for God only knows how long."

"Any more than I can leave other men to fight my country's battles." He sighed, knowing that she was right to stay, just as he was right to go. "It won't be forever, love. Two or three years, perhaps." He reached for her hand. "I promise I'll come home to you."

Avoiding his hand, she got to her feet. Her red hair was a blazing cloud that framed her pale face and bleak eyes. "Don't make promises you can't keep."

"I *will* return," he insisted as he stood.

And he had. But he'd never dreamed that he'd come home a broken shell of the man who'd left.

Roxie joined the countess and the dowager in what was usually the morning room. It was one of the spacious connecting chambers that ran along the south end of the house. When the sliding doors that separated the rooms were opened, the space became the grandest ballroom in this part of Northumberland. While servants removed furniture and carpets to make way for dancing, the countesses squabbled amiably over the decorations for the ballroom. Unsurprisingly, the countess preferred elegance while the dowager's taste was far more colorful.

Roxie loved them both, but she wondered about living under the same roof with them. Three strong-minded women at Holbourne was at least one too many! Particularly since Roxie had been mistress of her own household for several years.

Perhaps Roxie and Edward could live at Haywick Grange until he inherited? They'd have more peace and privacy, and she'd not have to leave her home.

As she wrote lists for the countesses and made notes of what needed to be done, she silently plotted how she might get in to see Kim. She'd made attempts before, but she'd stayed within the bounds of good behavior. Like his family, she'd reluctantly accepted that he needed time. Now time had almost run out.

A heavy, locked medieval door was the only entrance to the small apartment at the top of the tower. Kim talked to Edward through the peephole with some regularity, and she knew Kim had sometimes spoken with his parents, but he'd never talked to her. When she tried, Welles would say apologetically that Captain Stretton was indisposed.

Did Kim think that if they actually talked to each other, she might persuade him to come out? That suggested she still had some power over him, and she might have more if they met face to face. If only she could touch him!

Pain ached through her as memories of touch and taste and sound sparkled through her mind. The memories were particularly acute when she thought back to those stolen hours in their private retreat by the river. Everything she knew of passion and satisfaction came from those wicked, wonderful interludes.

Only the final consummation had been missing, During long, lonely nights in the years since, she'd dreamed of lying with him in the soft open air, the river flowing serenely by a dozen feet away while they feverishly explored each other's bodies.

As she lay sleepless, she also wondered if she should have married him before he left. If she had, she'd have more memories and perhaps a child. But his departure would have hurt even more, and it had been nigh unbearable as it was.

She didn't think she'd been wrong to refuse to marry then. But she was no longer sure that she'd been right.

"We'll need more scarlet ribbons," Lady Holly said. "Make a note of that, Roxie."

"We've already purchased every inch of scarlet ribbon in Bellsburn," Aunt Elizabeth said mildly. "Surely we have enough. There isn't time to send away for more."

"The greens need more red to set them off," the dowager said firmly. "If there's no red ribbon to be had, we'll need more holly."

"We harvested most of the Holbourne holly on Christmas Eve," her daughter-in-law pointed out. "By now the bushes whimper when the gardeners approach."

"There are a number of holly bushes near Haywick Grange that haven't been cut, and they have a fine crop of scarlet berries," Roxie said. "Adding those to the greens will brighten the ballroom nicely."

"A good thought," Lady Holly said approvingly.

Lord Gabriel Quinfroy chose that moment to peer into the morning room. The dowager's eyes lit up at the sight of his golden head. "We can send my scamp of a godson to collect them."

"What am I being enlisted for?" Lord Gabriel asked warily. "I stopped by to say hello to Roxie, but I don't trust that glint in your eyes, Lady Holly."

Roxie smiled. If the Strettons were her family, Gabriel was surely a cousin. As the dowager's godson and a friend of both Stretton brothers, he'd visited the Abbey often over the years. His blond good looks and lighthearted charm were always welcome.

"You are to be sent into battle with fearsome holly bushes, Gabriel," she explained. "Your mission is to collect shiny, spiky branches with lots of red berries. They're intrepid north country holly with *many* stabbing leaves. Expect to bleed."

Gabriel groaned theatrically. "Danger! Blood on my im-maculate white linen!" He bowed, one hand over his heart. "But I shall not fail to fulfill my ladies' wishes."

Amused, Aunt Elizabeth said, "Enlist the head gardener. He and a couple of his men can go with you, and he'll have leather gloves you can use."

"There is less honor to be won, but my linen will be spared. My valet thanks you," he said grandly.

As Roxie sketched a simple map to the holly bushes, she suddenly thought of a way to conquer the tower so she could confront Kim. And once she was finally face to face with him—well, she'd see.

CHAPTER THREE

It was time for Kim to start the day's round of exercises. This apartment at the top of the tower was mostly one large room, and now it looked like a combination of gymnasium, bedroom, and sitting room. Setting aside his cane, he began to walk the perimeter, his left hand skimming the wall to steady himself if his balance failed.

In the agonizing days after Waterloo, when he was half out of his head with pain and despair, he remembered begging the surgeon to let him die. The surgeon, a Scot with wise, tired eyes, heard him out.

Then he said thoughtfully that because Kim's battered body seemed determined to survive, he must consider his future. If Kim didn't want to spend the rest of his days in a bed or a wheelchair, he'd need to push his body ruthlessly. He must endure pain while forcing himself to move in ever more demanding ways.

Kim had asked if he'd ever be able to walk again. The surgeon had said that perhaps he could, but only after great effort. There were no guarantees.

His honesty had been refreshing, though at first Kim thought the surgeon had lied about the chances of walking again. He'd barely been able to wiggle his toes, much less lift his right leg from the mattress. But doggedly he wiggled his toes, and painfully attempted to lift his leg until the day when he could.

Similarly, he'd worked his damaged hand until he could squeeze the fingers shut. Being able to pick something up took longer.

Every day, with Welles's help, he'd pushed himself as far as he could, then a little further. His life was reduced to pain and exhaustion. When Kim had been improved enough to be moved, Welles, God bless him, had managed to get him home on a small ship that sailed into the fishing port closest to Holbourne.

Here in the Lucky Tower, he'd managed to master walking. Not well, but walking badly was infinitely better than not walking at all. With the aid of newly installed railings on both sides of the tower stairs, he'd managed to descend and ascend the tower, though at first he'd needed Welles's aid to ascend the last few steps. Now he could manage on his own, barely.

How many times had he circled the room this morning? Often enough that his muscles were shaking and he was close to collapse. He collected his cane and continued to walk, leaning on it as necessary.

Though he could now walk and had regained much of the function of his right arm and hand, he'd also accepted the harsh truth that no matter how hard he worked, he would never recover all he'd lost. Some damage was too great to be repaired.

There were no mirrors in the tower because he couldn't bear to see his own face.

After Lord Gabriel left to enlist his holly hunters, Roxie glanced at the clock. She'd have to move quickly to set her plan into motion. Rising from her chair, she said, "I need to stretch my legs. Lady Holly, Aunt Elizabeth, would you like me to perform any errands while I wander for a bit?"

Both declined, and then returned to discussing how to

arrange their guests at the dinner that would precede the ball. This was a monstrously complex task that would keep the countesses happily occupied for hours as they weighed precedence, friendships, romantic possibilities, gender balance, and more.

Roxie strolled from the morning room, but she accelerated as soon as she was outside. She knew that Welles descended to the kitchen three times a day to collect meals for Kim and himself, and it was time for him to pick up the midday meal. Reverting to her tomboy ways, Roxie raised her skirts a few inches so she wouldn't trip and raced down the steps to the kitchen.

She was almost too late. Welles had already returned the morning tray with its dirty dishes and was leaving the kitchen with a new, heavily laden tray. The cook and her maids did their best to tempt Kim's appetite and tantalizing scents wafted from the covered dishes.

Jamie Welles was a fair, strongly built young man who'd grown up on a farm near Bellsburn. As a younger son with a yen to see the world, he'd followed Kim into the army, and their relationship ran long and deep. When Welles was struck down by a dangerous fever in Spain, Kim had personally nursed him back to health. They were friends, and utterly loyal to each other. Getting around Welles would be almost as difficult as changing Kim's mind.

Roxie intercepted Welles in the corridor that ran from the kitchen toward the back of the house, saying, "I need to speak with you."

He regarded her warily, having dealt with her many attempts to storm the tower and see Kim. "The captain's lunch will get cold."

"It's cold by the time you've climbed the tower anyhow," she said. "Please. This won't take long."

She opened the door to a storeroom where they'd have privacy. Since he couldn't very well refuse her, he entered and set the tray on the worktable in the center of the room. "The captain still doesn't want to see you, Miss Roxie. Or anyone else."

Roxie swallowed hard. She should be used to hearing this. "What is his condition now? You've said he's improved."

"He has. More than the surgeons thought he would." Welles sighed. "But he'll never be the man he once was."

"Does he look like a monster? So hideous that women faint and children cry when they see him?"

"He's no monster," Welles said firmly. "But he's scarred and crippled, not that handsome lad you sent off to war."

"I didn't send him," Roxie pointed out acerbically. "He left all on his own. Now he's home, and he's cut off his whole family. The Strettons are good people, and they love him dearly. Do you think he's right to withdraw like this?"

He hesitated. " 'Tis not my place to say, Miss Roxie."

She snorted. "Don't hide behind a servant's façade, Jamie Welles. We all played in the same muddy creek as children, and you didn't lack for opinions then."

Welles exhaled roughly. "I understand why the captain has wanted to hide himself away, but I think it's time he faced the world. He can't hide forever."

"Lord Brentford told me that Kim is planning to move away from Holbourne soon. Is that true?" When Welles nodded, she continued, "Will you go with him? Leave Northumberland forever? I hear you've been courting Maggie Haines. Are you going to leave her? Or ask her to leave all her friends and family to move to a strange far place?"

Expression miserable, Welles said, "I couldn't ask that of her, and I don't want to leave, either. Bellsburn is home. I'm thinking I'll go with the captain, help him find a place, and hire a few servants. Then I'll come home."

"And Kim will lose his last connection to Holbourne," she said softly. "Do you think that will be good for him?"

Welles looked even more unhappy and didn't reply, which was answer enough. Changing her tack, Roxie asked, "Now that your soldiering days are behind you, how do you and Maggie want to spend the rest of your lives?"

Readily accepting the change of subject, he said, "First thing I want is to marry Maggie. My older brother will take over Hilltop Farm, but there are other places." He looked wistful. "Sure would be nice if Maggie and me could have our own farm someday."

Perfect. She said, "The tenancy of Shepton Farm will be available soon."

Welles looked startled, intrigued, and then wary. "Are you trying to bribe me, Miss Roxie?"

"I would if I thought it might work," she said candidly. "But you'd spit in my eye before you'd accept a bribe to do something you think would be against Kim's best interests."

Welles grinned involuntarily. "Yes, Miss Roxie. But I'd spit politely."

She smiled back, relieved. Her key words were "against Kim's best interests." Since Welles agreed that it was time for his master to return to the world, he'd probably help her if she handled this well.

"I've been considering who to choose as a new tenant ever since the Dodds told me they were getting too old to keep up the farm and they wanted to move in with their daughter and her family," she explained. "I thought of you immediately, but I didn't want to mention it while Kim needed you so much. If he's leaving and you want to live here, it's time I asked. I think you and Maggie would make splendid tenants. I also think you deserve a reward after all you've done for Kim. Even if he never speaks to me again, you still deserve this. Talk it over with Maggie and let me know."

"Oh, she'll want this right enough!" he said, his face glowing. Then his expression turned thoughtful. "But even if this isn't exactly a bribe, I'm thinking you want some help."

"You've known me too long, Jamie Welles! Yes, there is something you might do." How should she phrase this without causing him to dig in his heels? "You've made some good improvements in the tower. The railings on both sides of the stairs. The new lock that you installed on the apartment door."

He nodded. "The old lock was simple and too easy to open. The captain thought family members would want to visit, and he was right. Don't know how many times there was a rattling at the door as someone tried."

"Imagine that!" Roxie said with feigned innocence. "He's so lucky to have you. But you do go out sometimes. There's always a holiday assembly in Bellsburn the same night as the Holbourne ball. Are you going to attend?"

"Yes, the captain said I should go and enjoy myself with Maggie." Welles scratched his chin thoughtfully. "I'm thinking that I'll be so excited about the news I have for her that I might not lock the door properly. No real harm in that, though, this being Holbourne Abbey and safe as a church."

"No harm at all," she agreed. "Give Maggie my best wishes. I know the two of you will prosper at Shepton Farm. Sorry to slow the food delivery."

Now that they'd reached an understanding, he nodded politely and picked up the tray as she opened the door for him. When he was gone, she closed the door again and leaned against it, her eyes squeezed tight with relief.

The first essential step had been taken. The bigger question was how Kim would react when she forced herself into his lair.

With Holbourne Abbey packed to the rafters with guests, Roxie stayed at her own home, but she was invited to all the house party meals and events, so the next morning she set off early to ride to the Abbey for breakfast. After several days of uninspiring weather, this day dawned bright and crisp and invigorating. Her enjoyment helped reduce some of her tension.

Her dapple gray mare, Misty, was in a mood to run, so Roxie released her into a fast canter. She was halfway to Holbourne when she saw another rider, a woman who was coming down the next hill over. She rode beautifully, and since her mount was one of the Abbey's horses, she must be a guest.

The woman spotted Roxie and gave a friendly wave. The two riding paths intersected near the Abbey, so on impulse, Roxie made a sweeping arm motion in a wordless invitation to race.

The other woman understood, and they set their mounts into a gallop at the same time. After an exhilarating charge down the hill and onto the flat, Roxie reached the intersection in a dead heat with the other woman. Laughing, she slowed Misty to an easy trot. "Lovely!" she exclaimed. "I'm Roxanne Hayward. Are you a guest at Holbourne?"

The other woman was young and had an unfashionably tanned complexion, but it suited her. That thick tawny hair must be glorious when it was released.

As she fell into place beside Roxie, she replied, "Yes, I'm Lily Tremaine, one of Lady Holly's many godchildren. Are you another?"

"No, I'm a neighbor, from Haywick Grange. I've spent half my life at the Abbey, so I'm more or less an honorary niece." Roxie studied the other woman, admiring her exotic looks. "Is this your first Holbourne Christmas ball?"

"Yes, I've been in India for the last ten years." Lily Tremaine inhaled deeply, her cheeks pink and her eyes sparkling.

"Do tell me about India! I've always been intrigued by it, but I've never met a woman who lived there."

"I've ridden on elephants," Lily said obligingly. "Is that a good start to a monologue?"

"It certainly is! Please monologue on."

Roxie guessed that Lily Tremaine was generally reserved, but under the influence of Roxie's interest, she opened up and told amusing tales of her years in India. She would be a fine asset at a house party where most of the guests already knew each other's stories.

By the time they reached the Holbourne stables, the two were on a first name basis and Roxie's anxiety had eased. This made her better company at the house party breakfast. With Lady Caroline in London, Roxie moved comfortably into the role of daughter of the house, working in tandem with the countesses to ensure that all the guests were well cared for.

Luckily, her services weren't needed after breakfast so she could return home. Haywick Grange's needs didn't vanish just because the mistress of the estate was involved with house parties and impossible men.

CHAPTER FOUR

The next night Roxie took her carriage to Holbourne Abbey in deference to the formal evening and her silk ball gown. She was as nervous as a cat on a griddle, but at least by the end of the evening, she'd know for sure if Kim really didn't want her. She supposed that his plan to leave Holbourne made his rejection clear, but after all they'd meant to each other, she needed to see him at least once before he left.

The Abbey was glittering with lights and fragrant with the scent of greens. She'd been attending the ball since she was sixteen, and before that, she'd spent the night of the ball in the Holbourne nursery with the Stretton children and occasional other child visitors. They'd peer through the bannisters on the upper level of the atrium to watch guests arrive.

She and Caroline would ooh and ahh over the gowns, and as they became older, they made similar sounds over the handsome gentlemen. Later, after being firmly escorted back to the nursery, they'd have a children's feast from some of the delicacies being served downstairs. Those were simpler, happier days.

As a de facto member of the family, she was invited to the dinner that preceded the ball along with house guests and other particularly close friends. After handing over her cloak, she followed the laughter into the reception room where guests were chatting and sipping their pre-dinner drinks.

She was interested to see her friend Sarah Langsdale looking adoringly up at Kim's friend Ivo, now Lord Harris. Even more interesting was that Ivo was looking adoringly right back. When Sarah glanced away from Ivo long enough to see Roxie, she gave a slow, satisfied wink. Roxie grinned back. Later, she'd find them both and thank Ivo for saving Kim's life and pledge money to Sarah's new orphanage, but first she needed to find Edward and tell him of her plans for the night.

She was scanning the reception room looking for him when she noticed Lily Tremaine quietly standing by one wall, a glass of sherry in her hand. Since Lily knew few people, Roxie moved to her side and said, "Good evening! Your gown is very lovely, and I suspect that beautiful shawl is warm protection against our Northumbrian winter."

Lily smiled back. "Yes, but I've discovered the conservatory. I can go there when I feel the need for tropical warmth and color." A touch of mischief in her voice, she added, "Your golden gown is splendid, but I see you also have a shawl."

"I arrived layered like an onion," Roxie agreed as she accepted a glass of sherry from a passing footman. "That's a cold wind blowing out there! I shed my cloak at the door and the shawl will be set aside when the dancing begins."

Lowering her voice, she said confidentially, "My décolletage is rather dramatic, and I don't wish to distract the gentlemen from their dinner."

Lily chuckled, but they were summoned to dinner before the conversation could continue. Roxie was seated next to Edward. He nodded gravely and complimented her appearance, looking as tense as she felt. Was he having second thoughts about marrying her? He must know that she would never hold him to marriage if he changed his mind. More likely he was just anxious for the matter to be settled.

There was a ripple of surprise when Lady Caroline arrived and was seated just before the first course was served. She looked lovely in a silver gown, but tense. Roxie gave her a welcoming smile, then glanced inquiringly at Edward. He murmured, "I didn't know she was coming, either. I wonder where Piers is?"

That question was answered later when Caro's husband, Piers Camden, arrived in an advanced state of travel dishevelment. He had the unshakeable good manners of a politician, but under his polish he looked ruffled. He also watched his wife as if he wanted to sweep her off to the nearest bedchamber. Most interesting.

Knowing she'd hear the story eventually, Roxie applied herself to her dinner. She suspected that if she was more ladylike, she'd be unable to eat when anxious, but nerves had never come between her and a good meal.

Kim had always liked her robust appetite. On occasion, he'd murmured naughty comments about how her enjoyment of food implied she had other robust appetites.

Don't think about Kim until dinner is over!

The dinner party was far too public to speak with Edward seriously, so she concentrated on being a good guest through the endless meal. Finally, Aunt Elizabeth rose and gave the signal to withdraw. As Roxie stood, she said quietly to Edward, "I'm going to make my final attempt to see Kim now. Wish me luck."

Eyes grave, he said, "Always, my dear. If anyone can bring him back to us, it's you."

Grateful for his support and understanding, Roxie slipped away in the flurry of arriving local guests and the last-minute preparations for the ball. When she was out of sight of the other guests, she walked swiftly to the back of the house and the passage that led to the tower.

The passage was a pleasant place in summer, but bitterly cold in late December. Tugging her richly patterned Indian shawl tight around her shoulders, she crossed to the tower.

The door was heavy and medieval, with gouges from ancient swords hacked into the dark wood.

A small lantern hung inside, sufficient to light Welles's return later. Also sufficient for a lady storming the tower, where her future waited. At the top of the steps, she paused to catch her breath and collect herself. Then she reached for the recently installed doorknob, thinking that if Welles hadn't left it unlocked, she'd have his head.

The knob turned easily under her hand. Heart pounding, she swung the door open. The room was well lit with a fire and two lamps so it was easy to identify the man sitting by the fireplace, his long legs stretched out as he read a book. She studied his left profile, his too thin body and too long hair, drinking in every familiar detail hungrily.

Kim said in a rusty voice, "You're back early, Jamie. Did you forget something?"

"I have forgotten nothing, Kim," she said quietly.

"Roxie!" Kim lurched to his feet, his book spilling to the floor and chair legs scraping. He almost fell over, but he grabbed a cane and steadied himself as he stared at her with wide, shocked eyes.

He took a step toward her, then froze. He was almost gaunt, despite all the good Holbourne food Welles had brought up. His right arm moved awkwardly and clearly the cane was for serious use, not fashion.

And there were scars. Not one but several marked the right side of his face. One across his temple into his dark hair. Another from his cheekbone almost to his ear. A third slashed down his throat. That one looked particularly savage, and she guessed it was responsible for the altered timbre of his voice.

Trying not to think of all the pain he'd suffered, she said, "Welles assured me that you weren't a monster who would send children screaming, and he was right. You look remarkably like a man who once wanted me to marry him.

But he broke our betrothal without so much as a word of explanation. That was rather monstrous."

"Roxie," he said again, his voice hoarse. "You shouldn't be here!"

"Why not?" she lashed out, suddenly furious. "Because you're too much of a coward to face me and your family? How can you just lock yourself away from the people who love you? Your father, your mother, your brother, Lady Holly—you have been breaking their hearts!" Her voice cracked and she realized that tears were as close as anger.

She took a deep breath and said in a quieter voice, "Now that I'm here, speak to me." She caught his gaze, searching his haunted eyes to find the man she loved. "Surely, I deserve that much."

Kim squeezed his eyes shut, as if that could block out Roxie's words. Better yet, her very presence. *Welles must have left the door unlocked, damn him!*

But she'd always been a hard girl to elude, even when she was barely knee high to a pony. Opening his eyes, he said flatly, "You deserve more than a scarred cripple like me, Red. Marry Edward. He wants to marry you. He's admitted it in so many words."

Halfway across the room, Roxie perched on the edge of the table he used as a desk, her slippered feet swinging gently. "That certainly sounds like the Kimball Stretton I've known for twenty years. Pigheaded and noble to a fault."

He almost smiled. The comment was so very, very Roxie. "I'm just being realistic. I'm not the man I was. I never will be again. You need a husband who is whole and healthy, and Edward needs a woman as full of life as you."

She shrugged. "He needs to provide an heir for Holbourne since you seem to have abandoned the idea of marriage. He and I are the best of friends, our properties march together, and all those splendid practical considerations.

We could both do worse. That doesn't mean he needs me in particular."

Kim's bad leg was starting to tremble, so he sat again, glad his face was shadowed so she couldn't see him well. "Has he proposed to you yet?"

"Edward has offered." As Roxie replied, she regarded him with grave gray eyes. She wore a shimmering golden gown with a richly patterned bronze and gold shawl tied loosely over her shoulders, and she was shatteringly beautiful. "I told him I couldn't give an answer until I'd spoken to you."

So that was why she was here. "We're speaking now. You can see what I've become." He tried to keep the bitterness from his voice. "You've done your duty. Now you can head down those stairs and tell my brother it's all right to announce your betrothal at the ball."

She studied him reflectively. "A captain is by definition a leader of men. You've been giving orders to your troops for years. But that seems to have harmed your character because you've apparently acquired the delusion that you know what's best for Edward and for me."

"It *would* be best for you to marry him." He stared at her, trying to make her understand. "You are a bright, beautiful, sunny-natured heiress. Why weigh yourself down with a monstrous cripple?"

"Because I love you?" she asked softly. "Yes, I loved your flawless young face, but only because it was part of you. You were a handsome boy, now you're a handsome man who happens to have some scars. Still yourself. We all change with time. You loved my young girl's body. Would you have continued to love me after I bore your children and no longer looked like that young girl?"

"That's not the same thing!" he exclaimed, exasperated.

"Of course, it is!" she retorted. "That's why the wedding service says 'for better or worse, in sickness and health.' We never know what the future holds. Love is what carries people through what life gives us. Love and vows."

"But we aren't married. There's no reason for you to suffer along with me!"

"I fell in love with you the day we met, when you let me ride on your horse and said you'd keep me safe." She blinked hard. "You can't begin to know what that meant to me. I'd lost my parents, and then—I found you. There has been a connection between us ever since. Can you deny it?"

No, he couldn't, no matter how much he wanted to. The unbreakable thread of connection between them was thrumming like a violin string. But that didn't mean Roxie should ruin her life because of loyalty to their past.

She'd always been able to talk circles around him. He was better at physical responses. He used his good left arm to lever himself out of the chair. "Look at me, Roxie! I've recovered better than the surgeons thought possible, but I'll never be what I was. An artillery shell exploded next to me and I have scars all down the right side of my body. Skin and muscles were ripped up, bones were broken. I would have died if Ivo hadn't managed to get me to a field hospital, even though he was wounded himself."

With difficulty, Kim lifted his right arm as far as he could and showed her his mangled right hand. "I lost my little finger and half of the third finger." He tried to make a fist and showed her how badly he managed. "I've regained some of my strength, but my arm and hand will never be what they were."

"Then it's fortunate that you've always favored your left hand," she said calmly. "If the shell had fallen to your left, you'd be worse off."

He blinked. Again, that was so very . . . Roxie. "It isn't just my hand." He took a few steps, limping. "I'm rather proud that I can walk at all. It wasn't considered likely. But I need a cane if I'm taking more than a few steps, and even then I'm in danger of falling flat on my face."

"I can only guess at how maddening this is for a man who was as strong and healthy as you always were," she said, her eyes compassionate. "But your life isn't over. You still have your mind, your ability to speak." She gave him a swift smile. "Your stubbornness. You won't regain all of your abilities, but you've already done a great deal of healing, and you'll do more. It's only been six months."

"True," he admitted, knowing his strength and balance were still improving. "But I will always have limitations." His gaze dropped to his hand. Fingers didn't grow back.

She regarded his hand, unconsciously flexing her own fingers. "It looks like you could hold reins. Do you think you might be able to ride again? Not being able to ride would be almost as bad as losing the ability to walk."

"Actually, a few nights ago Welles and I went down to the stables," Kim admitted. "He saddled Slow Sally, the greatest slug there, and helped me mount her. I was able to stay on her back and guide her around. But I'll never be a neck or nothing rider again."

"That's not a bad thing," she said tartly. "I used to worry that you'd kill yourself taking insane jumps. Worse, you'd kill your horse!"

He couldn't help himself. He laughed. "I see your priorities haven't changed, Red."

"No, they haven't," she said softly. "I love you more than anyone or anything else in my life. I always will. Once you said you loved me. Have you changed so much that you no longer do?"

He hesitated, wondering if he could lie well enough to persuade her that he didn't love her anymore. But Roxie had always been able to see right through him. "Of course, I still love you. I read and reread your letters until they were in tatters. I dreamed of you. When I was out of my head after Waterloo, you came to me as a vision, taking my hand and telling me that I did not have your permission to die. But that doesn't mean we should marry."

"Are you sure?" Roxie slid from the table, landing lightly in her dancing slippers. With slow deliberation, she pulled off her shawl and dropped it to the floor. Underneath she wore a gown cut so low that she could stop a saint in his tracks.

In his months of pain and despair, Kim had wondered if desire had left him forever, but now he wondered no more. As he stared, forgetting to breathe, she untied a small bow on her right hip.

Her bodice was a crisscross arrangement that slid from her shoulders with sensual inevitability. Another tug undid her whole gown. The shimmering fabric glided over her shapely hips in a cascade of golden silk, leaving her wearing only stays, stockings, and a translucent shift.

"Where did you get that gown?" he asked in a strangled voice.

"I came up with the idea and my talented maid Betty was able to make it. I wanted a gown that I could remove without help. Naturally, the stays are specially made to go with the gown." She pulled a pair of ribbons and the stays fell away, leaving her barely covered by her shift.

"I can only think of one injury that would interfere with marriage." She walked toward him, her breasts swaying gently under the translucent muslin of her shift. "And from what I can see, that's one injury you didn't receive."

He knew he should retreat, or wrap a blanket around her, or do *something,* but he couldn't move.

She stopped in front of him and whispered, "Show me your scars, Kim. I guarantee there will be nothing worse than the thought of losing you." She raised both hands and drew his head down for a kiss.

At the touch of her sweet, warm mouth, the last of his resistance disintegrated as the connection between them blazed into passionate life. He fell into the essence of her and found not only her strength and love, but her loneliness and vulnerability. What a damnable fool he was! In trying to save her pain, he had caused her greater anguish.

Awed by her courage, he said hoarsely, "Ah, Roxie, my

love, I surrender! Marrying me may not be the best thing for you, but it's the greatest blessing imaginable for me."

He embraced her, and found more strength in his right arm than he'd believed he possessed. Later, he could never remember the details of how they ended up naked together in his narrow bed, but the joy and rightness of coming together seared him to his soul.

Their youthful explorations of each other's bodies made this final intimacy as easy as it was wondrous. Roxie was lithely curved and perfect, as lovely as a woman could be. He was imperfect, scarred, and weakened and very different from the young man who'd kissed and caressed her by the soft flowing river. But she didn't seem to mind.

She kissed his scars tenderly and by that simple act made them mundane, merely part of who he was rather than a reminder of unspeakable despair. And as she accepted him, he accepted himself and started to become the man he wanted to be for her.

After, as they lay twined together, firelight flickering golden over Roxie's skin, she murmured, "Does this mean you're finally going to marry me?"

"I think we just married ourselves, my love." He kissed her temple, feeling whole and happy in ways he'd imagined forever lost. "But for the sake of the family and the law, we can start the reading of the banns this Sunday."

"Good!" Roxie tilted her head and gazed up at him.

She'd also changed in the last years as the strength and warmth that had always been part of her deepened and matured. She'd lost both the grandparents she loved, and Kim hadn't been here for her. She'd taken control of her family estate and ruled it with skill and fairness. "You were the most beautiful girl," he whispered, "and you've become the most amazing woman. What have I done to deserve you?"

She smiled mischievously. "You're just very lucky, Kimball. Speaking of your family, do you feel well enough to make an appearance at the ball? It would make everyone so happy."

He froze. Yet, when he considered, he realized that the panic he'd felt at facing family and friends had faded. The prospect was still deeply unnerving, but now that Roxie had broken through his fear and despair, he could deal with any other reactions. "I can do that as long as you're beside me."

"Where else would I be?" She swung from the bed, graceful in the firelight. "Do you have your scarlet regimentals here? You look so dazzling in uniform that no one will even notice your scars."

"Not true." He climbed from the bed with much less grace, wincing at the pains in his right leg, though overall, he felt amazingly well. "But at least the uniform justifies the way I look."

They helped each other dress, Roxie matter-of-factly assisting him with fastenings that he had trouble managing with his damaged hand. As she twisted her hair up and pinned it into place, he said ruefully, "In spite of your best efforts, you look like you've just been tumbled."

"Well, I have," she said with a grin. "Since we'll be married in less than a month, I don't think it matters if my reputation is tarnished."

He laughed and caught her hand up for a kiss. "Anyone who looks askance at you will have to deal with me. I may be battered, but I'm a fierce veteran of the Peninsula, and I'm armed with a cane."

"When we announce that we're going to marry, our friends and neighbors will just smile indulgently and ignore all signs of misbehavior." She tweaked his sleeves and brushed a bit of lint from his chest with delightful wifeliness. "You're too thin, but the uniform makes up for all such shortcomings."

A thought struck that should have occurred to him earlier. "Before we make any announcements, do you need to speak with Edward? Even if you weren't officially betrothed, he did offer marriage and you didn't refuse him."

"Edward told me he couldn't lose because he'd be equally happy if I married him, or if I lured you back to the world," Roxie said seriously. "He may have a few regrets, but he won't be heartbroken."

He hoped she was right. For all Edward's quiet reserve, his feelings ran deep, and how could he not love Roxie?

Kim ushered her out the door to the steps. On the long descent, she carried his cane so he could use his left hand on the railing. In the last fortnight, he'd added going down and up these steps to his exercise routine, but even so, by the time they reached the bottom of the tower he was panting.

"How are you managing?" Roxie asked, her brow furrowed. "You don't need to do this tonight."

"I must face my world, and now is the right time." He exhaled roughly. "But I do need to catch my breath and prepare myself before I enter a ballroom full of people, most of whom knew me . . . before."

"Knew and loved you and will be incredibly happy to see you again," she said. "But after months of you seeing no one but Jamie Welles, I'm sure it will be rather overpowering." She gestured to the door on the right. "Let's stop in your father's study. It's a calming place."

He followed Roxie into the small, cozy room and sank onto the leather upholstered sofa. A single lamp cast warm light on the desk, furnishings, and bookshelves, and a faint scent of tobacco lingered from his father's pipe. The earl had deliberately chosen this location because it was far from the household bustle, but when the weather was bad, he sometimes welcomed his sons. Kim would play quietly with his toy soldiers while Edward read and their father worked on accounts or studied proposed legislation.

Kim smiled fondly as he remembered those times. "This is one of my favorite spots in the Abbey."

"It's very inviting," Roxie agreed as she sat beside him so close that their thighs touched. "But my very favorite place is the conservatory."

A brilliant thought struck Kim. "Shall I build you a conservatory at the grange?"

Roxie blinked. "I've never considered having one of my own! But that would be splendid. I've always wanted to grow pineapples."

Pleased that he could please her, he said, "Then you shall have a conservatory, my lady." He bowed with what grace he could muster. "My father built the Holbourne conservatory for my mother, so it's only right that I build one as my wedding present to you. Pineapples for my bride!"

With her fair redhead's complexion, Roxie blushed adorably. He curved his left arm around her. As she sighed happily and rested her head on his shoulder, he felt not only joy, but deep contentment. He'd come home for good and all.

But the sound of dance music drifting down the corridor was a reminder of what must be done next. "Shall we storm the ballroom? I'm as ready as I'll ever be."

Roxie frowned as she got to her feet. "I need to speak with Edward first. How about if I go into the ballroom while you wait outside? After he knows, we can make our announcement to the world."

"That's only fair," he agreed.

As they stepped into the corridor, Roxie said, "They're playing a slow waltz. Shall we see if you can still dance?"

"I seriously doubt it!" But he'd managed other things the doctors had thought unlikely. "Well, a reel would be impossible, but maybe I could manage a slow dance where I can hold on to you for balance. Shall we give it a try?"

Roxie smiled and moved into his arms. "If you stumble, fall on me. I'm soft."

"Please, my love!" he exclaimed. "Allow me this gallantry. If I trip over my feet and drag you down with me, I'll cushion your fall."

But they didn't fall, though there were a couple of near misses. He found that he could laugh at his own clumsiness, and since there was no one to see, they could hold each other wickedly close.

As he led Roxie into a slow turn, she asked softly, "Those years in the army, the pain you suffered—has it all been worth it?"

She's never been one to avoid the hard questions. A dozen measures of the music passed before he replied. "Yes, it was worth it even though the cost was high. Stopping Napoleon mattered, and I'm proud that I contributed to victory in some small way. I've seen many things I'd never have seen if I stayed home, and I've learned tolerance and patience."

"Patience? You?" she asked incredulously.

"*You* should talk!" he said with a laugh. "I may be damaged goods, but I think I'm a better man for my experiences." His gaze caught hers. "And I hope I'll be a better husband." He bent for a kiss.

Time disappeared for long moments. When they surfaced to breathe, he said softly, "I'm ready now to face my family and half of Northumberland."

Together, they headed toward the ballroom, but the closer Kim came, the harder his heart hammered. He felt as if he was going into battle.

His grip must have tightened on Roxie because she looked up, her eyes warm with confidence in him, and in their future. "You'll do splendidly, my love," she murmured.

His fear dissolved. He was home, and he and Roxie were finally together as they were meant to be. "I should call you Saint Roxanne because you work miracles on me."

She grinned. "You more than anyone know how far from sainthood I am!"

Head high and his hold on Roxie unbreakable, Kim

straightened his shoulders as they turned the corner. Mentally, he prepared himself for anything. There would be surprise, of course. And revulsion and anger, but also genuine welcome. He deserved the anger and accepted the revulsion. That would be a fair price for emerging from the shadows where he'd hidden himself.

But Roxie's plan to leave him outside while she searched for Edward was thwarted when they turned the corner and found that the double doors had been thrown open to let the heat out. Startled, they halted in the doorway.

To Kim's astonishment, his brother was dancing with a tawny beauty in the middle of the ballroom. The other guests had drawn back to watch, leaving a wide open space around Edward and his partner. The two of them gazed at each other as if they were the only two people in the world.

Roxie said gleefully, "I believe it's safe to say that Edward is not going to be heartbroken at my defection!"

The dance ended. Edward murmured something to his blushing partner, then raised his gaze. He was facing the open doorway and his face froze with shock as he saw his brother. His expression turned to blazing happiness. *"Kim!"*

On impulse, Kim raised his left hand and gave his brother a vigorous thumbs-up. It was the signal they'd used as boys to say that all was well. Laughing, Edward returned the gesture.

There was a rustling of surprise as people turned to follow Edward's gaze. Kim's mother saw the newcomers and gasped, raising her hand to her mouth in shock. *"Kimball!"* she cried out as she rushed toward him.

A moment later a tidal wave of jubilant people swarmed toward Kim and Roxie, blocking Edward from view. Lord Holbourne's usual calm expression fractured with emotion as he strode forcefully through the throng a few steps behind his wife. Lady Holly's jaw dropped and she was for once speechless. Kim's friends Ivo and Lord Gabriel, both almost as close to him as brothers, lit up with delighted smiles as they saw him.

Kim saw shock, but no anger or revulsion. Only glad welcome. His throat tightened as Roxie whispered, "I'm not the only one who loves you, my darling."

As Kim took a firmer grip on his beloved, the old chaplain who'd lived at Holbourne for many years said in a hushed, reverent voice, *"Unto us a son is given!"*

OLD FLAMES DANCE

Cara Elliott

～

In the darkest hours of winter,
old flames slowly dance to life . . .

CHAPTER ONE

December 26, two days before the ball

*M*emories. Keeping her snow-cold hands fisted deep in the folds of her heavy traveling cloak, Lily Tremaine glanced around the cavernous entrance hall, taking in the ancestral portraits, the ancient weapons, the stag head paying homage to the hunting prowess of a long-dead Earl of Holbourne. She had forgotten how the trappings of tradition hung so very heavily in the grand houses of England. Ten years in India had hazed her recollections. Life had been so different there—blazing colors, exotic customs, piquant spices, searing heat. . . .

Her fingers curled in the blessedly thick wool, seeking a whisper of warmth. *Oh, what she wouldn't give at this moment for a blade of tropical sunlight to cut through the chill of a northern winter.*

Had it been a mistake to come here? Some memories were best left buried in the past.

A discreet cough drew her from her reveries.

"Her ladyship will be with you shortly, madam," intoned the portly butler, who just now had returned from informing the countess of her arrival.

"Thank you." She drew a deep breath, hoping the traditional Christmas scents of fresh-cut evergreens would help loosen the clench in her chest. But despite the festive garlands of pine and holly decorating the walls—

Hearing the sound of rapidly approaching steps, Lily turned to see a flutter of pale silk emerge from the corridor behind the butler.

"Welcome to the Abbey, Mrs. Tremaine! I am much relieved that you have finally arrived." Lady Holbourne gave a graceful wave of her hand, punctuating her cluck of concern. "What beastly weather. I am so sorry your carriage was delayed by a broken spoke."

"Thank you," she responded. "The inn provided a very comfortable parlor for the wait. And it was kind of them to send a post boy on horseback to alert you to the delay."

"Mr. Fowlkes is an old friend of the family. He has tended to many of our traveling guests over the years. But enough on the travails of your journey. Now that you are finally here, we must get you comfortably settled."

Holding back a wry smile, Lily murmured a polite reply. Clearly, the countess did not recognize her face or her surname. A decade of sun had darkened her complexion to a very un-English hue, and time had dulled the first bloom of youth. As for her name, she had been twice widowed, so Tremaine meant nothing to any of the Holbournes, save for her elderly godmother, the dowager. . . .

"My mother-in-law will be upset that she's missed your arrival, but she was feeling a trifle fatigued after dinner and chose to retire early."

"I do hope Lady Holly is in good health," said Lily.

"Be assured she is as sturdy as an ox," replied the countess dryly. She gestured for the footmen who had just entered with Lily's trunks to proceed up the stairs. "And greatly looking forward to having a houseful of guests for the Christmas ball. She adores watching the young people dance, so the music will be swirling until close to dawn."

"It sounds like it will be a very festive evening."

"Indeed," agreed the countess. "And it may be made

even more festive by some happy news. My children are being exceedingly coy about things, but there have been hints that my eldest son will be announcing his betrothal."

Lily's hands, which had become pleasantly warm, suddenly turned to ice. "My congratulations," she replied, hoping any tremor in her voice would be put down to fatigue.

"Yes, we are all in alt—assuming, of course, that there is any truth to the rumors. I confess, I had all but given up on . . ." The countess clasped her hands together. "But here I am, prosing on when you must be famished and thirsty from such a long day. Some of the guests have retired, and some are enjoying postprandial refreshments and a game of cards in the drawing room. I shall have a table set up for you and ask cook to send out a selection of dishes from the evening repast—"

"Oh, please," interrupted Lily. "That is very kind of you, but to be truthful, the rigors of the road have been a bit grueling and I would just as soon retire to my quarters. A simple supper tray—a cold collation and a pot of hot tea—sent up to the room would be wonderful."

"But of course. You must be exhausted," exclaimed Lady Holbourne. "Munton will escort you upstairs while I see to your refreshments."

"I am very grateful," said Lily, barely able to muster more than a whisper.

"I hope you enjoy a good night's rest," replied the countess. "Sleep as late as you like, and we will go through all the introductions on the morrow. There will be many activities, both indoors and outdoors, to choose from. Do you like to ride?"

"Very much so."

"Excellent! We have a prime stable, and many of the younger set love a good gallop. The grooms will saddle you a suitable mount whenever you wish to go out." Lady Holbourne gave a motherly pat to her arm. "I shall see you in the morning."

Forcing a wan smile, Lily nodded and then turned to follow the butler to the massive staircase, whose age-dark stone curled up into the shadows. Only the flickering branch of candles softened the angular shapes half-hidden in the nighttime stillness.

Their steps silenced by the thick Turkey runner, they wound their way through several turns. Brief flashes of gold sparked as the wavering light caught on the gilt-framed paintings, illuminating for just an instant the family faces. *An imperious lady, a pair of laughing boys* . . .

Lily quickly averted her eyes.

"This way, madam," said Munton, his hushed tone further muffled by the chilly gloom. He crossed the landing and led the way down a long, dimly lit corridor. "You will be staying in the Turquoise Room."

Another turn, and the glow from the wall sconces grew even more muted. Drawing her cloak a bit tighter around her shoulders, Lily quickened her pace, anxious for the solitude of her quarters in which to reorder her unsettled emotions. Up ahead a door was half ajar, allowing a pool of warm light to spill out over the patterned carpet. As she passed, she cast a quick look inside—and for an instant her feet froze.

A man was sitting in a leather armchair, his long legs propped up on the brass fender surrounding the flames dancing up from the logs in the marble hearth. His head was bent over the book in his lap, the planes of his profile sharply defined by red-gold flames, even though tangled strands of silky black hair had fallen across his cheek.

Lily tried to breathe, but the hammering of her heart against her ribs seemed to thump all the air from her lungs.

His face was more austere. Time had chiseled away the softness of youth. There was a new firmness to his features—the cant of his eyes, the slant of his cheekbone, the shape of his nose. . . .

Oh, but the shape of his mouth still possessed a fullness that belied the serious expression tugging at its corners.

Seeming to sense the scrutiny, he slowly looked up from the open pages.

The slight movement broke the spell that held her in thrall. Lifting her skirts, she hurried to catch up with her escort, the agitated *swoosh-swoosh* of wool and lace skirling around her legs.

"Your quarters are here, madam." Munton opened the paneled portal and stepped aside for her to enter. Her maid had already lit the oil lamps and stirred the banked fire to a cheery blaze. "You have only to ring if you require anything."

"Thank you," replied Lily, her breath still feeling a little ragged.

He bowed, and the door closed with a discreet click.

"I've laid out your night rail and wrapper, Mrs. T." Her maid, Colleen, an Irish girl from County Kerry who had been with her for the last five years, came around the large four-poster bed chafing her arms. "Cor, I had forgotten how cold winter can be here. I never thought I'd say it, but I almost miss the sweltering heat of Bombay."

"It will take a little time to readjust."

"Aye, lots of things to get used to again," agreed Colleen. An even-tempered girl who had proved unflappable through any adventure, she had become a friend as well as a companion. "The weather, the peace and quiet, the food—though I won't miss that hot-as-hellfire curry."

Lily smiled and they continued chatting as her maid helped her to undress and ready herself for retiring. The supper tray arrived, the hot tea and still-warm meat pie helping to calm her jumpy stomach. She then dismissed Colleen for the night, wishing to be alone with her thoughts.

Not that they proved to be very good company.

Edward. She had thought that time—how many hours were in a decade?—had rubbed off all the sharp edges of longing. Her godmother's invitation to the ball had offered a chance to see him one last time before retiring to the snug little cottage she had leased on the coast—and she had told herself it was merely a mixture of curiosity and nostalgia that had compelled her to accept. A dispassionate glimpse back at her youth before heading to the future of living out her widowhood in comfortable peace and quiet.

Liar! In her heart, she should have known her feelings, however carefully locked away in the darkest depth of her being, had not withered away for lack of air or light. One glimpse—one fleeting glance at his face—and love had burst into bloom, its tender vines shooting out to curl around her consciousness. . . .

"Yes, it was a mistake to come here," she whispered.

A mistake magnified by the unexpected news that a betrothal was about to be announced. She had heard that Edward was unwed, and that fact had helped her make her decision. But now, it seemed, she would have to witness his engagement to another.

The only consolation was that she could do so in anonymity. Her appearance was unrecognizable—fine lines had chased away the first bloom of youth, the tropical sun had tanned her flesh and burned her hair a tawnier shade of gold. And her new name would be equally unfamiliar to him. *A stranger.* As well Mrs. Tremaine should be.

She mustn't stir up the embers of the past. What once was between them was long gone. But despite the admonition, her thoughts couldn't help straying back in time.

It had been her first Season, and in a letter to her godmother, she had confided how nervous she was about making her entrée into the glittering social whirl of the ton. *Lady Holly—or, more properly, the Dowager Countess of Holbourne—had asked her grandson, Edward, who was spending some time in London, to shepherd her through the first few balls. As Fate would have it, they had actually met on their own at Hatchards bookstore, where he had teased her over her taste in reading material. That had sparked a serious discussion on books, and they quickly discovered they shared a common interest in history and poetry. Dancing had followed, along with drives in the park. The mutual attraction soon deepened into love.*

Lily closed her eyes, feeling the sting of salt as tears pearled on her lashes.

Edward had asked her to marry him. But her father, whose coffers were dangerously low, had pressed her to accept the suit of a wealthy under-governor of the East India Company, no matter that he was years older than she.

Edward had appealed to his parents to give their consent—and enough funds—to allow him to match the other man's proposal. Thinking him too young to know his mind, they had refused. . . .

Hugging her knees to her chest, Lily tried to quiet her thoughts. It was pointless to torment herself with what might have been. Edward had likely long since forgotten the youthful infatuation. Like many handsome, titled gentlemen, he had avoided marriage, no doubt happy that fate's twist had given him the freedom to sow his wild oats.

If that were changing now, it was because the heir was eventually expected to settle down. Time and change—it was the natural order of things.

But after tossing and turning for yet another interminable interlude in the bed, Lily gave up trying to sleep and threw back the eiderdown coverlet. Deciding that a book might help quiet her mind and allow her to drift off into the land of Morpheus, she tugged on her wrapper, then padded to the armoire and wound one of her woven Indian shawls around her shoulders. An extra layer, however thin, would help ward off the unaccustomed chilliness of the night—and perhaps, she thought wryly, the fiery colors might add an extra spark of warmth.

She lit the candle by the door, and made her way out into the deserted corridor. All was silent, save for a flutter of cold air and a creak from the old floor as she started for the library.

One, two, three . . . Lily carefully counted the closed doors, hoping that in her agitation she had not become confused. Pausing halfway down the drafty length, she clicked open a latch and slipped inside. The chair, thank heavens, was empty and the fire banked down to glowing coals. The faint hiss and crackle stirred memories of past Christmases. She stood still for a moment, recalling jolly laughter echoing through halls hung with holly and mistletoe. It all seemed a world away.

Shaking off a clench of sadness, she moved to the tall bookshelves and, holding her candle high, began to make her way slowly along the rows of leather-bound spines, leaning close to read the gilt-stamped titles.

"You are looking in the wrong place." The low voice was like a finger of fire teasing down the length of her spine. "Mrs. Radcliffe's novels are on the next shelf."

Lily grasped the decorative wood molding to steady her stance. All of a sudden her skin was prickling with heat. *Steady, steady.* She drew in a great gulp of the night air, taking a moment to compose herself. Then, turning slowly, she managed a calm half smile. "Actually, I was hoping you might have *Pride and Prejudice,* the newest novel by the author of *Sense and Sensibility*. Having just arrived back in England, I've not yet had a chance to visit a bookstore and purchase it."

Edward, Viscount Brentford and heir to the earldom of Holbourne, moved out of shadows. "No visit to Hatchards?"

"No," she replied softly.

It *was* Lily. Any lingering doubt was put to flight by her

voice. The sound struck a chord deep within that had been silent for . . . too many years.

"I had very little time in Town before heading north," she added.

"Well, you are in luck. We do have a copy." Two strides brought him closer to her—close enough to inhale the scent perfuming her skin—a beguiling mix of neroli and jasmine, spiced with some exotic undertone to which he couldn't put a name. Reaching up, he plucked a slim volume down from the top shelf.

"Word is the author is a lady by the name of Jane Austen," he murmured as he held it out to her.

"Whatever her name, the story is said to be sharply observant, insightfully wise, and slyly clever," she responded. "Which of course doesn't surprise me in the least."

A chuckle rose in his throat. "I see that we shall still argue over whether women can write as well as men. But in this case, I shall have to concede that the book is exceedingly good."

"I—look forward to reading it." Lily tucked the little volume inside the folds of her shawl. She looked away, the shadows masking her face.

He wished he could read her thoughts.

As for his own . . .

To cover his confusion, Edward turned slightly and fumbled for flint and steel to light the branch of candles on the side table. The flames leapt to life, and yet, to his dismay, the light did not quite reach her profile.

"That is a very striking shawl," he observed in order to break the awkward silence that had settled between them. "All the different shades of red are quite extraordinary." Ye gods, had he really uttered such an addlepated comment? "They bring out the subtle coppery highlights in your hair," he added lamely.

Her head jerked around. "I fear the harsh sun has made

the copper none too subtle anymore. More than one acquaintance has commented that I often take on a Mars-like glow when I am roused to action."

Edward would have chosen a different god—or goddess— to mention. *Venus*. At that moment, she looked even more beautiful than he remembered. "I never thought of you as bellicose. Certainly wise, so your acquaintance would have been more accurate to call you Minerva rather than Mars."

"I suppose different people see different things." Lily hesitated. "I—I never thought that you would recognize me. My hair, my face—I daresay my whole appearance has changed greatly in ten years."

"I knew you in an instant," he replied. "It is the way you carry yourself, the way you move."

Her eyes widened ever so slightly, but before he could discern what emotion might be swirling within their hazel depths, her lashes lowered, shuttering her gaze.

"I would have thought that I had acquired a very peculiar sway over the years. Riding an elephant is not at all like riding a horse."

"No," he said quietly. "You are as graceful as before."

Biting her lip, she looked away again. It was a familiar quirk of hers and made him feel marginally less foolish. He knew she only did it when she was nervous.

"What does puzzle me is why I didn't see your name on the guest list," he went on. "Grandmamma asked me to go over the invitations with her weeks ago, and I am quite sure I would not have missed it."

"It was there," she assured him. "Mr. Carrington passed away in India six years ago. I am now Mrs. Tremaine."

The statement hit him like a punch to the gut, but Edward managed to shake off the pain and keep his expression impassive. Having lost her once, what did it matter if he had lost her a second time?

"Ah," he answered politely. "Mr. Tremaine did not choose to accompany you north?"

"I am a widow," she said. "Yet again."

He wished a hole—a very deep one—would open up beneath his feet and swallow him into the bowels of the Earth. "My condolences," he said, more gruffly than he intended.

"Thank you." Her voice held no hint of what she was thinking. "I . . . I should return to my room."

Loath though he was to let her go, he could think of nothing to say to keep her. "Yes, you must be tired from your travels."

"Not really." Her shawl fluttered, the deep scarlet and earthy cinnabar colors rippling like a flame against the iron-gray shadows. "But now I have a good book to read."

Edward felt his mouth twitch up at the corners.

Lily shifted and slowly turned for the door. As she did, her gaze fell upon a small round game table set in an alcove between the bookshelves. Centered on the inlaid pearwood was an antique chess set carved out of ebony and ivory. "You still play?"

"Yes, I have been practicing. But likely I am still not able to beat you." Drawing in a deep breath, he thought for a moment. Chess was all about strategy. For all her quiet, calm demeanor, Lily had never been one to back down from a challenge.

"Care to try?" he asked casually.

Yes or no? Lily knew which was the wise answer. But regardless of Edward's comment on Minerva, she wasn't feeling very wise.

"I would," she answered.

He moved around to the chairs. "Shall we take the usual sides—you play the fair-haired queen and I'll play the black knights."

"It does give me the advantage. I always warned you of that."

"You did," he acknowledged. "But I was too gentlemanly to want to take turns."

"Or too stubborn," said Lily dryly.

The shadows beneath his eyes seemed to lighten as the tautness around his mouth gave way to a smile.

Her rib cage suddenly felt as if it was filled with a flock of butterflies, fluttering their gossamer wings. *Yearning to break free.*

"That, too," conceded Edward, his face looking impossibly boyish in the soft flicker of the candlelight. "Besides, the coloring suited us—you so light." He tucked an errant strand of ebony-colored hair behind his ear. "And I so dark."

And yet, nothing is black and white, thought Lily as she took the chair commanding the ivory forces. They both possessed an infinite range of hues in between. Setting the book aside, she snugged her shawl a little tighter and looked at the board, considering her first move.

"Already intent on countering my best efforts?" he murmured.

"You never expected me to temper my abilities when we played in the past," she replied. "I'm assuming that hasn't changed."

"No." A wry twitch tugged at his lips. "And I doubt it would matter if I did."

She looked back to the checkered board, trying to make herself concentrate on the game. "Correct." Taking hold of a pawn, she pushed it forward.

He matched her opening, and for several minutes they played in silence.

"So, what brings you back to England?" he asked abruptly as he started to study the position of his bishop. "That is, if I may ask."

"You may," she answered calmly. "I simply decided that

after so many years in a faraway land, it was time to come home."

"You . . ." He left off to shift his chess piece another few squares.

"Yes?" prompted Lily when he didn't continue.

"You . . . you did not wish to remarry again?"

The question made her feel a little like an old dish, slightly chipped around the edges. "There are many exotic customs in India," she replied. "But none where a woman is the one who makes a proposal."

A slight tinge of color seemed to creep across his cheekbones. "Forgive me. I did not mean to be offensive."

"You weren't." Lily smiled and then slid her knight over.

"Drat," he muttered under his breath, seeing that no matter which way he moved, his bishop was lost.

"As for proposals," she went on, after removing his piece from the board. "Your mother hinted that you will have some news to announce at the Christmas ball."

Like her, he chose to answer obliquely. "Mother should know better than to take every rumor she hears to heart."

Deciding to steer away from such a dangerous subject, Lily quickly fell back on the usual polite platitudes. "Your mother is looking very well. I trust she is in good health?"

"As sturdy as an ox," replied Edward with a chuffed laugh.

"She said much the same about Lady Holly—whom I am very much looking forward to seeing. It has been a long time." She paused, taking a moment to survey the board and how the game was unfolding. "Your mother did not recognize me, which is just as well. I don't wish to stir awkward memories, especially at such a festive occasion."

Edward steepled his fingers and took several long moments to make his next move. "I hope," he said slowly, "they aren't entirely awkward, for I should like to hear more about your life in India. It must have been very . . . adventurous."

"I suppose it was," allowed Lily. "And you? I imagine you've had your share of adventures, too."

He made a wry face. "I am not sure Ireland and Scotland qualify as exotic destinations."

"A great many people would disagree with you," she quipped, and their shared laughter seemed to loosen the undercurrent of tension in the air. They had always been very comfortable with each other, so perhaps for this brief interlude they could recapture that spirit of friendship.

Friends. The word caused her chest to constrict with a painful pinch. But it would have to do.

"True," said Edward. "Hunting among the Highlanders is quite an experience." He went on to recount an amusing anecdote concerning stags and sheep.

Lily responded by recounting her first elephant ride.

"You've always had a wonderful seat in the saddle, so I doubt it was quite so embarrassing as you say. If you wish to ride at any time, simply inform the grooms. We have recently acquired a very handsome gelding with a sweet gait. I think you would enjoy putting Ajax through his paces."

"I shall leave off wearing brass bells and silken flags, so as not to spook him."

He laughed again—and then gave a low grumble as he glanced at the board. "Drat, you've distracted me on purpose!"

"But of course. All is fair when it comes to a chess match." She moved her queen diagonally. "Checkmate."

The grumble segued into a growl.

"You are getting too good at the game," she murmured. "If I didn't resort to such tactics, I fear I would have been soundly beaten."

"I should like to test whether that is true." He sat back and crossed his arms. "So I demand a rematch."

"You shall have it, but not right now." Lily stifled a yawn, telling herself it was only fatigue that had her imagining the candle flames had sparked an oddly fierce glint in his chocolate-dark eyes. "I really must get some sleep."

The glimmering gave way to a look of contrition. "I'm sorry, I shouldn't have pressed you to play, knowing what a trying day of travel you've had."

"I enjoyed it," she said.

A ghost of a smile passed over his face, but was gone in a quicksilver flash, leaving his features looking as if they were chiseled out of shadows and stone. "I shouldn't have, but so did I."

Uncertain as to what he meant by the cryptic statement, Lily dipped a vague nod and rose. "Well, then. Good night."

"Good night," echoed Edward as she moved to the door and slipped out to the corridor.

It might only have been the whisper of her steps on the carpet but a faint whisper of "Lily" seemed to hover behind her for just an instant before dissolving into the darkness.

CHAPTER TWO

*T*here was yet a steel-gray hue lingering in the shadows of the morning, but the clear winter sunlight was quickly burnishing it to a silvery glow. The sky was cloudless and the air very still. In the distance, the dark silhouette of the bare trees sparkled here and there with bits of frozen snow, setting off a winking of diamond-bright flashes against the snow-dusted landscape.

Edward squinted as a blade of light cut across his eyes, and then splashed some ice-cold water on his face. He had slept badly, plagued by strange dreams.

Plagued by fierce longings.

He had never thought to see Lily again, and yet here she was, at Holbourne Abbey. And free, though he hadn't been thinking clearly enough last night to inquire further on her reasons for returning to England.

Where was she headed? What were her plans?

Wincing, he took his head in his hands. *What did it matter?* The irony of the situation stirred a laugh deep in his throat, but it stuck there, reverberating painfully in his chest.

Of all the devil-cursed luck. A momentary glint of tawny gold, wrapped in a flutter of flame red—and all of a sudden his orderly life had been turned on its ear.

Moving to the mullioned windows of his bedchamber, Edward pressed his forehead to breath-misted glass, letting the chill seep through his heated skin. What had seemed like a reasonable idea just the day before now had him tangled in a hellish coil.

Damn, damn, damn.

Expelling a harried sigh, he wiped clear one of the glass panes and peered out toward the stables. Perhaps an early ride in the bracing cold before breakfast would help clear his muzzy head. He needed to think—how the devil was he going to deal with Lily? Her presence had sparked to life all the passions he had carefully locked away in the darkest recess of his brain.

They were now dancing like demons—wild, wicked fire-red flames swaying in time to the music of longing. Teasing, taunting his resolve.

"Damn." Edward was about to turn away when he saw two riders break free of the trees and spur to a canter over the snow-dusted cart track that ran between the pastures. Closer and closer they came, handling their mounts with easy grace over the treacherous ground. One of them was Lily, whose unexpected appearance had stirred to life sparks from the past. . . .

And the other was the lady whom he had so recently asked to become his wife.

Another oath suddenly slipped from his lips. Spinning around, he hurried to his dressing room.

"That was quite exhilarating," exclaimed Lily, her breath forming a cloud of vapor as she added a soft laugh. Sliding down from the sidesaddle, she handed the gelding's reins to one of the grooms. "I had forgotten how stimulating the chill of an English winter feels slapping against your cheeks."

Roxanne Hayward raised a brow, the arch of red nearly disappearing beneath her fur-trimmed shako. "You actually enjoy its icy fingers raking against your flesh?"

"After years of searing heat, it is a welcome change."

"For now," quipped Roxie—the young lady had insisted on being addressed informally, saying all the Strettons and their guests did so. "With no wind and the bright sunshine, the morning is quite mild for this time of year. Let us see how you feel when a howling blizzard blows in from the North Sea."

She dismounted from her spirited filly with a natural grace that Lily couldn't help but admire and casually tossed her crop to the grizzled stable hand who rushed over to greet her with a gap-toothed grin. "How are the kittens doing, Jock?"

"They be crawling around, making mischief in the loft, Miss Hayward," he replied. "Just like you and Lord Edward and Mister Kim."

"Aye, we were little hellions, weren't we?" she said without a hint of contrition.

The comment sparked a flurry of bantering comments from the men mucking out the stalls. Lily stood silently as Roxie traded good-natured barbs with them, feeling her spirits drop a notch lower with every clever quip. The lively redhead seemed so at home at the Abbey, she was beginning to have a sinking suspicion that this lady might very well be Edward's intended.

Looking out to the paddocks, she drew in a rueful breath. Her sleep had been fitful, and seeking to dispel her unsettled mood, she had decided to take a short ride before breakfast. But in hindsight, it hadn't been the best of plans.

She had encountered Edward's neighbor at the far end of the orchards, where the two properties abutted. Roxanne Hayward had come flying over the high stone fence, expertly steadied her horse as it landed on the slippery ground, and without breaking stride had cut between the trees to take a shortcut out to the cart track. Curiosity about the stranger riding on Stretton lands had, naturally enough, impelled her to canter over with a friendly hallooo.

Lily slanted a quick sidelong look at Roxie's animated face, framed by wind-snarled curls of glorious copper red. She had quickly learned of the young lady's history with Edward and his siblings, along with a number of facts about the Abbey and its surrounding lands. According to local legend, the ancient tower adjoining the main house was blessed with protective powers and was considered a talisman of good luck, which was why a previous earl had restored it rather than knocking it down.

Perhaps, thought Lily wistfully, a little good luck would rub off. . . .

"I'm famished," announced Roxie, interrupting her thoughts. After exchanging a last jest with one of the young boys sweeping around the feed bins, she added, "Shall we go in to breakfast?"

Lily nodded, noting that Roxie seemed to be treated as part of the Stretton family by everyone. "I will, of course, need to change out of my riding habit."

"Yes, yes, I know it's quite unfashionable for me to traipse into the breakfast room smelling of horse and sweat, but I've been running tame here at the Abbey since I was a bantling, so they will forgive me." She smiled. "Besides, I don't mean to stay for long. I just wanted to speak with Edward about something."

At this hour? A queasy feeling began to churn in Lily's stomach, one that had nothing to do with hunger. "It sounds as if the two of you are very good friends."

Roxie's face clouded for just an instant, but the shadow disappeared so quickly it might have been merely a quirk of the light. "Yes, we are."

They passed through the open stable doors and started up the path to the Abbey. The bright sun was making the morning very pleasant, but Lily was still grateful for the thick wool jacket and fur collar of her new riding clothes. Somehow, a chill suddenly seemed to be seeping into her bones.

"And what is your connection to the family?" asked Roxie after several strides. "If you have been in India for ten years . . ."

"The dowager is my godmother," replied Lily. "Edward was kind enough to obey her request to squire me through my first Season. I have not yet met his siblings."

Roxie remained silent, as if expecting more. But Lily had no intention of elaborating. Instead, she couldn't help probing for more information from her companion. "You said you are now the owner of the estate adjoining the Abbey? That must require a great deal of time and attention."

"It does, but I love the land and care very deeply about its tenants and its well-being. So I truly enjoy all the responsibilities."

Lily knew Edward felt the same way about Holbourne Abbey. "Well then," she said briskly, "you and Edward share much in common."

"We do." Roxie waved to a servant chopping wood by one of the outbuildings, and then began peppering her with questions about life in India. They were actually welcome distractions from the present. And the future.

Don't be maudlin, she chided herself, while giving an account of her first tiger hunt. To think Edward's heart might be unengaged after ten years was absurd.

"How very exciting," murmured Roxie. "It sounds like you've experienced a great many adventures."

"There were many exotic experiences," replied Lily. "But I am very happy to be back in England."

Roxie darted a quick glance at her, but the slanting shadows of a nearby oak tree made it impossible to read her expression.

Both of them seemed uncertain of how to continue, and for several moments, the only sound between them was the crunch of snow and gravel beneath their boots.

"Oh, look! I think I spot Edward," exclaimed Roxie, giving a vigorous wave in the direction of the pillared portico.

They were still some distance away, but Lily, too, instantly recognized the figure coming down the front steps. Suddenly desperate to escape seeing him greet his neighbor, she looked around and spotted a path leading through the opening in the yew garden and around to the ancient tower at the opposite end of the house.

"You have piqued my curiosity about the local legend. I think I shall have a look for myself before I go in to breakfast," she said, already angling her steps toward the safe haven of the greenery. "It was lovely to make your acquaintance. No doubt we shall be seeing each other again over the coming few days."

"Where did Lily go?" asked Edward, puzzled at how, in the short time it had taken him to stop and confer with one of the gamekeepers, she had disappeared into thin air.

"I told Mrs. Tremaine about the local legend. She wanted to have a closer look."

His gaze lingered on the hedge. "I would have been happy to accompany her. She doesn't yet know her way around."

"I doubt that she's in any danger of being swallowed by a tiger," quipped Roxie. Her smile thinned to a more enigmatic expression. "You didn't mention that an old friend was coming to the ball."

"I didn't know," responded Edward. Catching the skeptical slant of her brows, he explained, "She remarried when her first husband passed away in India, so I didn't recognize the name on the guest list. I wasn't aware that she had returned to England, or that Grandmamma had sent her an invitation."

"Ah."

"Which means?" It wasn't often that he couldn't read what she was thinking.

She dismissed the query with a shrug. "Nothing in particular." A pause. "Your Mrs. Tremaine seems to have led a very interesting life."

Edward felt his jaw tighten. "Has she? We've not yet had a chance to discuss her time in India."

"Tigers, elephants, spitting cobras—clearly she has the courage and composure to face any challenge. One has to admire such worldly experience." Roxie made a face. "In contrast, I feel a little like a provincial schoolgirl."

"Nonsense," growled Edward, though he couldn't help being curious about Lily's stories. Would he seem like a country bumpkin in her eyes after all the adventurous gentlemen she had met in her travels? "You have an impressive array of talents. Why, you run a large estate, and do it very well."

"Like you, she seems very bookish."

"Have the two of you been out riding since dawn?" he asked a little querulously. "You appear to know her whole life story."

In answer Roxie fixed him with a searching stare. "Is there a reason you are in an ill-humor this morning?"

Edward blew out his cheeks, feeling frustration welling up inside him. "In fact, there are several. Grandmamma's ball is supposed to be a festive family celebration, and yet I am concerned that all is not as it should be with Caro's marriage. And as for Kim . . ."

He glanced at the tower. "Any great plans yet on how to storm his defenses?"

Roxie replied with uncharacteristic silence.

Unsure of what else to say, Edward kicked at a clot of snow.

Evading eye contact, she shifted her stance to stare out over the sloping lawns. "Look, you are perfectly free to change your mind about—"

"What gives you the impression that I wish to renege on our arrangement?" he asked tightly.

Roxie drew in a sharp breath, and then let it out in a slow exhale. "I was simply pointing out—"

"I'm quite aware of all that we agreed upon." He cleared his throat. "Are *you* having second thoughts?"

She hesitated just a moment before shaking her head.

"Fine," he responded, in a tone he hoped would put an end to the subject. "Was there a reason you rode over here at this hour of the morning?"

"Other than cook's sultana muffins?"

He knew she meant it to break the subtle tension between them, but he wasn't in the mood to smile.

After a long moment, Roxie went on, "I was checking the mended fences along the north pastures and since I was close by, I thought I would stop and ask if you need any additional flowers from my hot houses for the ball."

"You would have to ask Mother or Mrs. Taft."

"I shall go do so." She waited expectantly for him to move. "Are you coming?"

"I had better go around and see whether Mrs. Tremaine is in need of any assistance. She's not yet been introduced to any of the guests, and entering a houseful of strangers can be daunting."

"Yes, of course," murmured Roxie. Without waiting for any further response, she turned and set off at a brisk pace for the pillared entrance of the Abbey.

Lily set a hand on the weathered stone. Perhaps it was merely the sun or the thought of a magical local legend, but it seemed that a curl of heat rose up through the fleece of her sheepskin gloves to caress her palm. She slowly rubbed back and forth along the wind-carved block, feeling at the edges where the mortar had long since crumbled away.

There was something about myths and legends that appealed to her imagination. Lucky talismans, wondrous enchantments, talking bears—

"Do you need some help? The footing is quite unstable around the base, and it's easy to twist an ankle."

She straightened, hoping he had not seen her rubbing the stones. "I was just examining the mortising. It is quite old, isn't it?"

"Yes. An old castle stood on this spot. When one of my ancestors built the main house a hundred years ago, he left the tower standing in deference to the locals, who—"

"Believe it bestows luck on those around it," she finished. "I know. Your friend Miss Hayward told me the story."

"Superstition," he muttered.

"You don't believe in the legend?"

Edward looked up at the shuttered windows built into the ancient openings. "I've seen no sign of it," he answered tersely.

Lily sensed a tension radiating from him—the stones seemed to react with a faint thrum. But something in his expression kept her from questioning him further.

Stepping back down to the path, she turned the talk to a more mundane topic. "I very much enjoyed taking out Ajax this morning. He's a lovely mount. And your lands are beautiful. I can see why you have always loved this place."

"It is special to me," he replied, then offered his arm. "Shall we go in? You must be hungry after a rousing ride, and Mother will be anxious to introduce you to the other guests."

The short walk back to the main house passed in pleasantries. She did not bring up Roxie, unsure of whether she wanted to know more about his redheaded neighbor. Likely she would learn soon enough about his relationship with her. Edward seemed preoccupied, but it was only natural that the ball, with its impending announcement, would be weighing on his thoughts.

They parted at the main staircase. "Please tell your mother I shall be down shortly, after I've made myself presentable for polite company," she said, brushing several windblown tendrils from her cheek. "It was so glorious to be back riding through the English countryside that I couldn't resist a good gallop."

His gaze held for a moment on her face, before he looked away. "I shall wait for you in the breakfast room, and help you through the introductions."

"You need not trouble yourself. I'm sure you have much to do, and Miss Hayward seemed very anxious to talk to you," replied Lily. A wry smile curled up the corners of her mouth. "I am no longer a shy, tongue-tied girl who needs a knight in shining armor to squire me through such rituals."

"I was a green cub without a bit of Town bronze, while you were always poised and polished."

"I shall not correct your memory," she murmured, the words trailing off in a whisper of wool as she started up the stairs. But in her mind, the image of the serious, solemn young man with the beautiful smile would never, ever tarnish.

CHAPTER THREE

*I*t did not take her long to dress and descend to the breakfast room. Edward, she noted, had taken her at her word and had not lingered. Instead, it was the countess who made the introductions of those who had come down—Lord Gabriel Quinfroy, Miss Minchington. . . .

Nodding politely, Lily moved through the social conventions by rote. By now, such things were second nature. She was, however, happy she did not have to meet Miss Hayward again just yet. Having a face—all that red hair and rosy cheeks—to go with the vague rumor suddenly made it vividly real. Until she had some quiet time in which to reorder her thoughts and prepare for the inevitable, Lily feared she might not manage to mask her feelings.

The countess announced a number of activities for the morning. The men were to tour the gun room, and she had organized a carriage for those ladies who wished to peruse the shops of Bellsburn.

Lily demurred, choosing instead to explore the large conservatory built in the latter part of the previous century by the current earl's grandfather, whose collection of exotic specimen plantings from around the world had been carefully maintained by the family. Edward, who had more than a passing interest in botany, had described it in great detail to her during their long-ago courtship, and so she couldn't help but be curious to see it.

As she pushed open the heavy brass-framed oak doors, a cloud of moist, warm air enveloped her, bringing with it the heady fragrance of life bursting into bloom—pungent grassy scents mixed with delicate florals and mysterious spices. Looking up at the soaring, sun-dappled glass, Lily stood very still and filled her lungs, hoping to chase away the shadows clouding her thoughts.

Up ahead stood a cluster of tropical palm trees, the long-fingered fronds stirring lazily in the gentle drafts of heat set off by the copper braziers placed around the perimeter of the cavernous space. The ruffling sounds reminded her of India, and she moved closer, letting the leaves brush against her cheek.

Strange how she felt suspended between two worlds. She had left one behind, but as yet was not sure how she fit into the other.

"Are you homesick?"

Edward's low voice startled her out of her reverie.

"No, not at all." Lily composed her expression before turning around. "I never really thought of it as my home. I think I always knew that I would return to England."

"Why?" he asked.

How to answer? She thought for a long moment before answering. "Because my heart is in England."

A muscle on his jaw gave a tiny twitch.

"I suppose the place of our birth has a powerful pull on us, no matter how long and far we travel."

He came closer—close enough that his shoulder kissed up against hers. "Yes, I do believe that elemental forces do have a hold on us, no matter the passing years."

Lily didn't dare look up to meet his gaze. As it was, the current connecting them through all the finely tailored layers of silk and wool was threatening to overwhelm her senses. Letting him see the emotion in her eyes would make her too vulnerable.

They stood side by side, silent amidst the soft flutter and

swoosh of the surrounding plants. From some hidden spot, a caged bird began to sing.

"Tell me more about your life in India," he asked abruptly. "Did you really hunt tigers?"

"It is not nearly as adventurous or dangerous as you seem to think. There is a veritable army of servants beating the bushes and priming the rifles." She made a face. "The truth is I did not enjoy seeing such a magnificent beast shot for our amusement. After being part of one hunt, I never went again."

"You've always had a sensitive soul," he murmured. "Surely there were some activities that captured your fancy."

"The art is fascinating. . . ." Lily wasn't quite sure how long they stood there within the leafy shadows discussing sculpture, which led to talk of books on the cultures and religions of the vast subcontinent. They had always shared an interest in intellectual pursuits and the spirited exchange of ideas seemed to come just as naturally as it had in the past. It was only after she finished describing a lengthy Hindu ritual that she realized she had gotten carried away by the subject.

"You should have stopped me from rattling on like a loose screw," she said, feeling a flush steal over her face. "I'm sure I've been boring you to flinders."

"On the contrary. I've found it all fascinating." Edward took her arm and drew her toward the far side of the conservatory. "By the by, I think you might enjoy seeing the specimen plantings the family has collected over the years. Many come from India."

There were half a dozen long rows of teak tables, separated by narrow brick walkways. Each held a profusion of unusual bushes and flowering plants. The perfume was more intense here, the lush scents making her feel slightly woozy.

Or maybe it was the warmth of his hand lightly gripping

her arm. Every time their bodies touched, she was aware of some ache stirring within her core.

Oh, how she had missed his company. *His voice, his laugh* . . . Lily looked up and felt her breath catch in her throat. *His smile.*

Desperate for distraction, she looked around wildly. Spotting a tall twisting mass of vines, she pulled free and went to finger the bright red clusters of tiny berries. "Oh, how marvelous. It's *Piper nigrum*—a pepper plant."

Edward nodded. "The spice you taste at dinner will come from here."

She bent over and inhaled deeply. "We had masses of it growing on our grounds."

Perching a hip on the tabletop, he traced his thumb along the length of a seedpod. "You've told me all about the sights and the sounds and the tastes of India. What about your marriages, Lily? Were you happy?"

Her hand tightened, snapping off the end of a pod. "T-They were both fine men," she replied.

His hand stilled. "That wasn't the question I asked."

Lily sought to control the pounding of her heart. "Y-You know very well that for the *ton,* happiness is not something one is supposed to consider in the matter of matrimony."

To her dismay, Edward rose and set his hands on her shoulders. He drew her closer, and all at once the subtle scent of his bay rum shaving soap overpowered all the exotic perfumes in the air. She wanted to draw away, fearful that the thrumming beneath her skin would give her away. But her body wouldn't seem to obey her brain.

Just for this one moment, she would savor the scent and the feel of having him close. A memory to hold in her heart for the long winters ahead.

"Lily . . ." Oddly enough, his voice seemed to betray a slight tremor, as if mirroring her own inner agitation. "But don't you think it should be?"

At that, she looked up, intent on asking why he was

making such a query when clearly her thoughts didn't matter. But as their eyes met, she found herself drawn into the depths of his gaze.

Could one drown in desire? she wondered, feeling the chocolate-dark currents pulling her under. She had never thought brown could be such an infinitely alluring color.

Perhaps expiring in a swirl of caramel and cinnamon wouldn't be so terrible.

Impelled by some unseen force, Edward slowly lowered his head, and all at once his lips were naught but a hair's-breadth from hers.

Her eyes fluttered half shut—

And suddenly flew open as a loud metallic *clink* and *clank* shattered the fluttery silence.

They both jumped back a step.

An instant later, a housemaid clattered around the corner of the bench in pursuit of a rolling kitchen pot cover.

"Sorry, sorry," she squeaked, skidding to a halt on seeing them.

Edward trapped the runaway lid with his boot, and then fixed her and the pile of pots in her arms with a quizzical stare. "Er, might I ask what you are doing in here with those?"

"Umm." Flustered, the maid looked down at her feet. "I, um, thought this was a quicker way to the kitchens, milord."

"You are one of the temporary girls hired for the ball, aren't you?" he asked gently. "If memory serves me correctly, your name is Martha?"

"Y-Yes, milord," she mumbled into the jumble of metal. "I-I shall do better, I promise, if you'll give me the chance."

"The kitchens are in the opposite direction, Martha," he pointed out. "And you need not look as though you've swallowed a mouthful of nails. You're in no danger of losing your position."

The maid dipped an awkward curtsey as he carefully placed the lid atop her pile. "T-Thank you, milord."

In spite of her own jangled nerves, Lily smiled as Martha scurried off in a welter of clinks and clanks. "Poor thing. She seems so very nervous. I take it she has no experience serving in a grand house."

Edward lifted his shoulders. "I don't know where Mrs. Taft found the girls, but my guess is she's never been in service."

Her thoughts quickly moved on from the maid to . . . the kiss? *Had he been about to kiss her?* More likely, her overwrought imagination had taken a wild flight of fancy. Edward had always been the soul of honor—if he was engaged to another lady, he would never be unfaithful to his promise.

And yet, a glance showed a very strange spark still lingering in his gaze.

Caught up in a coil of confusion, Lily turned back to the specimen plants. "And what of your happiness, Edward? Surely you have someone special in your life?"

Lily's question caught him by surprise. "I . . . I do. In fact, I have more than one," he answered, quickly choosing to make light of it. "Mother, Father, Grandmamma"—a pause—"my brother Kim and my sister, Caro." He stopped, aware that his voice had unconsciously pinched to a tight tone.

Lily didn't miss the change. "You speak as if something is amiss with them."

"Kim was badly injured in the war. Now that he's home, he's locked himself in the tower and refuses to see . . . any of his family or old friends," answered Edward. "I'm deucedly worried about him. He seems to have lost the will to live."

She touched his arm. "Don't give up hope. I have seen terrible injuries during my years in India. Such cases often take longer to heal, not only in body, but also in spirit. Love, patience, and time—I think you will find that very potent medicine."

Edward wanted to say that time was the one thing he had let slip through his fingers. "Perhaps you are right," he mumbled.

"Is your sister here? I have not yet met her."

"She arrives tomorrow with her husband. From her last letter I sense that all is not right between them, and well, I fear it is my fault. Piers is an old school friend and I should have pressed harder on them to wait. Caro was awfully young—"

"And she didn't know her own mind?" she said with a gentle wryness.

He gave himself a mental kick. "I did not mean to imply . . . that is . . ." Hell's bells, he seemed to be turning into a tongue-tied oaf around her. And if the confused maid hadn't interrupted earlier, he might have made an utter ass of himself by kissing her.

"I was just trying to tease a smile to your face, Edward," she said. "I know how seriously you take your duties to your family and your lands. But no matter how much you yearn to, you cannot hold yourself responsible for the well-being of others. Happiness is not something that can be wrapped up in fancy paper and satin ribbons and bestowed at will."

His lips quirked, though not upward. "Would that it could."

"Yes, would that it could." Sunlight caught on the curl of her lowered lashes. Was there a hint of moisture making it bead like tiny drops of tawny honey?

Before he could make any sense of it, Lily had turned again and wandered a few more steps deeper into the facing rows of foliage. Pink and purple blooms framed her slender form. Her curves had grown more womanly, and yet the years had not robbed her of the girlish grace that he remembered so well.

As she bent to sniff the flowers, he felt his heart clench. *Lud, she was achingly beautiful.* At that moment, he wished he had consigned all the confounded rules of Society to the devil and kissed her. No matter the consequences.

Sensing his scrutiny, Lily turned. "Forgive me if I am acting a little foolish, but I am still adjusting to the starkness of an English winter. It is nice to have an oasis in which to savor the smells and textures of the tropics."

"I am glad you like it," replied Edward. "I, too, find it calming to come here."

"Do you do so often?" she asked after a long moment.

He shrugged.

The wordless gesture provoked yet another uncomfortable question. "I've prosed on and on about my life. Now tell me about yours. How have you passed the last ten years?"

"Living a very quiet, ordinary life," he replied. *Without you.* "Compared to your colorful experiences, I fear it has been rather dull." As he spoke, Edward found an even more uncomfortable thought creeping into his head. Compared to the bold, colorful men she had met in India, he no doubt appeared rather dull as well. Even if he were not caught in the conundrum with Roxie, how could he imagine Lily would want to renew their old romance?

They had both changed—and he not for the better.

She had wandered to the end of the benches, and now turned to retrace her steps. "Taking on the stewardship of land that has been loved for generations cannot be called dull."

"There are no tigers or elephants in the backwoods," he quipped, "merely foxes and stoats, which hardly excite the imagination."

Lily looked about to reply when the conservatory door swung open and a tentative call interrupted her.

"Your pardon, milord," called the butler. "But her ladyship wishes to speak with you about the flowers for the ballroom."

Repressing an oath, Edward took in a measured breath and answered, "Tell her I shall be there in a moment, Munton." His gaze angled back to Lily, but she was now occupied with examining a bush bearing scarlet-colored berries. "It appears I am needed—though why is a mystery. Mother and Grandmamma have always had very strong opinions on how the decorations should look. May I escort you to the drawing room? There is a blazing fire in the hearth, making a pleasant reading spot."

"Thank you, but I think I shall stay here for a bit longer."

"I shall see you later, then." But in his heart he was sure that somehow he had mucked up the moment, and later would be far too late to make amends.

CHAPTER FOUR

$\mathcal{L}$ily passed the rest of the day quietly, and dinner was a small gathering which demanded no more than the usual polite pleasantries. To her relief, Lady Holly's godson, Lord Gabriel Quinfroy, was both witty and charming, and his bantering with the dowager saved her from having to make much conversation with the people seated next to her. The local vicar uttered nothing more than remarks on the weather, while Miss Finch seemed intent on remaining silent as a mouse—which suited Lily perfectly as she was in no mood for making idle chatter.

The meal was over quickly, allowing the ladies to move on to the drawing room while the men enjoyed their postprandial port. Hoping to avoid having any further contact with Edward, Lily planned to plead fatigue and return to her rooms early. However, as Lady Holbourne prepared to serve tea, the dowager summoned Lily to her chair with an imperious wave.

"Well, ten years abroad seem to have done you no irreparable harm—assuming your flesh is not permanently burned to that nut-brown hue," observed the dowager with a critical squint.

"The color will fade, Lady Holly," murmured Lily as she bent to kiss the parchment-pale cheek. "Alas, the wrinkles will not. But it doesn't matter. No one gives a widow a second glance."

"Hmmph." The dowager gave another low snort, and then beckoned to the countess. "On second thought, I find myself fatigued, and wish to take my tea in my rooms. My goddaughter will assist me upstairs and keep me company."

Lily dutifully offered her arm, though she had a feeling the elderly lady was spry enough to sprint up the curved staircase.

A maid was dispatched to follow with a tea tray, and in short order Lady Holly was enthroned in her favorite berry red chair by the sitting room's blazing fire, a cup of her favorite smoky lapsang suchong warming her frail hands. The fire screen shielding her from the direct flames displayed a finely wrought vase of flowers. But Lily remembered Edward telling her that it could reverse to show a gaggle of half-naked Grecian athletes. A great beauty in her youth, the dowager was still very fond of handsome young men.

"Sit," she ordered, indicating the chair beside her. "And tell me about India."

Lily had repeated the tale often enough on the long voyage home to have refined the account to a manageable list of highlights.

"Interesting," responded Lady Holly when she was done. "You have, of course, omitted all the most meaningful parts. But we shall discuss that at another time. Right now, I am more concerned with your future, not your past."

She forced a smile. "My future is not all that exciting, Lady Holly. I have leased a cottage for several months in Ashington, with the intent of finding a suitable place in the area to purchase. I intend to lead a quiet country life, tending to my gardens."

"Alone?" queried the dowager.

"Yes."

"You are still young and lovely. Why lock yourself away in widow's weeds?" Lady Holly narrowed her eyes. "And do not try to gammon me with talk of pining away for either of your late husbands. I read enough in your letters to know you held them in regard, but did not love them."

Lily did not attempt to argue. Her godmother had always been a sharp judge of character. Perhaps if she had been in London during the time Edward had proposed, his parents would not . . .

"So, for whom are you in mourning?" pressed the dowager. "And don't bother trying to fob me off with fiddle-faddle. I see that look of longing in your eye, gel."

Was it so very obvious? Lily thought she had long ago learned the art of masking her true feelings.

"It can't be someone you left in India—unless, of course, it was a Moghul prince," mused Lady Holly. "So it must be someone from your past. . . ."

Her face must have betrayed some telltale tic because the dowager's gaze sharpened. "What happened between you and Edward?" she demanded. "I've always thought the boy became even more quiet and serious after that Season. Did you break his heart?"

"No!" The word escaped her throat before she could stop it. A ragged inhale served to steady her voice. "If you must know, Edward and I fell in love. He proposed—but Lord and Lady Holbourne thought us too young to know our hearts. They refused to grant him an allowance, and without funds . . ." Lily needed another breath to go on. "Mr. Carrington generously offered to pay off Papa's debts and was willing to overlook my paltry dowry. My parents pressed me to accept his hand, and as he was a kind, decent man, I felt I had no choice but to do as they asked."

The dowager muttered a very unladylike word under her breath. "So, what is standing in the way of your mutual happiness now?"

"Miss Roxanne Hayward," whispered Lily. "Rumor has it the two of them will announce their betrothal at the ball."

"Roxie has spark and intelligence, I grant you that. But I was under the impression she was in love with . . ." Lady

Holly pursed her lips. "Be that as it may, I'm convinced that whatever the agreement, Edward's heart is not in it."

"Even if that were so, there isn't anything I can do about it."

"You intend to give up so easily?"

Lily flinched, feeling the comment unfair. "What would you have me do?" She gave a wry grimace. "If I were in India, I could, perhaps, hire a horde of whirling dervish warriors to kidnap Miss Hayward and sell her to white slavers. But this is civilized England."

Lady Holly sipped her tea, a pensive frown pulling at her mouth. But after several moments, her expression brightened. "You may not have a whirling dervish packed away in your trunk, but I daresay you have another exotic weapon."

"I don't know what you mean—"

"A sari," said the dowager triumphantly. "Wear something sensuously seductive to catch his eye and I promise you, he won't be announcing his engagement to Roxie Hayward."

The suggestion was outrageous.

"Oh, I couldn't," she mumbled.

"What have you got to lose?" demanded Lady Holly. "Save for the man you love?"

Lily looked down into her cup, as if the tea leaves might spell out some words of wisdom. She had always allowed reason to rule her emotions. Did she dare cast caution—and all her carefully constructed defenses—to the wind?

"I—I shall think about it."

"Do." The dowager set aside her tea and patted back a yawn. "I am getting sleepy, and Miss Finch will soon be here to read to me. You may toddle along now."

She rose and gathered her skirts.

"Don't be a fool, my dear," murmured Lady Holly as Lily started for the door. "One doesn't often get a second chance at seizing happiness."

CHAPTER FIVE

$\mathcal{E}$dward rose very early and headed to the stables, determined to distance himself from his inner turmoil by riding long and hard out to the remote reaches of the estate. Not to speak of distancing himself from Lily. And Roxie.

Hell's bells, what a tangle. The coils wrapped around him seemed to be constricting with every passing moment, cutting off air and light.

The hours passed, the wind and sun slapping his skin, trying to breathe some life into his clouded thoughts. And yet, the physical exertion and the natural beauty of the lands he loved, which usually worked wonders to dispel any blue-deviled mood, only left him feeling more dispirited. As he bathed and dressed for dinner, he found it harder and harder to breathe.

He knew what his own sense of honor demanded, and was fully prepared to do his duty tonight at the ball.

But his emotions felt as if they had been stuffed inside a powder keg whose lid had been nailed firmly shut. God forbid if one tiny spark were to flare close by—they just might explode.

Tugging the last fold of his cravat into place, Edward turned from the looking glass and headed down to begin the night of festivities.

Dinner featured a full complement of local friends and house guests seated around the massive table, but despite the flowing wine and cheerful toasts celebrating the fiftieth anniversary of Lady Holly's Christmas ball tradition, he found it impossible to get into the holiday spirit. His sister, Caro, who had arrived earlier in the afternoon without her husband, was flashing smiles, and yet he sensed there was something troubling her. . . .

The muscles in his shoulders tightened.

Roxie, who was seated next to him, seemed equally tense.

Was she having second thoughts?

Edward shoved aside the hope, and tried to make pleasant conversation with the very young lady on his left. To his relief, she was too tongue-tied to respond with anything more than monosyllables—which left him free to brood about Lily.

Lily hurried up the stairs. She had excused herself from the after-dinner gathering in the drawing room, saying she needed a little extra time to dress for the ball. The explanation drew a questioning look from Lady Holly, which she had quickly evaded.

Choices, choices. As her feet flew over the treads, Lily still wasn't certain what to do. Her maid was laying out two outfits—one daring to risk it all, one conceding defeat.

"La, just look at how this feather-light scarlet silk glitters in the candlelight!" As she entered her room, Colleen floated an end of the gold-threaded sari through the air. "Why, it's like a tongue of fire, darting soft as a whisper through the shadows."

"You've been reading too much of Lord Byron's poetry," muttered Lily.

"There's nothing wrong with being wildly, passionately romantic at times," shot back Colleen, adding a last little flutter. "Life would be awfully dull without a blaze of heat to warm yer cockles."

She reluctantly set the sari back on the bed and smoothed out the creases. Next to it lay a traditional ball gown fashioned in a muted shade of smoke-blue silk. "So, have you decided which one to wear?"

Lily picked up a silver box from the dressing table and slowly sorted through her jewelry. "I . . . I . . ." Taking up a long, dangling gold filigree teardrop earring—the pair had been the most exotic ornaments she had ever purchased—she closed her eyes.

"I shall let Fate decide," she said, and then tossed it in a high arc toward the bed.

She waited a long moment before letting one lid open.

"Well, it looks like Fate is a lady after me own heart," murmured Colleen with a grin.

Her maid's hands, noticed Lily, were carefully clasped behind her back.

"We had better start dressing, Mrs. T. It requires a great deal of pleating and pulling to get all the fabric to fall just right." Colleen rolled up the ball gown and shoved it back into one of the trunks. "And a handful of pins."

After a lengthy interlude, Colleen finally stepped back to admire her handiwork. "You look . . . like a goddess straight out of one of them fancy Moghul paintings," she exclaimed. "All the gentlemen are going to drop their teeth in the punchbowl when you float into the room."

"Let us hope not," said Lily dryly. "It would quite ruin the dowager's special mixture of champagne and strawberries." But after mustering the courage to look at her reflection in the cheval glass, she had to admit that the sari was rather striking.

"You don't think it's too flashy?" she asked, setting the silk in motion with a tentative twirl.

"It's perfect," answered Colleen. "It's a special night, and you deserve to set off a few sparks." She reached out and loosened one of Lily's honey-gold curls. "There—now go and dance until dawn."

"I may have to in order to stay warm." The sari bared more flesh than an English ball gown, and in very un-English places. Her breasts were . . .

Better not to look at the front of her sari, lest she lose what little courage remained.

A glance at the mantel clock showed the ball was about to begin. But deciding she needed an interlude alone to compose her nerves before facing Edward and Roxie, Lily took up her matching red shawl and made her way to the library. As she had hoped, it was deserted, though a fire was still burning brightly in the hearth. Wandering to the chessboard, she picked up the ivory queen, hoping it might serve as a talisman, allowing her to draw strength for the coming few hours. Chess, she mused, was an apt metaphor for life—the complicated strategies were all about risk and reward.

"But I must be realistic," she whispered. "It's all very well to dream of fairy-tale endings, but such enchantments rarely happen in the real world."

After a moment, Lily replaced the queen on its square and sat down to study the board. Someone had left a half-finished game. As of yet, it was impossible to see whether white or black held the advantage. Taking up the challenge, she slowly began to move the pieces.

"Have a care. The white knight is in danger."

Lost in thought, Lily nearly fell off her chair at the sound of Edward's voice.

He crossed the carpet, the glass of amber-colored whisky held close to his chest casting deep gold shadows over the intricate white folds of his cravat. His evening clothes were dark as midnight and finely tailored to show off the long, lean lines of his body. He looked so impossibly handsome, the chiseled planes of his face softened by the exquisite drape of the wool and linen.

The perfect English gentleman.

Acutely aware of her exotic clothing and her hopeless longings, Lily suddenly felt like a perfect fool.

Edward took a swallow of the spirits, then set down his drink beside the board. "Let me take a look." His gaze skimmed over the squares, hit the end of the board and slowly lifted.

His jaw dropped ever so slightly. "*What* are you wearing?"

"A sari," she answered. "Lady Holly thought it might add a unique twist to her fiftieth anniversary ball." It was dimly lit in the alcove, and his dark lashes made it impossible to read his expression. "But on second thought, I think I ought to change into a more conventional gown."

As Lily stood up, she heard the hiss of air leaving his lungs.

"Don't," he said in a whisper as soft as the silk. "Grandmamma is quite right. It will make for a memorable evening."

"I have a feeling the ball will be exceedingly memorable, but because of your announcement, not my attire." She somehow managed to keep her voice from quivering. "Again, I wish you joy, Edward. May you and your future bride be very happy together."

He continued to stare in silence.

Sure that she had shocked him to his very core, Lily was desperate to slink away. "I really ought to change. This wasn't a good idea."

Like a moth drawn to a flame, Edward moved closer. Like a flicker of fire rising up from the dark, she seemed to bring a sudden warmth and light to the shadowed space.

"Before you go, let us have a holiday kiss." He gestured vaguely at the unseen ceiling. "I'm sure there is mistletoe up there—they've hung it everywhere. And well, we ought to celebrate the season and our renewed friendship." The echo of his voice sounded a little ragged to his ears. "I—I am very happy to see you again, Lily."

"Our friendship was never sundered," she replied with an inscrutable smile.

"Yes, but you were very far away." *And the wife of another*. "I missed your company."

"As I did yours."

Did he dare hope? "Well then, as I said, let us celebrate the reunion with a kiss."

Edward leaned down and feathered his lips against hers.

Lily flinched, as if touched with a red-hot poker, and then her mouth softened.

The cold clench in his chest gave way to a flare of searing longing. *Of searing love*. He couldn't let her leave the room. *He couldn't let her leave his life*. In that instant he knew he couldn't live without her.

"Lily," he rasped, deepening his embrace. Clasping her close, he reveled in the feeling of her glorious body melting into his.

Two as one. They were meant for each other.

"Lily," he whispered against her skin. "I love you—I've always loved you. Dare I hope you might still care for me?"

She looked up, her eyes shimmering with tears. "My feelings for you have never changed. Never."

Edward framed her face with his hands. "We need not be ruled by anyone's command these days, save for the voices of our own hearts. Please say you will marry me. I can't bear the thought of life without you by my side."

"But—"

"This time, no 'buts' will come between us," he rasped.

Her mouth pinched in confusion. "But Miss Hayward . . ."

"Ah, Roxie." He allowed a wry smile. "It's not me she loves, it's my brother, Kim. But she had lost heart." He went on quickly to explain everything. "Tonight she is determined to make one last try. But however things turn out, she will understand and wish us joy, truly she will."

The shadows clouding Lily's gaze gave way to a luminous light. "Then yes," she said simply. "Yes."

Happiness bubbled up inside him, far more intoxicating than the finest champagne.

"Still, it seems only right that you should let her know before——" she added.

He cut her off with a kiss. "In a bit," he murmured, savoring the ethereal sweetness of her lips. "I've waited too long for this to end it so quickly."

But after a long moment, he reluctantly drew back. "However, you are right. I must find Roxie and explain things to her before we appear together in the ballroom."

"Of course, you must," murmured Lily. "I do hope she will not be hurt. I would like to think we could be friends."

"Perhaps I've become a hopeless romantic, but somehow I believe that love will find a way to conquer all—even the darkness that currently grips my brother's heart." Edward took her hand. "Come, why don't you wait in the conservatory while I go on to the ballroom."

Chapter Six

Lily wandered through the specimen plants, the warm, floral-scented air brushing a gentle caress to her already overheated skin. The light from the overhead brass lanterns was muted by the nighttime shadows, and yet as it flickered over the foliage, the darkness seemed to come alive with a glow of rainbow colors.

The thought of having Edward in her life from now on would light a spark of joy in the deepest gloom of midnight black.

Lost in such happy reveries, Lily moved to a cascading tumble of scarlet bougainvillea. The exotic flower had come to be a favorite of hers in India, its vibrant color always a cheerful tonic when her spirits plummeted. She would, she decided, shift this one to a special place as a reminder that hope should always bloom, no matter how dark the future looked.

"I'm sorry I've taken so long." Sounding harried, Edward pushed through the heavy door, in his haste leaving it slightly ajar. "Roxie's not in the ballroom, and I've looked everywhere I can think of." He joined her by the teak table and blew out a sigh. "I would like to believe it's a good sign. She did say she would be storming the tower and trying to bring Kim back to life. Dare I hope . . . ?"

Lily slipped her arms around his waist. "Hope is a very powerful force."

The tautness around his mouth softened. Reaching out, he plucked a bloom of the bougainvillea and tucked it behind her ear. "You are right—it's a beacon of bright light when all else seems black as Hades."

"Hope, love, and Miss Hayward," murmured Lily. "I doubt any demons will dare stand in their way."

"As for love . . ." Their eyes met and Edward hesitated.

"Yes?" she encouraged, after the silence had stretched on for several heartbeats.

"I—I am not sure I've expressed my feelings clearly enough. Allow me to try again."

Words proved unnecessary. Love had a language all its own.

"You are very eloquent," whispered Lily when after a lengthy interlude he finally released her lips.

His smile sent a skittering of heat down her bare arms. "Actually, I've a great deal more to say." He pressed a kiss to her brow. "But I suppose I had better wait until later. Grandmamma is likely on the verge of marshaling a search party to find us, so we had better go join the festivities."

"You don't want to make one last try at finding Miss Hayward?" she asked.

"I have great faith in Roxie—and it seems I've come around to having great faith in the legendary luck of the family tower." Edward guided her out to the corridor. "Besides, the guests expect an announcement." He cocked an ear. "And I think I hear the musicians tuning their instruments for the next set."

"Yes, I think you're right," said Lily. Or perhaps it was just the fugue of joy playing inside her head.

As he took her hand and led her toward the rising sound of the music, her emotions were spinning in dizzying circles. Everything seemed to blur together as they entered the ballroom—the festive evergreen garlands, the brightly colored gowns, the floral perfumes, the curious stares.

Lily blinked to clear her gaze and saw Lady Holly sitting

in her place of honor. The brilliant sparkles of light from the crystal chandeliers glittered overhead as their gazes met.

The dowager gave a tiny wink. *A silent salute?* Lily flashed a grateful smile and then Edward placed a steadying hand on the small of her back, turning her with a flourish into the first figures of the waltz.

Time stood still. The years fell away. The only thing that mattered was the perfect harmony between them. All her doubts, all her fears seemed to melt away. In his arms she felt like liquid fire. An elemental flame burned bright in her heart, spreading warmth and light to every fiber of her being.

Love.

"I love you," she whispered.

Their palms pressed together, Edward twined his fingers with hers, basking in her glow as joy chased away the darkness that had shadowed his spirits for a decade.

"I love you." Three small words, filling an immeasurable void.

Round and round they spun. Silk rippling, folds flaring, Lily was a bright blaze of color, the gold-threaded scarlet fabric trailing a flicker of rose-tinted sparks in her wake.

His mother, who was standing by the dowager's chair, began to fan herself.

The other guests had slowly stopped dancing, and the buzz of voices was beginning to rise above the notes of the violins.

"Everyone is staring," murmured Lily. "Perhaps we ought to stop now and announce the news to dispel the idea that you are marrying Roxie."

"My love, after seeing us dance together, I don't think anyone here is the least confused as to whom I am marrying," drawled Edward. "But Grandmamma would be disappointed without a Grand Gesture."

A signal to the musicians brought the melody to an end.

"I think I need a glass of champagne," said Lily faintly, after a glance around at all the expectant faces.

He plucked two glasses from the tray of a nearby footman and placed one in her hand. "I have a special announcement to make, but before I do, I would first like to propose a toast."

The whispering ceased.

"To Lady Holly, to family," continued Edward as he turned in a slow circle to salute everyone in the room. "To friends, to the spirit of Christmas, and to—"

His gaze reached the entrance, where the double doors were open wide, and suddenly his heart leapt into his throat, making it impossible to speak.

Kim. And Roxie clasping tight to his arm, a delightfully rumpled pillar of support.

Shock gave way to a surge of pure joy. "Kim!" he cried, finding his voice as his brother gave him a quick thumbs-up, their brotherly signal that all was well.

The others in the room all turned to follow his gaze. His mother cried out and darted forward—and then suddenly Kim and Roxie were engulfed in a sea of well-wishers.

Edward drew Lily closer and softly clinked his glass against hers. The frothy fizz bubbled over, and they both laughed.

"And to Love," he finished, before pressing a champagne-sweet kiss to her lips.

A SEASON FOR MARRIAGE

❧

Nicola Cornick

CHAPTER ONE

London, December 1815

*L*ady Caroline Camden, pretty, witty and rich, with a beautiful home in London and another in the country, a happy disposition, and a handsome husband, had lived nearly twenty years in the world and most people would have said she had very little to distress or vex her.

Little did they know.

This afternoon was an excellent case in point. Caroline had gone shopping, as she was wont to do just about every day except for the sabbath, but matters were not going to plan.

"I am very sorry, madam," the modiste said, and Caroline could tell that the woman was on the contrary not sorry at all, "but I can extend you no further credit. Mr. Camden has announced that he will no longer honor your debts."

Caroline felt her face burn with humiliation. The shop was full, of course, full of the matrons and widows of the *ton* and their debutante daughters all madly purchasing new clothes for the Christmas season. Out of the corner of her eye—because she most certainly could not look them *in* the eye—Caroline could see their covert smiles and spiteful glances. She knew that in one hour—less than an hour if Lady Royston was present—Town would be buzzing with the news of her disgrace. The scandal sheets would be speculating that she had bankrupted her husband.

She turned on her heel and made for the door, eyes straight ahead, head held high. She had not really wanted the puce silk gown anyway. It was very aging, much more Lady Royston's sort of thing than hers.

She did not trouble to visit Madame Duval farther down Bond Street, nor Madame Devy, nor the perfumier nor the milliner. She knew her reception would be the same at all the shops. Her husband, Piers, was nothing if not thorough. No shop in London would offer her credit now.

"Perhaps there has been a mistake, my lady," Pershore, her maid, said timidly as, empty-handed, they ascended the carriage steps.

"I don't think so," Caroline said. "Mr. Camden does not make mistakes." But he had, she thought. He had made an enormous mistake when he had married her.

She could vividly remember the night it had happened. She had been nineteen and had already had two Seasons without attracting a suitor who met her exacting requirements. She had not lacked offers; there had been fourteen in all. None of them, however, could match Piers Camden, friend of her elder brother Edward, with whom she had been in love since she was old enough to understand what love meant.

That summer night she had been sitting on the steps of the family home, Holbourne Abbey, trying not to cry because she had overheard her father telling her mother in exasperated tones that if she did not accept one of her suitors soon, he would betroth her to Lord Drysdale with or without her agreement. There was a ball going on, a beautiful, exciting, summery occasion and she had never felt less beautiful, excited or summery in her life.

Piers had found her outside and asked if he could help her.

"No," she had said tragically. "No one can help me."

Piers had smiled then, that attractively rakish smile that always made her heart turn over, and had sat down on the step beside her. "Tell me," he had said.

To her surprise she had told him everything: how Lord Drysdale was old—at least forty—and already a widower, and how he had hungry eyes and a wet mouth. How she knew she had to marry well, but that she would rather enter a convent than marry Lord Drysdale.

"Have you found a suitable convent?" Piers had asked.

"No," Caroline had said. "There are no suitable convents in Northumberland."

His eyes had gleamed with amusement. "That is probably for the best. I don't think you have the temperament for the religious life."

"But I had also thought I might take a governess post," Caroline said eagerly.

"Another startlingly bad idea," Piers had said. He had shifted a little beside her, running one hand through his thick, dark hair. "I am sure this is all a misunderstanding, Lady Caroline. Your parents, I am persuaded, would do nothing so Gothic as to marry you off if you were unwilling."

"I heard them talking about it!" Caro burst out. "There is no mistake." She had started to cry and Piers had proffered his handkerchief and then somehow—she was not at all sure how it had happened—her parents had rushed out onto the terrace accompanied by Lord Drysdale, who was furious, and various other guests, who were everything from shocked to curious, and everyone wanted to know what she was doing out there in the dark with Piers. She supposed it *had* looked rather scandalous because they were sitting close to one another and Piers had an arm about her and was wiping the tears from her eyes, but even so there had been no need for him to propose to save her reputation.

Her parents, naturally, had been delighted. Piers was

young, only six or seven years older than Caro was herself, handsome, rich, and the heir to a barony. He was her brother's friend. It was a perfect match.

Except that it was not.

It was a match born out of honor. Caro had felt hideously guilty. Piers had shown her kindness and she had repaid him by trapping him into marriage. When she had told him she did not wish him to feel obliged to wed her, he had told her that she should feel no guilt; theirs would be a good match. It all sounded dreadfully passionless and cold. When Caro had gone to her mother and tried to back out of the arrangement, Lady Holbourne had told her in the kindest but plainest terms that if she did so she would be ruined. So here she was six months later in a marriage of supposed convenience where the biggest inconvenience was that she was hopelessly in love with a husband who barely noticed her.

With a tiny sigh, Caro sat back in her seat and watched the streets of London roll past the window. Dusk was starting to fall, even though it was barely three o'clock. There was a scattering of frost on the bare branches of the trees in the squares. Everything looked cold and a little bit lonely, and she gave an involuntary shiver.

Caro knew it made matters much, much worse that she was in love with Piers. She knew he did not love her. He had wanted no more than an aristocratic alliance and a hostess for his political dinners. True, he had consummated the marriage, but the experience had not been a success. Stricken with guilt, she had lain as still as a board when he had made love to her. It had been mortifying. Afterwards, Piers had brushed the hair away from her face and kissed her gently and said: "You need time. We will wait."

She had not wanted time. She had wanted forgiveness for compromising him into marriage. She had wanted him to love her as she loved him. Her heart cried out to him for that love, but all he offered was kindness, and somehow that seemed to make matters worse.

Piers had not come to her bed again. She had tried to broach the subject with him once or twice, but he brushed the matter off. There was always a reason, always an excuse. He was very busy. He spent all of his time working. Caro felt as though she had become one of his causes. Piers's life was dedicated to helping others. Barely a day seemed to pass without his establishing a new school for the poor or a hospital for the indigent sick. Admittedly, he did not usually wed his charity cases, but it felt as though her marriage was based on the same principle of duty and sacrifice that motivated him in his other work.

The carriage jerked to a halt outside their town house in Cavendish Square. Everything looked uncommonly pretty with a powdering of snow on the street and the lanterns giving a warm twinkle to the chilly air. Not that Caro was in the mood for Christmas cheer. Now that Piers had withdrawn his funds, she could not even dress well to perform the one part of her role she thought she had perfected, that of elegant political hostess. She had only been so profligate in her spending to please him. She had so wanted him to be proud of her. Younger than all the other matrons, she had tried at least to appear poised, buying confidence from the modistes.

She was so angry that she marched straight into Piers's study without waiting for Portland, the butler, to announce her.

Piers was seated at his desk in the window. The last of the late afternoon light gleamed on his thick black hair, burnishing it with shades of rich chestnut. There were lines about his eyes and mouth that Caro had not noticed before. She wondered suddenly if he was as unhappy as she and her stomach felt hollow at the thought.

Not that that was any excuse for his ungentlemanly behavior. She drew herself up to her full height, which was an impressive five feet nothing.

"Why are you refusing to honor my debts?" she demanded.

Piers looked up and his dark, dark eyes met hers. Caroline's heart gave an errant thump. It was so lowering to be desperately in love with one's own husband when he preferred to spend time with his government papers to spending time with her.

He raised his brows very slightly.

"Good afternoon to you, too, my love," he said. "I hope you are well."

They seldom saw one another so he would not know if she was in good health or if she had contracted typhus. The realization lodged another cold shard in Caroline's heart. She made a quick gesture dismissing his enquiry. "Well? My debts?" Her voice was sharper than she intended because of the sting of the words. *My love.* Never had an endearment rung so empty.

"I will of course honor your debts," Piers said.

Caroline released her breath in a huge sigh of relief. Pershore had been right; it was no more than a misunderstanding.

"However, I will advance you no more money," Piers continued. "You will have to wait until your next quarterly allowance and try to make it last better this time."

His gaze was unnervingly direct. Caroline felt as guilty as she had at the age of fourteen when summoned before Mrs. Blanket, headmistress of Mrs. Blanket's exclusive seminary for young ladies, for sliding down the main staircase on a wooden tray. She had done that to garner attention. She had cut a swathe through Piers's inheritance for the same reason, but only because she wanted him to notice her, to be proud of her, to approve. She had tried her best with this inconvenient marriage, had tried to assuage her guilt by doing all she could to please him.

Yet still he rejected her efforts.

Even now it was clear he was bored. His fingers were beating an impatient tattoo on the pile of documents on the desk. She could tell he longed to be rid of her. She felt her heart shrivel a little more.

"I cannot afford you, Caroline," Piers said. "You are too expensive for me."

"You make me sound like your coach and four," Caroline said.

Piers smiled. "There are similarities. You are very elegant—"

"And highly bred," Caroline said. "With clean lines and marvelous upholstery." She could not quite keep the bitterness from her voice. She had thought Piers would want a wife with high polish. He was ambitious, already a junior minister in Lord Liverpool's government. She was doing her best to support him.

"I really do need a new gown for Lady Aston's ball next week," she said. "You said yourself that it is an influential event—"

"I am sure you will find something suitable in your wardrobe," Piers said. "You will look delightful."

His words reminded Caroline precisely why men should never be consulted over matters of dress.

"I cannot wear something I have worn at a previous engagement," she said. "Everyone will notice." By which, of course, she meant every female guest, and they were the only ones who mattered.

Piers raised an indifferent shoulder. His hand had strayed to the paper on the top of the pile before him. Reading upside down, Caroline could see that it was headed "proposed laws for the restriction of shooting game." Evidently, he preferred the plight of pheasants and partridges to hers.

"Very well," she said, drawing her tattered dignity about her. "I shall do my best, of course."

She went out. Piers did not appear to notice. That, she thought, was precisely the problem.

Upstairs in her bedchamber she kicked off her shoes, then remembered that they were made of very delicate French silk and if Piers really was not going to fund her in future she could not afford to damage them. There would be no more where those came from. No more shoes, no more gowns, bonnets, scarves, or gloves. She would have to make do.

She crossed to her closet and wrenched open the door. A cacophony of gowns shouted for attention from within, gowns in every shade of the rainbow and in every style that was fashionable. She could arrange for some of them to be altered so that she could wear them again, but the ladies of fashion who attended the same social events that she did would still recognize them. It was humiliating.

Abruptly, she sat down on the edge of her bed. She knew this was not really about clothes, or money, or even Piers's career. It was about love. Piers had married her out of a sense of obligation. That made her unhappy. So she had tried to please him by being what she thought he wanted: a trophy of a wife, a dazzling hostess. Yet it made no difference to how Piers felt about her. It was a lost cause.

She stood up, suddenly restless. Something had to be done. Her grandmother, the redoubtable Dowager Countess of Holbourne, would doubtless tell her that no cause was hopeless and she should devise a plan. And already she had an idea, but to put it into practice she needed some help. She knew just the person; her godmother, Lady Eleanor Noel, one of her grandmother's oldest friends, was currently in London and would surely be prepared to advise her.

Caro crossed to her writing box and taking out pen and ink, sat down to write.

* * *

As soon as the door had closed behind his wife, Piers Camden threw down his pen, spattering ink across the pile of papers he had been trying to concentrate on for the past several hours. In the beginning, he had found his work a useful distraction from the problems of his marriage. These days, however, he found little solace in the endless wearying business of government. All his ambitions, all his plans, seemed hollow if his marriage to Caroline was unhappy and unfulfilled.

Marriage, in fact, had not been remotely as he had imagined it would be. His decision to wed Caro had been a rational one based on mutual profit. For a couple of years he had been thinking vaguely that it would benefit him to have a wife. He needed a hostess to help promote his political career and Caroline, pretty, well-bred, and elegant, seemed an excellent choice. He had been foolish to compromise her—he and Caro's brother Edward had been sharing some excellent brandy that evening and perhaps it had affected his judgment—but since he was not averse to marrying, it did not really matter. And he liked Caro, of course. He liked her a very great deal. It seemed an ideal match.

That feeling did not outlast the wedding ceremony. He had seen Caro coming up the aisle on her father's arm looking both radiant and a little bit shy. Her fingers had trembled as she put her hand into his. And then she had smiled at him.

He had seen that smile before.

It was the smile he had seen on his mother's face as she had gazed up into his father's eyes, a smile of such love, such trust, that he felt himself turn to ice, for he knew the damage such love could do.

Caroline loved him. He had not realized.

He did not want her love.

The difficulty was that it was too late. There and then he had felt an odd sort of shift in the region of his heart, a fierce protectiveness and a desire to make her happy. The sensation had been unexpected, disturbing, and unwelcome. Aristocratic marriages should be business arrangements as far as he was concerned. His parents had made a spectacular love match and it had consumed them. One of the reasons Piers had spent so much time at Holbourne growing up was because his parents were utterly engrossed in each other to the exclusion of all else. He and his sister had been an irrelevance, important only as proof of their parents' love.

Piers shuffled his government papers impatiently. His latent feelings for Caro were a weakness. He could not allow himself to love her or he would be as vulnerable as his father had been, a man profligate in love and with his money, a fool and a laughingstock. Reginald Camden had had no self-control. He had been the type of aesthete who had worshipped at the feet of his wife and wept at the beauty of a flower. Piers shuddered at the thought.

Not that he was indifferent to Caro's attractions. She might not be a statuesque beauty, but she had fine glossy dark hair and very expressive brown eyes. When he had first known her, she was always smiling. It had been her warmth and sweetness that had first drawn him to her. These days she smiled less and less.

His hand strayed towards the brandy bottle, but he knew that was no way to settle his problems. With another sigh he returned to the papers on his desk. His work was his mistress now.

CHAPTER TWO

"Lady Eleanor Noel." Portland opened the door of the music room with a grand flourish and bowed the visitor inside. Caro, who had been sitting at the pianoforte rather listlessly playing a sonata by Haydn, jumped up as her godmother swept into the room.

Lady Eleanor was fabulously wealthy, splendidly outspoken, and completely unconventional. She was a tall thin woman with a beaked nose and determined expression. As a child, Caro had been terrified of her. It was only as she grew older that she had come to see the kindness beneath Lady Eleanor's terrifying exterior.

"Good gracious, it is like a funeral in here!" Lady Eleanor exclaimed, twitching back the drapes to allow the winter sunlight to flood in. She embraced her goddaughter. "You look peaky, my love," she commented, with all the tactlessness of an old family acquaintance. "You are only nineteen; far too young to be so haggard. Besides, it is almost Christmas—a time of joy!"

"The sun is rather too bright to be kind today," Caroline said by way of excuse. She did feel haggard and not in the least joyful. She had not slept all night for loneliness and misery. She wondered if Piers would remember that it was Christmas in a couple of weeks' time or whether he would see it merely as an irritating interruption to the political calendar.

"I suppose it is Camden," Lady Eleanor ploughed on, ignoring her. She tossed her reticule onto the table and subsided into a wing chair. "I heard about his financial troubles. Everyone has. They say you have bankrupted him with your extravagance."

It had occurred to Caroline that her attempts to shame Piers into opening his wallet might give rise to such widespread rumors, but now she felt ashamed, wincing to think that the scandal might damage his political standing. She had not wanted to ruin him, only to make him pay attention to her.

"There's no truth in the gossip," she said. "Piers and I had a small disagreement about money. I have been trying to . . . persuade him . . . to increase my allowance."

"By shopping as though it is going out of fashion?" Lady Eleanor regarded her with indulgence. "That seems very unlike you, Caroline. You have never been extravagant." She tilted her head to one side, observing her goddaughter thoughtfully. "I dare swear there is more to this than your desire for seventeen gowns in the same shade of pink—so tell me, what is really going on?"

Caroline sat down abruptly. "I was trying to look . . . older," she admitted. "More authoritative." She raised her gaze to meet that of Lady Eleanor. "I know I am very young in comparison to the wives of Piers's colleagues and I wanted to impress them—and to make Piers proud of me."

"But he is!" Lady Eleanor looked surprised. "Everyone has observed it. Why, Sally Jersey was commenting only the other day how he dotes on you!"

"Lady Jersey must be confusing me with some other person," Caro said dryly. "I think that Piers holds me in dislike."

Lady Eleanor's brows shot up. "I should be *astonished* if that were the case," she said. "Whatever gave you such an idea?"

"He avoids me," Caro said. She had been bottling up her

feelings for a long time and now they all came pouring out. "We are like strangers. We barely see one another. I think he cannot forgive me for compromising him into marriage."

"Pshaw!" Lady Eleanor said energetically. "No such thing. Has he said so?"

"No," Caro admitted. "We do not discuss it. We talk about nothing but the weather and the food cook serves. And that is only when Piers joins me for dinner. Often he is at the House or at his club. I have tried to talk to Piers about our marriage, but he rejects all my attempts."

"Does he come to your bed?" Lady Eleanor asked bluntly.

"No." Caro blushed at her godmother's outspokenness. "He did—once. It was not a success."

Lady Eleanor's brows, already high, now disappeared into her hair. "Well! I would have trusted Camden not to make a mess of *that*," she said disapprovingly.

"It was my fault," Caro said. "I felt so guilty and miserable for trapping him into marriage that I think he believed I had a disgust of him. And now it does not matter what I try to do for Piers rejects any attempt I make to draw closer to him."

Lady Eleanor gave an exasperated sigh. "The two of you have woven a tangled web indeed." She eyed her goddaughter thoughtfully. "You said that you needed my help, my dear. What can I do?"

"I would like to borrow a carriage and four, if you please," Caro said.

Lady Eleanor smiled. "Would you, indeed! What for?"

"I am running away," Caro said bluntly. "I need to shock Piers. He will never listen to me whilst we are here in London, for he will always have the excuse of burying himself in his work. But if I can lure him away, I can confront him about our marriage and—I hope—have a last chance to put matters right."

"You are a woman after my own heart." Lady Eleanor's

eyes gleamed with amusement at her goddaughter's determined expression. "And where might you be going?"

Caro got up and crossed to the window. Already the shadows were lengthening, the short winter's day past its peak. She would need to go soon if she were to make any distance before nightfall.

"I am going home to Holbourne Abbey," she said. "I am going to the Christmas ball."

The clock on the Church of St. Andrew's was chiming two as Piers Camden arrived home after a long evening discussing the Corn Laws with some of his political colleagues. He was cold and bone weary and wanted nothing more than to sleep. As he entered the darkened hallway and was struck by the absolute silence of the house, he was also struck by an odd sense of loneliness. He realized that he did not want to sleep, at least not alone. He wanted Caroline. He wanted to talk to her, laugh with her, make love to her, lie with her curled up at his side. The realization turned him cold with horror. This had been his father's weakness. Seduced by intimacy, seduced by love, Reginald Camden had been unmanned. His son could never show such frailty.

"Good evening, sir." Portland was approaching him like a ghost in the sepulchral gloom of the hall.

"For heaven's sake, Portland." Piers tried not to take out his frustrations on the man. "There was no requirement for you to wait up for me. Get to your bed."

"I have a letter for you from Lady Caroline," Portland said. "It is most urgent. She said I had to deliver it to you as soon as you returned."

"I'm sure it could have waited until the morning." Piers divested himself of his coat and gloves and took the note the butler was proffering. He grabbed the candle from the table, taking it into the study, where he threw himself down in a chair and unfolded the note.

My dearest Piers . . .

He sat back.

I am leaving . . .

He sat bolt upright, heart suddenly pounding.

*For a few weeks in the country. You may recall that a
month or so ago my mama wrote to invite us to the
traditional Christmas ball at Holbourne Abbey . . .*

Piers did not recall it at all. He searched his memory but
the detail remained tiresomely elusive. He knew that there
was always a Christmas ball at Holbourne. He had attended
a number of them before he and Caro had been married.

We did discuss the possibility of attending this year . . .

Had they?

*But, alas, you considered yourself too occupied to
spare the time for a trip to Northumberland.*

Had he? He ran a hand through his hair again in exasperation, making it even more disordered.

*I, however, have very little to occupy myself if I am not
shopping . . .*

Was that sarcasm he detected?

*And so I have set off today. Pray do not be
concerned—Lady Eleanor Noel has loaned me her
general factotum, the most marvelous fellow called
Shepherd, who is taking care of every last detail of the*

journey and my comfort. I have Pershore with me, too. It is all perfectly safe and respectable. I wish you a very Happy Christmas, Piers, and will see you when I return.

Piers ground his teeth. Perfectly respectable it might be, but he could just imagine the speculation when his wife arrived at her parental home without him. Already there were rumors flying over a rift in their marriage. Lady Royston had been quick to spread the story of Caro's humiliation. Piers had been furious. He was even more furious now that Caro had added fuel to the fire by running away.

His conscience smote him. He knew he had neglected Caro shamefully. He had been cold and aloof because he had not wanted her love. He had not wanted to hurt her, but inevitably he had done so.

Leaping to his feet, Piers dashed out into the hall where Portland was waiting, still as a piece of statuary.

"Portland, send to the livery stables for their best horse," he said, cursing the fact that he kept no stable of his own in London. "I want to be ready to leave within the hour. I am going to pack a bag."

"Will you be traveling alone, sir?" Portland was impassive.

"Yes." It would be quicker to ride than to take a carriage, Piers thought, and much quicker not to take his valet, who was maddeningly slow and precise in everything he did. This was perfectly fine in the tying of a neck cloth, but not in the rush to catch up with Caroline on the road.

"The livery stables will not be open for a number of hours, sir." Portland nodded to the clock, whose hands stood at a quarter past two.

"Then make them open!" Piers snapped. "This is an emergency." He took the stairs two at a time.

The butler's voice stopped him on the landing.

"The weather threatens snow, sir," Portland said.

"Thank you," Piers said politely. He supposed that snow in December was no surprise and it certainly was not going to stop him from pursuing his errant wife.

CHAPTER THREE

*C*aroline's journey north progressed smoothly. Shepherd was a treasure. At every change of horses there was a fresh team waiting. At every inn, there was hot food and chocolate or coffee if she wished it. The beds were comfortable, which was fortunate since some heavy snowfall had made the roads slower than normal. They had no major problems, however, and thus it was Caro arrived at Holbourne Abbey on the evening of December twenty-eighth.

As the carriage rolled up the long drive, Caro saw the house ahead at the top of the slope, lit up so brightly that it seemed to gleam with joy and hope. Snow was falling now, gently, languorously, dusting everything with a glittering whiteness. Even the old tower, the only bit of the ancient castle that remained, looked like something from a fairy tale. Caro felt a lump come into her throat, nostalgia and longing all mixed up together. This was her home. She had forgotten how much she had loved it here.

For a moment she wanted everything to go back to the way it had been before she had married Piers. She wanted to start over again. But she could not. She had to go on. She hoped that her plan was going to work and that Piers would come after her. She had half-expected him to overtake them on the road, but he had not and with every mile that passed her spirits had fallen a little lower. If Piers did not come, then she would know that he truly was indifferent to her and she would not get the opportunity to put matters right between them in the way she wanted.

The carriage drew up in front of the main door, which swung open with joyous alacrity, spilling light outwards to draw her in. Caro could see Munton, the butler, waiting. He looked just the same, a little more portly perhaps, a little grayer, but so familiar and reassuring that she felt another pang of longing for the past.

"Lady Caroline," Munton said, "welcome back to Holbourne Abbey." Not by a flicker of an eyebrow did he express any surprise to see her so unexpectedly.

"I hope you are keeping well, Munton?" Caroline said. "I am sorry to arrive unannounced and throw you all into confusion."

"It is always a pleasure to see your ladyship," Munton said grandly. He summoned a couple of footmen to help Shepherd with her luggage. Their green-and-gold livery looked very festive, matching the swags of greenery that decorated the pillars of the hall. There was an air of suppressed excitement about the house. It seemed she had arrived just in time for the ball.

And here was her mother, dressed for dinner in blue silk and diamonds, hurrying forward to greet her.

"My dear"—she kissed Caro's cold cheek—"how lovely to see you!" She looked around as though expecting to see Piers lurking behind some statuary, then drew Caro to one side, behind one of the grand pillars that soared up to the landing. Guests were starting to arrive for dinner and it was clear to Caro that her mother did not want to make a scene in front of them.

"Caro—" This time her mother was whispering, a very quiet murmur in her ear. "What is going on? Why are you here? Where is Camden?"

"I am here because you invited me," Caro said. "You wrote several months ago to tell me about the ball. And Piers will be . . . joining me later."

She crossed her fingers behind her back and hoped as hard as she could that Piers would appear.

"Is that true?" The countess's voice had dropped still further to a sibilant whisper. "Even here we have heard the rumors, Caroline. They say you have run through Camden's fortune to the point that he cannot even afford to clothe you. It is the latest *on dit* at every dinner table in the county!"

She might have known, Caroline thought. Scandal traveled as fast as the best horse in the stables. If Piers did not arrive, the gossip would become deafening. She felt a cold knot of fear lock tight in her stomach.

"Mama!" She put a soothing hand on her mother's arm. "The rumors are quite false, I assure you."

"Well, I hope so." The Countess's gaze scoured her face. "You look tired, my dear, and more than a little washed out. Perhaps"—she brightened at the thought of minimizing the latest scandal—"you would prefer to take a quiet supper in your room after such a long journey? Although, I do not know which room that will be for Mrs. Tremaine has your old bedroom and Mrs. Taft will be quite beside herself to learn she has to find additional space—"

"I would not dream of missing supper and the ball," Caro said firmly. "If I might wash and change in your room, Mama, I shall be ready and downstairs and out of the way to give Mrs. Taft the time to find me somewhere to sleep. Now"—she gave her mother a gentle little push—"you have guests arriving. Please do not worry about me."

With one long, thoughtful backward glance, Lady Holbourne walked away and Caroline beckoned to Pershore and went up Holbourne Abbey's imposing stair. The house was gloriously decorated for Christmas. Swaths of greenery gave a wonderful fresh scent to the air. Red berries and ribbons gleamed amongst the boughs of pine, rosemary, and mistletoe.

She was the last guest to be seated for dinner, but she arrived before the first course and counted that a triumph. It was clear that her arrival had been accommodated at the last minute as she was squeezed in between Andrew Wright, son of one of her parents' neighbors, and her father's secretary, Mr. Wolverton.

"Well, miss," her grandmother the dowager countess said tartly as she took her seat, "this is an unexpected pleasure. We hear tales of your racy life in London. Come to empty your father's purse, have you, now that you've run through Camden's fortune? And where is that handsome husband of yours?"

Caro squirmed a little. Her grandmother never hesitated to call a spade a spade and was forever meddling, but she was kind of heart and Caro could see the spark of anxiety in her eyes. Like everyone else, the dowager was worried that Piers had banished her for her extravagance. And since there was still no sign of him, Caro began to wonder if he really had washed his hands of her.

One of the other guests, Mrs. Tremaine, tactfully came to her rescue with a question about the weather on her journey. Caro, despite her own preoccupations, noticed that her elder brother Edward cast frequent glances across the table at the elegant Lily Tremaine. He seemed to be taking an inordinate amount of interest in her, which was curious since Pershore had already told her that the gossip in the servants' hall was that Edward planned shortly to announce his engagement to Roxanne Hayward, their neighbor of many years. Roxie had given Caro a cheerful little wave of greeting as she had come into the room, but Caro thought she looked very pensive and not in the least like a woman who was happy about her future. And as Roxanne had once had a *tendre* for Caro's younger brother Kimball, it seemed all the more odd. Love, it seemed, was playing havoc with them all this Christmas.

The courses came and went, the conversation ebbed and flowed. Caro painted on a bright smile and tried not to wilt. Her gamble had failed. Piers had not followed her.

The sound of voices from outside the dining room cut across the conversation within and for a moment there was a lull as everyone tried not to gawp at what was going on. Then Caro heard a step in the doorway, a familiar, impatient step and a familiar deep voice:

"Thank you, Munton. I'll announce myself."

Caro looked up, her fork clattering from her hand.

There in the doorway was Piers, dark, disheveled, the expression on his handsome face hard and remote as his gaze swept around the table to pin her to her seat.

CHAPTER FOUR

$\mathcal{P}$iers knew he looked unforgivably bedraggled to be arriving directly into his hosts' dining room, but he could brook no further delay. He had had the most appalling journey. He had fallen in a snowdrift twice, his horse had gone lame, he had been obliged to hire a carriage and then one of its wheels had come off in a frozen rut. He had tortured himself with the thought that if he had had such a dreadful journey, then Caro must have suffered equally. Perhaps she was marooned in an inn or benighted in some cowshed, sheltering from the weather. If he got to Holbourne and found her missing, he vowed to venture out immediately to rescue her. . . .

"Mr. Camden!"

Munton was not to be cheated of his announcement. As he stood back and Piers entered the dining room, he saw Caroline at once. She was not marooned, benighted, or bedraggled. On the contrary, she looked dazzling. Gone were the rather aging gowns he had been accustomed to seeing her wear at dinners and balls throughout the past six months. Instead, she was radiant in a stunning silver gown that seemed to caress each curve, shimmering and sparkling as she moved. She paled a little on seeing him and dropped her fork, but she covered up the lapse quickly enough, raising her chin, meeting his eyes, a spark of something intriguing, something challenging, in her own.

The air between them hummed with awareness. Piers blinked, standing riveted to the spot, staring at Caro until the dowager countess cleared her throat very pointedly.

"Well, Camden?" she said. "Are you going to keep us all from the rest of our dinner by standing there dripping on the floor? Sit down, man, sit down!" She applied herself to her beef with renewed vigor.

"My dear!" Caroline said sweetly. "How glad I am to see you. I hope you did not have *too* difficult a journey?"

There was a glimmer of amusement in her eyes as she took in his state of disarray. Piers almost growled as he bent formally to kiss her smooth cheek.

"Not in the least, thank you," he said. He was startled by a powerful and entirely inappropriate urge to drag Caro into his arms and carry her out of the room to settle their differences in the most fundamental and satisfying way possible. He blinked, wondering what on earth was the matter with him.

He realized that the dowager countess still had her beady eye on him—in fact, everyone was watching him—so instead of following his baser instincts, he was obliged to apologize to the company for his late arrival and to Munton for upsetting the seating plan. The elderly chaplain, who was seated next to Caro, swept his apologies aside as he stood to make way for him.

"There is no difficulty at all, sir, I assure you. I have eaten very well already."

As he settled himself next to Caro, Piers found that he was seething—with relief and frustration and less definable emotions. Pulling himself together, he found himself faced with a plate of beef and a lady on his left who introduced herself as Mrs. Lily Tremaine. She was showing a lively interest in the byplay between him and Caroline. Across the table his old friend Edward glowered at him in a somewhat unnerving fashion, as though in speaking to Lily he was committing some cardinal sin.

The long and elaborate dinner continued. Piers doubted that he did justice to any of the courses for they all tasted like ashes in his mouth. He was exerting himself to be courteous to the delightful Mrs. Tremaine whilst simultaneously being utterly distracted by Caro on his other side. He imagined that he could feel the warmth of her body. He definitely did feel the brush of her arm against his and the slippery slide of her silken-clad thigh against his leg beneath the table. The gown seemed to be working some sort of perverse enchantment on him. He was so accustomed to seeing Caro bundled up in high-necked creations with voluminous skirts that the clinging sinuousness of the silver gauze fascinated him, as did the swell of her breasts above the modest edging of lace at the neckline.

The ladies withdrew. Caro left with one long, unreadable backward glance at him that made Piers feel quite hot. He had no idea what was wrong with him. All he knew was that somehow the balance between himself and Caroline had changed and he felt uneasy and not in control. Either that or his fall into the snowdrift had given him a fever.

The port circulated. There was some conversation of a political nature. His opinion as an MP was widely sought. He hoped to heaven that he had made sense. Finally, the gentlemen rose to join the ladies. Piers felt an inordinate sense of relief. At last he would be able to get his wife to himself and they could talk.

"Glad you were able to join us, Camden." Edward caught up with him in the doorway, offering his hand. He lowered his voice, his tone clipped. "Everyone is aware that matters are somewhat awry between yourself and Caroline. I suggest that you smooth them out as swiftly and discreetly as possible."

And he walked off, leaving Piers staring after him.

When Piers entered the drawing room, it was to find that Caro was playing the piano and singing softly, a sweet counterpoint to the buzz of conversation about them. Piers recognized the melody as an old Northumbrian folk song, "The Oak and the Ash." It sounded sad, and his heart gave an errant lurch to hear the poignancy in her tone. Had he made her so very unhappy? He had thought that they would deal well together. It was a shock to realize that his judgment had been so flawed.

Caroline played the last chord and the room broke into a smattering of applause. "We must have a duet before the ball begins!" the Countess of Holbourne exclaimed. "Caro, darling, will you and Piers sing for us? A carol would be lovely."

"I am afraid that Piers does not care for music," Caroline said, before Piers could agree. "We have not been to a single concert nor recital since we wed."

Piers was silent. Caro was right, of course; he knew that she was extremely talented at both playing and singing, and yet over the past six months he had never encouraged her to indulge her love of music. He remembered visiting Holbourne in years past and hearing Caro as he passed the schoolroom door, her voice soaring, effortlessly beautiful. The memory felt bittersweet. When had he lost that open pleasure in Caro's accomplishments? Was it when he had realized that she cared for him, and had run from that emotion like a coward?

He stepped forward, intending to offer to join her, but already Caro was bending a dazzling smile on Andrew Wright. "I know you have a fine voice, Mr. Wright, for I have heard you sing in church. Would you care to sing with me?" She held out the sheet music for "Christmas Day in the Morning." "We are a little late," she said, "but we may still celebrate."

Piers subsided, glowering, into a chair at the countess's side. "Caro is so kind," Lady Holbourne whispered. "She knows how shy Mr. Wright can be and wishes to draw him out."

"How generous of her." Piers gritted his teeth as he watched the bashful young man bend a worshipful glance on his wife. Wright did indeed have a fine tenor voice, but Piers did not enjoy listening to it much, nor did he like the way in which Wright was smiling at Caro with such obvious pleasure as their voices entwined.

"Delightful," Lady Holbourne enthused, tapping her foot in time to the music.

The song came to an end and the audience applauded enthusiastically this time. Wright was bowing gallantly to Caro, kissing her hand. Piers repressed a growl. Caro looked flushed and pretty and very, very desirable, her eyes sparkling and one tendril of hair escaping from her elegant chignon and curling in the hollow of her throat.

Unable to keep still a moment longer, he leapt to his feet. "Caro—"

As Caroline turned towards him, Lady Holbourne laid a hand on his arm, restraining him. "It would be splendid if you and Caro were to open the ball, Piers, but I think perhaps"—her gaze assessed him critically and clearly found him wanting—"you really do need to change into something *clean* first." She glanced at the clock. "You have a few minutes to spare. . . ."

"Of course," Piers said, smothering the impatience he felt. Out of the corner of his eye he could see Caro moving towards the door on Andrew Wright's arm. "If your housekeeper would be so good as to show me which room I will be in," he said, "and if Edward could perhaps lend me his valet—"

"Of course," Lady Holbourne said. "I am afraid that Mrs. Taft is run off her feet but Caro will be able to show you. The two of you will be sharing a room for we are monstrous short of space. I do hope"—she looked dubious—"that arrangement will be satisfactory?"

Piers had the pleasure of seeing Caroline stop dead in her tracks. The look she cast at him was suddenly a great deal less assured.

He smiled at Lady Holbourne. "Indeed, ma'am," he said smoothly. "That will be delightful."

CHAPTER FIVE

"I can sing," Piers said, falling into step beside Caro as she led the way towards their room. There was a note of chagrin in his voice. Caro hid a smile.

"Can you?" she said lightly. "I do apologize. I did not realize." She had known full well that Piers had a very good voice. She could remember each and every childhood theatrical they had performed together at Holbourne, the songs they had sung, the fun they had had at summer festivals and winter caroling. It gave her a pang of sadness to remember those long ago days and all the ease in each other's company that they had lost.

"I must have forgotten," she said, "since you have shown no interest in music these six months past. Besides"—she flashed him a sweet smile—"Mr. Wright was more than happy to oblige me."

"So I observed," Piers said, an edge to his voice.

Caroline kept the smile painted on her lips. This was not the time or place for a private conversation: housemaids scurried across their path, footmen passed by with trays and harried expressions. But a touch of jealousy was no bad thing, she supposed, even if poor inoffensive Andrew Wright was the target of Piers's wrath. Certainly, she had succeeded in jolting her husband out of his complacency. He was here—he *had* followed her, just as she had hoped. Even better, he was no longer sure of her, no longer in control. It was extremely gratifying, but it also felt rather dangerous, as though she had a tiger by the tail now.

She repressed a shiver.

"We are in the Green Bedroom." She gestured to a corridor that turned off to the right. After the bright lanterns and Christmas sparkle of the hall and stairs, it seemed dark and a little gloomy. "Though I cannot imagine why you need my guidance, Piers," she added. "You have been visiting Holbourne this past age and know the house as well as I do."

"Perhaps I simply wish for your company." Piers's voice had hardened. "After all, I have come a long way for it."

Caro's heart jumped at his tone. He sounded as though he expected an apology from her and she was damned if she was going to offer one. Could he not see that she was the one with a grievance? He had shut her out, rejecting all her attempts to draw close to him. If she had chosen to eschew the dubious pleasures of a Christmas alone in London whilst he attended to government business, and had preferred a family Christmas in the country, then surely that was understandable.

"There was no need for you to join me if you did not wish to do so," she said stiffly. She could feel her fragile hope of developing a better understanding with him melting away like the snow in the spring. How foolish she had been to think there could be something stronger between them, if not love, then at least a mutual regard. They seemed always at daggers drawn.

"No need?" Piers stopped dead and turned to her. In the shadows of the corridor she could not read his expression. "Our marriage is already the *on dit* from here to London," he said grimly. "How would it have appeared had I *not* come?"

"It would have appeared exactly as it is!" Caro lost her temper. "It would have appeared that you dislike me!"

Piers had gone very still.

"I beg your pardon?" he said. He was looking at her as though she were quite mad.

"Our chamber," Caro said, ploughing on determinedly, "is here on the right—"

Piers brushed her direction aside. "What did you mean by that?" he said. He looked impatient, demanding, and formidably annoyed. Caro felt like stamping her foot.

"You dislike me!" she repeated. "Can you pretend otherwise?" She put her hands on her hips and stood up very straight. "You make it quite clear that you prefer politics to everything else, Piers. You spend endless nights at your club or in the House. You only speak to me when you wish me to attend a political dinner with you. You behave as though spending any time in my company is akin to torture—"

Piers took a step towards her and Caro stepped back instinctively, feeling her back come up against the door. The handle dug painfully into her waist. Somehow Piers had trapped her between his body and the panels. He was so close that Caro could feel the brush of his leg against her skirts and suddenly she was overwhelmed by his physical proximity. Her throat turned dry. Her heart hammered.

"You *can't* deny it!" she finished, trembling a little. "You dislike me!"

"Your deduction is false." Piers's lips were suddenly very close to hers. "Just because I avoid you, it does not mean that I dislike you."

"Oh." Caro was very definitely trembling now.

Piers laughed, short, unamused. "Let me demonstrate to you just how much I dislike you, Caro," he murmured.

His kiss was like no other he had given her before. It was hard and demanding, full of passion and heat and desire. Caro's head spun. It was like her wildest dreams, better, the pent-up longing of the past mingling with the excitement of the present. Piers was holding her now, his arms close about her, and she was glad because she was not at all sure her legs would hold her up.

He nudged her lips apart and then his tongue was tangling with hers and suddenly she was swept away by hunger and desire and kissed him back in full measure. Little tingles like licks of flame sent shivers along her skin. His lips brushed the sensitive hollow beneath her ear, making her gasp. His tongue traced a path lower, flicking into the base of her throat and lower still, touching the lace that edged her bodice. It was delicious, wicked pleasure.

His mouth returned to hers, plundering, seeking, and she felt the spiral of desire ache and tighten inside her.

When he finally let her go, they were both breathing hard.

"Sweet Caro," he murmured. "Surely you cannot believe I dislike you?" He cupped her face in his hands. His touch was gentle, his eyes tender. "I thought that I had given you a disgust of *me* by coming to your bed. I thought you found my embraces distasteful."

"Oh, Piers!" Caro touched her fingers to his lips. "You cannot surely still think so?"

His eyes were dark with desire. He was looking at her mouth. "No," he said hoarsely.

"I was only so still and cold because I was stricken with guilt for compromising you into marriage," Caro said. "I was certain you must blame me for trapping you."

Piers seemed to find no better response to this than to kiss her again, a course of action with which Caro wholeheartedly agreed. She slid her arms about his neck and gave herself up to the kiss, lost in a sweet, sensual haze.

"I love you," she whispered, against his mouth.

She felt the change in him at once. It was only the slightest hesitation, a sense of withdrawal, but it was enough. She drew back. His expression was blank now, utterly unreadable.

Caro felt a chill envelop her, like the rush of icy air when a door opened. She could see she had made a mistake. She had not thought for one moment to dissemble her feelings for Piers. She was too open to pretend and she had been too swept away by her feelings to be anything other than honest anyway. Yet now she saw that just because Piers desired her, it did not mean that he loved her. Men, she had heard, were adept at separating physical love from emotion, whereas she could not unravel her feelings for Piers even if she wanted to.

For one long agonized moment she stared at him and saw the regret in his eyes. He knew he had hurt her. He was sorry for it. But that was all. And it was not enough.

Someone cleared his throat nearby, a loud, deliberate sound that had them both jumping apart.

"Excuse me, sir." Edward's valet, a bowl of hot water in his hands, was standing a mere four feet away. "If you are ready . . ."

"Thank you." Piers touched Caro's cheek. "You are well?" he asked softly, the words for her alone.

Caro nodded. "Very well. Thank you." But she was not. Of course, she was not. She felt as though her heart had broken all over again.

Piers bowed. It felt very formal all of a sudden. "I will join you directly, Caroline."

The door closed behind them. Caroline was left alone. Her heart was still racing from the kisses they had exchanged and she pressed a hand to her bodice as she tried to calm her breath. It was odd to feel so excited and yet at the same time so utterly bereft. Her thoughts seemed cold and strangely objective. She wondered whether in future she would feel better or worse when Piers came to her bed. They could have a physical relationship that was exciting and full of intimacy and yet it would always lack love. There was a hollow feeling of loneliness beneath her breastbone at the thought.

She turned towards the stair and the light and chatter of the ball below. Down in the hall were her parents standing beneath the mistletoe bough. They had not seen her and for once on this busy night, they were alone. As Caro watched, she saw Lady Holbourne put both her hands into those of her husband and stand on tiptoe to press a kiss against his cheek. The candlelight reflected the happiness in her eyes. Lord Holbourne smiled down at his wife and then he put his arms about her and they sped away back to the ball, as light of step and happy as young lovers.

Caro felt a lump in her throat. *That was love,* she thought, the enduring joy they took in each other's company, come sickness or health, riches or poverty, building a life together. That was what she wanted, and she wanted to give that gift to Piers, too; she wanted to build a family with him and experience the shared joy, the love. But would he take that from her? Could he learn to love her, or was it too late?

He had hurt her again. He had not intended to but he had hurt her nonetheless and he felt like a cad. Caroline was so generous with her love, so sweet, and so giving. There was no artifice in her. She loved him and so she had told him. It was as simple as that. Yet once again he had rejected her love.

It seemed to take Piers an inordinate amount of time to dress for the ball. He was in an agony of impatience to find Caro again. He was afraid she might have gone off alone somewhere to lick her wounds, but in that he was mistaken. As he entered the ballroom, he saw her twirling through a country-dance in the arms of a rather sturdy gentleman who looked as though he suffered from the gout. Caro was smiling and giving him her entire attention and the gentleman looked dazzled, as well he might.

As Piers watched the dance came to an end and Caro thoughtfully steered her wheezing companion to a rout chair before stopping to chat with the lady sitting on his left. She had a smile for everyone. She knew them all and clearly she cared about them and their affairs: the families, the children, the Christmas festivities, the weather. She had a word for everyone and an easy charm that set them smiling in return. It made Piers feel inordinately proud of her.

She looked up and caught him watching her, and for a moment she stilled and the happy light died from her eyes. But then she smiled at him and Piers felt his heart shift and an odd sensation make his chest tighten. He did not seem able to help himself. His rational mind warned him to beware, that he was slipping into dangerous waters, but his heart did not seem to care.

Caro's next partner arrived to claim her for the set that was forming and Piers watched again as she lit up the dance, sparkling in her silver gown, exuding a light and warmth that drew everyone to her like moths to the flame.

He cut Andrew Wright ruthlessly out for the next waltz.

"Really, Piers," Caro said, as he spun her into the dance, "there is plenty of space on my dance card. You need not have been so precipitous."

"I could not wait," Piers said, without apology. "You draw all eyes, Caro. Is that a new gown you are wearing tonight? You look different."

Her smile cooled. "No, it is not. I have not spent any more money, if that is what you mean."

Piers cursed himself for a clumsy fool. "I meant only that you look beautiful," he said truthfully, "but it is different from the style you have previously chosen."

"I was trying to look older before," Caroline said baldly. The dance swept them onward, their feet moving automatically in time to the music but neither of them concentrating on it now. "All the political events we attend are very daunting. I wanted to"—she paused—"to make a good impression."

Piers sensed something wistful behind her words. He glanced at her face, but she looked quite serene.

"You always made a good impression," he said. "Everyone has remarked upon it. Why would you doubt it?"

"Because you never told me so." Her candid gaze rose to meet his and his heart lurched. "I was trying to please you, Piers," she said with devastating simplicity. "I dressed to please you. I knew you needed an elegant hostess and so I tried to make you proud of me."

Lord, but she was making him feel uncomfortable tonight! Piers acknowledged it ruefully; acknowledged, too, that there was no reason why she should pander to his feelings. He had chosen to shut her out. He had rejected the intimacy she craved from him, not because he wanted to punish her but because he had been too much of a coward to risk loving her. He knew he had to take responsibility for that.

"Caro." His voice sounded husky. He cleared his throat. "I am so very proud of you. I want you to know that. I realize now that I haven't been kind—"

She stopped him with a touch of the hand. "You are the kindest man I know," she said softly. "You do so much to help others."

Yet he had failed his own wife.

There was silence between them. The music swooped, lilting and romantic, and they moved through the throng as though in a separate world.

"Tell me"—Caro's voice sounded conversational and she was smiling for the benefit of the other dancers—"was there ever a time that you felt you belonged here, Piers? You spent so much time with us—did you ever see Holbourne as home?"

"No," Piers said. It felt as though time was rolling back and he was the child, fresh on holiday from Eton, looking through the Holbourne bannisters at the family scene below. He had seen what Edward and Kim possessed, the love of hearth and home, but it was alien to him.

"I don't feel as though I have a home," he admitted. "I

was very young when my parents died and although I was my uncle's heir . . ." He stopped.

"It was a material inheritance," Caro said softly, "not an emotional one."

He felt devastated by the truth of that. He was materially wealthy but it felt hollow without something—or someone— to add warmth to his life.

"My parents were madly in love." He spoke gruffly. It did not feel like a non sequitur but suddenly, desperately important. He had spoken of this to no one. People knew the facts, not the feelings behind them. "My father doted on my mother. He loved her to the exclusion of all else. When she died, he could not deal with the grief. He took his own life."

"I'm so very sorry, Piers." Caro's eyes were full of kindness. It was not pity, he realized. He would have shrunk from that. No, Caro was watching him with understanding and compassion, and suddenly he wanted to crush her to him and slake all his loss and grief in her sweetness. But first there was more to say. He had to be honest now, as honest with her as she was with him.

"I grew up to spurn that sort of love." The words were wrenched from him. "For me it meant nothing but misery and weakness and a loss of control."

"I understand." Her touch on his arm was still gentle, as though she took his words for the apology he wanted them to be. "You have seen only the dangerous side of love, the obsession and the damage it can do. Yet, you should not be afraid to love, Piers. You are not your father. You are a different man. And love is worth the risk of loss." A rueful smile touched her lips. "I know that to be true."

He understood what she meant. She had dared to risk loving him, had continued to do so in the face of his rejection, and now she was still offering him that love no matter how little he deserved it.

"I think you are almost too loving, my darling Caro," he said roughly. "I cannot bear to see you hurt."

"Oh, Piers." Caro had her arms about him. It was not an accepted part of the dance, but suddenly he did not care. Everyone was staring at them. He did not care about that either. All he wanted was Caro and the solace she could give him.

"Come with me," he whispered, his lips brushing the delicate tendrils of hair that framed her face. "I need you."

She did not hesitate. She slid her hand into his and together they walked across to the door, ignoring the curious stares and the stifled whispers, up the stair, along the gloomy corridor, into the warmth and light of the Green Bedroom where the fire burned bright in the grate. Caro felt light and fragile in his arms and yet at the same time she was the strongest and most precious thing he could ever wish for. He reached for her greedily, needing her, taking with an eagerness that bordered on desperation, his kisses fierce and urgent. She responded with the generosity he recognized in her now, holding nothing back, returning caress for caress. And in the end, when at last he abandoned all fear and simply lost himself in her, he heard her tell him again that she loved him and this time he did not run from it. This time it felt good and right and true.

CHAPTER SIX

Caro opened her eyes. She felt warm, sated, and very wicked in the most delightful way imaginable. The night had been everything she had longed for—passionate, tender, and exciting. After the initial urgency of their lovemaking had been satisfied, they had lain entwined in tenderness, talking a little, kissing, as the fire died down and the shadows took them. Then they had made love again and this time Piers had devoted himself to her pleasure, such pleasure as she had never imagined. Caro thought that perhaps her grandmother was right. Marriage was indeed an ideal state.

She rolled over and realized that she was alone. Piers was sitting on the edge of the bed with his back turned towards her, head bowed. His dark hair was tousled. She felt such a wave of love for him then that it almost stole her breath. She wanted to touch him, to pull him back down into her arms, to lose herself again in their newfound happiness. Yet there was tension in the line of Piers's shoulders. She caught a glimpse of his profile as he half-turned towards her. His jaw was set in a grim line.

Cold anxiety breathed goose bumps down her spine.

Not again. Not now.

She had been so sure that he loved her, too, even if he had not said the words aloud. He had shown it in every touch, every kiss.

She put a hand on his bare shoulder. He felt warm and vital, his skin smooth beneath her fingertips.

"Piers? Is something wrong?"

He turned to look at her. There was such desolation in his face that it felt as though her heart snapped in two. She had allowed herself to believe that all would be well now. She had thought Piers loved her in the same way that she loved him—wholly, deeply, completely. Yet he looked stricken, hardly the expression of a man in love.

Her hand fell to her side. There was something about his rigidity that forbade her touch. There was such misery in his face and yet such longing, and in that moment she saw the child behind the man, the little boy who had seen his father ruined by intemperate emotion, who had lost any vestige of a family that he had known, and did not want to risk loving and losing again.

Swiftly, following instinct, she wrapped her arms around him and drew him close.

"I love you." She spoke firmly. "I love you, Piers, and I know that you love me."

She saw the flash of emotion in his eyes, deep, disturbing, infinitely satisfying. He did love her. He loved her as fiercely as she loved him. Emboldened, she ran her fingers along his jaw, and kissed him. He did not move away. That encouraged her.

"Tell me," she said.

For a moment she thought he was not going to answer her, but then he took her hand in his, his fingers tightening convulsively around hers.

"I don't want to lose you." He sounded hoarse. "I never thought I would feel like this." He pulled her to him and held her as though he would never let her go.

Against the warm skin of his throat, Caroline smiled. "You will not," she said. She thought of the lonely little boy who had come to Holbourne Abbey for the first time as a child. "You will not lose any of us," she said. "You are part of our family now."

"I loved you from the start," Piers said against her hair. "For so long. You were like a flame that drew me, so warm and so bright and so loving. I wanted that love for myself, but at the same time I was afraid to claim it in case I lost it." He smiled, but there was sadness in it. "My beautiful, bright girl," he said. "I don't deserve you."

"Now you are just feeling sorry for yourself," Caroline said, smiling to soften the briskness of her words. "Who was it who let me tag along with the boys' games, who taught me to ride, who rescued me when I got stuck up a tree? You even rescued me from marriage to Lord Drysdale." She cupped his face in her hands. "What is life without risk, Piers? What is love without loving wholeheartedly?" She kissed him softly, sweetly. "I love you with all my heart, holding nothing back for fear of hurt."

For a moment he looked down into her eyes and then he was kissing her, with passion and demand until her head spun and she tumbled back down into the engulfing bedcovers with him.

"Darling Caro—" His lips were pressed against her throat, sending delicious shivers over her skin. "I love you like that, too—truly, madly"—he kissed the hollow at the base of her throat—"deeply and forever. I cannot help myself."

It was a very long time before they spoke again. Caro, lying sated and very happy in his arms, turned her head against Piers's shoulder to look at him. The lines of weariness and grief had gone from his face. He opened his eyes and they were soft and drowsy with sleep. He smiled at her and she saw her own love for him reflected in his eyes.

They had been abed so long that the pale light of a winter dawn was creeping around the bed curtains.

"I suppose we should go down for breakfast," Caro said

with a sigh, "although I am tempted to hide away and have mine here. I have no great desire to be berated for my shocking lack of conduct at the ball last night."

"Coward." Piers kissed her bare shoulder. "I will be with you. And besides"—he smiled—"I suspect that there will be plenty of other matters to talk about. There was more than one romantic entanglement developing at the ball."

Caro's eyes opened very wide. "Really? How exciting! Who?"

"Did you not see Edward dancing with Lily Tremaine?" Piers asked. "Or Kim appearing with Miss Hayward?"

Caro's mouth dropped open. "But I thought Edward was to marry Roxie? And I did not even know that Kim was here!"

"I fear we have been very wrapped up in our own concerns," Piers said. "So even if there is some disapproval of the way in which I hurried you away to ravish you, I am sure that everyone will be happy for us. Your mother will scold, but beneath it all she will be glad we are reconciled, and your grandmother—"

"Will say she always maintained that marriage was the best and happiest state in the world," Caro said, giggling. She reached for her wrap and slipped out of bed, padding across to the window in her bare feet. "It has been snowing again. How very pretty it looks, all fresh and bright!"

Piers had come to stand beside her, his arms about her. "It is a time of new beginnings," he said. "Happy Christmas, my darling wife."

MISS FINCH AND THE ANGEL

Jo Beverley

CHAPTER ONE

December 26, Boxing Day

*F*our steaming horses swept the post chaise up the slushy drive of Holbourne Abbey and were halted by their postilions, snorting and stamping, before the impressive pillared entrance. Liveried footmen hurried out, their own breath white in the crisp air, to open the carriage door and extract luggage from the boot.

First emerged a black-clad valet. Then followed a fashionable young gentleman in a many-caped buff greatcoat and a glossy beaver hat set at an exact angle on golden hair. He regarded the house, smiled slightly, and strode forward to climb the steps.

"A pleasure to see you, Munton," he said to the portly butler who stood waiting in the entrance hall to take his hat and gloves and pass them to a liveried footman.

"And you, my lord. May I offer season's greetings?"

"I'm sure you may," the young gentleman said pleasantly. "All in order?"

"In general, my lord. Mr. Kimball still chooses a contemplative life."

"Even at Christmas?"

"Indeed, my lord, but the ball will take place as usual."

"Of course, it will, especially as it's the fiftieth. Where will I find Lady Holly?"

"In her rooms, my lord."

Lord Gabriel Quinfroy nodded his thanks and surveyed the hall, which was lushly decorated with greenery that scented the air with bay, rosemary, and pine. So typical of the Stretton family to plunge so generously into Christmastide. He was well accustomed to Holbourne and the Stretton family. The Dowager Countess of Holbourne was his godmother, and he was distantly related to the family, so he'd paid many, long boyhood visits. His father, the Duke of Straith, had not thought his "spare" should become too attached to his home, which had suited Gabriel to perfection. Holbourne was much more fun. He left the hall and ran lightly up the wide, carpeted staircase.

Soon he rapped at a door and was summoned to enter the dowager countess's domain. She'd been known to the world since her marriage as Lady Holly—sprightly, beloved, but not without spines, which could even draw berry-red blood if she was outraged.

The old lady sat enthroned in a berry-red chair by the fireside, shielded from the direct heat by a fire screen depicting a scene that involved half-naked Grecian athletes. He knew that if she was minded to present a different impression, it could revolve to show a vase of flowers.

Thespia Holbourne had been a beauty in her youth and known for her saucy ways. She was a beauty still, in her way, with a plumply wrinkled face, clear blue eyes, and frothy white hair beneath a lacy cap, which he saw with amusement was now trimmed with a sprig of mistletoe.

He obligingly went over to kiss her cheek.

"So you came," she said.

"You commanded, dear heart."

She snorted. "It must have suited you."

"It did. Crampton's bride was trying my temper, and

quarrels are so very unseasonal, don't you think?" Crampton was his older brother, heir to the dukedom of Straith.

He subsided elegantly onto a sofa at a distance from the roaring fire, glancing once at the slender lady who sat to one side quietly stitching something plain and white. Her simple, high-necked gown was in an odd shade he could only think of as mouse-gray, and her plain cap revealed nothing more than that her hair was straight and brown.

"Don't know why he married her," Lady Holly said and he turned back.

"Forty thousand pounds," he said. "All my fault, of course. Uncle Milius left me his fortune, but until Father joins the angels poor Cramp must subsist on the income from the heir's estate. So he's married money. Now, tell me why you summoned me. Kim?"

He referred to the younger son of Holbourne, who'd been wounded in the war in more ways than one, and who, he'd been told, was living a hermit's life in the medieval tower still attached to the classical modern house.

"If you can do anything to the purpose there, I'm sure we'd all be grateful. They say time heals, but it's being demmed slow about it. No, I bade you here for other charms."

"My dearest dear, you want to set me up as your flirt!"

"Impudent puppy! Though if I were thirty years younger and not your godmother . . ." She waggled a beringed finger at him. "You're too attractive for anyone's good."

"It does *me* good," Gabriel pointed out mischievously, and shot another glance at the mouse. He caught her in a frosty glare, but she immediately looked down. Who was she? A distant dependent of the family? If so, someone should dress her better. Where was the jolly Miss Bunting, Lady Holly's friend and companion since he'd been a grubby urchin?

"I asked you here," the dowager said, "to enhance the charms of some young ladies who will attend the ball."

He stared. "Enhance? You think I'm a dancing master?"

"I'm sure you could be if you waste your all."

"Devil a bit."

Did his language cause a stir to his left?

"I have taken an interest in some young ladies, and I wish you to bring them out a bit. Make them blush. That always does a girl good. Why so many refuse to use rouge these days I've no idea. Help them to relax and show to greatest advantage. I'm hoping at least one will find a husband. Merely being asked to dance by you will raise their appeal."

"Only with idiots. There's more to choosing a wife than snatching another man's fancy. Money, for example. I assume your charity cases have none."

"None or very little," she admitted.

"Beauty?"

"Not to any remarkable degree." Lady Holly was known for her eccentricities as well as her enthusiasm for Christmas, but this seemed an odd start all around. "Every gel should have at least one grand ball," she stated, "if only to remember. Wearing a pretty gown, flirting with eligible gentlemen, and only sitting out if she needs to catch her breath. For these, it might be their last chance to attract a suitor."

"I never knew you had such a romantic heart."

She pursed her lips at him, but then admitted, "I was mainly thinking of a goddaughter of mine, who seems likely to go off into servitude. But I didn't want Alice to look particular, and when I considered the matter I found another worthy case. Miss Langsdale."

"And I'm to make them show to good effect on the market stall. Very well, but in case your plan is devious, note that I will not marry either of them."

"I hope they'd have too much sense to consider it. You're a rake and a rascal and will never make a good husband. A scholar or clergyman will probably suit for my gels, or a gentleman of modest estate. I've made sure all the suitable ones in the locality will attend."

If they were local people, the suitable gentlemen would already know the last-chance ladies, but perhaps his god-mother's plan would work on some. To see a Plain Jane blushing, smiling—and yes, the chosen partner of a rake and rascal who was also the wealthy son of a duke—might open a man's eyes.

He rose. "With such exertion before me, I must find whatever corner has been urgently cleared for my repose."

"The Angel Room, of course."

One of the finest guest rooms, correctly called the White Room, but known as the Angel Room because it had a ceiling painted with cherubs. When he'd reached the age to have a room outside of the children's area, he'd chosen it and always used it when he visited.

"You were so sure I would come?" he said.

"Was I wrong?"

"You're a witch, I'm sure." Aware of chilly disapproval as much as of the hot fire, he asked, "Where, pray, is the delightful Bunting?"

"Ha!" his godmother exploded, mistletoe jiggling. "Run off with a man. At her age!"

He laughed. "Bunting eloped? Good for her."

"Miss Bunting married in the chapel here, in perfect order."

That was the gray mouse, voice cool as the water one might pour over a drunkard's head.

"All the same, good for her."

"Abandoned me," Lady Holly complained. "Now I've . . ." She stopped what she'd been about to say, probably out of kindness. "Now I have the pleasure of Miss Finch's companionship."

Joan Bunting had been a cheerfully trenchant lady of about forty who'd been the perfect foil for Lady Holly's eccentricities and whims. Gabriel felt little optimism about the Finch's future. Another charity case, he was sure, and none of his concern. Yet, as he left the room, he glanced back at her again, and was disappointed not to catch her in another disapproving stare.

He strolled along the corridor toward his room, needing no one to show him the way. Pity about Kim. He'd find out more from Edward, Holbourne's heir. He'd always rubbed along with Edward and Kim much better than with his own brother, the Marquess of Crampton. Always Crampton. Any use of his baptismal name, James, had been sharply discouraged, but here Viscount Brentford was comfortably Edward to the family.

A passing maidservant flickered him a smile and he winked at her. She giggled and hurried on, and yes, her blush had made her prettier for a moment.

"So you came when summoned."

Gabriel smiled to see Edward. He was lean and dark and could appear a sober sides, but he was a good friend with a lively sense of humor. "I was pleased to escape."

"Family still as frosty? Have you just arrived? Come to my room for refreshment."

They were soon settled in Edward's bedroom, which was large enough for a substantial desk and some bookcases, but cozy with two well-worn leather armchairs and a small sofa. When he'd been moved into it at sixteen, they'd all tagged it the "heir's lair."

"I've drinks," Edward said, waving to a selection of decanters. "Need more solid sustenance?"

"I paused to eat."

"Care to try some Scottish whisky?" Edward picked up a decanter. "Gift from northerly relatives."

"Is it civilized?" Gabriel asked dubiously.

"Try for yourself." Edward poured for them both and they took the chairs on either side of the large fireplace.

"The Setons were supposed to be here for the ball, but they've sent their apologies. Weather."

"Yesterday I wasn't sure I'd make it here." Gabriel sniffed at the liquid in his glass and was encouraged to take a sip. "Not bad. It's not cognac. . . ."

"And couldn't be expected to be. I like the smoky notes. It's more substantial."

Gabriel toasted him and took a larger mouthful.

"So, life at Straith?" Edward asked. "I heard Cramp married."

"To forty thousand, which unfortunately came attached to Lady Juliana Pole. She looks around the place so avidly, I fear she'll slip rat poison into Father's soup, and she disapproves of me."

"The Pole family is rather strait-laced."

"Pole up the arse, as some have said. But her main grievance is my money, not my morals. Enough of that. Tell me about Miss Bunting and Miss Finch."

Edward chuckled. "Such a turmoil. I think Grandmamma tried to put some spokes in the wheels, but once it was settled she was too kindhearted to make difficulties, and dear Bunting positively bloomed. Odd really, when her beau was gone fifty, fat, and bald, but it's a love match."

"Delightful to think that even when we're fat and bald ourselves, there'll still be hope."

"Hard to imagine you reaching that stage."

"You think I'll die of dissipation first?"

"I think, like your father, you'll become all bone and sinew, and retain your hair."

The idle chat was pleasant enough, but Gabriel found himself wanting to know more about the Finch.

"The new companion," he said. "Will she last?"

Edward grimaced. "No love match there. Mama's tried to hint Miss Finch to a livelier wardrobe and manner, but to no effect. Of course, having taken her on, Grandmamma won't dismiss her, but it's not a happy situation."

"Lady Holly should recommend her to someone else and give her a good reference."

"But she won't. Don't know why."

"Perhaps she hopes to bring joy into her life. Any idea where the Finch flew in from?"

"Herefordshire, I think. Solid gentry family, recommended by one of Grandmamma's old friends who knew she'd take in a waif."

"Waif?"

"Has to be."

"An orphan of impoverished parents," Gabriel speculated, "left without the means of survival. In that case, she'd do better to be obliging."

"People can't change to suit. It seems my fate to be responsible, and your fate to be . . ."

"Not?" Gabriel supplied without offense. "If you mean I lack responsibilities, I agree, but those I have I respect."

"And most of us envy you the lack of burdens. Do you have nightmares about Crampton dying?"

"Many. I rejoiced at his wedding and will throw a grand party when he has a son. An even grander one for a second. I can't imagine why anyone who's comfortably situated wouldn't dread such high rank and responsibilities."

"To have the rest of the world grovel," Edward said bluntly.

"Unpleasant, but true." Gabriel dragged the conversation back to where he wanted it. "So you think Miss Finch was born to be a blight on every feast?"

"Too harsh. Rather, I'd say, born to be invisible."

Gabriel had not found her that. "If she were invisible, she wouldn't be blighting Lady Holly's life. She has a gray presence."

"Is that why you're here? To brighten the gloom in Grandmamma's life?"

"After a fashion, but it's to do with other burdensome

spinsters—the ones she's invited to the ball for their last chance at wedded bliss."

Edward groaned and topped up their glasses. "That. We all predict disaster."

"What inspired her? It being her fiftieth Christmas ball?"

"Perhaps. A remarkable record. The first one was when the king was sane, the Colonies ours, and Versailles still a pleasure palace."

"When the roads were atrocious, smallpox ravaged, and we would have had to wear powder and paint. We live in better times. Why will Lady Holly's plan lead to disaster?"

"If her protégées had been going to find husbands in the area, they would already have done so. And neither of them is accustomed to a grand occasion. It'll be a shame if they're awkward."

"Behold, my part. I'm to put them at ease, charm them into blooming, and make them trophies in other men's eyes."

"Be careful, or one of them'll hook you!"

"I'm well accustomed to all the ploys—but what of you? You have the duty to wed."

Edward shrugged, but he looked away. Did he have something to hide? An unsuitable attachment? Gabriel remembered that years back he'd had a notion that Edward had formed an attachment to someone unsuitable, but if so, it had been a temporary flicker of irresponsibility. If he'd done it again, Gabriel would do his best to support and encourage. Suitable brides were so damned tedious.

"Perhaps Lady Holly is hoping an atmosphere of romance will inspire you," Gabriel teased. "Is Miss Finch another of her last-chance ladies?"

"Finch? No."

"Why not?"

Edward opened his mouth, and then shut it. "No point, surely. Dull thing."

"But," said Gabriel, "if a fever of romance brought her a suitable offer, it would solve a number of problems, wouldn't it?"

"By gad, it would. You think you could make her appealing?"

"No squint, warts, or humped back. She's not beyond all hope."

"Lay you a monkey you can't do it."

"Done," Gabriel said, smiling with anticipation.

CHAPTER TWO

*T*wenty sat to dinner that night. Ten were the permanent household of family and high-born attendants, only lacking Kim. The rest were relatives and close friends invited for the Christmas season.

Gabriel noted that Miss Finch had been seated some distance from the dowager. Not a good sign. She was between the elderly chaplain and a plump gentleman who was principally interested in the food. She seemed content.

All the same, he caught her looking at him once, though he couldn't read her expression. She'd changed out of mouse gray into a dull shade of green he couldn't begin to describe. Surely it hadn't been dyed that color on purpose so it must have been reduced to it through time and laundering. The neckline was somewhat lower than her day dress, but filled by a fichu which might even be starched. Yet again her hair was beneath a plain white cap.

Get thee to a nunnery, mouse, if you're so determined not to play the game.

But then he noticed that a tendril of brown hair had escaped whatever pins she used to discipline it. Gently, it curled against her ear.

He smiled as he turned to pay attention to Lady Garway. She had been a Stretton, and was worldly-wise and handsome. All the same, he'd rather have had Roxie Hayward by his side. She was opposite, next to Edward, lucky fellow.

Roxie was a neighbor and when they'd been children she'd tagged along on their boyhood games as often as she'd been allowed. She'd grown up into a lovely woman, spirit untamed, and Gabriel was surprised she hadn't been snatched up. As well as her charms, she owned a large estate.

When the meal was over, the ladies left, but the gentlemen didn't linger beyond an hour. No one seemed inclined to talk politics, and Lord Holbourne had never encouraged disreputable talk. The port passed generously, but their host rose before anyone slid under the table or, worse, would be staggering when they joined the ladies.

Gabriel strolled into the drawing room to find the ladies sitting in groups and Lady Garway playing the piano, very well. His quarry was sitting at a distance from the fireplace talking to a large older lady. Ah, that was Mrs. Pennard, a distant relative of the countess's who'd been given the sinecure of companion so as to have a home and income.

The gentlemen spread out to mingle with the ladies. He strolled over to the quiet couple.

"Mrs. Pennard," he said. "How delightful to see you again."

The older lady smiled, and even blushed a little. "So kind of you to remember me, Lord Gabriel."

"It's not much over two years since I last visited, ma'am."

He turned to the Finch, but she rose. "I should relieve Lady Garway at the instrument."

He glanced over. "I believe Miss Minchingham will beat you to the opportunity to shine before the gentlemen."

Ah-ha! A blush. And it did improve her, but he noticed that she'd re-imprisoned that wanton lock.

"Please don't hurry away, Miss Finch. I hope to hear more of Miss Bunting." Her eyes flickered around as if seeking escape, but then she sat again. He moved a chair closer and sat down. "Was it truly a love match?"

"I wasn't here, my lord. Mrs. Pennard knows much more."

Mrs. Pennard obliged with a full and boring account of courtship, hesitations, and final connubial bliss. Miss Finch sat, hands in lap, and Gabriel saw why Edward thought her invisible. She was trying to disappear. Perhaps he should call her the "gray ghost." The "pallid green ghost" did not have the same ring.

"Will you attend the ball, Mrs. Pennard?" he asked when he had the chance.

"Oh, yes, my lord. I always do. So kind. Of course, I do not dance much. Such exertion as one gets older, and unpleasant to perspire. But I do enjoy a quieter set."

"And you, Miss Finch?"

"I will not attend."

Mrs. Pennard obliged with the protests. "But you must, my dear! The dowager will be most disappointed if you do not."

Miss Finch frowned. "Why? Will she need my services?"

"She likes to see people enjoying her Christmas ball," Gabriel said. "It has a long tradition, and it's been the spark for a number of happy unions. You can have no objection to a ball, can you?"

"I don't think it's suitable for someone in my position, my lord."

"Mrs. Pennard plans to attend," he reminded her.

Her lips tightened in annoyance at being caught out on that. "I didn't mean to imply . . ."

"Of course not, dear," Mrs. Pennard said, patting her hands. "And I'm sure in some houses ladies such as we would not be invited, but I assure you that's not the case at Holbourne. You will be welcome, indeed obliged, to attend."

"Then, of course I must." Surely no other lady had heard sentence of dancing with a heavier heart.

Gabriel's idle interest turned to sharp curiosity.

Who are you, Finch?

What is your story?

"Do you perhaps need practice in dancing, Miss Finch?" he asked. "We have a day before the ball, and I'm sure any number of people would enjoy an afternoon dancing party to learn some new steps."

"I will attend, my lord, but I won't dance. I assume *that* is not an obligation."

"Goodness, dear, do you have moral objections?" Mrs. Pennard asked.

"I simply do not care to dance." Distinctly harried, the Finch rose. "Excuse me. I must see if Lady Holly requires anything." She went to the dowager. A moment later she left the room.

Full retreat.

"Odd lass," Mrs. Pennard said. "Never know what's going on in her head. But very obliging."

In general, Gabriel wouldn't indulge in this sort of gossip, but he felt the need. "Do you know her background? Daughter of a clergyman, or such?"

"A country family, I believe—squirearchy—but I've heard no details." She lowered her voice. "It's clear she's a charity case, of course. Probably gaming. Father ruined. Blew out his brains. Left daughter destitute."

It wasn't impossible, but Mrs. Pennard had a taste for overblown drama.

"Or simple misfortune or mismanagement." He'd mined Mrs. Pennard for all she had to offer and was pleased when the chaplain came to invite her to make up a table for whist. Three tables were forming, but Gabriel evaded involvement there. He had a wager in hand. He'd wanted a word with Roxie, but she must have already left.

Lady Holbourne was merely supervising the whist, so when all was settled, he went to her. "A word with you, Aunt Elizabeth?"

He'd called her that since a lad. She smiled and sat on a

sofa a comfortable distance from other non-players. "Are you about to confess a sin, Gabriel?"

"Would you give me absolution?"

"Probably. I've never known you to do anyone harm. The dowager is already brighter for your arrival."

"Then I'm pleased, but that leads to my topic. Miss Finch."

She pulled a face, sighing.

"Do you know her background?" he asked. When she frowned, he said, "I'm not digging for gossip. I want to make Lady Holly happier. She's invited a couple of ladies to the ball with an eye to matchmaking. Might it not serve to add Miss Finch to the number?"

Lady Holbourne was startled, but quick. "Find her a husband? But who would be interested?"

"She's not entirely an antidote," Gabriel said, surprised by a spurt of annoyance. "Before I meddle there, I need to know who Miss Finch is."

"Ah, I see. No, we wouldn't want to countenance a misalliance. You'll have to ask Lady Holly. She said a friend had asked her to take in a lady who'd been left destitute."

"But of good family."

"I assume so."

"Herefordshire?"

"Or Hertfordshire. Does it matter? She has the manners of a lady from birth, but no money. I wish her well, but rate her chances slim."

"She'll present better in a fetching gown."

"If one was found, she'd not wear it. I've offered to improve her wardrobe and been frozen out."

He knew women who lacked taste, and others who chose sober styles for moral reasons, but why would any woman choose to be badly and bleakly dressed when offered an alternative?

Pride?

He was sure the offer had been made tactfully.

"She's a servant," he said bluntly. "If Lady Holly and you insist that she dresses suitably for the ball, she'll have to bend."

"Or break. What are you up to?"

"You think I'm expending this effort in a cruel trick? I want Lady Holly happy, and though I don't have her blissful view of marriage, surely a suitable one would improve Miss Finch's state?"

Lady Holbourne considered, and then said, "Very well. I see nothing wrong with your trying as long as you don't press her too strongly. You seem to have overlooked a substantial obstacle, however. I'm sure she owns no suitable gown and it's far too late to obtain one."

"Any obstacle is merely a challenge. I have a plan."

She rolled her eyes. "When any of you boys said that it predicted disaster."

He chuckled. "I can think of many, but this won't be one." Sobering, he asked, "Would Kim welcome a visit?"

Her face revealed the depth of her concern. "I don't know. He does speak to us, but through the door. I fear he thinks his wounds make him unfit to be seen. It's as if he's retreated into a shell, and none of us knows how to break it. Or whether he wants us to. Or," she added, "if shattering it might do him harm."

"I see. I know any number of men left scarred by the war, and not always visibly. I'll send him a note to say I'm here, but I'll leave it at that unless he invites me."

"Thank you. Perhaps someone new, someone not directly of the family. . . . As for Miss Finch, I could make it clear to her that she's expected to attend the ball, but might that not be cruel, given the state of her gowns?"

"I'll make sure she's suitably clothed and presented."

"You suddenly have miraculous powers?"

"Am I not named after an angel?"

"Not all angels are on the side of good," she pointed out.

She glanced behind him and rose. "I see a footman looking portentous. Probably some problem with supper." She fixed him with a stern look. "I shall be very angry if you make Miss Finch unhappy, Gabriel."

"I promise. I won't do that."

Alone again, Gabriel surveyed the room. Twelve were playing whist, and Miss Minchingham was still at the piano, looking annoyed to be abandoned to the task. Best to leave before she summoned him to her aid.

Problem with supper or not, Holbourne Abbey was calm and quiet once he'd closed the drawing room door. He remembered how much he'd always enjoyed strolling about the house at night when the servants were mostly below stairs or asleep and family members were in various rooms, leaving the corridors deserted.

Why not? Oil lamps hung in the main corridors at night. They were widely spaced, leaving areas of darkness, but they gave enough light for a stroll. He headed to his right, leaving the hall for a quiet corridor. He paused at the short passageway that led to the solid oak door into the old tower, where Kim had gone into hiding.

When the first earl had set about building a grand new house to suit his station, he'd wanted it on top of Abbey Hill, which gave a view for miles around. The hill had once held an abbey—a well-defended one, for this area was close enough to the Scottish border to be raided. The abbey had been dissolved in the sixteenth century and the Strettons had been given the land. They'd built themselves a handsome manor house near the river, using stone from the abbey until only the tall watchtower remained, a jagged memorial to the violent past.

The first earl had brought in men to tear it down, but the local people had been thrown into an uproar. They called it the Lucky Tower, and according to them it had survived because it had blessed properties and protected the area from all harm. Instead of trampling on their feelings, the first earl had persuaded them to let him repair the tower and then he'd incorporated it into one end of Holbourne Abbey. According to the story he'd said, "Only a fool tears down blessings."

Sensible people, the Strettons. Kim had been sensible once. Gabriel thought of knocking, even hammering on his door, but it was late and he didn't know what would help and what would harm. He suddenly wondered if Kim had walled himself off not only to lick his wounds, but to protect the rest of the household from whatever demons weighed him down.

He climbed the north staircase and then passed the library to go into the long gallery, where family portraits hung along with other fine works of art. Holbourne Abbey was less than a century old, but it had a deep mellowness. It came from excellent design and well-chosen furnishings, but he thought it also came from generations of good and mostly happy people. The place was having its soothing effect, but that made him realize how rattled he'd been by his own family's situation.

The Quinfroys weren't close or warm, and he rubbed along with his brother, Cramp, because they rarely met. All the same, he didn't like to think of the irritation Cramp's wife seemed likely to bring. And, he realized, he wished Cramp had married for love.

He was as bad as Lady Holly! But truly, if people did marry, it was better that they loved. He wondered if part of the reason for his sister-in-law's vinegary nature came from knowing she'd been married for her money. If so, she'd not have been sweetened when she realized that until the duke's death she'd be second-in-command to a bullying duchess.

Was it fair to attempt to push the Finch into marriage for the convenience of others? She must as least find a congenial husband. What sort of man would that be?

Disturbing to realize he had no idea. He doubted the gray ghost façade was the whole of her. He continued through the gallery and onward, along corridors and up and down stairs, enjoying furniture and paintings that were old favorites, as well as a few that were new.

Somewhere along the way the odd notion came to him that he might like a home. He had rooms in Town and they housed some objects and art of which he was fond, but he couldn't say his rooms were truly a home. Perhaps it hadn't struck him before because the only other home he was likely to have would be Straith and it was a ghastly place.

In fact, home to him had always meant Holbourne. He rolled that new idea around in his head as he walked. He didn't hunger to own Holbourne Abbey, but the idea of owning something of the sort unfurled in his mind.

He had money.

He could purchase something.

A much simpler place, of course. A manor house, close to London and the life he enjoyed there. He didn't want a substantial estate to run, but a home farm would be pleasant, along with a decent-sized park.

He paused by a rather primitive painting of Stretton Manor—the modest Tudor house that had been built near the river. The painting was probably Jacobean, judging by the clothing of the three riders approaching the house. A woman stood at the door, and three children ran as if to welcome Papa home.

He shook himself as if escaping a spell. If a manor house meant wife and children, it was better avoided. And, indeed, why else would any man want such a place?

He turned away and saw a skirt disappear around a corner. A dull green skirt. He pursued. When he turned the corner she was walking briskly away. He almost ran after her, but came to his senses and called, "Miss Finch!"

She halted and turned, as she must. He strolled to join her.

"My lord?" she asked.

The distantly spaced lighting gave her smooth features interesting contours.

"So you, too, enjoy walking the house in the quiet hours," he said. When he saw a flicker of alarm, he added, "I don't accuse you of anything. I've always found it pleasant. It's a comfortable house, despite its grander aspects."

She relaxed a little. "It is, my lord. And I enjoy the exercise."

"The park is pleasant, too."

"Not with inches of snow on the ground."

"Perhaps you need sturdier footwear."

"And shorter skirts." The tart note made him smile.

"Women are unfairly dressed, are they not?"

"Women are unfairly treated in a great many ways, my lord. Good night."

She dipped a curtsey and walked away, leaving him surprised. Was he the sort of popinjay who thought every young woman should blush and simper if he spoke to her? No, but it was generally the case.

He watched her until she turned out of sight, noting a pleasing vigor that probably meant she was accustomed to enjoying more exercise than she got here. Even when the weather was suitable for outdoor walks, the dowager would merely stroll near the house for a half hour or so.

No, the gray ghost wasn't the real Finch. The tart, brisk woman he'd just encountered would be much better off wed, and his challenge was to get her to the ball suitably dressed.

CHAPTER THREE

Gabriel planned his campaign, which would begin with a ride over to Hayward Hall to coax Roxie to help him. As he sat to breakfast, however, she arrived, so he drew her aside.

"Bad news?" she asked, which was odd.

"Of course not."

"Oh." She laughed as if nervous, which was most unlike her.

Roxanne Hayward had never allowed being female to hinder her. She'd shrugged off all limitations imposed on women and lived life to the fullest, so what was worrying her now? He couldn't imagine, and he had his plan. He was realizing that Roxie was the exact opposite of his gray ghost, which could be a fatal flaw.

"I need a gown," he said, "and I hoped you might have one I could borrow. A ball gown."

She stared at him. "Whatever jape you're planning, I've nothing that would fit."

He laughed. "Not for me. For a ghost. No, I'm not mad. Do you know Miss Finch?"

"The dowager's new companion? Ghost. Yes, I see."

"She's to attend the Christmas ball, but has nothing suitable to wear."

"Why are you involved in this?" She frowned. "It's not some trickery, is it?"

"Why the deuce does everyone assume I'd indulge in cruel jokes?"

She blinked at him. "I suppose it is unfair. It's only that you seem so light."

"Better than dark, surely."

"Yes. I'm sorry. I have a number of distracting matters at the moment."

"Unlikely, I know, but is there anything I can do to help?"

She smiled. "Probably not, but I'm glad you're around, Gabriel."

It seemed an odd thing to say, for he knew nothing of estate management or any local problems she might face. Best to stick to the matter in hand.

"I judge that you and Miss Finch are of a size and height," he said, "so I'm shamelessly asking you to donate a ball gown to her cause. And before you question my motives again, it's in the faint hope of marrying her off so that Lady Holly can hire someone more in tune with her nature."

"Ah, I see. Yes. You're welcome to any of them except for a few of my newest gowns, but I don't have time to hunt through them with you. There are matters to do with snow and sheep. But if you want to ride back with me, I'll have my maid help you."

"Thank you. I'll be with you shortly."

They were soon walking to the stables, talking of the weather and the chances of the ball coming off as it should, and then Gabriel enjoyed a brisk ride cross-country to Hayward Hall.

As soon as they were inside, Roxie said, "I'll summon my maid. She knows which are new or favorites, and there are any number of older ones. I never have time to sift through and decide what to get rid of."

"Thank you."

She smiled. "I am glad you're here, Gabriel. You always make things brighter."

"As a talent, that's not too bad a one."

"No, it's not."

In minutes he was following a plump, middle-aged maid to Roxie's rooms, which he'd never had occasion to visit. Clearly, she hadn't expended much effort on refurbishment. The decoration and furnishings looked generations old. He rather liked it.

"The older clothes are in this press, my lord," the maid said, pulling out the top drawer of five. "I've been trying to get Miss Roxie to give some away. I'd be pleased to be rid of dozens."

Gabriel was tempted to carry off a whole new plumage for the Finch, but he'd be cautious in the first step.

"I need a ball gown," he said and the maid began pulling out muslin-wrapped bundles to put on the bed. He peeled back the wrappings on one and found a confection of rainbow silk.

"Not so flamboyant."

"Miss Roxie does like bright, my lord. Ah."

The next shroud revealed ivory and pearls.

"Too virginal. Not that the lady isn't," he added quickly, "but she's nearer thirty than twenty."

The maid replaced the offerings, shut the drawer, and began on the next.

Gabriel kept out a blue, though he wasn't sure the vibrant shade would do, and a buttercup yellow satin muted by an over slip of white gauze. It felt too flighty, but perhaps the Finch should take flight. Then the maid unwrapped a green.

His first reaction was rejection because it reminded him too much of her dismal evening gown, but then he reconsidered. It was a soft moss green and beautifully made, with details of beading and embroidery. All the same, it was quiet.

"Unusual for Miss Hayward," he commented.

"She takes this start to be different sometimes, my lord,

but generally regrets it. That one's years out of fashion. It'd need a lot of refurbishment to be acceptable now."

It was indeed old-fashioned, falling simply from the high waist to the floor. The square neckline was modest and the short sleeves would fully conceal the shoulders, but he was beginning to think it was just the thing.

The green silk was sprigged with green flowers of the same shade, giving a plain first impression, but the rich texture soon became apparent. Neckline and hem were enlivened by delicate beadwork, again in the same shade. Under candlelight or in motion, as in a dance, the beads would shine.

"It's perfect as is," he said, and saw the maid's thought—that some poor lady shouldn't have entrusted this task to him. He hoped she was wrong. A bright fashionable gown would be too much of a change for Miss Finch, but this wouldn't startle. It could even be something of her own from better days.

"A pair of long gloves, if you please, and our work is done."

Roxie came in then. "Progress?" Then she asked, "That one?" as surprised as her maid.

"Not one of your treasured favorites, I hope."

"I'm surprised it's still here. I had it made in a low period. It's beyond hope."

"Not at all." He took the pair of long white gloves and thanked the maid.

"If you're sure," Roxie said. "Tessa, find something for Lord Gabriel to carry the gown in on horseback." When the woman had gone, she added, "If Miss Finch throws it in your face, you can return to plunder again." She touched the gown. "Odd how time passes, isn't it?"

"Natural, I'd say."

"I mean how things change. Fashion. Us." She glanced at him. "We're none of us the people we were as children. What nonsense I'm talking."

"No. Kim is much changed."

"Yes . . ." The maid returned with a satchel. "Ah, perfect." As the maid carefully folded the muslin-wrapped gown away, Roxie asked, "Have you spoken to him?"

"No. I sent a message to say I was available, but he hasn't replied. He'll come out of it eventually. He has to."

"Yes," she said, but with the same doubts he felt.

One problem at a time, he reminded himself, and the Finch's plumage was the more urgent. He thanked Roxie and rode back to Holbourne with his prize.

He stored it in his room and plotted the next steps. He had two goals—to talk to Lady Holly without the Finch nearby in order to learn more about her, and to get the Finch alone so he could persuade her to wear the gown. Unfortunately, the Finch took her duty to attend Lady Holly seriously, and he couldn't hover all day hoping they would separate. He was obliged to take part in the amusements provided for guests, and even assist with them. As everyone in the family was busy, he hosted an afternoon billiards party for some of the gentlemen.

After dinner, he lay in wait. He took up position on a bench in the long gallery, armed with a decanter of port and two glasses. The gallery was excellent for walking and a natural passage between different parts of the house.

CHAPTER FOUR

$\mathcal{T}$he clock struck half past ten before the door at one end opened and she came through. She closed the door and walked briskly along the gallery, not noticing him.

He rose. "Miss Finch."

She started, and then stared, hand to chest. "My lord, you alarmed me."

"My apologies. May I offer you wine?"

"No, thank you."

She turned, but he said, "Don't go."

She turned back. "Why not?"

"I have a matter to discuss with you."

"At night, here?"

He smiled. "On my honor, Miss Finch, I have no designs on your virtue."

"Why should I believe that when you've been brought here to seduce innocent young ladies out of their good sense?"

"But not out of their virtue."

"Unless they're weak."

"Then I will be strong. You do have a low opinion of me, don't you?"

"'A rake and a rascal'?" she quoted at him with that brisk tartness he was coming to admire.

"I'm not a model of chastity," he said, "but I don't seduce and I don't ruin and I do need to discuss something with you."

"Then we can do so tomorrow. In the garden, in full view of the house."

"You have your duties to Lady Holly and the slush will soil your gown. It's to do with the Christmas ball."

She went still, but that meant she wasn't leaving.

"You are to attend, I believe, but I suspect you don't have a suitable gown."

"As the dowager's companion, what I have on will do."

"It will not, and you know it."

"I have nothing else, my lord, so it will have to. You know I don't wish to attend."

"But when you do, you should be suitably dressed." He gestured to himself. "Am I not Gabriel?"

"I do hope you're not about to announce the hand of God, my lord."

She startled a laugh out of him. "Only a gown. For you."

Had there been a flicker of echoing amusement? If so, it had disappeared. "And how have you achieved that?" she asked.

"Honorably, I assure you, and I lay you a guinea that you'll like it."

A glint appreciated his challenge. "You'd lose."

"Shall we put it to the test?"

She glanced around. "Where is it? Your bedroom? No, sir."

"How clumsy you think me. I've put it in the library. A room, yes, but a public one, and we can leave the door open. It will only take a moment for you to come to a conclusion."

She hesitated, as wary as a finch, but alert as a hawk. Then she said, "Very well. I could use an extra guinea." She set off at a brisk pace.

Gabriel abandoned the port and followed. What a fine, clear spirit shone beneath the shrouds.

He'd gambled on no one wanting to use the library at night and left the gown spread out on the central table beneath the light of a number of lamps.

She halted when she saw it.

"Surprised?" he asked, coming up behind her.

"It's quite plain."

"Disappointed?"

She turned. When she realized how close he was, she backed away before turning and walking up to the table. "No."

"Because you see it isn't entirely plain. Of course, you might object to it being years out of date."

"I might." But she reached out and touched the silk before pulling her hand back again.

"How honest are you, Miss Finch?"

He was referring teasingly to their wager, but she turned sharply to him. "Completely!"

Suddenly he knew. He reviewed things she'd said and words she'd reacted to.

"Who betrayed you?" he asked.

Stupidly.

She fled. He raced after and blocked the door. "Don't, please. I mean you no harm. . . ." Suddenly tongue-tied, he managed, "I wish I could thrash whoever it was."

"My lord . . . Please."

"Finch . . . Damnation, what's your first name? Come on. You know mine."

"That's because you're a duke's son!"

"Lady Holly will tell me."

Her lips went tight, but then she said, "Clio."

"The muse of history. Your father was a scholar?"

"My father is a landed gentleman of as little education as he could get away with. My mother thought classical names would elevate the family."

Her father was alive. Now he felt sure of the story. Some man had ruined her and her family—the ones seeking elevation—had thrown her out. Had she borne a bastard?

He wanted to thrash someone, to fight battles for her honor. Where had this madness come from? Concentrate on the purpose at hand. She was no longer trying to run away, so he could relax and speak more moderately.

"Please take the gown. You'll feel more comfortable at the ball, and you'll note I've chosen one that's superficially plain and old-fashioned. It could easily be a gown you've worn in the past."

"Chosen? From what heavenly storehouse?"

"Do they have wardrobes in paradise? I coaxed it from Miss Hayward, who is happy to be rid of it. You'll wear it?"

"I can't afford a guinea."

He'd forgotten the wager. "I'll take a substitute."

She tensed again. What games had her seducer played with her? She was expecting him to demand a kiss.

"To see your hair," he said.

She touched her cap. "My hair? Why?"

"Because I don't think you'd show me your knees or anything even more adventurous."

"Are you never serious?"

"As little as possible. I'm not so much angel as jester. Well?"

She rolled her eyes, but undid the bow beneath her chin and took off the cap to reveal neatly pinned dark hair. It looked thick and wavy. Without thinking, he reached and pulled out a pin. He'd taken out two when she started and moved out of reach.

"Stop that!"

He raised his hands, shocked at himself, but he couldn't ignore that for a moment there she'd been as enthralled as he, and then she'd reacted as he might want her to react if he were . . .

Good God.

"You'll wear the gown?" he asked. It came out rather hoarsely. "Please."

She glanced between the gown and him, eyes wide, three locks of hair sliding down to torment him. She was feeling everything that he felt, including disbelief and alarm.

She dashed to the table, grabbed the gown and gloves, and headed for the door.

He was in the way.

He stepped back, but she still brushed close enough to send a shock through him. When she'd left, he went to the door and watched her walk away. A long tress slithered down her back. She paused to try to tuck it up again, failed, and continued. That thick, rich hair must fall to her waist when freed.

He realized she'd dropped the cap on the carpet. He picked it up. Many women wore caps. Certainly when married, but often when single and of a certain age. They need not be as plain as this.

Clio Finch had been hurt and betrayed so badly that she was trying to be invisible, but beneath the gray ghost lay a vibrantly alive woman and he was reacting to her in an extraordinary way.

He shook his head and extinguished the lamps. She wasn't a woman for unmarried pleasure, and she was certainly not one for marriage. A nobody would be scandalous enough, but a ruined one? His family would refuse to meet her.

With a wry smile he saw the advantages of that, but it wouldn't do. If he were a more ordinary specimen perhaps no one would delve into his wife's background, but he was the very wealthy son of a duke. His marriage would be a nine-day's wonder, and the *ton* would hunt down every detail about his wife.

All he could do for Clio Finch was get her married to a suitably undistinguished gentleman. That way, she'd have a chance of happiness and he wouldn't be tempted toward disaster.

But, he realized, if her scandal was public knowledge, it could make any marriage impossible. Tomorrow he must get the full story out of Lady Holly before the fateful ball.

CHAPTER FIVE

The next day the house was in ferment with last-minute preparations for the ball, but there was something else in the air—something out of tune and ominous. Kim hadn't responded to his note, Edward had been in a harried mood and had then disappeared, and even Aunt Elizabeth seemed distracted by more than the preparation of the ballroom and food for the supper.

Gabriel couldn't even question Lady Holly. For once, she was unattended by Clio Finch, but ensconced in a chair in the hall, supervising the enhancement of the decorations there. Or rather, interfering. Gabriel decided his good deed for now could be to distract her.

He moved a chair beside her. "Dear heart, stop harrying the troops."

"Why? I enjoy it."

"But they're not your troops anymore."

She pulled a face at him, but didn't argue.

"Where's the Finch?" he asked. "Acting as courier?"

"I sent her to spy on the kitchens."

"Cruel. She'll be shot. Will she attend the ball?"

"It seems so. I gather you persuaded Roxie Hayward to lend her a gown."

"An easy task."

"Since you have meddled that far, I expect you to dance with her."

"Your wish is my command." And my pleasure. Perhaps he could learn something here. "Is she accustomed to dancing?"

"I doubt she'll shame you," she said, but she was glaring across the hall. "Look at that! We have always put the gilded roses over the fireplace for the ball."

He distracted her by asking, "Herefordshire or Hertfordshire?"

"What?"

"I have been told by one person that Miss Finch comes from Herefordshire, and another Hertfordshire. There's a considerable difference."

"Hertfordshire. What is it to you? Don't make trouble."

"Trouble?"

"You're up to something," she said, but her reaction had been alarm. His suspicions were true. Before he could probe further, she said, "Go and tell them to put those roses where they ought to be."

He'd get no secrets from Lady Holly here, especially not in this mood, so he did as bade, even more concerned about the storms brewing at the Abbey. He hoped the ball would be accomplished without an explosion.

Clio Finch emerged from the rear of the house and went to report to Lady Holly. Gabriel walked over to join them, but Clio rose again and went to the harpsichord that sat in one corner of the hall. It was rarely played, but she began a sprightly performance of traditional Christmas songs.

The pianoforte was more complex and sonorous, but the plucked strings of the harpsichord suited the old music. As "The Holly and the Ivy," and "God Rest Ye Merry Gentlemen" tinkled out, people smiled and jigged in time as they worked.

She played very well. He suddenly envisioned a manor house filling with music well played. . . .

He turned and left the hall, seeking refuge elsewhere, anywhere.

* * *

In late afternoon, he compelled a private word with Lady Holly. He went to her room and claimed to want to discuss some private family matters.

"Off you go, Finch," Lady Holly said. "I'm sure you need time to prepare for the ball." As soon as they were alone, Lady Holly said, "What problem do you have?" in as truculent a manner as he'd ever heard.

"What has you out of curl, my dear?"

"Oh, I'm just being silly. But I had such hopes. Caro and Camden were supposed to be here. I've been so worried about her."

Gabriel knew there was reason to worry. The couple lived separate lives in Town and he doubted Camden could afford Caro's extravagant ways. But he made it a golden rule never to meddle in marriages. He'd have thought Lady Holly felt the same.

"I need to talk about Miss Finch," he said.

"Why?"

"If she's to be introduced to the locality, shouldn't we know more about her?"

"If I countenance her, who is to question her?"

"My dear," he said gently, "if there's any possibility of her engaging a gentleman's interest, it becomes important."

She sighed and he could swear her sprig of mistletoe drooped. "I know. I never thought she'd want to attend, and if she did, in her unbecoming way of dressing . . ."

So his meddling had caused this problem.

"What's her story?" he asked.

"It's not mine to share."

"Then let me guess. Some handsome schemer seduced her for amusement. She believed his claims of love, but once he'd had his way, he abandoned her."

She stared at him, distressed. "How did you know?"

"A few things she said. Put together with the rest, it seemed bound to be true. Did she bear a bastard?"

"No, thank heavens, but her foolish family cast her out. If they'd explained away her absence, all might have been well. She came into the care of a friend of mine just when I'd written to complain of Bunting abandoning me, so she asked me to take her in."

"So if anyone looked into her background, they'd discover all."

"Perhaps not. Northumberland is a long way from Hertfordshire."

"Word gets around, my dear. These days people travel up and down the country on a whim and half the world gathers in Town for the Season."

She sighed again. "Best if she doesn't attend the ball, then. I could claim to be ill and need her attention."

"And miss your fiftieth Christmas ball? I have a better idea. I'll add Miss Finch to my ladies, and attend her so devotedly that other gentlemen will be warned off."

She brightened. "Would you? But what about later? You'll have raised hopes. Will you then jilt her?"

"I'll make sure she understands, and for the world's eyes, I'll make it clear she refused me, having come to her senses."

"Who'd believe someone like Miss Finch would turn down the son of a duke?"

"Anyone with sense. I'm not marrying material." He took her hand and kissed it. "Don't fret, dear heart. I'll make sure your Christmas ball is a perfect success."

It should not be a great challenge, but Gabriel prepared for the ball feeling as if he faced Waterloo. His lighthearted wager with Edward had created possible disaster, something was amiss with his friend, and Kim's situation felt like a keg of gunpowder, needing only a spark. He scandalized his valet by pulling on a pair of boots and going down to leave the house near the Lucky Tower.

There was the well-worn spot on the tower wall, where for centuries the local people had rubbed the stone for good luck or blessings. He circled his fingers there, calling down peace and joy on Holbourne.

Clio read Lord Gabriel's note and was very inclined to cry off from the ball. So she was an object of shame, was she, from which gentlemen must be protected? To her alarm, she was also inclined to weep.

She'd brought this situation on herself by her stupidity and wickedness, and she'd accepted the consequence—that she must be grateful to live quietly for the rest of her life. But she'd never expected to meet someone like Lord Gabriel. It didn't help to know that he charmed women as carelessly as he breathed. She was charmed, and so she raged against her fate.

Oh, don't be silly. He'd never marry you if you were a beauty of perfect virtue, and if you had any sense, you'd not want him to.

She looked at the gown, spread out on the bed, unable to ignore the fact that he'd gone to some effort to get it, and had chosen well. He must care a little.

Very well. She'd wear it to the ball, and she'd enjoy his attentions in full awareness that he was playacting. She'd never have another opportunity to frolic like that again.

Gabriel was to escort Lady Holly in to the dinner that preceded the ball—at her command. "This is my fiftieth Christmas ball, and I'll begin the evening on the arm of the most handsome man present." That was going to cause some disruption in protocol, but Aunt Elizabeth would cope.

They gathered in the hall. Lady Holly was magnificent in red silk, including a turban pinned with a holly brooch made of emeralds and diamonds, a gift from Lord and Lady Holbourne. Even so, Gabriel saw concern in her eyes, and wasn't surprised, for not long before, Caro had arrived— alone. Caro said her husband was on his way, delayed by important matters in Town, but how many believed that? Perhaps a divorce was in the offing. That was bad enough, but something else had Lady Holly out of curl. What else could be going wrong?

Caro was brittle in her good spirits. Aunt Elizabeth was watching everything as if alert for a gunpowder explosion, and Lady Holly was frowning. One of Lady Holly's last-chance brides, Miss Langsdale, had arrived for dinner in excellent spirits, on the arm of Lord Harris. Gabriel didn't think she needed his help to have roses in her cheeks, and he'd think Lady Holly would be cock-a-hoop. Was she peevish because her assistance hadn't been needed?

Then Gabriel saw Mrs. Tremaine look at Edward. The twice-widowed lady had arrived a day ago in an aura of mystery. It probably simply came from her having spent a great many years in India, but now Gabriel wondered exactly what she was up to. Then another guest, Lord Kelsey, claimed to feel unwell and dashed up to his room.

Were they all to be felled by food poisoning?

The elderly chaplain was summoned to take Kelsey's place at table, and then they all processed into the dining room to "God Rest Ye Merry Gentlemen," played on the harpsichord by one of the professional musicians. Gabriel hoped nothing would dismay them all tonight.

The man played no better than Clio, who was looking wonderful in the gown. She was behind him in the procession, but he'd noted at first glance that the embroidery and beading shimmered by candlelight exactly as he'd thought they would. Her hair was uncovered and neatly dressed, decorated with pearl pins. She wore modest pearls around her neck and at her ears. Borrowed? They might be her own, taken with her when she was cast out.

For this occasion, Lady Holly's place was at the head of the table with Lady Holbourne taking a seat in the middle. Gabriel seated her, and then nipped down the table to the seat he'd arranged at Clio's side. She was startled, but then she smiled warmly. For a moment he forgot that they were playing parts. . . .

He hadn't prepared for the effect of having her by his side for over an hour. For the effect of light conversation and the brushing touches as they were served and reached for glasses. For her ease. Where had the gray ghost gone? It was as if she'd thrown off a disguise and was revealed to be a lost princess. A pity he had fat Lady Claymott on his other side, demanding an ear for endless chatter whenever she could.

He smiled and nodded as she went on, keeping an eye on the table, though heaven knows what he could do if anything went amiss. The alluring Mrs. Tremaine was a few seats to his right, so he couldn't tell what she was doing, but he caught one hot look from Edward in that direction that had him wanting to sound an alarm bell. There was nothing impossible about the attraction, but then why did it seem Edward was eyeing forbidden fruit?

Lord Holbourne, bless him, claimed Lady Claymott's attention and Gabriel turned back to Clio.

Quietly he asked the question that had been plaguing him since the dinner began, "How is it that you weren't snapped up in your teens?"

She blushed a little, but also laughed. "There's no need for such flattery."

"It's not flattery. I'm truly curious. If not in your teens, then years ago."

She looked down at her plate and cut through some meat. "I was. He died."

Dolt not to have thought of that. Her dismal clothing could even be mourning. "My condolences. Military?"

"Yes. Not in a famous battle. In a skirmish somewhere in Spain. Three years ago."

"But you still feel it."

She looked up at him. "I always will, but I'm not sunk in grief."

"May I know his name?"

"Michael Partington. His family lives close to mine. We'd known each other all our lives, though he was four years older." She picked up her wineglass and sipped. "It was hard to have him gone from the world. I'd not seen him for over a year, but we wrote. His last letter arrived after the news of his death."

He took her left hand in his beneath the table. "I'm sorry you had to endure that."

She gently disengaged. "Many did. Let's not talk more of it or I'll cast a pall over the evening with tears."

He wanted to take her in his arms and let her weep, but he smiled. "We'll be enthusiasts for Christmas frolics, then."

As if summoned, a flurry brought Caro's husband, Camden, apologizing but looking at his wife in a way that carried hope. The chaplain was sitting at Caro's side. He immediately offered his place. "There is no difficulty at all, sir, I assure you. I have eaten very well already."

After much demurring and persuading, the chaplain left and Camden sat in his place as new dishes and cutlery were provided.

"One situation improved," Gabriel said quietly to Clio. "Lady Caroline and her husband are at least not stabbing one another with forks."

"Two situations," she said. "Mr. Lupscombe does not eat large meals. He'll be much happier away from here. Do you think Lord Brentford and Miss Hayward will make a match of it?"

Gabriel glanced their way, surprised. It would be an excellent match in practical terms, joining two large estates, but he'd never thought of it. In the past, Roxie had shown a preference for Kim, but perhaps that was over now. Was she taking Edward as substitute? That might not be good. And what of Mrs. Tremaine?

He told himself there was nothing he could do, but dammit, he cared about what happened to the Stretton family. They were his anchor in the world.

When the ladies left, the atmosphere eased a little. Were women always a cause of turmoil among men? Talk turned to politics, with local gentlemen keen to hear what Camden had to say. By the time they rose from the table, more guests were arriving for the ball. Servants were taking greatcoats and cloaks and in the room set aside for it, guests were changing their outdoor footwear for dancing slippers.

Gabriel went to the ballroom, still alert for dangers he could avert, but mostly anticipating spending as much of the night as was decent with Clio Finch.

CHAPTER SIX

The minuet was falling out of fashion, but Lady Holly's Christmas ball always began with one. Nowadays it was particularly slowly paced so that she could take part, and she danced it with Colonel Percy, who was almost of an age with her and willing to flirt.

Gabriel led out Clio, who confessed to having rarely danced it, but managed well enough.

"An expert partner is certainly an advantage," she said as they slid past each other, eyes locked.

"Polished in every social perfection!"

She chuckled, eyes bright, cheeks tinted by natural good spirits.

When the dance was over he had to surrender her, but there was no shortage of candidates for her hand. She was flustered for a moment, but then strolled off with a young sprig, probably because he seemed harmless. Gabriel hoped that was true.

Miss Langsdale didn't need his help, and the other young charity case, Miss Fenton, had failed to appear. Aunt Elizabeth came over. "Will you ask Miss Kelsey to dance, Gabriel? The poor girl's brother has deserted her and she's rather shy."

"Of course."

He was duly introduced, and though Miss Kelsey seemed overwhelmed, she blushed and agreed. The dance was a lively country one, and she'd been well trained in such things, so he could work at putting her at her ease. He thought he succeeded. Certainly, she didn't lack for partners for the next.

He was too late to claim Clio for the next set, and her partner this time was older and smiling at her dangerously, but he could hardly drag her away. Looking around, he noticed that Edward and Roxie had disappeared. He tried to be pleased, but he didn't feel that was the right union for either.

Then he realized Mrs. Tremaine was also absent.

He was tempted to go in search, but why get himself blown up? Whatever was going on, there was nothing he could do. He partnered safe Mrs. Alsop. Then he secured Clio again. As they strolled about the room, waiting for the next set to begin, he asked, "Enjoying yourself?"

She smiled. "Yes. I determined to, you see. There won't be many such occasions."

"There'll be another Christmas ball next year."

"I probably won't be here by then. Lady Holly is very kind, but I don't suit her and the situation doesn't suit me. I'd prefer to be more useful."

"Useful? You mean, as a governess?"

"What horror!" she teased. "I don't think I'm suited to be a teacher, but there must be truly useful work to be done. Perhaps for the poor in London."

"Good God."

She laughed in surprise. "It horrifies you?"

"I wouldn't want . . ." All kinds of idiotic words almost spilled out.

"You wouldn't want to do such work. I see that. But as I can't take a more conventional path, I'd like my life to have purpose."

"But you'd prefer conventional? Marriage, children, and such."

Stop it. You can't offer her that.

"I suppose I would. But I'd still want to help those in need. Having been in need. Not of my daily bread, but needing help, which I generously received."

"I see."

"I don't suppose you do. I wouldn't have before my life fell into pieces."

He couldn't help it. He paused them in a corner where no one was nearby. "What led you to it, Clio? If he wooed you, why not demand marriage?"

She turned away to look at the crowded room. "I don't intend to talk about it, Lord Gabriel."

Her statement was absolute, and he had to respect it. However, her position showed him the nape of her neck, where soft curls brushed small, gleaming pearls against her creamy skin, which he desperately wanted to kiss. The gown's neckline rode some inches lower, giving him a glimpse of her spine and inviting completely improper visions of her naked back down to her rounded bottom. She liked to walk, and she danced lightly and with ease. She'd be lithe and lovely by candlelight in his bed. . . .

He forced sanity on himself, welcoming the summons to the next dance, and that it was a lively reel. He was in danger of doing something disastrous.

Then he saw Edward come into the room with Mrs. Tremaine, and the woman was extraordinarily dressed in an Indian sari! Outrageous, but she looked magnificent.

Edward said something to the musicians, and the music changed to a waltz. Edward and Mrs. Tremaine moved smilingly into the steps. They might as well have made an announcement then and there!

But what of poor Roxie? Had she had hopes? Was that why she'd left the company? Perhaps he should offer his battered heart to her.

But then, bright with delight, Roxie came in with Kim in his regimentals. Kim's scars and limp shocked Gabriel, but he couldn't feel sorrowful when his friend looked so happy as he and Roxie joined the dance. Everyone watched the two couples dance, entranced by each other, but Aunt Elizabeth sent him an urgent look.

"I assume you can waltz," he said, and drew Clio out onto the floor. After a startled moment, she complied, and then other couples joined.

"How extraordinary," Clio said, turning gracefully in his arms.

She probably meant the situation, but he agreed with respect to the dance. Many thought it scandalous, and perhaps it was, but he'd never found it so marvelous before.

The dance was over too soon. Gabriel should be seeking his next partner, but he took Clio with him when he went to congratulate Kim and Roxie, and then Edward and his lady.

"We were in love many years ago," Edward said, "but we let the chance slip through our fingers. Never again."

"Never," Mrs. Tremaine said, looking into his eyes as if nothing else in the world mattered.

Chance slip through our fingers . . .

Then Lord Holbourne called for attention, and champagne was being brought around.

"Christmastide is a time of joy, and we are all enjoying my dear mother, Lady Holly's, fiftieth Christmas ball."

Everyone applauded.

"But we have even greater cause for joy. Tonight, not one but both of my sons have found a bride. Edward, Lord Brentford is to wed Mrs. Lily Tremaine, and Kimball, my younger son, is to wed our dear neighbor, Roxanne Hayward. Let us all toast to their happy futures!"

Everyone did, and Lady Holly was dabbing her eyes and looking blissful.

Gabriel joined in the toast wholeheartedly, but inside something was crying, "Why not for me?"

The music struck up again and he turned to Clio, but she'd moved away and was about to let some other man lead her into the next dance. Gabriel snatched her away and onto the dance floor.

She went, but said, "My lord?"

He didn't try to explain, only saying, "Surprisingly good news."

"I had wondered if Lord Brentford and Miss Hayward were truly suited, but I had no idea of an attachment between her and Mr. Stretton."

"No one had. They squabbled their way through childhood."

"Perhaps that's the way it begins."

Something in her smile made him ask, "For you, too? You said your betrothed was a neighbor."

"For me, too."

The dance started, but Gabriel said desperately, "I want you to be happy, Clio. You deserve that."

She smiled as she moved into the steps, but the sad smile said, *No, I don't.*

The ball ended at two and the guests from nearby departed, with lamps on their carriages and outriders carrying extra ones. When all was quiet, Gabriel walked the corridors of the house, half hoping, half fearing an encounter with Clio Finch.

He paused again in front of the picture of Stretton Manor and imagined riding home to find Clio at the door, smiling a welcome, a child or two running out to meet him. The idea in the abstract had horrified him, but now he yearned.

Even without her scandal it was too early to think of such things, but no one had told his mind or heart that. He could see it. He could feel it.

But it was impossible.

Not for his sake, but for hers, he reminded himself. She'd be shunned by his world, and probably shunned even by the worthy world she thought she'd find a place in. If she turned up in some city to help the poor, no one would ask questions. Once her story was out, however, the "good people" involved in such work would drive her away. The world was very unforgiving to a wanton woman.

And she had been wanton. Clearly, she'd encountered a clever, unscrupulous man, but to run off with him without marriage had been foolish. She was no fool, so she had to have been driven by lust. She had lusted for another man.

He turned from the picture and headed back to his room. He'd leave tomorrow and put all this behind him.

CHAPTER SEVEN

$\mathcal{T}$he next day started sleepily at Holbourne Abbey. Most of the servants had been given leave to rise late, and the guests slept on. Gabriel found himself awake at ten, however, and restless. He'd like to simply leave, especially to avoid another encounter with Clio, but he needed to take farewell of his hosts and Lady Holly, and he also needed to send for a chaise from the nearby town.

He wandered down and found the minimum of a breakfast laid out in the morning room on the ground floor. A footman brought him fresh coffee and he made do with ham and bread.

Morning had not brought sanity. He still wanted to woo Clio into becoming his bride, but the obstacles remained and he could see no way around them. He'd thought of their living abroad, but they'd be bound to encounter English people, and the curiosity would start up. Perhaps if they went beyond civilization and changed their names, but he doubted they could be happy that way.

He was finishing his second cup of coffee when someone rapped on the front door. The morning room door was open so he heard a man demand, "Is Miss Finch here?"

Gabriel rose and went to observe. The arrival was a raw-boned sort of man in a heavy greatcoat of good quality. The seducer racing to correct a wrong? He appeared to be at least fifty.

The footman was uttering the standard defense. "I will ascertain, sir. If you would wait in here, please?" He indicated the reception room across the hall.

"But is she here?"

A choleric gentleman, and Gabriel had a suspicion. He couldn't say there was a resemblance to Clio, but perhaps something. . . .

He strolled out. "You find the house somnolent, sir, because of a grand ball last night. May I offer you refreshment as you wait? You may want to shed your outerwear?"

The man looked thwarted, but he let the footman take his greatcoat, gloves, and hat. "I'd appreciate a cup of tea, sir."

Gabriel nodded to the footman to provide it and took the man into the morning room. "I'm Lord Gabriel Quinfroy, sir, a connection of the house. And you are?"

"Henry Finch. I've been told my daughter is here."

There seemed no point in denying it. "She is, sir. She's companion to the Dowager Countess of Holbourne."

"Ha! So I was told. I'll go odds the lady don't know the truth about her."

"I suspect you might lose that bet. Why are you here?"

Mr. Finch frowned at the tone. "My daughter. Her welfare."

"Yet you seem to have lost her."

"Your pardon, my lord, but this is none of your business."

The footman brought the tea and laid it out on the table, then looked a question at Gabriel. Gabriel waved him away.

"I seem to be the representative of the family at the moment, Mr. Finch, and I am the dowager's godson, so I can perhaps claim a spiritual connection. Miss Finch has become one of the family and is much valued. Are you come to take her away?"

Clio's father stirred sugar into his tea and drank some. Gabriel didn't like the look of him, but he knew he might be prejudiced.

"I am," the man said at last. "She has received a very flattering offer of marriage."

Gabriel had to take a moment to absorb that. "How very fortunate. And yet you mentioned a truth we might not know."

"Fensham knows."

"The Earl of Fensham?" Gabriel didn't try to keep the astonishment out of his voice.

"Know him?"

"I know nearly everyone, Mr. Finch. He's buried three wives."

"Unlucky."

"And yet you'd entrust your daughter to his misfortunes?"

Mr. Finch jutted out his jaw. "She'll be a countess, and damned lucky to be so."

"You think she'll accept this offer?"

"Of course, she will," the man growled. "What hope is there for her otherwise?"

Gabriel poured himself more coffee to buy time to absorb all this. "Lord Fensham doesn't worry about his fourth wife's reputation?"

"Rumors only, and if he and we deny them, they'll blow over. Has she been sent for?"

Gabriel rose. "I'll go and find out."

In the hall he saw Aunt Elizabeth coming down the stairs. "I understand we have a visitor?"

"Clio Finch's father," Gabriel said quietly to her. "Hold his attention while I go and talk to her."

"She's probably still in bed."

"Never mind."

He ran upstairs and then realized he didn't know which room was Clio's. It would probably be next to Lady Holly's. He picked the most likely door, knocked, and went in.

She sat up staring, and clutched the covers up high. She

wore a plain white nightcap, but her hair was plaited. She was astonishingly beautiful. "What are you doing here?"

"Don't scream," he said, shutting the door behind him. "Your father's here."

Her eyes widened in alarm. "What? Why?"

"Because you've received an offer of marriage from Lord Fensham."

"No!"

He smiled at her instant horror. "I hope that's refusal rather than disbelief."

"Both. I'd never marry him, but why would he even offer?"

"Because there aren't many families in the land who'd let him have a daughter after the way he treated his first three wives. Your father can't force you."

"No, thank heavens. I suppose I must go down and tell him so. Go away so I can dress."

He wanted, desperately, to go to her and kiss her. Good God, they'd not yet kissed. He wanted so much more. He wanted to climb into her bed and ravish her, but first things first.

"Wait a moment," he said. "According to your father your disgrace is only rumors. Can that be true?"

"Rumors are bad enough."

"But not fatal. What exactly happened, Clio?"

"Why are you angry with me?"

I'm mad with lust for you, and yes, angry that you may have implied a greater ruin than is true.

Gabriel made himself calm down and talk sense. "I'm not angry. Irritated, perhaps. Desperate for other reasons. Please tell me the story."

She frowned at him, but did so. "The man—I'll call him Lovelace—wooed me. He was good company and I was lonely. I'd been engaged to marry Will, so I'd kept other men at bay, and then I'd mourned him. Not exactly mourned, because I couldn't believe it. For a while I clung to hope that there was a mistake. That he'd be found alive. But then one of his friends came to see me and give me some mementoes. He'd been there when Will died. . . ."

She used the sheet to dab her eyes. "Lovelace took me away from such thoughts and didn't seem to mind that I was still dressing plainly out of mourning. I thought I was in love, but he had no money. When my father saw my interest, he forbade me to see him again. It seems mad now, because my father was right, but I rebelled and when Lovelace asked me to elope with him, I saw it as proof of love. Lovelace didn't mind that I was penniless. Of course, he simply wanted me. After two nights on the road he slipped away, leaving me a few guineas to survive on and a note to say that the name I'd known him by was false."

"I do hope to meet him one day."

"And what? Fight a duel? That would compound the folly. It was as much my fault as his."

"Nonsense. I was told your family threw you out."

"They did, in effect. The innkeeper sent for the vicar, and the vicar and his wife proved to be truly good people. They took me in without a word of reproach and persuaded me to write to my parents, asking their forgiveness. They told me never to return. The vicar contacted a local lady. She wrote to the dowager, and so I came here."

"Still wearing mourning for your one true love."

"Yes."

"Was that green gown that color originally?"

"What has that to do with anything?"

"Idle curiosity."

"You're mad. No, it wasn't. It was bright green and I tried to dye it black. The dye didn't take so it ended up like that. It served for half-mourning. I didn't care about such things."

He had to go closer, even though he knew it was dangerous. "Your father claims the scandal was merely rumors, so your parents must have made some explanation. They'd not want to scream to the rooftops that you'd eloped, and especially that you'd been abandoned."

"I suppose not. Why does it matter?"

"Because," he said, hand tight on the bedpost, "you aren't ruined in the face of the world."

She stared at his tone. "I'm still *ruined*. Two nights on the road, Gabriel. We didn't behave chastely."

Suddenly, he relaxed. He could even smile. "You called me Gabriel."

"Probably because we're engaged in an inappropriately intimate discussion in my bedroom!"

"I look forward to many more. Clio, I think I love you."

She frowned. "You think?"

"Let's not push insanity too far."

"Insane, is it?"

"Completely, because it's too fast and furious, but I've been fighting the need to act on it and ruin your life."

"It's already ruined, or have you forgotten that?"

He waved a hand. "A trifle."

"I am not a virgin," she said carefully.

"That's a natural result of two nights on the road spent unchastely."

"You don't mind?"

"I'm not a virgin either. Rather more absolutely than you, if that makes sense. I'm not worthy of you, Clio. Remember what Lady Holly said."

"That you're not suitable for marriage or some such. Is that true?"

"I don't know. But I'm willing to try if you are. I think it would be a very good idea if we kissed."

"I don't. Not here at least."

"Then get dressed and—"

There was a knock on the door and Aunt Elizabeth put her head in. "Decent, thank heavens. I don't know what's going on, but I can't fob off Mr. Finch much longer. He's becoming concerned that we've done you some harm, dear."

"Oh. Right. Go away," Clio said to Gabriel. "Whatever nonsense is in your head, we'll discuss it after I've dealt with my father."

He had no choice but to leave.

Out in the corridor, Aunt Elizabeth demanded, "What nonsense is in your head, Gabriel?"

"I want to marry her. I think."

"Only think?"

"I'm trying to be sensible! But I don't think I can live without her. I thought we couldn't marry, because if she's ruined . . . You do know about that?"

"Of course. Lady Holly told me before inviting her here."

He paced the carpeted corridor. "It seemed it was public knowledge in her home area, and you know what would happen if I married her."

"Everyone would dig for information. I see."

He stilled to look at her. "But if it's not. . . ."

"It doesn't seem to be, but I don't have the full details. What are you going to do?"

Gabriel stared at the wall and suddenly all was clear. "Marry her. I'll go mad otherwise. If the situation's bad, we'll go abroad. We'll find some place on the globe where no one will care." He smiled at her. "At least I'll be spared encounters with my family."

She put a hand on his arm. "But for this family's sake, I hope it will not come to that, my dear."

Aunt Elizabeth went away. Gabriel waited. Clio emerged wearing the gray and the cap, but this was no ghost. Her chin was up and she was ready for battle.

She blushed, however, when she saw him. "I won't hold you to anything you said."

He took her hand. "Let's settle it with a kiss." She resisted a little, but not very much, and then she was in his arms, so perfectly. He sank his fingers into her thick hair beneath the dratted cap, and finally, at last, kissed her. He felt her relax and blend into the kiss so he could deepen it and taste her and sink entirely into her, home at last.

"Gabriel!" It was hissed rather than shouted, but it made him emerge from bliss.

Aunt Elizabeth was glaring down the corridor at them. "Now!" she said, but she was smiling at the same time.

"Come on," he said, and linked arms with his beloved as they went downstairs and into the breakfast room.

Clio's father rose. "There you are at last! Have you been told? Pack your bags and we'll be off home."

Gabriel closed the door. "I do beg your pardon, sir, but before this goes any further, I wish to ask for your daughter's hand in marriage."

The ruby color rose in Finch's face again. "What? *You?*"

"Me."

"But . . . Who exactly are you, sir?"

"Lord Gabriel Quinfroy, son of the Duke of Straith."

"Duke . . . ." The man's jaw dropped.

"And Clio does me the honor of preferring me to Lord Felsham."

"Be damned to that!" Mr. Finch had recovered. Clearly, he was the sort of man who didn't like his plans overturned, not even for the better. "You don't know the truth about her."

"I believe I already intimated that I did. However, despite your being my lady's father, I regret to have to say that I shall take great objection to any further mention of the matter."

"What? *What?*"

"Sit down, sir, before you have an apoplexy." Gabriel steered Clio into a chair opposite her father and sat beside her. She was tense now, and perhaps even trembling, so he kept hold of her hand. "Mr. Finch, what story did you tell at home to account for Clio's absence?"

Finch set his jaw as if he'd refuse to answer, but then said, "That she'd been called away to attend to a sick aunt."

"Which aunt?"

"Does it matter?"

"It will if anyone checks the story."

"My sister, Marjorie. She's always ailing with something or other."

"She's a widow," Clio said quietly. "Lives in Nottinghamshire. I was never near her."

Gabriel asked, "Does she know about this story?"

"Of course, she does," Finch said. "What's the use of a story if it won't be backed up?"

"But it won't stand if anyone looks closely," Clio said. "Gabriel . . ."

"Hush, my dear. Do I have your blessing, sir?"

Finch was still frowning, out of pure bloody-mindedness. "What sort of life can you offer her, sir? I know about you younger sons."

"My dear sir, duke's sons are rarely penny-pinched, but I happen to be a very wealthy one. She will want for nothing." He turned to Clio. "I never asked if you have brothers and sisters."

"Two brothers. One sister, married."

He turned back to Finch. "Clio's family will doubtless benefit from her marriage, if that counts with you."

It did. Mr. Finch was unpleasant, but not stupid. "The Duke of Straith, eh? Influence?" He was probably envisioning visits to Straith. Gabriel thought it unlikely, but wished him well of it.

"I have your consent, sir?"

"I . . ." Still it seemed likely to choke him, but he managed, "You do, my lord."

Gabriel rose, taking Clio with him. "We thank you, sir."

He took her across the hall into the reception room and closed the door.

"You haven't exactly asked me," she said, "and I haven't accepted!"

He went on one knee. "Clio, my dear, please marry me."

She bit her lip. "How can I know if I should? I won't like other women."

"I'll keep my vows."

"Are you sure you can? Oh! That's a horrid thing to say, but I'm . . ."

"You're afraid. Fate cheated you once, and delivered a cur another time. I won't betray you, my dear. That is my solemn promise. Take flight. Say yes."

She stared at him, but then whispered, "Yes."

He rose and captured her for their second kiss, which was every bit as splendid as their first. And more so. He felt her move, and remembered thinking she'd been driven to folly by lust. It had bothered him then. It didn't now. He wished they were married now, but as they weren't, he broke the kiss and held her tight.

"I'd set off now for Scotland and a hasty marriage, my love, but I'd prefer to wed you in good form and splendor."

She drew back to look at him. "From my *home*?"

"Not if you don't want. We could marry from here. Lady Holly will want to be present, and it's no season for traveling."

"Will it do?"

"It will do. If you don't need time to be sure. I want to seize you now, chain you to me forever, but if you need more time . . ."

"I want to seize you now as well. I'm afraid. Afraid this, too, will slip away."

"It won't. I won't." He took her by the hand and led her upstairs, to the painting of Holbourne Manor. "I thought to buy a place a little like this, but close to London. I wanted a home. It took me longer to realize that I wanted you by the door."

"And our children running to greet you?"

"And our children running to greet me. We can hunt for it together. Soon."

She turned from the picture to smile at him. "How perfect that will be. Perhaps you are an angel, after all, my love."

MISTLETOE KISSES

❦

Anne Gracie

CHAPTER ONE

"*Teach?* Good gad, gel, you can't possibly go off and teach in some dreary girls seminary," the Dowager Countess of Holbourne, known to her friends as Lady Holly, declared. "It'll be the end of life as you know it!"

"There's no other alternative," Alice Fenton told her. "Papa's cousin has inherited the estate, he and his family are returning from Jamaica in the New Year, and I have nowhere else to live. Besides, his commitments in Jamaica gave me a whole extra year here at The Oakes, for which I'm very grateful." It had given her time to mourn in peace, and time to make a plan for her future. "Now it's time to move on."

"He's pushing you out in the *cold*?" Lady Holly said, outraged. "From the home of your *birth*? And that of your father and his father before him and goodness knows how many Fentons before that?"

"On the contrary, he told me I was welcome to make my home with him and his wife and children—"

"Hmph! The fellow has some family feelings then."

"He has been everything that is honorable and sympathetic," Allie assured her kindly neighbor.

"Then why this dreary seminary?"

Allie wondered how to explain it to Lady Holly. She didn't want to make her cousin seem ungenerous, and in fact he hadn't been—not at all. He just happened to mention—in the same paragraph as he offered her a home at The Oakes for as long as she needed it—that his wife would welcome her help with the children. All five of them.

And while Allie was fond of children, if she had to spend her life tending to other people's children, she'd rather be paid for it. The never-ending role of "poor relation" was not one she wanted to step into.

"I've always had a fancy to be a teacher," she said lightly. "And the idea of earning my own living appeals. Besides, it wouldn't be fair to my cousin or his wife. If I were to stay on at The Oakes it would cause—with the best will in the world on my part—divided loyalties."

The old lady sniffed. "Pride, that's what it is. You've ruled the roost here all your life."

Allie laughed. "Precisely, and you know as well as I do that if I stayed on, the servants and tenants would be forever referring to me, instead of Papa's cousin, who is the rightful heir."

"Selfish! That's what he was."

"Oh, I hardly think it's Cousin Howard's fault—"

"Not him, your father. Now I don't wish to speak ill of the dead, but there's no denying it. He buried himself in his books and left everything to you all these years, never once considering your future. You never even had a chance of meeting eligible young men, stuck at home as you were, first looking after your poor dear mother, and then your papa—not to mention keeping the estate running."

Allie said nothing. It was true, more or less—Papa had been devoted to his studies and had no interest in the estate, or how Allie spent her time, but what Lady Holly failed to understand was that Allie had enjoyed it, far more than was ladylike.

She liked meeting with the tenants, deciding on what improvements to make, what crops to try, liked balancing the books and working out ways of increasing their income. She enjoyed it and was good at it.

But Lady Holly didn't approve, let alone understand. To ladies of her generation—and to men like Papa's cousin—a young woman should be spared all that nasty masculine responsibility. A young woman's only task was to obey her parents. And to dance and look pretty and to make a suitable match.

And had she ever had a chance to dance and look pretty and make a suitable match, no doubt Allie would have been perfectly content, too, but poor Mama had become ill just before Allie was due to make her come out, and the dreadful wasting disease had taken five years to do its ghastly work. Papa had not been able to bear watching Mama suffer; he'd buried himself in his studies, and hadn't ever emerged. So Allie had done what needed to be done, nursing Mama and seeing to the running of the estate. And then Papa had sickened . . .

Now, at seven-and-twenty, Allie was not only too old to make a come out, she was well and truly on the shelf. Still, she was looking forward to her new career. She'd spent so long dealing with illness and death, the idea of living and working with lively young girls held a strong appeal.

"You'll come to my Christmas ball, then," Lady Holly told her. "Don't bother trying to think up any excuses—you're coming and that's that. Your year of mourning will be up, and you have no reason to stay here moldering away when I've gathered an excellent range of eligible gentlemen for your perusal."

Allie laughed. "For my perusal? As if I'm going shopping?"

"That's exactly what you'll be doing."

"Don't the gentlemen have any say in it?"

The old lady sniffed. "Women have been making men believe they have a choice for generations. Now don't be frivolous, Allie—I am determined to give you one last chance to find a husband before you go off and bury yourself in this, this school of yours." She pronounced "school" as if she really meant "zoo."

Allie smiled. For all her caustic tone, Lady Holly had a very kind heart. "I would love to attend your ball, Lady Holly . . ."

The old lady frowned. "I hear a 'but' coming."

"Not really—I would truly love to dance and flirt and be madly frivolous, and your Christmas balls are legendary, and you know I've never been able to attend. But the only ball dresses I have were made for the eighteen-year-old me, and not the seven-and-twenty version. Alas"—Allie indicated her hips and bosom and grimaced—"I'm no longer the slender young thing I was."

Lady Holly snorted. "You were a scrawny young twig back then—no bosom or hips to speak of. Now you've a fine womanly figure. Besides, I've thought of that. Took the liberty of getting a dress made for you—left the box with Meadows. It should fit—got Mrs. Meadows to take your measurements from one of your current dresses."

Allie blinked in surprise. "You had a dress made for me? A ball dress?"

"Now don't get all stiff-necked on me, Allie Fenton," the old lady said in a fierce tone that didn't deceive Allie for an instant. "I was very fond of your dear mother and this is for her, as much as for you. She was so looking forward to your making your come out and was devastated that her illness prevented it."

"I'm not being stiff-necked, truly I'm not. I'm just . . . surprised." There was a lump in Allie's throat. She was deeply touched by the old lady's brusque kindness. And thoughtfulness. A ball dress . . .

Lady Holly reached over and patted her hand. "Now don't look like that, my dear—I promised your mother I'd see you dancing in the arms of a handsome man, and though circumstances have prevented it in the past—and I quite see that it would have been the height of impropriety for you to go dancing when first your mother and then your father lay dying—there is nothing to prevent you now, and you will come to my ball!"

Allie smiled mistily. "Just like Cinderella. And you've even provided the gown."

The old lady chuckled. "It's my fiftieth annual ball. I wasn't going to have you coming dressed like a crow, was I?" She eyed Allie's mourning clothes and wrinkled her nose. "You'll be putting off your blacks tomorrow, I hope."

Allie nodded. It was a year since Papa's death.

"Good. Then you'll come to my ball." It wasn't a question.

"Thank you, I would love to come—I cannot think of anything I would love more, to dance at your fiftieth Christmas ball and to say farewell to all my friends." Allie hugged the old lady. "You've always been such a good friend to me and my family. Thank you, dear Lady Holly, with all my heart."

Lady Holly, deeply pleased, said gruffly, "Pish-tush, girl, no need to gush. Come and stay at the Abbey from Christmas Eve onward—the ball's not 'til the twenty-eighth, but you won't want to be alone for Christmas." She stood, ready to leave.

"Thank you, it's very kind of you, but I won't come for Christmas," Abby said. "It's my last Christmas here, and I want to spend it at home."

Lady Holly frowned. "Here? Alone? On your first Christmas without your father?"

"I won't be dismal, I promise you. I know it sounds as if it would be a melancholy occasion, but Papa loved Christmas and so do I, and I want to make this a Christmas to remember—my last Christmas in my own home." And though there would inevitably be moments of melancholy, Allie would rather be here at home having a small, special, personal Christmas, than with a crowd of smart London people in Holbourne Abbey, where she didn't belong. And where Christmas would be a noisy, rollicking affair.

The old lady gave her a troubled look. "That's all very well, but . . . alone?"

Allie linked her arm through the old lady's and walked slowly with her toward the front door. "I won't be lonely, truly I won't. I'm very used to my own company. And I want a last precious Christmas at home to remember." She added with a laugh, "And when I'm in the seminary, surrounded every minute of the day and night by clamoring schoolgirls, no doubt I'll reflect fondly on the joys of solitude, too."

Lady Holly gave a delicate shudder. "Can't see it, myself, but if that's what you want . . . But if you change your mind, come on Christmas Eve. Or before."

Allie hugged her again. "I won't, thank you, but I'll definitely be there for the ball. And thank you again for my dress."

Meadows had taken the parcel containing the dress up to Allie's bedchamber, so the moment Lady Holly's carriage had driven off, Allie hurried upstairs, consumed with curiosity. And excitement—how long was it since she'd had a new dress? Years.

She didn't count the three new dresses she'd ordered from the village dressmaker—she hadn't worn them yet, and besides, they'd been ordered with a view to her role as schoolteacher, so they were sober in color and cut—a deep blue kerseymere and a sage-green wool for everyday wear, and a dress in amber silk for when she needed something dressier.

Lady Holly liked lighter, brighter colors. So did Allie.

The parcel, tied with string and wrapped in brown paper, lay on her bed. She untied the string and under the wrapping paper found an elegant box with a stylish gold emblem on the front. She swallowed. This was no dress from the village seamstress—it was from Lady Holly's own London mantua maker.

She eased off the lid, parted the layers of protective tissue paper and gasped. Almost holding her breath, she drew the dress from its nest of tissue. It was beautiful.

The underdress was a light shimmering lilac shade that she just knew would go perfectly with both her recent mourning, and also her coloring. But the lovely silk underdress was quite cast in the shade by the delicate overdress in some kind of gauzy fabric through which the lilac silk shimmered. Embroidered here and there with tiny rosebuds in silver thread, it was finished with bands of delicately gathered silver lace around the hem and at the elbows of the puffed sleeves, and a line of silver embroidery around the neck.

In the box, hidden beneath the dress, was underwear—not the kind of underwear that Allie had ever in her life worn—delicate, lacy, flimsy, exquisite underwear—a chemise, a petticoat, the daintiest, most feminine drawers, and even a corset. All were trimmed with lace, and everything but the corset was practically transparent. Almost scandalous.

She remembered Lady Holly's comment that she had the figure of a woman now, not a girl. Allie had never really given it much thought. But now . . . these were certainly underclothes for a woman, not a girl. Smiling to herself, she put the lovely, naughty underclothes back in the box. She'd probably die a spinster, but she would treasure these forever.

She picked up the dress again, held it against her body and turned to gaze at her reflection in the looking glass. It was the most beautiful dress she'd ever owned. And it suited her perfectly. The lilac color complemented her pale complexion and her dark hair, and even seemed to make her very ordinary gray eyes look almost exotic. The silver thread gleamed and shimmered in the light. It was a dress made for dancing. . . .

How many years since she'd danced? And never at a ball.

Delight bubbled up in her. After what felt like years wearing mourning black and gray, this dress felt like a breath of spring. And yet even the highest sticklers could not look askance at her—lavender and lilac were approved colors for half mourning.

But would it fit? She stripped off her old black gown and, holding her breath, she carefully slipped the ball gown over her head. And breathed. It was perfect. It was more than perfect.

She gazed at her reflection, gave a sudden laugh and twirled around and around, as if she were a giddy, carefree girl again.

She felt just like Cinderella. And she was going to the ball.

CHAPTER TWO

"Take the horse and gig—I insist," Allie told Meadows and Mrs. Meadows, her butler and cook.

"But you'll be all on your lonesome, Miss Allie." The motherly cook's face crumpled with concern. "You can't stay here without a soul to care for you."

"For a few days?" Allie laughed. "I can and I will. There's enough food to feed an army, sufficient wood to keep me warm for the whole of winter, and you'll be gone less than a week."

She'd given the servants a holiday. Since her father's death, when Cousin Howard had assumed the reins of control, albeit from Jamaica, they'd had to work doubly hard.

Cousin Howard had seen no reason to keep on what he called "a horde of servants" to care for one young woman, and he'd put most of them off, instructing Allie to close off all the rooms of the house except those she herself would need.

The Meadows family was all that remained of the former staff. They did everything, except for two village girls who came in twice a week to clean and do laundry. The Meadows's son, Albert, did whatever else was needed, including caring for the one remaining horse Cousin Howard had deemed necessary for Allie's use.

Allie had only met Cousin Howard a few times when she was young, but since Papa's death, the letters that came regularly from Jamaica had given her a fairly clear picture of the man's character; he was not a man who liked to spend his money on other people's needs. And since Allie had very little of her own, she couldn't afford to pay servants herself. She'd had to be content with giving them a small Christmas bonus from her own purse. And a holiday.

"Maybe Albert should stay, just so as you have someone else here."

Allie shook her head. "And have a Meadows party go without music because Albert's not there to play his fiddle? I wouldn't think of it. No, you must all go."

She was fairly certain they would not be getting holidays, or even appreciation once Cousin Howard was here in person, so she was determined to give them a holiday before she left. And enable them to attend the christening of their first grandchild.

"But what if you need the gig?"

"I won't—not until the twenty-eighth, to go to Holbourne Abbey for Lady Holly's ball, and you'll be back the day before that so—no, don't shake your head at me like that—I insist. I can walk to church, as long as the weather holds, and if it doesn't . . ." She shrugged. "It won't hurt to miss one day. Besides, you'll need the gig to visit Susan and your beautiful new granddaughter—it's much too far for you to walk, and you must stay on for the christening. You have the little gift from me, don't you?"

"Yes, Meadows packed it safe and sound, but—"

Allie pushed the woman gently toward the door. "Then go. And don't worry. I'll be perfectly all right. It's only a few days. Have a very merry Christmas, and pass on my best wishes to the rest of the family, and in particular to Susan and the baby."

Susan was a few years younger than Allie, but they were friends, having grown up in the same house. Susan had been married for five years and had begun to despair of ever having children, but now at last she had her own dear little baby daughter to love.

Allie waved good-bye, trying not to feel envious.

The following morning, Allie waxed and polished all the furniture in the sitting room, polished the brass fenders and the fire screen with its old-fashioned sailing ship design, mopped the floor, beat and straightened the rug, and plumped the cushions on the settee. When she finished, the room smelled pleasantly of beeswax and brass cleaner. And of the wood burning in the fireplace.

Tomorrow, she would go out to cut greenery. In years past, they'd decorated the whole house, but this year it would just be the sitting room.

Next she went up to the attic and fetched down the Christmas box. Made of oak from a tree grown on the estate, the wood had been sanded and polished until it was silky smooth. She dusted it and set it on the rug in front of the fire in the sitting room.

It had been made for Allie when she was a child by Old Peter, an elderly workman on the estate. Every year he'd made something new to add to the box.

Each item was wrapped in tissue; first the stable—just three walls and a roof—then the holy family, carved and painted by Peter, and dressed by Allie and her mother; Mary in a blue cloak and dress made from an old dress of Mama's, Joseph in a red flannel robe tied around the middle with a piece of string; and the three kings and the wise men in rich robes cut from an old dressing gown of Papa's and some scraps Allie had begged from the dressmaker one year. The kings were distinguished by gold paper crowns. Then came the manger and the tiny baby Jesus, wrapped in a square of white wool, hemmed in clumsy stitches by an eight-year-old Allie.

No nativity scene was complete without animals and Old Peter had carved an ox, a donkey, a few chickens, a cat, two tiny mice, a couple of camels—slightly oddly humped, as Old Peter had never seen a camel—and a handful of sheep, along with the requisite shepherds with their ragged striped robes and crooks.

Allie's favorite piece was a carved and painted version of her beloved dog, Gippy, a gift from Old Peter the Christmas she was twelve. Every detail was perfect, from the little tan eyebrows on the black-and-white face, to the feathery tip of white at the end of his black tail.

Gippy was long gone, but his spirit remained in this little carved figure. And on one of the shepherds, whose body bore a clear line of puppy teeth dents. Each year those teeth marks made her smile.

She arranged the nativity scene on the mantelpiece. The paint was worn, the clothing faded, and the gold of the kings' crowns was dull now, instead of shiny, but Allie wouldn't change them for anything.

After a simple lunch of soup and cheese on toast, Allie put on her warmest coat, hat, scarf, gloves, and boots. There had been a severe frost the night before and it was still bitterly cold outside.

She fetched a basket and a pair of stout shears and tried not to think about previous Christmases when the collecting of greenery had been laughter-filled events, punctuated with snowball fights. . . . And fingers, toes, and noses all cold, and tingling with the joy of being alive, and coming home to hot drinks and mince pies and soup and toasted crumpets. And the smell of the house filled with fresh fragrant greens . . .

She always loved collecting the pine and laurel, holly, ivy and . . . maybe, she wouldn't bother with mistletoe this year. With nobody but herself in the house, what was the point?

The grass crunched under her feet as she set out. Last

night's frost still lay on the ground in some parts. The air was crisp and cold and invigorating. She breathed in great lungfuls of it, feeling more alive by the minute. Her breath coiled in smoky puffs, then dissipated, along with the faint melancholy that had overtaken her earlier. She found herself humming a Christmas carol, and smiled. She loved this time of the year.

She headed toward the river that bordered the road that passed their front gates. The berries were always reddest on the holly that grew there—she didn't know why.

She was almost within sight of the gates when she heard the sound of hooves and a carriage. Then there was a shout, the screaming of a horse, and a loud, sickening crash.

Allie dropped her basket and ran toward the sound. She reached the road in time to see a yellow traveling chaise tipped on its side, slipping slowly down the riverbank to land half in the river. The two horses pulling it were plunging and struggling to escape, the postilion still somehow clinging to the back of the lead horse.

A pale gloved hand flailed at the carriage window— there was a woman inside the carriage.

Allie raced across the road, and skidded down the bank of the river. She had to climb onto the wheel to reach the handle of the door. She wrenched it open and the white, frightened face of a girl looked out.

"Here." Allie held out her hand. "Let me help you." She pulled the girl to safety and as she jumped down, a tall man appeared in the chaise doorway, his face covered in blood.

He dashed the blood impatiently from his eyes, saying, "Lucilla, are you all right?" The girl nodded, and the man said to Allie, "Thank you. You girls move to a safer place— I'll deal with the horses."

"But you're hurt—" Allie began, but he took no notice. He jumped down from the chaise and hurried to see to the panicking horses.

Allie pulled the shivering girl back onto the edge of the

road, watching helplessly. The horses plunged and struggled, the postilion yelled—it was complete chaos.

"Stop that caterwauling, you fool," the man snapped. "Calm them." The postilion gave him a fearful look and the yelling ceased, but he did nothing else. He remained clinging to the back of his horse looking frightened.

The tall man cursed under his breath, produced a knife from his boot, and proceeded to cut the traces of the panicked horses who, freed of the dragging weight of the chaise, calmed somewhat. He cut the last trace, the horses scrambled up the bank, and the chaise slid farther into the water.

"Now," he said grimly, turning to the postilion. "What the hell—"

The postilion took one horrified look at the sinking chaise, and the furious, bloody face of the tall man and galloped away, taking both horses with him.

"Come back!" the man shouted, but the horses turned the corner and were gone from sight. The man swore again to himself, pulled out a handkerchief and, wiping blood from his face, turned to Allie and the girl.

"That's the last we'll see of him, I'll be bound. Blasted fellow was drunk. I could smell it on him when I cut the horses free."

"It's a dangerous corner," Allie said. "And there was ice on the road."

He gave a curt nod of acknowledgment, but all his attention was on the girl, who was ashen and shaking. "Are you sure you're all right, Lucilla?"

The girl said nothing, but shivered convulsively in Allie's arms. Allie said, "I think she's just shocked and wet and shaken up, but what about you, sir—"

"I'm fine," he brushed her off. "But my sister—"

"You're not fine—you're bleeding like a stuck pig," Allie said bluntly.

He glanced at her then, and his lips quirked. "It's

nothing—a small cut from when the window smashed. Head injuries bleed easily. But I need to get my sister out of this cold. Her skirt is soaked, it's freezing, and she's very susceptible to chills."

"I live just up there." Allie pointed to the drive that ran from the big wrought-iron gates. "Come up into the warmth and we can decide what to do when you're dry and"—she indicated his injury—"I've tended to that."

The girl called Lucilla gave a little shriek and pointed to the chaise, which was sliding deeper into the water. "John! All our things."

He muttered something Allie didn't catch. "Take my sister up to the house," he snapped. "I'll try to retrieve the luggage."

"But—"

"Just go!" he told her and without waiting for her response, he slithered down the riverbank, climbed onto the precariously listing chaise, grabbed a bandbox from the swirling current and hurled it up onto the riverbank.

He saw her hesitating, and yelled, "Go on up and get warm. I'll join you as soon as I've dealt with this."

Seeing no alternative other than getting even colder as they watched him, Allie took the shivering girl up to the house.

CHAPTER THREE

$\mathcal{A}$llie took Lucilla straight to the kitchen, the warmest room in the house. The fire in the cast-iron range was kept burning through winter, the kettle was always hot, and she'd put on a large pot of soup to keep warm against her return.

"Now let's get you out of these wet things."

Lucilla hesitated and gave a wary glance around her.

Allie smiled. "It's all right, there's nobody else in the house—the servants are gone for the holidays."

"All of them? Then who . . . ?" Again she looked around. Clearly, she was wondering what kind of establishment did without servants.

"We look after ourselves," Allie said. She stripped the shivering girl of her wet clothes, toweled her briskly dry, wrapped her in a blanket and sat her down at the kitchen table with a bowl of hot soup with a little added brandy. While Lucilla addressed the soup, Allie hurried to fetch some clothes for her to wear.

Dusk was falling, so she lit a couple of lanterns and placed one at the front entrance to guide the man called John to the house. Then she went upstairs and went through her wardrobe.

Luckily, she and Lucilla were of a similar build. She grabbed a gray woolen gown, a flannel petticoat, woolen stockings, a warm shawl, and a pair of slippers. The girl's brother would no doubt be in need of a change of clothing, too, so Allie fetched some of her father's clothing, adding his dressing gown to the pile, in case Papa's things didn't fit.

She had only the vaguest impression of the girl's brother, that he was tall and dark and autocratic. And that he was bleeding. She hurried back to the kitchen.

"I hope you don't mind the color," she said as she helped Lucilla into the dress. "I'm only just out of mourning."

"No, not at all, it's very kind of you." She gave a worried glance at the door. "Do you think John will be all right?"

"He looks very capable to me," Allie soothed her. Capable and quite bossy.

"Oh, he is. He was a soldier, you know, but he had to sell out when our older brother died—he broke his neck on the hunting field. Papa died when I was a little girl, you see, and so Mama quite depended on John coming home."

Lucilla, thawed and warm, proved to be quite a chatterbox—or possibly it was the brandy—and in no time at all Allie learned that she was Lucilla Kelsey, that she was almost eighteen, that she was making her come out in the spring, and that she and her brother were on the way to Holbourne Abbey to attend Lady Holly's ball. She was thrilled by the prospect.

"It will be my first ever ball, you see, and Mama was going to bring me—she is a friend of Lady Holbourne—Lady Holly's daughter-in-law—only Grandmamma has come down with the shingles, which is the horridest thing, so, of course, Mama had to stay home to tend her because Grandmamma hates to be ill and is a very difficult invalid and Mama is the only person she will mind, and, of course, I was simply devastated when she said we couldn't go, because I was so looking forward to it and I had a special dress made and slippers dyed to match and everything." And here she went into a rapturous description of her dress which was white hail-spotted muslin with the palest green silk underdress and a row of the sweetest little green satin bows around the hem, with crimson satin ribbons tied in the most elegant knots—"Christmas colors, you see—holly and berries."

Allie smiled and made appropriate responses as Lucilla chattered on. The girl's liveliness was endearing, even if it made Allie feel rather dull by comparison. Had she ever been so young and eager and full of life?

Allie stirred the soup, cut bread and cheese and thick slices of ham and set the kitchen table. John Kelsey would be arriving any minute and he'd be wet, hungry, and half frozen. She hoped he wouldn't mind eating in the kitchen. Bad luck if he did.

She fetched her medicine basket. For all his protestations that it was nothing, that cut on his head needed tending. She glanced outside. Dark was falling fast and it had started to snow.

Lucilla rattled happily on. "All my life I've heard about Lady Holly's Christmas ball—Mama and Papa met there, you know, more than thirty years ago—so romantic it was, even though they only had old-fashioned dances and nothing like a waltz—do you waltz, Miss Fenton—I've had lessons, but I've never danced it properly at a ball, not with a real partner—so I was utterly cast down when Mama said we couldn't go. And then dearest, darling John said he would take me—he was to stay with friends over Christmas—a hunting box in Leicestershire—horrid stuff, but men seem to enjoy it. But instead"—she beamed at Allie—"he is taking me to the ball."

Allie smiled. "He sounds like a very good brother."

"Oh, he is. Mama told me most men would not give up a week's hunting to take their little sister to a ball, and that I was not to plague him by chattering nonstop in the carri—oh!" She broke off, clapping her hand over her mouth, looking comically dismayed. "Mama says my tongue runs on wheels. I've been plaguing you, haven't I?"

Allie laughed. "Not at all. I'm enjoying your company

very much." It was true. She found the girl's innocent chatter refreshing and the reflection that she would be working with young girls like Lucilla in the New Year cheered her immensely.

The front doorbell rang and Allie hurried to answer it. John Kelsey, carrying a valise and a couple of damp-looking bandboxes, stood on the front portico stamping snow off his boots. The single lantern bathed him partly in light, partly in shadow. Behind him, snow swirled and drifted against the darkness.

He was hatless and his thick, dark hair lay on his forehead in damp clumps. A dusting of snowflakes lay on his hair and across his shoulders, his very broad shoulders. His skin was lightly tanned, his cheeks were ruddy from the cold and he looked very big, very masculine, and very handsome. The cut on his forehead was no longer bleeding profusely, but was slowly oozing blood.

His jaw was firm, his nose was bold, his mouth was stern, and his eyes burned blue in the golden lamplight. They gleamed quizzically down at her, as if he were waiting for something.

Allie, realizing she'd been staring, gathered her wits, and stepped back. "Oh, I'm sorry. Please come in out of the cold, Mr. Kelsey."

"Thank you." He stepped inside and the entrance suddenly felt quite a bit smaller.

Allie shut the front door against the bitter cold and turned to face him. She picked up the lantern, suddenly at a loss for words.

His blue eyes glinted. "My sister has recovered from her fright, I take it?"

"Yes, she's perfectly well. She's changed her clothes and had some pea and ham soup with a little brandy in it and it seems to have done the trick."

"Thank you for taking care of her, Miss—?"

"Fenton. I'm sorry, I should have introduced myself

earlier"—*instead of staring,* she added silently—"I'm Alice Fenton. Welcome to The Oakes."

"And I am, as I'm sure Lucilla will have told you, Kelsey, of Kelsey Manor in Yorkshire. Thank you for tending to my sister and for offering us shelter." He glanced around, frowning slightly, and Allie knew he was wondering where the servants were.

There was no point trying to conceal the fact that she was alone here; he would find out soon enough, so she said, "I'm afraid you picked the wrong place to be stranded in, for I've given the servants a holiday and we will have to fend for ourselves."

He frowned. "Do I understand that you're alone here?"

"For a few days," Allie said tranquilly. "I'm perfectly capable of looking after myself and a couple of guests. Come this way. You won't mind the kitchen, I hope—it's the warmest room and the best place to tend your injury."

She led him to the kitchen, where Lucilla exclaimed over the damaged hatboxes. She anxiously examined the contents, several elegant hats that proved to be only slightly dampened.

"Lucilla, would you help your brother remove his coat and boots, please? Mr. Kelsey, if you would sit here please?" Allie indicated the chair closest to the fire.

"It's Lord Kelsey," Lucilla corrected her as she put a hat down and hurried to help her brother with his boots.

"Lord Kelsey." Allie handed him a towel to dry his hair. She should have realized he was titled from the way he'd introduced himself earlier: Kelsey of Kelsey Manor.

She placed a bowl of hot soup in front of him, added a generous splosh of brandy, and handed him a spoon. "Drink this while it's hot. It will warm you from the inside."

He took it, eyeing her with an expression she couldn't quite read. His steady blue gaze made her oddly flustered.

She took refuge in busyness. "Lucilla and I will leave

you to change out of those wet things. There are dry clothes there." She indicated a pile of folded clothing on a chair. "I hope they fit. My father was not as tall as you, nor quite as broad in the shoulder, but should they prove insufficient, his dressing gown should cover you well enough."

"There's no need—"

"There is hot water and more soup on the stove if you need it, and the brandy is on the table—help yourself. We shall return in fifteen minutes and I will tend to that cut on your forehead."

"It's perfectly all right."

She smiled. "Of course. Nevertheless, you will indulge me in this."

His brows rose and his lips twitched in a hint of a smile. "Will I?"

"You will," she said, quite matter-of-factly. "A gentleman must always indulge a lady. Besides, my house, my rules. Come, Lucilla, let us make up the beds."

Lucilla blinked but, with a bemused expression, she followed Allie upstairs.

John Kelsey hid a smile. Lucilla, making beds? As he drank his soup—very good it was, too, and the brandy a welcome addition—and ate the bread and cheese and ham, he considered his hostess, Miss Alice Fenton.

She had the sweetest face. His mother and Lucilla would probably say it was too round to be considered beautiful, but John found no fault with it. That small, decided chin balanced the roundness perfectly, as did the tip-tilted, rather imperious little nose, and the big gray eyes. Add to that a flawless creamy complexion, a luscious, very kissable mouth, and a figure that was rounded in all the right places, and Miss Fenton made a very fetching armful.

He stripped off his sodden breeches and dropped them

on the stone-flagged floor. He'd had to wade into the river to retrieve one of the bandboxes and his lower limbs were half frozen. He toweled himself vigorously.

What the devil was she doing here all alone, with not so much as a single servant to attend her? The house didn't look impoverished—he'd noticed dust sheets over the furniture in some of the rooms as he came in, but it was all clean and well-kept and the kitchen was clearly lavishly stocked—not that he was much acquainted with kitchens.

Her clothes were dark and not particularly fashionable. Was she some kind of superior servant—a governess or a paid companion, perhaps? And the family had gone away and left her behind, dismissing the rest of the servants for the holidays?

He felt mildly indignant on her behalf. Nobody should be left alone at Christmas, let alone in an isolated house in the country. And what if he and Lucilla had been villains? She would have been at their mercy.

He stripped off the rest of his clothes and toweled himself briskly until the feeling crept back into his frozen extremities.

Miss Fenton was quality born. The assurance with which she'd invited them in, and the way she'd taken command of Lucilla—and she hadn't exactly held back from contradicting his orders, either, and the way she'd told him to sit and be taken care of indicated a habit of command. But was it simply a governess-y habit or natural assurance?

She wasn't intimidated by him or his title. He found himself grinning as he imagined his sister making a bed—he doubted she'd ever made a bed in her life—ladies didn't. But Miss Fenton was clearly familiar with both bed making and cooking.

But "my house, my rules," she'd said, as if she owned the place. She was a mystery, one he'd very much like to unravel—in more ways than one.

He sipped the brandy slowly and pondered the enigma

of his hostess. It was very good brandy—another indication that it was not poverty that had caused her to be left alone at Christmas.

A few minutes later, Lucilla and Miss Fenton entered the kitchen. "Ah, I thought Papa's coat would not fit," Miss Fenton said, gathering up his discarded clothing, which still lay in a sodden heap on the stone flags.

John felt instantly embarrassed, seeing her clear up after him like a maid. He hadn't given his wet clothing a thought. Lucilla wasn't the only one who wasn't used to taking care of herself.

"Let me—" he began.

"No, it's quite all right." She pulled a chair closer to the fire and hung his coat and breeches over it. "Lucilla can rinse out the shirt and your smalls and stockings."

At Lucilla's shocked expression, she laughed. "Sorry, have I assumed again? It's just that my mother insisted I learn to do every job in the household—she said if I learned how everything ought to be done, and knew how difficult or easy various jobs were, I'd be in a better position to run my own household when I grew up. Leave it then, Lucilla. I'll do them after I've tended to your brother's injury."

John opened his mouth to assure her he needed no such tending, but she caught his gaze and gave him such a look that he found himself laughing and saying, "Oh, very well, if you must."

A dimple appeared in her cheek. "I must," she said with mock severity. She put a basket on the table beside him, and said to Lucilla, "Men think it unmanly to tend small injuries, but cuts can infect so easily—we had a gardener once who died of the tiniest scratch from a rosebush. Do you want to watch, Lucilla, or does the sight of blood distress you?"

"Not at all." Lucilla came eagerly. Miss Fenton had made a conquest of his sister, John saw.

He sat silently while Miss Fenton tended his injury and

explained to Lucilla what she was doing and what the salve she was going to use was made of. "Mrs. Meadows, my cook, makes it herself and it's very good." She began to list the ingredients, but John wasn't listening.

His attention was wholly engaged by the proximity of his lovely hostess—the very close proximity. With no apparent self-consciousness she'd stepped between his knees to tend his cut—well, it was the obvious position to do it, and if she'd been a physician John wouldn't have given it a second thought. But she was a luscious armful of femininity and what she obviously didn't realize was that in this position the only thing he could look at was her bosom. Her lush and fragrant bosom. Just inches from his nose.

Not that it was in any way exposed—her dress was high cut, warm, and modest—but beneath the sober fabric he could see her breasts moving—right in front of his eyes—as she gently washed the dried blood off his forehead.

He ought to be ashamed of himself for looking, ought to close his eyes in simple decency, but he couldn't help himself. It was an entrancing sight.

He held his breath as she lightly smeared pungent ointment over the cut, then bound it with a long strip of gauze that she wound around his head. Her breasts lifted and fell with each turn and once or twice they brushed against him as she reached back to straighten the bandage.

He fought the impulse to put his arms around her waist and just draw her to him, burying his face in those soft, lush, hidden breasts.

"There, that's better than vinegar and brown paper," she said as she stepped back and surveyed her handiwork. "I never understood why brown paper, though I suppose Jack and Jill's mother had to use what was to hand."

"You look quite dashing, John," Lucilla said. "Like a wounded hero."

"Thank you, Miss Fenton," John said softly, his eyes on hers.

A faint rosy flush crept into her cheeks. "My mother taught me well before she died," she said gruffly, and turned away to put his wet shirt and smalls into a bowl of soapy water. "They'll be dry by morning; we never let the kitchen fire go out—oh! The sitting room fire! I meant to put more wood on it when I came in."

She made to hurry from the room, but John stopped her. "That's a task for me," he said firmly. "Along here, is it?" He indicated the corridor he'd entered through.

"Yes, it's the only door that's closed—to keep the warmth in. There is wood—"

"I can manage," he told her with a faint smile. But he didn't feel like smiling. She ought not to be here on her own, worrying about keeping fires going and looking after stranded guests. But he could do nothing about it.

He built up the sitting room fire to a good blaze, then returned to find Miss Fenton hanging his wet clothes on a drying rack she'd set up in the corner of the warm kitchen.

"I'll do that," he said brusquely, taking the damp shirt from Miss Fenton. It wasn't right that she had to care for his things the way a servant would.

"Your valise looks quite wet, John," Lucilla said. "I think you should open it in case water has leaked inside."

"I know." He opened his valise and, as expected, all the items in one corner were damp. He hung them on the drying rack.

Lucilla exclaimed over the number of damp items. "I'd better check the contents of my trunk," she said. "Where did you put it, John?"

John glanced at Allie, then said, "It's still in the boot of the carriage."

"Still in the boot, but—"

"It's jammed shut by the angle of the carriage and I couldn't get it open."

"But all my things are in the trunk," Lucilla wailed.

"Now don't fuss, Lucilla," he said firmly. "The trunk is

stuck in the boot, and that's where it will have to stay until we get the carriage pulled back up on to the road. My valise and the bandboxes were, as you know, strapped to the top of the carriage, which is why they almost got washed away. Your trunk is perfectly secure. I know you want your things, but it's not as if anyone can steal them, can they? If I can't get to it, nobody can."

Lucilla opened her mouth to argue, and Allie realized a distraction was called for. "Let us go into the sitting room," she said. "Lucilla, you will find some games in the cupboard beneath the window. Let us play and take our minds off our woes."

"Excellent notion," Lord Kelsey said crisply, and held the door for his sister, who trailed reluctantly from the room.

CHAPTER FOUR

$\mathcal{A}$fter dinner they played cards for the rest of the evening, and Allie found herself laughing more than she had for a long time.

You got to know people quickly over cards; Lucilla was daring, impulsive, intensely competitive, but hilariously inconsistent. Her brother, on the other hand, was a demon card player, intelligent, observant, and cunningly strategic, but on the rare occasions he was beaten, he took his defeat lightly and well.

The three of them soon fell to behaving like old friends, abusing each other good-naturedly and laughing when disaster struck or a daring win was achieved. But all the time, Allie was subtly aware of Lord Kelsey's attention. He was a powerful distraction.

Finally, it was time to go to bed. Earlier in the evening, Lord Kelsey had lit a fire in each bedroom, so they waited, warm and welcoming.

"What are your plans for tomorrow?" he asked Allie as she packed the cards away.

She glanced out of the window where snow was falling steadily. "It depends on the snow. I was hoping to collect greenery to decorate the house for Christmas."

"Are you expecting visitors?" he asked.

"No, it's just for me." She hesitated and decided there was no point in hiding it. "This will be my last Christmas at The Oakes—I'm moving to Bath in the New Year, so I want to celebrate Christmas the way I used to as a child, a kind of farewell to my childhood home."

He said nothing, made no intrusive query, but he looked at her with that steady, unsettling gaze that seemed to see much more than she wished.

"Oh, I love decorating for Christmas," Lucilla exclaimed. "Can we help? John, can we, before we leave, I mean?"

He said with a rueful expression, "We might not be leaving tomorrow at all if this snow keeps up. I could no doubt make my way to the nearest village, but whether the road would be passable or not is another matter. We might be forced to trespass on Miss Fenton's hospitality for more than a night."

"You're very welcome to stay for as long as necessary," Allie said warmly. "We've plenty of food, and I've enjoyed your company very much." And it was true. She couldn't recall when she'd had such a delightfully cozy and pleasant evening with such easy and congenial company.

"Then we'll collect greenery tomorrow?" Lucilla asked. She seemed to have put all thoughts of her trunk aside.

"Yes, if the weather allows it."

The next morning was Christmas Eve. Light, powdery snow continued to drift down, but it didn't deter them from going out to collect greenery, so after a hearty breakfast of porridge, ham, and scrambled eggs, they bundled up well and set off.

They gathered lengths of green ivy, sprigs of holly vibrant with red berries, and fragrant boughs of pine. And even though Allie insisted it wasn't at all necessary, Lucilla sent her brother up a tree to cut a large bunch of mistletoe. As he handed his prize to his sister, he gave Allie a smile that set her cheeks glowing—and not just from the cold.

Lucilla waited until Lord Kelsey's back was turned and sent a snowball whizzing through the air that caught him square on the back of the neck.

He turned. "Oho, war, is it?" and the fight was on. Snowballs whizzed back and forth and the air rang with laughter and shrieks. Lucilla was a surprisingly good shot—brothers who played cricket, she explained—and she and Allie ganged up against her brother. Then the snow started to fall again, this time in earnest, and they gathered up their greenery and made their way back to the house, cheeks and fingers and tips of noses glowing with cold and life and laughter.

Once inside they changed into dry clothes and met in the kitchen for luncheon—sausage and vegetable hot pot that Allie had popped into the oven before they went out.

"Unless this snow stops soon, we might not get to Lady Holly's at all," Lord Kelsey commented, looking out of the window. "Not that I'd mind. I'd be happy to stay here for the whole of Christmastide, if Allie would have us." At some stage during the morning, they'd become Allie and John; a snowball fight had a way of melting formality.

"John, don't you dare say so!" his sister exclaimed, then blushed and hastily added, "I'm sorry, I don't mean to be rude, Allie—your hospitality has been wonderful. It's just that I do soooo want to dance at Lady Holly's Christmas ball."

Allie laughed. "I know, and I'm not the least bit offended. And I'm sure the snow will stop in time for you to make the journey. It's not far to Lady Holly's, and we have four whole days before the ball. Now, anyone interested in decorating the house?"

They'd gathered far too much greenery for just the sitting room and so they decorated the hall and even the kitchen as well. Allie produced a thick roll of red tartan ribbon and Lucilla set herself to fashioning bows and bunches of tartan-enhanced greenery, which Allie and Lord Kelsey hung, draped, and suspended from every possible position. By the time they'd finished, the house looked gloriously festive and smelled fragrant and Christmassy.

While Lucilla and her brother tidied up the mess, Allie went to prepare supper—leek and potato soup, with cheese and ham on toast followed by apple tart.

"Do you need a hand?" a deep voice behind her asked.

"Thank you, but it's just a matter of heating things and not letting them burn," she told him. "My cook left me extremely well provided for."

"As I see." He eyed the apple tart with approval.

"You could bring some wood in," Allie suggested. "The woodpile is through that door."

Lord Kelsey went to fetch the wood, and Lucilla entered. "Could you set the table please, Lucilla?" Allie asked.

"I'm not sure where everything is. Couldn't I stir the soup instead?" Lucilla suggested.

Allie handed her the spoon. "Go ahead," she said and began to set the table.

Lord Kelsey brought in the wood and was stacking it in the wood bin beside the stove, when Lucilla said, "Allie, can you check this soup please?" in an odd-sounding voice. Allie hurried over, just as Lord Kelsey straightened.

"Oh, look, mistletoe!" Lucilla exclaimed, pointing. Allie looked, and there, over the fireplace where it had not been a minute ago, hung a bunch of mistletoe tied with a tartan ribbon. "Now you have to kiss her, John."

Lord Kelsey looked down at Allie. "I'm afraid my sister is a minx." His deep, quiet voice seemed to vibrate right through her.

Allie felt a blush rising. She tried not to look too self-conscious and lifted her face, expecting a lighthearted buss on the lips, which was her experience of mistletoe kisses in the past.

Instead, he cupped her chin in one big hand and gazed

for a long moment into her eyes. It felt as though he was seeing her clear through to her soul. She waited, breathlessly, and finally he covered her mouth with his. His lips were firm and warm and a streak of heat flickered through her, startling Allie.

She blinked and swallowed and found she was clutching his arms. He stared down at her a moment, seeming to ask a silent question, then his eyes darkened and he bent to kiss her again. His kiss was warm and firm and possessive and it seemed to fill an aching void in Allie she hadn't realized was there until this moment. She leaned into him, kissing him back with a hunger that surprised her.

Lucilla's laughter and clapping broke the spell. "Oh, famous! The first kiss of Christmas! See, Allie, I told you we needed mistletoe!"

Fighting her blushes, Allie returned to stirring soup. It was, after all, just a kiss—well, two kisses—and prompted entirely by mistletoe. A tradition, pure and simple. So she'd gotten a little carried away. She would not think any more about it.

But of course she couldn't get it out of her mind. It wasn't as if she'd never been kissed, but never had a kiss been like that. Like a small lightning flash passing between them.

Had he felt it, too?

For the rest of the evening, whenever John Kelsey's blue gaze settled on her—which it did too often for her peace of mind—she felt herself warming.

Her card game went to pieces. Each time he looked at her, she forgot entirely what cards she'd played before. Thankfully, Lord Kelsey didn't seem to mind, and when Lucilla restlessly got up and walked over to the pianoforte, he tossed his cards aside and said, "Yes, Luce, give us a tune."

And because it was Christmas Eve, Lucilla chose a

carol, and then they were gathered around the piano singing, their voices blending, the fire blazing, the air inside fragrant with pine and beeswax, while outside the snow continued falling, softly and silently.

It was a Christmas Eve to remember, Allie thought.

After mince pies washed down with hot milk and honey—brandy in Lord Kelsey's case—they collected their lanterns to go up to bed. Lucilla went first.

Halfway up the stairs, she suddenly stopped and turned around. "Well? Are you two blind?" Another bunch of mistletoe hung over the stairs.

"Go on up to bed, baggage," Lord Kelsey told her. "We can manage without you."

Laughing, Lucilla went. Allie made to follow her, but a large hand stopped her and a deep voice said, "You're not going to run out on me, are you? When there's mistletoe waiting?"

"Oh, it's just a silly old country tradition," Allie mumbled. She didn't meet his eyes; she was afraid her desperate desire for his kiss would be embarrassingly obvious.

His eyes gleamed in the lamplight. "Some traditions are worth preserving," he murmured, and drew her against him.

At the touch of his lips, she trembled and without thinking slid her hands up over his chest to twine around his neck. And pull him closer. At his prompting, she opened her mouth to him and the taste of him flooded her senses, a dark masculinity laced with a hint of brandy. Intoxicating. Addictive.

Finally he broke the kiss and eased back a little. Slowly, reluctantly, she loosened her grip around his neck and let her hands slide down his chest. His breathing was ragged and uneven. As was hers. She could feel his heart thudding beneath her palms.

"Well," he said after a long moment spent just looking down at her. "This mistletoe is dangerous, isn't it?"

She didn't know what to say. Was the kiss just a lighthearted Christmas pastime for him? He was a sophisticated man of experience. No doubt he was used to such exchanges. She was not.

She took refuge in convention and propriety. "Good night, Lord Kelsey," she murmured, and forcing herself to let go of him, she grabbed her lantern and hurried up the stairs on legs that were distinctly rubbery.

Safely in her bed, shivering between cold sheets, she relived the kiss in every detail. The way he smelled, tasted, the way he'd held her against him, his strength, the way he'd made her feel. She curled up, her body so alive and throbbing.

Only a few more days until Lady Holly's ball. Would he dance with her? He would, of course, even if it was only out of politeness, but she wanted, oh, how she wanted it to be the waltz. To twirl in his arms under the glittering lights of the crystal chandelier, be touched by the magic that happened year after year at Lady Holly's Christmas ball. When people fell in love.

She fell asleep hoping he would dance the waltz with her. After that, it was in God's hands. As Lady Holly had said, it would be her last chance. . . .

But then, was that not what Lady Holly's ball was all about? Last chances.

She hugged the thought to herself.

CHAPTER FIVE

 C hristmas morning dawned white and cold. The snow was lighter now, sifting down like feathers. There was too much snow for them to get to church, but Allie didn't mind. A hush had fallen over a landscape etched in shades of silver and white.

"The world looks so quiet and peaceful," she said. "As it should be at Christmas."

"Certainly it'll be more peaceful now that Napoleon is safely incarcerated," John Kelsey commented.

The Kelsey siblings helped Allie prepare the Christmas dinner—John had insisted, and Lucilla was happy to join in—it was a novelty for both of them. Under normal circumstances, Lord Kelsey and his sister would never even step into a kitchen, let alone help with the cooking or fire tending.

Mrs. Meadows had left a fat capon to be baked, with strict instructions for the stuffing, so Lucilla was crumbling a stale loaf of bread, while John was chopping onions.

From his demeanor, last night's shattering kiss might never have happened. Allie found his attitude confusing.

When he'd come down to breakfast that morning he'd wished Allie happy Christmas with a light kiss on the cheek, but he'd kissed his sister the same way a moment later. Not by word or glance did he seem to be affected by it. Unlike Allie.

"John saw Napoleon once, you know," Lucilla said, frowning in concentration as she grated a crust of bread into a bowl.

"Only because I'm tall and could see over the heads of some other fellows," her brother said. "For all that he cast a long shadow over Europe, he's quite a small man."

"Were you a soldier for long?" Allie asked.

He nodded. "From the age of sixteen. Being a younger son, I needed a career. I was a hey-go-mad young buck and the army appealed. It suited me perfectly."

"Do you miss the army life?"

"It suited me then, and I miss the comradeship at times, but . . ." He smiled. "Peace is a fine thing. And though learning about such things as crop rotation and drainage occupies my time, it turns out to be a great deal more interesting than I would have imagined at sixteen."

Allie laughed. "I know. It sounds terribly dry, doesn't it, but the more you learn, the more fascinating it becomes." Seeing his surprised expression, she explained. "We've been experimenting with different crops here, too. It's amazing the difference it can make."

"You have?"

"I've been more or less managing the estate for the last five years," she said, adding with a droll expression, "but please don't mention it in public—it's terribly unfeminine, Lady Holly tells me. I think she fears I might introduce the subject of manure to the drawing room."

He laughed, and for the next few minutes they talked about the experiments in agriculture that were changing the face of farming and estate management in England.

Lucilla mixed herb, sausage, and chopped onion into the breadcrumbs. "I didn't know you knew Lady Holly, Allie. Are you going to the ball, too?"

"Yes, I've known her all my life. Lady Holbourne and my mother were friends," Allie said. "Now for the pudding."

The Christmas pudding had been hanging in its cloth in the cold larder for the last month. Allie carefully lowered it into a kettle of boiling water.

"That's a sizeable pudding," John Kelsey commented, watching. "You certainly have been left well provided for."

Allie laughed. "I know. Thank goodness you two are here to help eat some of it. Mrs. Meadows is used to cooking for a much larger household. Since Papa died and my cousin inherited, the household is much reduced."

"Your cousin?"

And she found herself telling him about Cousin Howard. He frowned. "You have to leave here?"

She wiped down the table with a damp cloth. "There's no need to look so concerned. I have a small nest egg from my mother, and I am planning to move to Bath. Such an interesting place, Bath, and I will have a much more social existence—as long as I remember not to talk about manure."

That made them laugh. She didn't tell them the nest egg was miniscule and that she would be working in Bath; she had no desire to be an object of pity—and besides, working with lively young girls would be more sociable.

She finished stuffing the capon and put it in the oven to roast, and set them to peeling potatoes, parsnips, carrots, turnips, and celery root, which would roast with the capon.

She asked him about Spain then, and about being in the army, and he told them stories about his days as a soldier, and some of his adventures. He even touched lightly on some of the grimmer times. He portrayed them as amusing adventures, but Allie could read between the lines.

They talked and talked while the pudding bubbled in its pot and the fire crackled and the kitchen filled with delicious smells, while outside a light southerly wind soughed softly through bare branches.

Lucilla seemed as interested as Allie in her brother's tales, and when he left the room to tend the sitting room fire, she said, "This is all new to me—John never talks about being in the army—not to me or to Mama or anyone else I know. But he seems to like talking to you."

Allie felt a small glow of pleasure at that, but she didn't let herself refine too much on it. They were snowed in and making the best of an accidental situation. John Kelsey hadn't given her any indication that the kisses they'd shared had affected him in any way. She'd been lacking the companionship of like-minded people for so long, she'd forgotten what it was like. That was most likely the reason for the strong sense of connection she felt.

They moved in very different circles, she reminded herself. He was Lord Kelsey of Kelsey Manor; she was simply the woman whose doorstep he'd landed on. He was kindhearted—the sort of man who would give up a week of hunting so that his little sister could attend a ball. Allie was a country girl—no, not a girl, a spinster, well and truly on the shelf—who'd never been anywhere, not even to a ball, a lady of birth, but no fortune, who was going to be a teacher.

He was being kind and gentlemanly, that was all. And if she wished it were otherwise, well, that would be her secret. A girl had her pride.

Christmas Day passed quietly and pleasantly, with good food, good conversation, and music, mainly Christmas carols. Allie was filled with warmth and happiness—she couldn't have imagined a lovelier last Christmas at home. The day ended with a highly ridiculous and fun game of charades, followed by a glass of wine and chestnuts roasted by the fire.

And for Allie, there was another bone-melting good night kiss under the mistletoe by the stairs. And while she told herself it was just a tradition and he was just doing what was expected, she couldn't stop herself from wishing. And hoping. And dreaming . . .

Perhaps Lady Holly's Christmas ball would perform the magic she so longed for. . . .

CHAPTER SIX

*B*y morning the snow had stopped, the wind was blowing steadily from the south and it was clear the snow was melting. In the distance they heard the sound of the traditional Boxing Day hunt, though as John Kelsey said, it was risky weather for it; there was still a lot of iced-over snow, as well as ice beneath snow, which was more treacherous.

Allie was half pleased, half sorry about the thaw; pleased they'd be able to get to Lady Holly's ball after all, but sorry that the Kelseys' visit would soon come to an end.

The day passed quickly. They ate well on leftovers from Christmas dinner, played cards, and talked. In the afternoon, a knock at the door surprised them.

It was one of Allie's tenant farmers, who'd come to check that she was all right. He'd spotted the carriage half tipped into the river, too, and was relieved to find that the travelers were safe, and that they'd turned out to be gentry.

"The wife'll be pleased to know you had suitable company over Christmas, Miss Allie," he said. "She were that worried about you bein' alone." He glanced at the sky and nodded slowly. "I reckon your guests'll be able to travel on to Lady Holly's tomorrow or the next day. I'll organize some men tomorrow to pull that there carriage out of the river."

Lucilla brightened at the good news, and in the evening

she announced that she needed to practice her waltzing because she was certain that she was going to meet someone special at the ball and she didn't want to make herself memorable by stepping on his feet.

So after dinner Lord Kelsey rolled up the carpet in the sitting room and moved the furniture back, and Allie played several waltzes while Lucilla and her brother danced.

He was an excellent dancer, which surprised her. "I didn't know soldiers danced."

"Staff officers do," he explained. "Very big on the social graces is The Beau." Which, as he explained, was a nickname for the Duke of Wellington.

"And now it's your turn," Lucilla said after half a dozen dances. "I'll play and you and John can dance."

John Kelsey held out his hand and, fighting a blush, Allie rose from the piano. His long, warm fingers closed around hers. No gloves, as there would be at a ball. Skin to warm skin. Could he feel how fast her pulse was beating?

The music started and, holding her in a light, firm grip, John Kelsey swirled her into a waltz. It was nothing like the lessons she'd had. Despite her fluttering heart and her mind—totally blank—she didn't even have to think about her steps; he commanded her every movement with a sure grace that made her feel like a thistledown maiden, instead of an inexperienced country spinster dancing the waltz for the first time with a man.

His sister played waltz after waltz. Allie floated dreamily, twirling to the music, abandoning herself totally to the command of his big, strong body. She closed her eyes, feeling utterly safe, utterly transported. It was magic.

If it snowed again for weeks and she never went to the ball, she would, at least, have had this.

Finally it came to an end. They were both breathless and, in Allie's case at least, not wholly from the exertion. She managed to curtsey her thanks and maintain the illusion of the ballroom. He bowed in return, his blue eyes seeming to look right into her soul. Aware of his sister's speculative interest, Allie collected her scattered thoughts and hurried away to make supper.

Lucilla followed her into the kitchen, leaving her brother to return the sitting room rug and furniture to their original positions. She hovered, eyeing Allie with a troubled expression.

"Is something the matter, Lucilla?"

Lucilla glanced at the door and bit her lip. "It's . . . it's— I saw the way you looked at my brother, and, well . . ."

Embarrassed that her feelings must have been so transparent, Allie tried to think of something to say, but before she could form a coherent sentence in her mind, Lucilla blurted out, "There's this girl, you see, Julia Courtenay, whose property adjoins ours and . . . and she's pretty and suitable, and we've known her family forever. Mama expects—well, we all expect that John will propose to her any day now. In fact"—she gave Allie a guilty glance— "when Mama knew John would be attending this ball, she wrote to Lady Holly and asked her to invite the Courtenays."

Allie busied herself with supper for a moment. Of course, he was already spoken for.

"I'm sorry, I should have told you sooner. And for the mistletoe. I didn't think . . ."

Allie manufactured a laugh from somewhere. "I don't know what you've been imagining, Lucilla, but there's nothing to forgive. Your brother and I have been entertaining ourselves, that's all. There's nothing at all between us, and I certainly have no expectations that there ever could be." Dreams, perhaps, expectations, no.

Lucilla gave her a doubtful glance. "Are you sure? Because—"

"My own future is all mapped out for me," Allie said in a light tone. "Bath, remember? I'm so looking forward to it. And while it's been delightful, flirting a little and dancing with your brother, it's just a little bit of Christmas nonsense. Don't worry. Now, will you set the table for supper, please? It may well be the last time you get to do it, for my servants will be returning tomorrow and Mrs. Meadows has Opinions about Ladies in the Kitchen."

For the rest of the evening, Allie did her best to appear cheerful and lighthearted, and if her laughter sometimes sounded brittle and a little forced, well, that was too bad. She was aware of John Kelsey's blue gaze resting thoughtfully on her from time to time, but she managed to carry on with, she hoped, her dignity intact.

They had what she called a nursery supper that night, scrambled eggs and ham, followed by hot cocoa and crumpets, all eaten on a rug in front of the sitting room fire.

Allie would never forget the sight of John Kelsey sprawled elegantly on the rug in front of the fire, his long booted legs crossed, as he manned the toasting fork, toasting crumpets that they ate dripping with butter and honey. Later, they sipped sweet muscat wine and talked and talked.

Their last night together; she would never forget it.

But when it came to bedtime, all her resolutions about keeping her distance came to nothing when, at the bottom of the staircase, he detained her with a light touch on her arm and an upward glance at the mistletoe.

She did try, saying, "Oh, but Christmas is over now," as she made to pass him.

"But the mistletoe remains," he said softly, and her determination crumbled. One last kiss, she thought, and gave herself into his arms, kissing him with all the misplaced passion inside her.

His embrace tightened, and he gave her long, intoxicating, drugging kisses that had her sagging at the knees by the time he was finished.

"Shall I carry you up to bed?" he asked in a deep ragged

voice—he was breathing heavily, too—and for a moment she was almost tempted.

A simple "yes" and she would know once and for all what it felt like to be a woman, how it would feel to lie in his arms, his body pressed against hers, skin to skin. What would it be like to be possessed by him?

But she wasn't made that way. And the possible consequences of such a night would ruin her more certainly than anything. She had no desire to travel that road, so she managed to pass it off with a shaky laugh and forced herself up the stairs with a cool, "Good night, Lord Kelsey."

Men came in the morning with poles for leverage and two huge draft horses, and the news that though the roads were icy in places, and mushy in others, the way to Holbourne Abbey was clear.

With a great deal of noise and fuss, they hauled the mud-covered yellow post chaise from the river and set it back on the road. Several panels and a wheel were smashed. The men brought the contents of the boot up to the house—a valise, muddy and damp, and an iron-bound trunk with one corner smashed in.

With a cry of dismay, Lucilla knelt on the stone flags of the kitchen and unbuckled the straps that held the trunk closed. She pulled out a series of wet items. "Oh, no," she wailed. "My beautiful ball dress! It's ruined—utterly ruined!"

"Let me see." Allie lifted the dress up. "Oh. Oh, dear."

The dress was—or had been—white. Now it was . . . well, blotchy was the best description. The dye of the red and green ribbons around the hem had run, and the dress itself had been packed on top of a blue spencer, and the dye of that had run, too, staining the dress with blue blotches as well.

Lucilla burst into tears.

"It might not be as bad as it looks," Allie assured the distressed girl, but her heart sank. She was fairly sure the dress was ruined.

And so it proved. First, she tried blotting the stains with cornstarch, and though it did absorb some of the dye, the blotches remained. She tried soaking it in milk next, which used to help with Papa's ink stains, but again, enough of the residue remained to make the dress unwearable.

"Never mind," she told Lucilla. "We'll try bleach, that might help." If it didn't ruin the silk, and Allie thought it might. But now there was nothing to lose.

Lucilla was inconsolable. "My first ever ball, and now I will have nothing to w-w-eear," she sobbed. "Oh, my beautiful ball gown . . ."

Allie tried every household remedy she knew, but they'd made no appreciable difference. The Meadows family returned by mid-morning, but even Mrs. Meadows's encyclopedic knowledge of stain remedies failed to remove the blotches. Lucilla's dress was unwearable.

Allie left Lucilla being consoled by her brother, while she made arrangements for Albert to drive them to Holbourne Abbey in the gig. She returned to the sitting room just in time to hear Lord Kelsey saying quietly, "I know you're upset, puss, but you must try to be brave about this. It's a disappointment to be sure, but you might be able to borrow a dress from someone. In any case, our hostess is in a difficult situation—I suspect she's being forced to leave her home, but it's Christmas and she has guests, so she's putting a brave face on it. Do you think you could do the same?"

Lucilla sniffled. "I'll try."

"That's my girl," he said softly. Allie entered the room, giving no sign she'd overheard the exchange. But his words had given her an idea.

For the following hours, as the rest of Lucilla's clothes were cleaned and dried by the extremely competent Mrs.

Meadows, it was clear that the girl was trying to put a brave face on it, as her brother had asked. It made Allie warm even more to her.

Finally, everything was dry and Allie helped Lucilla pack her things into an old trunk of her father's.

"I'll just have to wear this old white woolen dress," Lucilla said miserably. "It's not a ball dress, and it's last season's, but Mama made me bring it because Northumberland gets so cold in winter." She eyed it in disgust. "Why couldn't that have been the one that got leaked on?"

Allie looked at it and sympathized. The dress was practical more than pretty.

"I wish I hadn't come now," the girl confided. "I was so looking forward to my first ever ball. But John gave up his own holiday for me, and Mama is hoping he will propose to Julia tomorrow night, so I'll have to pretend to enjoy myself anyway. I don't want to be a wet blanket." A tear trickled down her cheek.

She darted a glance at Allie and added, half-embarrassed, "You'll think me foolish, but I was certain I was going to meet my true love there—Lady Holly's ball is famous for making people fall in love. But now . . . what man is going to look twice at me in this?"

Allie could see her point. The white wool was a dress for keeping out draughts, not for charming young men. She looked at it again and found herself saying, "I have a dress you could wear."

Even as she said it, a small voice inside her cried, nooooo.

But it was the right thing to do. She'd been facing unpalatable facts all her life. This ball wasn't going to make any difference to Allie's future.

Despite several earth-shattering kisses—to Allie, anyway—and a connection and companionability she'd never before experienced, Lord Kelsey seemed unaffected. He hadn't once referred to the kisses, or given any other in-

dication that he was interested in her in a romantic sense—
he was, as she'd told herself a hundred times already, just
being a charming and obliging guest. He was a man of experience and sophistication.

And a Miss Julia Courtenay was expecting his proposal.

It wasn't as if he'd mislead Allie. He'd never said a word
to make her think it was anything other than a little holiday
fun. It was Allie's own lack of experience that had led her
to read more into a few mistletoe kisses than she should
have. Spinning dreams out of nothing.

And though she would have loved to waltz with him at
the ball, she knew now it would lead nowhere, and any
pleasure she might have would be spoiled by the knowledge that Lucilla was miserable in her practical white
woolen dress.

And that Miss Julia Courtenay was there, waiting, expecting to be asked for something far more significant than
a waltz.

No, Allie had already danced her waltzes in Lord
Kelsey's arms. Plenty of women never experienced anything as remotely magical. And even if he hadn't meant
them, he'd given her kisses to dream on for the rest of her
life.

It would give Allie more pleasure to make his sister's
first ball a magical experience than to attend the ball herself.

Besides, this was Christmas, and Lucilla and her brother
had given her a priceless gift—a wonderfully happy last
Christmas at The Oakes, a happier Christmas than she'd
imagined possible—a Christmas to remember. She could
give this sweet young girl an equal gift.

She fetched the white box with the elegant gold design.
She kept all the beautiful underclothes for herself, though,
except for the corset which had been specially designed to
enhance the fit of the gown.

Lucilla gasped when she saw the dress. "Ohhh," she said

on a long sigh, lifting it out of the box. "It's the most beautiful dress I've ever seen. But . . . will you not want to wear it yourself?"

"I have another new dress," Allie said. "It arrived from the dressmaker just last week." It wasn't a lie.

"Ohhh," Lucilla said, holding the dress against herself and gazing at her reflection in the looking glass, swaying to imaginary music, just as Allie had. "Are you sure?"

"I'm certain," Allie said, and Lucilla embraced her. And in that moment she was sure. Regrets might come later, but it would be too late. She knew she was doing the right thing.

Lucilla had told her brother about the dress, and as they sat down to lunch he said to Allie, "Thank you so much for lending my sister a dress. You cannot know how grateful I am to be saved from an evening of Utter Gloom and Misery."

"It was my pleasure."

"I have something for you, too—a small thanks for the hospitality you've given us." Ignoring her polite disclaimers, he placed a parcel in her hands. "I hope you will remember this Christmas every time you wear it."

Allie unwrapped the gift and gasped with pleasure. It was a Kashmir shawl, softer and finer than anything she'd ever worn, cream wool, with a deep border of exquisite embroidery in crimson and blue and a long silk fringe. "Oh, it's beautiful—you shouldn't have—truly it was my pleasure, but—"

"Put it on," John Kelsey said.

She rose from the table, but he rose before her. Taking the shawl from her hands, he shook it out and wrapped it around her shoulders. He stood looking down at her. "Perfect," he said with a slow smile, and Allie felt herself blushing at the expression in his eyes.

"Will you save me a couple of dances tomorrow night?" he said softly in that beautiful deep voice that she was sure would haunt her dreams for years to come.

Allie looked down and mumbled something incoherent, but he seemed not to mind her apparent confusion.

The Kelseys left The Oakes with repeated thanks and Lucilla's avowed intention of remaining in touch; Allie must write to them at Kelsey Manor and let them know her direction in Bath. Allie, waving them off, smilingly agreed, but knew she would not.

Once she was in Bath, they would inhabit vastly different worlds. Besides, Lord Kelsey had said not a word about keeping in touch—it was all his sister.

"You were very quiet, John," Lucilla said as they drove away. "Won't you miss Allie?"

"No." John kept his own counsel; he wasn't going to explain his thoughts to his sister. Besides, he'd see Allie at the ball the following night.

Lucilla chattered on about the ball, and who might be there, and about the gown, and the shawl he'd given Allie, but John paid her scant attention. He'd actually bought the shawl for Lucilla as a memento of her first ball. But he was glad he had a gift worthy of Allie Fenton.

The accident had not only turned their coach upside down; he suspected it had turned his life upside down as well.

The truth was, Allie Fenton had knocked him for a six and he wanted a little time apart from her in which to examine his feelings. The few days they'd spent together were like something out of a fairy tale, and he needed a cold blast of everyday reality to test his feelings against.

Not that Lady Holly's annual Christmas ball was exactly cold hard reality.

His sister's voice pierced his reverie. "Have you got the note Allie gave you for Lady Holly?"

"Yes." John patted his pocket. "It's safe here." It was an odd thing to ask of him—to give a note to Lady Holly before the ball started when Allie was attending herself, but it was probably some female thing—a reminder or something. His mother and grandmother were constantly forgetting things and wanting reminders.

CHAPTER SEVEN

On the evening of the ball, just before they went in to dinner, John handed Lady Holly the note. "Miss Fenton asked me to give you this."

He went to leave so she could read it in private, but she seized his coat sleeve in a clawlike grip, staring past him at Lucilla coming down the stairs. "Where the devil did your sister get that dress? As if I didn't know! You, sir, will stay while I see what the wretched gel has got to say for herself!"

She broke open the seal, read the note, and made a disgusted sound. "No idea of how to act in her own best interest, that gel." She glared at John. "Heart as soft as butter!"

He frowned. "I don't understand."

"No, I don't suppose you do. It's all in here." She thrust the note into his hand and stalked off to tend to her other guests.

John read the note.

Dear Lady Holly, please accept my heartfelt apologies for missing your ball. Please don't be angry with me. I'm sure you have dozens of eligible gentlemen lined up for me, but truly, I am so much happier to let Lucilla wear the beautiful gown you gave me. It will make her first ball an occasion to treasure, when she would otherwise have been miserable. She and her brother have given me a wonderful last Christmas at home and memories to cherish the rest of my life. The gift of my lovely dress is but small recompense for that.

With love and apologies, Alice Fenton

John crushed the note in his hand, then smoothed it out, folded it, and slipped it into his pocket. Dammit, she'd given up her chance to go to the ball so that his sister might have a happy time.

Throughout dinner, he brooded over the contents of the note. Eligible gentlemen lined up for her? Be damned to that. But he'd been looking forward to dancing with her.

During the third course, he hatched a plan. The moment dinner was over, he approached Lady Holly again. She was standing with her son.

"Lady Holly, could I ask you to keep an eye on my sister, please? I'm afraid I'm going to have to leave the ball."

The old lady raised an eyebrow. "Leaving, are you? Anything to do with that note from Allie Fenton?"

He didn't answer but turned to her son. "Lord Holbourne, may I borrow a horse, please?"

"Take a carriage," the old lady said before her son could respond. "And ask Cook to make you up a basket of delicacies. Mrs. Meadows is a good plain cook, but if you're going a-wooing, you'll want something special. And take some champagne. Nothing like champagne for setting a mood."

Lord Holbourne, well used to his mother's autocratic ways, added with a smile, "Help yourself to whatever you need, Kelsey. One of the grooms can drive you. And don't worry, my wife and I will look after Lucilla."

John hurried to make the arrangements. So much for that dose of cold hard reality. It seemed he was going "a-wooing."

* * *

He arrived at The Oakes shortly after ten, and was relieved to see lights still burning in some of the windows. The journey had only taken an hour, but the night was cold and John was starting to have second thoughts about his impulsive action.

But a good soldier knew better than to change his mind once an action was begun. The thing was to make your decision, then do your utmost to ensure the result was a success.

And while he might doubt the wisdom of coming unannounced so late at night, he had no doubts at all about his feelings toward Allie Fenton.

Cloth-covered basket in hand, he rang the front doorbell and waited. After a few minutes, a bemused-looking Meadows opened the door.

"Lord Kelsey?"

"Is Miss Fenton still up?"

"Yes, but—"

John stepped inside and handed the basket to the butler. "Cinderella did not go to the ball, so I've brought the ball—or a small portion of it—to her. Lady Holly said I must bring champagne and a few delicacies if I were to, er, go a-wooing."

Meadows took the basket with a fatherly grin. "Indeed, m'lord. Miss Fenton is in the sitting room, I'll just annou—"

"I'll announce myself, if you don't mind." He strode down the hall and knocked on the sitting room door. He opened it to find Allie sitting curled up with a book by the fire, wrapped in his cashmere shawl. Her hair was down, falling in curls around her face. She was so lovely.

She gasped at his entrance and scrambled to her feet. "What—has something happened? The ball—"

"Is proceeding as expected," he said smoothly. "My sister is in seventh heaven, looking very beautiful in your dress—though you would have looked even lovelier in it."

"Then why—"

"I missed you," he said simply. "And I couldn't enjoy myself knowing you'd given up your chance to attend the ball so that my sister could enjoy it instead. It was foolish and generous and apparently—according to Lady Holly— typical of you."

She blushed. "Well, I—"

"So I thought I'd come and keep you company and bring you a small taste of the ball." At that moment the door opened and Meadows entered with a tray laden with delicacies, an open and gently fizzing bottle of champagne, and two elegant flutes. He must have been listening at the door to have timed things so well. He set out the supper, and reached for the bottle.

"I'll pour," John told him, and Meadows bowed and silently exited.

John poured two glasses and held one out to Allie. She didn't move.

"Don't you like champagne?"

"It's not that, it's . . . What about Miss Courtenay?"

"Miss Courtenay? What abou—oh, I detect the fell, clumsy hand of my little sister in this. I suppose she told you Julia Courtenay and I are on the verge of becoming betrothed." He rolled his eyes. "The truth is my mother and the Courtenays have been hoping for such an alliance ever since Julia was born."

She opened her mouth to say something, but he held up his hand and continued. "First they hoped she would marry my brother, though Julia was still a child when he was killed. Then they expected me to step into his shoes—in all ways. But the truth is, neither Julia nor I have the slightest interest in marrying each other."

"But isn't she at Lady Holly's ball? Lucilla said your mother had asked Lady Holly to invite her."

"Good lord, did she? Well, at least Julia had more sense than to accept. She's not there. And even if she were, there would be no announcement. Not for Julia and me—not ever. I have other plans." He held out the champagne glass to her, and this time she took it.

He held up his glass. "To 1816. May it bring us all our hearts desire."

From her expression she didn't seem to expect much from 1816, but she accepted the toast and drank. "Now what have you brought me from the ball? Oh, my goodness—it's a feast!"

It was a feast indeed; fluted pastry shells filled with mushrooms in a creamy sauce, slivers of smoked salmon on rounds of buttered bread, crab cakes encased in toasted breadcrumbs, quails' eggs in caper sauce, sliced roast duck, wafer-thin slices of ham, spears of asparagus, tiny medallions of preserved fruit—quince, oranges, cherries—gleaming like jewels in the lamplight, sugared violets, star-shaped ginger biscuits, and to finish, a whipped-cream confection layered with berries and cake and served in long, elegant glasses.

She laughed. "We can't possibly eat all that."

"Then let us work up an appetite first." Setting down his glass, he held out his hand to her. "Miss Fenton, you owe me a dance, I believe."

She laughed. "Here? With me in my old gown and slippers?"

"Why not? We are at a ball, are we not?"

"Without music?" But she put down her glass and came into his arms.

"Can you not hear the music? A waltz, I think." And he took her in his arms and began a slow, silent waltz. She was supple and soft and she nestled in his arms as if she was born to be there. And she was, he thought. Their steps slowed and as he bent to kiss her, a musical chord sounded.

"What the—?" he exclaimed, and then, from the hallway, a violin began to play a slow waltz.

Allie gave a soft, delighted laugh. "It's Albert, Albert Meadows—he plays the fiddle at every village celebration."

The whole blasted Meadows family must have been listening at the door, John decided, but he had no quarrel with the result. Albert played on, and they danced and danced, waltz after waltz, twirling around the sitting room, avoiding chairs and other furniture, pretending they were other couples, dancing and laughing until they were breathless.

"Thank you, Albert, that's enough," John called out and the music stopped.

"Time for feasting," he said. "Sit down and I'll bring you your supper as a good partner should."

But instead of a chair, she sat down on the rug in front of the fire. He brought the dishes over and placed them on the floor around her like a picnic. Then, bringing the champagne and glasses, he joined her in front of the fire.

They ate, talking in soft voices, tasting each dish, talking about everything . . . and nothing while the fire hissed and crackled gently and the wind nibbled at the eaves.

And when the dishes had all been tasted and the champagne drunk, another feast began as John pulled her into his arms.

She tasted of wine and sweetness and warmth and . . . everything he'd ever dreamed of in a woman.

John might have gotten carried away—the intoxication of the woman in his arms, the way she returned his kisses with such sweet, unpracticed passion—he almost forgot who he was, forget he had claims to be a gentleman.

But the clock in the hall chimed loud and sonorous, and there was a knock on the door and Meadows called through it, "It's midnight, Miss Allie. Lord Kelsey, do you want me to tell Lord Holbourne's driver to wait? Only he's been told to be ready to drive some of Lady Holly's local guests home from one o'clock onward."

John groaned and forced himself to sit up. "Five minutes, Meadows."

He looked at Allie, so sweetly mussed and flushed and rumpled, and gazing up at him with an expression that just . . . shattered him. He cupped her face in his hands and kissed her again, a long, slow promise of a kiss. "I have to go, love, or else your reputation will be in shreds—and for good reason. Go to bed now and dream of me. I'll come back tomorrow." He rose and, mustering all his resolve, left the room and the house without looking back.

The ball was still in progress when he returned, but he wasn't in the mood. He glanced in, saw his sister, as merry as a grig in a noisy group of young people her own age, and quietly took himself up to his bed.

He slept lightly that night, full of plans and dreams and possibilities.

But at breakfast an urgent message arrived from his mother: John and Lucilla must return home immediately. Grandmamma was dying.

Lord Holbourne offered them the use of his carriage to the nearest town, and sent a rider ahead to arrange the hire of a post chaise for the remainder of the journey.

John just had time to scrawl a note to Allie. He gave it to a footman, and paid him a guinea to deliver it as soon as possible. The man, busy sorting luggage for a variety of guests all leaving at the same time, pocketed the note and promised.

But as the carriage passed through the gates of Holbourne Abbey, the footman, carrying a lady's highly perfumed luggage, began to sneeze. As he pulled out a handkerchief to blow his nose, Lord Kelsey's note fluttered to the ground and landed in a puddle. It melted into the muddy water unnoticed, and was soon forgotten.

CHAPTER EIGHT

Miss Minchin's Seminary for Young Ladies, Bath

She'd forgotten all about him, Allie told herself. Lord Kelsey? Who was that? Nobody she thought about—or wanted to think about.

But she couldn't help herself.

Go to bed now, and dream of me. I'll be back tomorrow.

Why say that if he didn't mean it? But clearly he hadn't. She had gone to bed and dreamed of him. And she'd waited—all day she'd waited, until it was time to go to bed, and dream of him again.

He was busy, she told herself that first day. He couldn't get away. Lady Holly had organized her guests into some kind of activity and he had obligations as a guest. He had to look after Lucilla.

She'd waited all the next day, too, and the next. But still there was no sign of him, and no word of any kind. Eventually, she'd stopped making excuses, and decided she'd read too much into the events of that evening . . . magical and wondrous as it had been for her. But only for her, it seemed.

Like the mistletoe kisses, they'd been an amusement— she'd been an amusement for a sophisticated gentleman.

She'd burned the Christmas greenery and packed her

possessions—her precious keepsakes, her favorite books, and her beloved Christmas box into a large trunk. She kept one sprig of mistletoe pressed carefully between the pages of an old book—whether as a keepsake or a symbol of a lesson learned, she wasn't yet clear.

After a tearful farewell to the Meadows family, and a surprising number of other local people who called to say good-bye and wish her well, Allie left The Oakes on the second of January, two days before Cousin Howard and his family were due to arrive. It wasn't polite, she knew, but she didn't want to see him or his wife and children take possession of her home. She just wanted to be gone.

She reached Bath more than a week later, and despite being exhausted by the long and arduous journey, she started teaching the very next morning. And it was good, she told herself. She liked the girls, liked the work, and if she was kept so busy from morning to night that she barely had time to think, let alone sleep, well, that was good, too.

Because she didn't need to think, and she didn't sleep well anyway, her rest stolen by dreams of a tall dark man with eyes of deepest blue. Who kissed like . . . well, never mind that. She wasn't thinking about kisses either.

"Miss Fenton?"

Allie blinked and looked up. "Yes, Melisande, what is it?"

"Miss, you said if the sun came out, we could practice our French conversation in the courtyard and, well, it's out." The girl gestured to the window, where weak winter sun shone.

Allie nodded. "Very well, but make sure you bring your wraps with you. The sun might be shining, but that breeze is cold and we don't want you to catch a chill. Top of the stairs in five minutes."

There was a clatter and a rush to fetch wraps and in minutes the girls were assembled at the top of the stairs, jostling and giggling and staring down at someone who, from the sounds of things, had just arrived in the hall below.

"Girls, girls, please," Allie said crisply. "Young ladies do not shove and giggle and gawk at visitors. Come along now." She started down the staircase.

Halfway down she stopped. Froze. It couldn't be . . .

The gentleman in the hall looked up. "Ah, there you are," he said in the deep voice that haunted her dreams.

She swallowed, saying nothing. What was he doing here? How had he found her? Behind her there was a buzz of speculation and a few stifled giggles.

He handed his hat and cloak to the maid and strolled to the foot of the stairs. He looked up at her and smiled. "I see you're wearing the shawl I gave you."

"This?" She gave a careless shrug.

"She wears it every day, sir, practically never takes it off."

"Be quiet, Melisande," Allie said. In a glacially calm voice she told Lord Kelsey, "I'm sorry, I don't know why you've come here, but if it is to speak to me, I'm afraid it's not possible."

"Why not?"

"I'm busy." She gestured behind her, to the girls crowded excitedly on the stairs.

"Oh, I think these young ladies are perfectly capable of looking after themselves for a while, aren't you, ladies?"

There was a chorus of enthusiastic yeses from behind her. "Go on, miss, talk to the gentleman. He's come all this way and he's soooo handsome."

"That's enough, Melisande!" To Lord Kelsey she said, "Miss Minchin is out at present. I am in charge and cannot leave the girls unattended."

His brows rose. "So you refuse to speak to me in private?"

"Correct." Because if she saw him in private, she'd weaken, and he'd break her heart all over again.

"But you have something of mine." He moved up a couple of stairs toward her. "You took it the night we waltzed in your sitting room."

"Waltzing in the sitting room, ooh, miss."

Allie felt her color rise. She said coolly, "If you left something behind, you must apply to my cousin. He owns The Oakes now."

"I met him. He doesn't have it." He added chattily, quite as if there weren't upward of twenty pairs of ears listening to every word, "By the way, you made a good escape there. Those children of his are complete savages. Unlike these delightful young ladies."

The girls giggled. He mounted another two stairs.

Allie would have moved backwards up the staircase, except twenty eager schoolgirls were pressed against her back. "I don't have anything of yours. Unless you want the shawl back."

"No, that was a gift. The other was something you stole."

There was a chorus of shocked gasps, one of them Allie's. "I did not!" she said indignantly. "I've never stolen a thing in my life!"

He reached the landing. His face was just below hers. "You certainly stole this."

She gripped the bannister rail tightly. "What? What do you say I stole?"

"My heart."

There was a sudden hushed silence. Slowly, he lowered himself to one knee. "I love you, Allie Fenton. Will you do me the honor of becoming my wife?"

Allie stared down at him, dazed, hardly able to believe it wasn't a dream or some kind of joke. The silence stretched.

She felt a firm little hand in the small of her back. "Go on, miss, say yes!" There was an immediate chorus of whispers. "Say yes." "Tell him yes."

He rose to his feet and held out his arms to her, his eyes glowing with love and humor. "Do as your girls tell you, Allie. Say yes."

She couldn't say a word. Her heart was too full, her eyes were too full.

"She says yes," Melisande declared and shoved Allie off her step and into his arms.

He caught her against his chest. "Thank you, Melisande, but the decision is Miss Fenton's." He looked down at Allie and added softly, "You thought I'd abandoned you, but I was called away urgently to my grandmother's deathbed. Luckily, it turned out to be a false alarm, but when I returned to The Oakes, as I'd promised, you were gone, and your cousin refused to tell me where. But Lady Holly knew, thank God, and so I tracked you down." He cupped her chin. "Allie, my love, can you forgive me? And will you marry me?"

"Yes, of course," she said mistily, and reached up to kiss him, oblivious of the delighted onlookers.

You never knew how life was going to turn out. She'd been so miserable as the new year began, but now . . . Lord Kelsey's arms tightened around her. Allie sighed with happiness. 1816 had brought her her heart's desire after all. It was going to be a good year. A very good year indeed.

He bent to kiss her again and despite their audience, she made no move to stop him. Girls, after all, needed to learn about happy endings, as well as French verbs.

Connect with Us

Visit us online at
KensingtonBooks.com
to read more from your favorite authors, see books
by series, view reading group guides, and more.

Join us on social media

for sneak peeks, chances to win books and prize packs,
and to share your thoughts with other readers.

facebook.com/kensingtonpublishing
twitter.com/kensingtonbooks

Tell us what you think!

To share your thoughts, submit a review,
or sign up for our eNewsletters, please visit:
KensingtonBooks.com/TellUs.

Books by Bestselling Author
Fern Michaels

___The Jury	0-8217-7878-1	$6.99US/$9.99CAN
___Sweet Revenge	0-8217-7879-X	$6.99US/$9.99CAN
___Lethal Justice	0-8217-7880-3	$6.99US/$9.99CAN
___Free Fall	0-8217-7881-1	$6.99US/$9.99CAN
___Fool Me Once	0-8217-8071-9	$7.99US/$10.99CAN
___Vegas Rich	0-8217-8112-X	$7.99US/$10.99CAN
___Hide and Seek	1-4201-0184-6	$6.99US/$9.99CAN
___Hokus Pokus	1-4201-0185-4	$6.99US/$9.99CAN
___Fast Track	1-4201-0186-2	$6.99US/$9.99CAN
___Collateral Damage	1-4201-0187-0	$6.99US/$9.99CAN
___Final Justice	1-4201-0188-9	$6.99US/$9.99CAN
___Up Close and Personal	0-8217-7956-7	$7.99US/$9.99CAN
___Under the Radar	1-4201-0683-X	$6.99US/$9.99CAN
___Razor Sharp	1-4201-0684-8	$7.99US/$10.99CAN
___Yesterday	1-4201-1494-8	$5.99US/$6.99CAN
___Vanishing Act	1-4201-0685-6	$7.99US/$10.99CAN
___Sara's Song	1-4201-1493-X	$5.99US/$6.99CAN
___Deadly Deals	1-4201-0686-4	$7.99US/$10.99CAN
___Game Over	1-4201-0687-2	$7.99US/$10.99CAN
___Sins of Omission	1-4201-1153-1	$7.99US/$10.99CAN
___Sins of the Flesh	1-4201-1154-X	$7.99US/$10.99CAN
___Cross Roads	1-4201-1192-2	$7.99US/$10.99CAN

Available Wherever Books Are Sold!
Check out our website at **www.kensingtonbooks.com**